Murder
at the
MIKADO

Center Point
Large Print

Also by Julianna Deering and available from Center Point Large Print:

The Drew Farthering Mysteries
  Rules of Murder
  Death by the Book

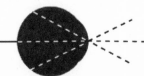

Murder *at the* MIKADO

— A Drew Farthering Mystery —

Julianna Deering

Center Point Large Print
Thorndike, Maine

This Center Point Large Print edition is published in the year
2014 by arrangement with Bethany House Publishers,
a division of Baker Publishing Group.

Scripture quotations are from the
King James Version of the Bible.

This is a work of historical reconstruction; the appearances
of certain historical figures are therefore inevitable.
All other characters, however, are products of the author's
imagination, and any resemblance to actual persons,
living or dead, is coincidental.

The text of this Large Print edition is unabridged.
In other aspects, this book may vary from the original edition.
Printed in the United States of America on permanent paper.
Set in 16-point Times New Roman type.

ISBN: 978-1-62899-223-6

Library of Congress Cataloging-in-Publication Data

Deering, Julianna.
Murder at the Mikado : a Drew Farthering mystery / Julianna Deering.
pages ; cm
Summary: "Set in 1930s England, Drew and his fiancée, Madeline,
answer a plea for help from an old flame of Drew's, discovering
murder—and more—behind the scenes of a theater production"—
Provided by publisher.
ISBN 978-1-62899-223-6 (library binding : alk. paper)
1. Murder—Investigation—Fiction. 2. England—Fiction.
   3. Large type books. I. Title.
PS3554.O3414M87 2014b
813'.54—dc23

2014019471

To the One who remembers me
according to His love

— One —

"Actors," the barman muttered to no one in particular as he wiped a freshly washed glass.

The Knight and Steed was empty but for the dozen or so customers clustered around the big table in the middle of the room and two others off by themselves in the corner. From the gramophone, a quartet sang the jaunty American tune "Nobody's Sweetheart."

They all knew one another, of course. All of them came from down the street at the Tivoli. Mostly they came in late, after performances, with the rest of the theater crowd. But Mondays, when the theater was closed or when they'd had an early rehearsal, they might come in for a little something, often with friends and hangers-on.

This was one of those early days. It wasn't even five o'clock yet, a grim, blustery afternoon, and they'd only just started to drink. The large group was boisterous, chatting and laughing, sometimes roaring when one of them displayed a spark of wit. The two in the corner were huddled together, talking so low no one could have heard them even if the others had been utterly silent.

The man was well known, lead actor and owner of the Tivoli. His leading-lady wife was sitting at the large table with the others. The woman with him was a reporter for one of the local scandal sheets. As he spoke to her, his eyes gleamed with a passion that had nothing to do with love or even lust, yet it was vivid and urgent all the same.

"Not much more," he was saying when the barman brought them a second round, sherry for him and pale ale for the woman. "It's exactly what they want, you'll see. And it's got plenty of—"

He broke off, glaring until the barman hurried away. Then he and the reporter put their heads together, conspiring once more as the group at the large table called out their orders.

"Coming," the barman singsonged. "Coming."

Before he was again behind the bar, the door swung open with a jingle of the bell and a rush of November wind and then clattered shut again. A tall woman swathed in furs hurried over to the corner table.

"Fleur, darling." The actor smiled lazily and did not rise. "I didn't think we'd see you again so soon."

Seeing he was not going to take her coat, the woman removed it herself, revealing an alluring body clad in the latest fashion. She brushed a few determined snowflakes off her sleek black hair and looked pointedly at the unoccupied chair next to him.

He shrugged. "Some other time, love. I have business to attend to."

She sat anyway, ignoring the other woman at the table. "We have to talk, Johnnie. I mean it."

His wife glanced at him from the middle of the room, her expression a mix of boredom and disdainful amusement, and then she turned, laughing, to her companions again. The actor lifted his glass to her and took a sip of sherry before turning his attention back to his uninvited guest.

"You'd best get used to the idea, love. I'm absolutely going to—"

He scowled at the barman, who had brought the other table their drinks and was making a great show of not listening in, and then he dropped his voice. The conversation was again low and intense, until the lady reporter gave a shrill, mocking laugh.

The room fell silent. With a dull screech of chair legs, the newcomer sprang to her feet and snatched up her furs.

"You don't really want to do that, Johnnie." Her black eyes snapped in her pale, perfect face. "I promise you don't."

The actor merely gave her a wink and a grin. "Do pop round again, darling, when we're not so busy, eh?"

"Come on, Fleur," cried one of the men from the other table, a character actor, bald and rotund. "Have a drink with us. Leave those two to their plotting. It's all monstrously dull. Come and hear all about when I played Hamlet in Berlin. I was all of twenty-two."

"Don't be absurd," said the bored young man who played all the juvenile leads. "When you were twenty-two, Hamlet hadn't even been written."

"Yes, do join us, Fleur," the leading lady drawled over the good-natured jeering that followed his remark. She leaned back so she could pull up a chair from an empty table. "Johnnie seems to be quite done with you."

With an icy glare the other woman shrugged into her furs and stalked into the cold.

"Oh, dear." The leading lady traced one slender finger over the rim of her wineglass. "What a shame."

"Lovely as always, darling." Drew Farthering took his fiancée's hand and pressed a light kiss to the back of it. "You look a positive angel in that gown."

Madeline Parker's blue eyes sparkled, and she did a half turn, displaying the cream tulle interspersed with little satin motifs like swallows' wings. "Like it?"

"Very much. Mrs. Landis is bound to ask the name of your dressmaker."

Madeline stopped before the mirror in Farthering Place's upper hallway and smoothed her already flawless dark hair. "What's she like anyway? Have you met her?"

"No, but judging by Landis, she's comfortably forty, extremely pleasant, and absolutely respectable. I'm certain you two will get on famously."

He moved over beside her, studying the totality of the reflection. In the stately surroundings of his ancestral home, he saw a beautiful girl with a sweet face and eyes that showed more than her fair share of intelligence and good humor. Beside her was a young man who looked far happier than he deserved. Well, why shouldn't he look happy?

It was November, and the grim events of the past summer were behind them now. His company, Farlinford Processing, had survived embezzlement, fraud, and near bankruptcy, and now, under experienced management, it was recovering nicely. He had himself—through what seemed little short of a miracle—survived near death. And after a whirlwind courtship, though he couldn't help thinking her consent was because of that near death, Madeline had at last agreed to marry him. In just one month she would be forever his own. What more could he want?

She brushed an imaginary speck of dust from his shoulder and straightened his tie just a fraction of an inch.

"How are you and Plumfield getting along?" she asked.

He chuckled. "Perhaps you ought ask how he and Denny are getting along. I'm not used to having a valet, even though it has been a local scandal the past decade, but Denny has enough to do just to look after the house without having to tend to me, as well. I believe there is a silent war going on between him and Plumfield over whether I should wear gold cuff links or platinum and whether having them monogrammed is overly ostentatious."

"Oh, dear," she said, feigning horror.

"Yes, it's been frightful. I feared I would have to wear one of each, you know, just to keep the peace. But now I wonder if that might not have actually brought them to blows."

He offered her his arm and was accepted.

"Where is Aunt Ruth?" he asked as they turned to go down the sweeping stairs. "Shall we go and fetch her?"

"No need to fetch anyone, young man. I'm coming."

Ruth Jansen bustled down the hallway, always swift and purposeful, despite her cane. She wore black as she always had since she had come to Farthering Place as Madeline's chaperone, as she had since losing her fiancé just before their wedding some thirty years ago, but her gown was simple and attractive.

Drew made a slight bow. "Good evening, ma'am. You're looking quite charming this evening."

"Flatterer," she said half under her breath, yet there was a twinkle in her eye as she took his free arm. "I hope you and this Landis fellow aren't going to talk business all night."

"We'll try to keep it to a minimum, Aunt, I give you my word on it." He patted her hand. "And I promise you'll like Landis. He's a good man. He's done wonders with Farlinford already. You know I know nothing about the oil business, and he's come in as if he'd already been there twenty years. Things are improving exponentially. By the time he's been there a year he'll have saved us at least three or four times the price of his salary, I'm certain of it."

"Hard worker, is he?" she asked, eyes narrowed.

"Decidedly. But you needn't worry he'll talk business all night. He's far more likely to tell you at length about his little son."

Madeline beamed at him. "A little boy? How old?"

"Four, I believe. And a marvel unmatched in modern memory, if I've heard properly."

Madeline laughed. "Oh, I think it's too sweet. I like Mr. Landis already."

At that, the front bell rang, and Dennison crossed the foyer to the door. In another moment he came to stand at the foot of the stairs.

"Mr. and Mrs. Landis, sir."

Drew escorted Madeline and her aunt down the last few steps and into the foyer, smiling at the amiable, fortyish-looking man waiting there. Brent Landis's hand was already outstretched.

"Mr. Farthering, good evening. So good of you to have us. Afraid we're a few minutes early. I hope that's not too much of a bother."

"Heavens, no, Landis. Not at all. Good of you to come." Drew shook his hand. "Aunt Ruth, Madeline, darling, this is Brent Landis. Landis, my fiancée, Madeline Parker, and her aunt, Miss Jansen."

Landis bowed to the ladies, and Aunt Ruth gave him a serene nod.

Madeline also shook his hand. "Drew tells me you've done wonders at Farlinford already."

"It's been only four weeks, Miss Parker. Wonders take at least five." Landis chuckled and then looked around. "Now where's my wife got to? Come along, darling. You look glorious as always."

Mrs. Landis turned from the hall mirror, still patting the thick black hair that was twisted into a chignon at the nape of her neck. Her lips, as red and glistening as rubies, were pursed into a knowing little smirk, and her black eyes gleamed as she held out one slender hand.

Drew's smile faltered. "Fleur."

She dropped her chin to her white shoulder, giving him a coy glance from under her black lashes. "Surprise."

Landis looked at her, then at Drew, then at her again. "You and Mr. Farthering know each other, do you? Why didn't you tell me?"

14

Her smile was hardly more than a knowing quirk of her full lips. "Well, I thought it would be rather fun to surprise you both. It's been simply ages, hasn't it, Drew?"

"Rather," he replied.

No one said anything for a moment, and then there was the sound of swift footsteps on the stairs as Nick Dennison came to join them.

"I do beg your pardon, ladies and gentlemen. I had a bit of estate business to see to and couldn't get away." He slicked back his tawny hair, still damp, and looked at Drew. "Introduce me, won't you?"

"Certainly." Drew nodded stiffly. "Mr. and Mrs. Landis, this is Nick Dennison. He is taking over the managing of the estate and otherwise gets me into and out of mischief. Nick, Mr. and Mrs. Landis."

Fleur smiled at him with a pretty tilt of her head.

"Mrs. Landis." Nick obliged her with a look of somewhat-stunned recognition, and then he and Landis shook hands. "Good to meet you, Mr. Landis."

Just then the bell sounded, and as his duty as host required, Drew offered Fleur his arm. "May I, Mrs. Landis?"

She accepted, her slim hand white against his dinner jacket, and with a bow, Nick held out his arm and escorted Aunt Ruth.

"Miss Parker?" Landis said, and with an

uncertain smile she took his arm and went last into the dining room.

Madeline and Drew took their places at opposite ends of the long, gleaming table, with Landis and Nick on Madeline's right and left and Fleur and Aunt Ruth on Drew's.

Drew glanced at his guests. Just as he and Nick did, Landis wore eveningwear that was absolutely correct in every respect. Fleur was wearing a beaded net gown, black to show off her pale, perfect skin, the daring bodice open to the waist in back and on both sides, and the skirt slit up high on the right. He was used to seeing women in such gowns. Bare backs and arms and sides were all the fashion these days, but Fleur . . . Fleur was Fleur, and there was always something a bit bold, a bit wild about her, even when she was seated quietly at the dinner table as the soup was served.

Madeline was her near opposite, demure in creamy white tulle, the ruffled, transparent sleeves flowing like angel wings from her shoulders. He smiled across the table at her, a subtle, intimate smile just for her, and she returned it just as subtly before turning to Landis.

"How have you liked working at Farlinford, Mr. Landis? Drew tells me it was in a bad way before you came."

"Oh, it wasn't too terribly bad, Miss Parker. Certainly there were some places that needed shoring up, a few rather thorny knots to untangle, but nothing that can't be put right in time."

Drew nodded as he took a sip of mock turtle soup. "You see, darling? I soon won't be needed at Farlinford at all. Then you'll have to figure out how to keep me entertained day in and day out."

"You never go in to work as it is, and you seem to have no trouble getting into mischief all on your own," Aunt Ruth observed with a twinkle in her eye.

He laughed. "I suppose not, ma'am, but at least when I do I won't have to worry about the business going south, as well."

"Drew tells me you have a great deal of experience in the oil business, Mr. Landis," Nick said.

"About twenty years now," Landis replied. "I'd been with Anglo-Persian Oil for the past sixteen, but I thought it was time I tried something new." He glanced at Drew, a touch of sympathy in his expression. "Well, after everything that happened this past summer, I knew it would take some work to get Farlinford back running as she should, and I thought that was just the challenge I'd like to take on. I'm glad Mr. Farthering agreed to let me give it a go."

"No doubt Anglo-Persian wasn't at all pleased with me stealing you away from them," Drew said. "But all's fair, eh?"

Fleur huffed, looking only good-naturedly put out. "Must you discuss business all night, Brent?

Don't you have enough of that at the office?"

Landis bowed and said, "I beg your pardon, ladies."

"Sorry," Drew added. "How about something a bit more congenial, darling?"

"Well, Mrs. Landis has told us hardly anything about herself." Madeline took a taste of her soup. "How long ago did you and Drew meet, Mrs. Landis?"

"Oh, heavens." Fleur's laugh was light and silvery. "Such ancient history. How long ago was it, Drew, love? Five years?"

"Six." He knew the word had come out more sharply than it should have, and he forced his expression into something more pleasant. "It is six, I believe. I remember because it was my first term there."

"What children we were." Fleur dipped her spoon in her bowl, toying with it. "But what lovely times we had. I so enjoyed Oxford. So pretty and so, oh, I don't know, just brimming with knowledge. One could feel it in the air, didn't you think so, Drew?"

"I know I learned a great deal there, yes."

Madeline was looking at him, trying to read his thoughts as always, and then she turned to Fleur. "Were you at the university too, Mrs. Landis?"

Again Fleur laughed. "I was with a repertory company there in the city. Light opera. Gilbert and Sullivan mostly. It was great fun."

Madeline glanced at Drew once more, but kept her attention on Fleur. "That must have been terribly interesting. Do you still act?"

"Oh, no." She bit her lip, and a certain wistfulness came into her eyes. "I left it all for dear Brent." She looked at her husband, her lips turned up on one side. "And then we had Peter, and that was the end of my time before the footlights. Of course, a woman's figure is always a bit frumpy afterward."

With a regretful pout of her full lips, she slid one hand from her slender waist to her hip and looked at the men seated at the table, obviously waiting for at least one of them to object. Nick glanced at Drew, smirking slightly. She knew exactly how she looked, and it certainly wasn't frumpy.

"Nonsense, sweetheart," Landis said. "You haven't aged a day since we met. If anything, you've grown only more beautiful."

"There, you see? That just proves that love is in fact stone blind." She laughed softly and lifted her wineglass in a silent toast to him. "You turn my head terribly, darling."

He toasted her in return, a sudden warm softness in his brown eyes. "It is one of the great pleasures of my life, my love."

She gave him a secretive little smile and then faced Madeline again. "I suppose Drew is just as bad. Worse, I'd guess. He was always such a romantic when I knew him back at Oxford."

19

"I trust we've all grown up a bit since then," Drew said.

"Oh no." Fleur wagged one finger at him. "I know your type, Drew Farthering. Death before dishonor. Utterly devoted. Quietly and deeply passionate. Eighteen or eighty, you'd be just the same."

Drew ate another spoonful of soup, hoping his face wasn't turning any uncomfortable shades of red. Madeline, bless her, was quick to shift the conversation to something not so awkward.

She turned to Landis. "I understand you and Mrs. Landis have a little boy."

"That's right." Landis's eyes lit. "Peter. He turned four this summer, and I tell you, the boy's smart as a whip."

He reached in his jacket pocket for his wallet, and Fleur rolled her eyes.

"Oh, dear. Please, Brent, you mustn't bore everyone with your pictures."

"Just one, Fleur."

"I'm so sorry," Fleur said to Madeline with good-natured regret. "I told him before we arrived—"

"Oh, I'd love to see." Madeline leaned toward Landis, waiting for him to find what he was looking for. "Four is such a darling age."

Landis beamed at her and handed her a photograph. "Sorry, my dear, but I can never resist. A bit proud, don't you know."

Madeline gave him a warm glance and then looked at the picture. "Oh, how sweet. Look, Nick."

Nick leaned over to look, too. "Cute kid."

"Aunt Ruth, you must see."

Madeline passed the photo to her aunt.

"A lovely child. He favors you, Mrs. Landis," Aunt Ruth said. "Very much, apart from the blond hair."

Fleur patted her black chignon and gave Aunt Ruth a pert grin. "You'd never know it to see me now, Miss Jansen, but my hair was just as blond when I was that age. I'm afraid it didn't last, and yet I've never cared for bleaching. It seems so . . . so false."

Drew looked over at the photograph Madeline's aunt still held. It showed a fair-haired little boy holding a stuffed rabbit. His expression was solemn for the camera, but there was a brightness to the eyes and a sweetness to the mouth that were altogether appealing.

"You've every right to be proud, Landis," Drew said as Aunt Ruth handed the picture back. "He's a fine little chap."

"All right, dear, I've put it up." Landis replaced the photograph in his wallet, a touch of mischief on his face. "Won't happen again."

Fleur leaned forward in her chair to get a better view of Madeline around Nick. "You mustn't misunderstand me, Miss Parker. I'm quite the doting mother myself, but I know how tedious hearing about other people's children can be."

"I think Peter is charming," Madeline assured her. "Anyone would be proud to claim him as his own."

Fleur simpered as if Madeline were thirty years her junior rather than just seven or eight. "Isn't she sweet, Drew? Just the sort of girl you were looking for when you were at Oxford."

"True enough," Drew told her, keeping his expression bland. "But I've found since then that they're exceedingly rare."

The creamed chicken, spinach, and new potatoes arrived, and the conversation shifted to food and then to staff. Landis and Aunt Ruth discussed Chicago at length, since Landis had visited there many times on business, and Fleur told several amusing stories about her time onstage. By the time the pears a la conde and then the port were served, Drew let himself relax, at least a little. It seemed the evening would not be a disaster after all. At least it wouldn't be until he had to talk to Madeline alone, and he was sure from the look in her eyes that she would insist on it.

Once the Landises were gone, Aunt Ruth retired for the night, and Nick, claiming some estate business to attend to, made himself scarce. Madeline sat beside Drew on the sofa in the drawing room, her hand on his arm. She had once teasingly accused him of never believing a woman could do any harm.

"Oh, no," he had told her then. "I've been taught to know better. I have the scars to prove it."

"I'll want to know someday," she'd said to that, her voice tender and sympathetic. She hadn't pressed to know more, and he had known she would wait until he was ready to tell her about those scars.

He sighed. Now that someday had come.

"Madeline . . ." Why did this have to be so difficult? "Madeline, I—"

"You both handled it extremely well. I think her husband believed her story."

He shrugged. "It's true, you know. Everything she said. We met about six years ago when I was at Oxford. I haven't seen her since."

"But that's not the whole story."

"No."

She studied his face for a long moment. "I suppose it was exactly what I'm thinking it was."

He nodded. This was supposed to be behind him. God forgive him, did it have to come up just now? Right before the wedding?

Her mild expression did not change. "Will you tell me about it?"

"There's not much to it." He drew a deep breath. "I was eighteen. I'd been away at school before, of course, but I was just beginning to feel as if I

23

were truly on my own. I saw Fleur in a production of *Ruddigore* at the local theater. I thought she was amazing, but I never expected to see her except on the stage. But when my friends and I went to have dinner afterward, there she was with three or four other girls from the troupe. I just went to tell her how much I had enjoyed the performance, and she asked us all to join them."

There was a touch of wryness in Madeline's faint smile. "And you were smitten."

"I was. I won't deny it. But I never thought anything would ever come of it. I didn't think we'd ever even meet after that, but the next day I ran into her in a tea shop near my college, and again she invited me to sit with her. Here she was, an older woman by five years and an actress, God save us, just the sort I'd been warned away from, and she was as sweet and ladylike as any of the girls I'd been told were proper company. I asked if she'd dine with me after her performance the next night, and she said she would. I saw her almost every night after that. We'd go to dinner after the show was over and talk for hours about nothing."

"Sounds harmless enough."

"Perhaps. It should have been. It was." He shrugged again. "It was until a couple of weeks later. I had taken her to dinner at a little French place, and I could tell the whole time that she was upset. She kept saying it was nothing, but when I took her to her door, she started to cry. She held on to me and cried as if her heart were breaking. I couldn't leave her that way, so I took her inside. I'd never even stepped foot in the place before. It's . . . well, it was something I was always careful never to do with any of the girls I saw. Call me Victorian if you like, but I'd seen too many of my friends get into trouble too easily. Anyway, that night I told myself it would be all right, that I couldn't just dump a lady on her doorstep when she was in such a state."

Madeline nodded. "So you took her inside."

"I did." He let the air seep out of his lungs. "At first she wouldn't tell me why she was so upset. Then she said it was because the troupe were moving on after the Saturday night show and we'd likely not see each other again. I told her if she married me, she wouldn't have to go with the troupe at all. Then she was kissing me and, well, it wasn't anything like the good-night kisses we'd shared before." He felt his face getting hot. "Do I need to say anything more?"

She shook her head. "Did you love her?"

"I thought I did. I was infatuated with her. I wanted her. But, no, I didn't love her. There was always something . . . distant about her, as if she were playing a role and not letting me see her true self."

"And that didn't bother you?"

His smile turned bitter. "It was a very charming role."

"When you were with her, why didn't you just stop?"

"I couldn't. I . . ." He trailed off, laughing faintly. "Forgive me, darling. I mean to be always and entirely honest with you, and that's not precisely true. I didn't stop because I chose not to. Whatever else I've told myself since, that's how it was. I thought we were in love. I thought we were going to be married. I thought that would make it all right. There are a lot of little decisions one makes between good night at the door and good morning under the coverlet, and I made all the wrong ones. Still, that was the last time I saw her."

She squeezed his arm. "At least that was the end of it."

"The end of it," he said, "but not the worst of it."

There was a touch of wariness in her eyes. "What do you mean?"

"Afterward, though I knew it would be a scandal back in Farthering St. John, I proposed to her. I thought surely she would want to marry me then. I thought surely we must be in love. After what we'd just done, what else could it be?" He leaned over, elbows on his knees, head in his hands. "The more fool me."

"Why do you say that?"

He cringed inside, his pride smarting from what he'd already told her, but she deserved to know it all. She shouldn't, God forbid, hear it from anyone else.

"When I said I would be quite honored if she would consent to be my wife, she only laughed and said her husband wouldn't think much of the arrangement."

Madeline's eyes went wide. "She was already married?"

He nodded, searching her face, trying to read her thoughts.

"To Mr. Landis?"

He shook his head. "Her name was Hargreaves then. I believe her husband was an older chap, MP or something, though they were already living apart. I didn't much care by then. Whether he died or divorced her at that point, I can't say." He gave her a grim little smile. "I got the distinct impression at the time that I wasn't her only intrigue, so maybe it wasn't solely because of me that the marriage ended. The divorce ruined his political career too, I've heard."

"Either way, she must have married Mr. Landis not long after."

"Right." Drew sat up straight again, forcing his expression into more pleasant lines. "He mentioned they'd been married five years now."

She didn't say anything to that, and for a while they just sat there. She studied her engagement ring, the one his grandfather Elliot Farthering had given to his grandmother Amelia. The band was an elegant crisscross design filled with round channel-set diamonds, accented with round pave diamonds all the way around. Crowning it was a brilliant square-cut white diamond, lavish without being gaudy. Over the past three months he had grown accustomed to seeing it there on her hand.

"What are you thinking?" he asked finally.

She shook her head, still staring at her ring.

"Come on, darling." He pushed a stray lock of her hair back behind her ear. "Tell me what's on your mind."

"Nothing really. Nothing important."

"It must be important to put that look on your face." He looked at the ring and then into her eyes. "Regrets?"

Again she shook her head, and he bit his lip. What was he to say to her?

"Darling, I have no excuses for you. I was foolish. I hope you can forgive me."

"She's very beautiful, isn't she?" Madeline smoothed the cream-colored tulle of her dress. "And very . . . dramatic. It's no wonder you were taken with her."

"One always knows when she's in the room," he said with an attempt at lightness. "I daresay she was born to be on the stage."

Madeline looked at him, her gaze piercing. "Are you sorry you couldn't marry her? I mean, if she hadn't already been married, would you have truly wanted to marry her?"

"I did at the time, certainly. I'm sure after . . . after that night, I would have. As wrong as it was, I thank God now that she was married already. I can only think it would be torment to be her husband."

"Mr. Landis seems taken with her."

"He does, poor chap. Perhaps, and I hope so sincerely, she has changed her ways. Sometimes motherhood has a settling effect."

Madeline shrugged. "And sometimes people merely grow up."

He was silent for a long moment, and then he put his arm around her. "Do forgive me, darling. If there were any way I could change the past, I swear I would. I wouldn't hurt or disappoint you for all the world."

Her fingers were light and gentle in his hair. "You were still just a boy. You made a mistake."

He looked away from her. "It was cheap. It was tawdry. Good heavens, I was looking for something grand and glorious and real, and she was only playing."

She turned his face back to her. "It's been six years, darling. I think it's time you forgave her and yourself."

He searched her eyes. "And will you forgive me, as well? For not being the paragon you were looking for?"

"I was looking for a man, darling. You're already nearly too perfect anyway. And if you were any better, what would you want with me?"

He chuckled. "Not perfect, my love, as you well know, but perfectly happy and perfectly in love."

The sparkle came back into her periwinkle eyes. "I don't suppose I could ask for more than that, could I?"

"Not and reasonably expect to be satisfied, no."

She looked into his eyes for a moment more. Then her lashes fell to her cheeks. "Will you do something for me, Drew?"

"If I am able, yes. What is it you want? Buckingham Palace? The Taj Mahal?"

She shook her head, completely somber. "I would like it very much, though, if we didn't have to have the Landises to dinner again."

He winced. "That would be rather awkward at this point, wouldn't it? Consider it done. If I need to socialize with Landis, I'll have him round to my club. How would that be?"

She put her arms around his neck and smiled into his eyes once more. "That would be perfectly perfect."

— *Two* —

Three mornings later, Drew was sitting at the breakfast table. Along with Mr. Padgett, Nick was up in the master suite seeing to the workmen who were remodeling it for Drew and Madeline to occupy once they were Mr. and Mrs. Farthering.

Madeline and her aunt had been staying in his mother's old suite of rooms in the west wing ever since Madeline had accepted his proposal. Drew had not himself moved into the master suite after his stepfather's death, but once Madeline had agreed to marry him, he had begun to have the rooms redone to suit them both.

They had agreed to keep the furniture. Old and heavy and steadfast, it had served the Farthering men for decades, and Madeline liked it. But the murky browns and greens of the carpet, curtains, and bedding had to go. They decided instead on a buttery tone of ivory with dark sage, plum, and a bronzy gold. It was rich without being heavy, breezy and fresh but not girlish.

Evidently there had been difficulties today with the wallpaper Madeline had chosen, but Drew and Nick had agreed it would be best to simply see to the matter and not worry Madeline with it. Madeline herself had hurried off to see to the caterer with Aunt Ruth. So with Nick attending to the workmen, Drew was left to linger over his newspaper and the last of his liberally honeyed tea.

"A Mrs. Mallowan to see you, sir."

Drew looked up at Dennison and chuckled softly. "Mrs. Mallowan or Mrs. Christie?"

Denny's face was as impassive as ever. "I was given the name Mallowan, sir. Shall I enquire again?"

"No, no, that's all right. Did she give you her card?"

"No, sir. Do you wish me to tell her you are not at home to visitors?"

"Nonsense," Drew said. "Send her in, if you would, please. I think I'm up for an adventure this morning."

"Very good, sir."

"But, uh, I say, Denny?"

"Yes, sir?"

"What does this Mrs. Mallowan look like? Anyone we know?"

"I couldn't say, sir. The lady is wearing a veil and seems rather determined to remain unknown."

Drew grinned. "Not Miss Parker in disguise, is it?"

"No, sir. Unless I am much mistaken."

"Well, that's too bad, I suppose. All right. Ah, please show her into the drawing room on second thought. I'll be right there. And ask Miss Parker if she would do me the favor of coming down too, eh?"

Denny made a slight bow. "At once, sir."

He disappeared into the hallway, and Drew folded his newspaper. Agatha Christie's married name was Mallowan. So unless it truly was the celebrated Mrs. Mallowan herself, surely someone was having him on. Well, that was all right. It was as much tradition to harry the groom-to-be as it was to fête the bride.

He swallowed down the last of his tea and then straightened his tie. "Whoever you are, dear Mrs. Mallowan, I hope to give you as good as you send."

The lady was sitting on the sofa when Drew came into the drawing room. She was tall and slender and, as Denny had said, draped in a heavy veil. And she was dressed all in black as if she were in mourning. Drew's expression sobered. Best not treat this as a joke until he was certain it was one.

"Good morning," he said, making his voice pleasant but not too cheerful, just in case.

She extended one black-gloved hand. "Thank you for seeing me."

Her voice was a husky whisper, but he was certain he had heard it before.

"Mrs. . . . Mallowan?"

She nodded once. "Will you shut the door so we may speak in private?"

He inclined his head. "Forgive me, but I've asked my fiancée to join us. I hope you don't mind."

She made a petulant little huffing sound that he recognized at once.

"Fleur?"

She used both graceful hands to lift her veil just enough so she could peep out from under it. "Must she, Drew? I'd much prefer—"

"I do hope you'll pardon me, but, yes, she must.

33

If you wish to speak to me, she absolutely must."

"But Drew—"

"Otherwise I really have to bid you good morning."

She pouted and let the veil fall over her face again. "Can she at least be trusted not to let anyone know I've come to see you?"

"If that's necessary, I'm certain she can. Madeline is always very—"

"Always very what, darling?"

Madeline stood in the doorway, smiling and spring fresh in a flowered frock and pink jumper.

Drew held out his hand to her. "Come in, Madeline, and shut the door if you would."

She lifted an eyebrow, but did as she was asked and then came to stand at Drew's side. "Won't you introduce us?" she asked.

Fleur put back her veil again and discarded her hat altogether. "I'm sure you remember me, Miss Parker."

Madeline glanced at Drew, her expression suddenly cool. "Yes, Mrs. Landis, I do. Forgive me, but I wasn't expecting—"

"No, forgive *me*." Fleur's dark eyes were pleading and helpless. "Both of you, please, I really can't have anyone know I've come to you today. Will you promise not to say anything?"

Drew settled Madeline on the love seat and then sat next to her, putting her arm through his.

"Say anything?" he asked. "To whom?"

"To anyone. Please, Drew. I know we didn't part the best of friends back in Oxford."

She turned those eyes up to his, shining with unshed tears, and he remembered now why his eighteen-year-old self had been so easily smitten. He wouldn't again be such a fool.

"I daresay."

His voice was coolly polite, and no one said anything for a moment. Madeline looked at him, her delicate eyebrows lifted just the slightest bit.

He turned again to their guest. "I take it there's a reason you've come? Why go through the pretense of saying you were Mrs. Mallowan?"

"I know you like mystery novels, and I thought the name might pique your interest. I couldn't risk your not seeing me. I . . ." Fleur had a lace handkerchief crumpled in one hand, and now she touched it to her trembling lips. "I'm in the most awful trouble, Drew, and I was hoping you might be able to help me."

"Perhaps you ought to be talking to the police. I know a Chief Inspector Birdsong who—"

"No." She shook her head, again pressing her handkerchief to her mouth. "Oh, Drew, no. You don't understand. The police are the ones I'm going to be in trouble with!"

Madeline gave Drew a subtle glance, one he knew meant she didn't want him to get involved with anything that would interfere with their wedding plans. He squeezed her arm in acknowl-edgment.

"Perhaps a solicitor then. I could give you the name of the firm we use. Or if you had rather keep the matter separate, I'm certain they could give you a referral to someone who specializes in whatever sort of case you have."

"No, no." Fleur's voice was nearly a sob now. "I need someone unofficial, someone who can keep my name out of it."

"A private investigator perhaps."

"I couldn't possibly go to someone like that. Poor Brent, the scandal would kill him."

Drew narrowed his eyes at her. "Just what are you afraid you'll be accused of?"

"Haven't you seen the morning paper?"

He shook his head. "At least not all of it. I was reading it over breakfast, but I always start at the back and work my way to the front. Save the headlines for last, as it were. Shall I have it brought in?"

She sniffed and then nodded. "I couldn't . . . Oh, Drew, I couldn't possibly tell you the awful details."

He tried to figure out how much of her fright was real and how much of it was put on to sway him. But it didn't matter. Whatever this was, it wasn't his place to help her. She had a husband, and he seemed a very good man. Surely he would stand by her whatever the problem was.

He rang for Denny, and in just another moment Drew had that morning's paper in hand. One bold headline caught his eye.

ACTOR RAVENSWOOD MURDERED

Drew looked up at Fleur. "Ravenswood? It was his troupe you were in back in Oxford, wasn't it? What happened?"

"Read it." A single tear traced down her porcelain cheek, and she immediately blotted it away, forcing herself to sit up straighter. "You'll want just the facts, and that will tell you better than I would be able to."

Madeline was already reading over his shoulder, and he hurried to catch up.

Local celebrity, actor John Sutherland Ravenswood, born Henry Percival Sutherland, was found at two o'clock this morning in his dressing room at the Tivoli Theater, bludgeoned to death with an empty champagne bottle. Ravenswood's wife and leading lady, Miss Simone Cullimore, already having gone home after last night's performance, called the theater to speak to Ravenswood before he left for the evening. Conor Benton, another of the actors, and one of the workmen found the star's dressing room locked, and receiving no reply to repeated knocks and calls, they forced the door open.

"He was lying there with his head bashed in, mind you, and fair wallowing in his blood," said Grady Hibbert, the Tivoli's longtime stageman. "I never had nobody killed in my theater, barring onstage of course, nor seen a dead body since I was at Ypres in the Great War."

"We had all been drinking champagne," Miss Cullimore said. "It was the fifth anniversary of our opening night at the Tivoli, and everyone was in a jolly mood. Johnnie said he had a few things to see to before he went home, so I went on alone. Now I'll never see him again."

Chief Inspector James Birdsong of the Hampshire Police declined comment except to say his men were investigating the matter and that they were not prepared to name any suspects.

Again Drew looked up at Fleur, skipping the remainder of the article. "What does this have to do with you? Did you kill him?"

"Drew!" Tears sprang to her eyes, and once more she pressed the frothy bit of lace to her mouth, her body shaking. "I know what you think of me after . . . after Oxford, but you can't believe that of me. Not murder. Please tell me you don't."

"I haven't seen you in six years, Mrs. Landis," he told her. "And even back then, I can't say I really knew you. How would I know what you're capable of?"

"Drew," Madeline murmured.

He pressed his lips into a tight line. "Sorry, darling."

Fleur studied them for a moment, then looked away. "I just thought you might be able to help me."

"Is there some reason in particular you think the police will suspect you?"

"Well, I . . . I knew Johnnie Ravenswood. We were . . . we used to be an item, but that was years ago. When we were in that repertory company in Oxford."

Drew glanced at Madeline. "Was that before or after you and I met?"

Fleur looked down and somehow had the grace to look ashamed. "Before and after. I know. I know. It was insane. I was sowing my wild oats, and now I suppose I get to reap the harvest."

"That's hardly any reason for you to be a suspect now, is it?" Drew asked, his voice cold. "There must be more."

She bit her lip and nodded. "I still kept in touch with him. Well, with all of them. That's often how it is in the theater. Sometimes, especially with small companies that have the same players in them for years at a time, it's like a little family. I was friends with his wife, believe it or not, and with several of the others. I missed it, being onstage, and I liked chatting with them about old times. Sometimes I'd sit in and read a part when they were rehearsing or trying out some new bit of business. Johnnie would sometimes use one of my suggestions, especially if it was one of the women's roles. Brent never understood, so I never told him that's what I was doing. But there wasn't any harm in it. It was just . . . fun."

Drew exchanged a look with Madeline. She looked no more convinced than he.

"And this 'fun' is enough to make you a suspect?" he pressed.

"Oh, I don't know." Her eyes filled with tears once more. "The police came to talk to me this morning. Evidently someone claims he saw me at the theater last night after everyone else had gone, but I tell you I wasn't there! I was at home all night—you can ask Brent."

"The police haven't talked to him yet?"

"He had already gone to the office, but I suppose they've gone there to question him. I don't know."

"And who is it that says you were at the theater last night?"

Fleur pursed her lips. "A perfectly odious man. Conor Benton. He plays all the juvenile leads, and *juvenile* is the perfect word for him. He and Johnnie were always at it hammer and tongs over blocking and stage business and how lines ought to be delivered." She frowned. "I suspect too they had a bit of not-so-friendly competition over the girls in the chorus and any stagestruck young things who threw themselves at the two of them. I mean, fair's fair. Johnnie was more handsome than any man ought to be. More than that, he knew how to charm anyone out of anything. Benton's not much better. He fancies himself something of an Adonis, though I think he's got a bit of a weak chin. Still, he draws the ladies, and that's what he was engaged to do."

"I see," Drew said. "But why would he claim to have seen you at the theater if you weren't there?"

She glanced at Madeline, and a blush touched her cheek. "A few months ago he tried to seduce me. I told him I wasn't interested, that I loved my husband. He called me all sorts of filthy names and said I was a hypocrite. He couldn't believe I was different now, that I wasn't who I used to be." Again there were tears. "You have to believe me, Drew. I'm not who I was. I'm not that thoughtless girl you once knew. I love my husband and my son. I don't want to hurt them. I don't want to ruin them. Please help me."

Drew sighed and again looked at Madeline, knowing her grim expression was a mirror of his own. This was bad. Very bad.

"And you want me to do what exactly?" he asked at last.

She squirmed in her chair, dark eyes pleading. "I merely thought that you could investigate the case yourself. If you could find out who really

41

killed Johnnie, then they couldn't suspect me, could they?"

"I suppose not. But I'm not—"

"If you could start work right away, and work very quickly, then Brent doesn't have to deal with all this." She clasped her hands together, almost in an attitude of prayer, and there was more than a touch of desperation in her expression. "And nobody has to know."

"If you are innocent," said Drew, "then what does it matter if your husband or anyone knows you might briefly be a suspect? You will be cleared by the police in time, won't you?"

"It's just . . ." Again the dark eyes were pleading with him. "You know already, Drew, how foolish I've been in the past. I'm not proud of how I treated you once. I'm not proud of how I've treated other men." She glanced at Madeline and then back at him. "But I've tried to change my ways. The police suspect me. They might even arrest me before long, but I didn't do it. You must believe me, Drew. You must."

Drew stared at her. Was she a murderess? He couldn't quite imagine it of her, but he didn't trust her either, not after what had happened in Oxford. Her distress seemed genuine, but perhaps it would be even if she had killed Ravenswood. Maybe more so. He liked to think himself discerning, but just how good an actress was she?

He glanced at Madeline, trying to read her

reaction, but her expression remained determinedly cool.

"Why did you stop seeing Mr. Ravenswood, Mrs. Landis?" Madeline asked. "Were you the one to break it off or was he?"

"I was," Fleur said. "I had my little boy, you see. I thought what it might be like for him in a few years to know his mother was . . . well, talked about."

"And your husband?"

She lowered her eyes. "Brent's been nothing but good to me. No matter what. He's why I've come to you now. I don't want to hurt him more than I have already. He doesn't deserve that. He doesn't deserve the scandal that would surely come if I were to be accused of something like this." She smiled wanly. "You like him, Drew. I could see you did right from the start. Everyone does, you know. Couldn't you help me for his sake, if not for what you and I once were to each other?"

Something flickered in Madeline's eyes at that, and Drew abruptly stood.

"We were never anything to each other, Mrs. Landis. You made that quite clear the last time we met in Oxford, and I quite agree with you."

"But Drew—"

"I'm sorry you're rather in a bind right now. Sorry for Landis and for your little boy more than anyone. But I think you need to find someone who can actually help you."

She took a deep breath, and her laugh was almost soundless. "It's been a long time, Drew. I thought perhaps you would have forgiven me by now."

He shrugged. "It *has* been a long time. We've both moved on. I'm not angry anymore, Mrs. Landis. I just haven't anything to say to you. And there's nothing I can do for you now."

She looked up at Drew, still pleading with those fathomless dark eyes of hers. Then she gave Madeline a desperate look, but Madeline merely turned away from her.

Fleur slowly nodded, her expression stiff, and stood with her black-lace bag clutched in her hands. "Well, I suppose that's it then. I'm sorry to have bothered you both." She smoothed her already sleek hair and replaced her hat, drawing the veil once again over her face.

"I'll see you to the door," Drew said. He turned to Madeline. "Don't get up, darling. I'll be back in a moment."

"All right," she said. "Goodbye, Mrs. Landis."

Fleur inclined her head, regal as a queen. "Miss Parker."

With just the lightest touch to the back of her elbow, Drew accompanied her out of the drawing room and into the foyer.

"I take it you didn't drive your own car here," he said, keeping his voice low. "Shall I phone for a taxi?"

"I have one waiting," she said, her voice also low, just as it had been when she'd tried to pretend she was a Mrs. Mallowan.

"Excellent," he said. He touched her elbow again, meaning to see her down to the drive, but she stopped. He couldn't see her face, yet he could tell by the angle of her head that she was looking up at him. He could feel her eyes on him.

"Will you forgive me, Drew? I know I hurt you. I knew all along, you see, that first night you took me to dinner. I knew. That's what made the game so much fun."

"Knew what? What game?"

Her head went down again. What was that? Regret? Shame?

"What game?" he pressed.

"My friends, the ones I was with that first night we met, they said you were a rarity. Being on the stage, of course, we were all used to proposals of one kind or another. They said you were too posh to propose marriage to somebody like me, and too much the gentleman to propose anything else. I told them I'd get one or the other from you before the week was out."

"How proud you must have been to tell them you'd been so successful."

"I'm not proud of it now, Drew. I know I broke your heart. I know—"

"Don't flatter yourself. You never had my heart to break. You hurt my pride, I'll give you that much, but maybe I was a bit too sure of myself back then anyway."

"Back then?" Her laugh had a touch of derision in it, but it was soon gone. "I meant it, Drew. I'm sorry for what happened. All of it. I'd like you to forgive me if you possibly can."

He studied her for a moment, imagining her sweet face turned up to his under that veil. Imagining her dark eyes sparkling with unshed tears. Then he saw those same eyes glittering with amusement back there in her Oxford flat, her flawless features smug and twisted as she told him she was already married, and his heart turned icy inside him.

He opened the front door. "Your cab is waiting."

— *Three* —

"I'm glad you turned her down." Madeline put her arm through Drew's when he came back and sat beside her on the parlor sofa. "I don't like her being around you."

He put his hand over hers, giving it a gentle squeeze. "You needn't worry, darling. I was decidedly cured of her six years ago."

He felt her laugh rather than heard it. "I'm not worried about that. I just know she's not a pleasant memory for you, and I don't want you to be unhappy."

"Unhappy? You love me, don't you, darling?"

She looked up at him, a warm softness in her eyes. "Very much."

"Then I could never truly be unhappy."

He put his arm around her, but she pulled back a little, her expression troubled.

"Darling?"

"Is she . . . ?" She frowned just the slightest bit. "Is she why you've been so careful with me? Making sure we don't get into any compromising situations?"

"Partly, love."

"And the rest of it? Is it because I'm not as irresistible as she was?"

He looked deeply into her eyes. "It's not because you're not driving me mad every moment I'm with you, and even when I'm not. It's just I don't want us to have any regrets. If I resist you, it's because I'm trying my best to do what is right, not at all because it's easy. I've told you before, it's because I love you even more than I want you. And that, Madeline, is much more than I could ever put into words."

She tightened her hold on his hand.

"Maybe . . ." he began. "Maybe if I had loved Fleur, if I had really loved her instead of just wanting her, I wouldn't have let things go too far."

"And if she had cared anything for you, she would have let you alone in the first place." There was a touch of wryness in Madeline's expression. "Charming way for her to amuse herself."

"She has an interesting sense of fun, does Mrs. Landis, but I realized long ago that I don't care to play along."

She twined her fingers into his and tilted her head to one side. "Shall we talk about something a little more pleasant, Drew?"

"Brilliant idea, darling. What did you have in mind?"

She gave him that pert look of hers. "Would you like to know who I've invited to come help me with the wedding plans?"

"Very much. Anyone I know? King George? Mrs. Hoover?"

"Don't be silly. George is one of *your* friends, not mine. And from what I hear, Mrs. Hoover is packing her things and preparing to move out of the White House."

"Very well, that leaves us with just the population of the world minus two. How about a hint of some variety?"

"Hmm, let me see." She pursed her lips for a moment. "Well, if I were Yum-Yum, they would be Peep-Bo and Pitti-Sing."

"Ah, I see. 'Three Little Maids from School,' eh? Well, then who could it possibly be but the delightful Miss Holland and, ahem, Miss Brower."

"And I'm sure they're just perishing to see Adorable Drew again."

Drew pretended to scowl. "Oh, joy unbounded."

"You love it and you know it," Madeline said with a giggle. "Anyway, you know Nick has been pining for Carrie for months now."

"Has he been? Pining? I hadn't noticed any pining."

She shook her head, looking faintly disgusted. "You men never notice anything. All right, maybe *pining* isn't quite the word, but they got along very well when she was here this summer, and she didn't end up marrying any English lords before she went home, so I think that's pretty significant."

He laughed. "If you say so, darling. And, yes, I expect Nick will be quite pleased to see her. She seems an awfully nice girl, and I'd like Nick to find someone who suits him. At least better than Barbie Chalfont." He pulled her a bit closer. "I'd like him to be as happy as I am, though I don't know how he could possibly manage it."

He brought her hand to his lips and was puzzled to see something like wariness in her eyes. In another instant it was gone and she was all smiles again.

"And what if he decides to move to America to be near her?"

Drew's eyes widened. "Nick? In America? For good?" He shook his head. "No, no. That would never do. That wouldn't do at all."

"My father did it. He was English, but he seemed pretty happy living in America."

Drew looked at her, incredulous. "My girl, your father was not heir presumptive to the office of Estate Manager of Farthering Place. Nick is as much a part of Farthering as . . . as Denny! If he decides he cannot manage without Miss Holland, then she shall simply have to come here. We've plenty of room and a perfectly good auntie to chaperone until they decide whether or not to marry."

Madeline laughed. "You know Aunt Ruth isn't going to live here, either. Not permanently."

"Why not? The more the merrier, I say. We have acres of room for everyone."

"The next thing you'll suggest is that we marry *her* off."

Drew made a great show of considering this. "You know, that's not a half-bad idea."

"Don't be ridiculous. Aunt Ruth?"

"Why not? Just because she's reached a certain age, that doesn't mean she doesn't still have a heart. Don't you think she's been alone long enough?" He sat up a little. "Oh, I know. We could have a double wedding. You and me and Aunt Ruth and her long-awaited love. No, wait, there's Nick and Miss Holland, as well. A triple wedding! Won't it be jolly?"

She crossed her arms. "Now you're just being silly. And who exactly is going to walk me down the aisle? Neither of us has any family to speak of, and my uncle Calvin isn't really up to making such a long trip."

"We'll think of something, darling. The doctor perhaps. Or the vet." He grinned at her. "So when are the other two little maids meant to arrive from school?"

"Carrie and Muriel won't be here until a week before the wedding. Carrie's father was absolutely against her coming back so soon, but since it *is* for the wedding, he finally gave in."

"What about Miss Brower? I never heard about her family when she was here before. Do they also object?"

"She's practically an orphan, too," Madeline told him. "Her great-aunt raised her and pretty much lets her do as she pleases about most things."

"Ah," Drew said, "this explains a great deal."

Madeline shook her head. "Muriel's a good sort. Just a little brassy at times."

"Like a euphonium."

"But you like Carrie, don't you?"

"Miss Holland is a delight, and I have yet to meet anyone who seems more appropriate for Nick. I'm glad she's coming back for a while. It will give them a chance to get better acquainted."

"Give who a chance to get better acquainted?" Nick asked as he came into the room.

"You, my good fellow," Drew said. "We've decided to marry you off, as well."

"Oh, all right." Nick considered for a moment. "Anyone I know?"

"You remember Miss Holland who came to visit with my Madeline this past summer, don't you?" Drew asked.

Nick's eyes lit. "Oh, I should say I do."

"Well, she's coming to Farthering Place."

Madeline nodded. "She and Muriel are coming to stay for a week before the wedding. Won't that be fun?"

"Oh, capital! I didn't think she'd be back over so soon. She never mentioned it in her letters."

Drew gave him a knowing look. "You've exchanged letters, have you?"

"A few," Nick said. "You know, just keeping in touch."

"I see you were right after all, darling," Drew said. "Young Mr. Dennison has been pining."

"Pining?" Nick asked. "Me? It's a monstrous lie."

"Thinking fondly?" Drew suggested, and Nick smiled.

"Well, perhaps that. She was jolly nice to have around, and I shouldn't be unhappy to have her back again."

"You don't think Barbie will mind, old man?"

Nick made a face. "Barbie and I are on the outs again just now."

"Carrie suits you better anyway," Madeline said.

Dennison stepped into the room, clearing his

throat with utter correctness. "Pardon me, sir, but Miss Madeline's dressmaker is here."

"Oh." Madeline glanced at her watch and then touched her lips to Drew's cheek. "I didn't realize it was so late. You boys try to behave."

She hurried out, and still Dennison stood there, lips pursed. "And you, Nicholas. Haven't you any business to attend to?"

"That's what I came in here for, Dad."

"We're just seeing to it," Drew added. "Thank you, Denny."

Dennison bowed. "Very good, sir."

Drew laughed softly once the butler had gone. "You'd think you were working for him and not me."

"Good old Dad." Nick chuckled. "He's always afraid I'll overstep my place."

"Couldn't be done, old man. Couldn't be done. What, after all, would I do without my Watson?"

There was a little glint in Nick's eye as he sat down next to Drew. "That, actually, is what I came to talk to you about. Don't say anything to Dad."

Drew nodded, suddenly grim. "You noticed our visitor earlier, I take it."

"The Black Widow. Yes, I did. Who was it? More important, what was it and do you have another case?"

"No case this time. Well, to be precise, yes, there is a case, but no, I will not be looking into it."

"No? What case? And who was the woman?"

"Did you read about that actor who was murdered last night? Ravenswood?"

Nick nodded.

"That's the case," Drew said. "And the woman was Mrs. Landis."

He quickly filled in the details of the case, Fleur's involvement in it, and what she had asked of him. When he was done, Nick shook his head.

"She always was bold. What about Landis?"

Drew frowned. "I feel rather bad about him. No doubt our chief inspector has already been to see him about the case."

"But you're not going to look into it?"

"Afraid not, old man. My bride-to-be has expressed her extreme displeasure at the very notion, and to be frank, the idea of being around Fleur again doesn't appeal to me in the slightest."

"After what happened in Oxford, no doubt." Nick gave him a wry grin. "Those bad pennies. Always turning up, eh?"

Drew shrugged. "So, no, I will not be investigating this case. I will merely enjoy the preparation for my upcoming nuptials, and you can pursue Miss Holland unimpeded."

"I rather like that idea. This thing with Barbie's a bust anyway."

"What is it now?" Drew asked. With Barbie it was always something.

Nick said, "I ought to have known better. She's one of your crowd, not mine."

"Nonsense. You've been running with my set most of your life. Barbie's never minded before."

"Well, I suppose she likes me well enough. I mean, for myself."

"Of course she does."

"But now we've gotten down to serious matters," Nick added, "and I can see it's never likely to work."

"Serious?" Drew hadn't thought Nick and Barbie were that keen on each other. "You don't mean . . . ?"

"Oh, yes, very serious. She's come to realize I can't afford to take her to the posh places she likes, not often anyhow, and that I won't let her pay. Not even under the table."

"No," Drew said. "That simply isn't done."

"Well, when the Right Honorable Sir Giles Nincompoop or Lord Tommyrot ask her to those places without a thought, what's a chap to do?"

"Sorry, old man."

Drew wouldn't insult his friend by offering him money either, but it was a rotten spot for Nick to be in.

Nick shrugged it off. "I expect, to the right girl, it won't matter, and there's no use getting tangled up with a wrong one. What's that Scripture verse? Something about if you take fire into your lap, you can expect to be burnt?"

"Something like that."

Nick was thoughtful for a moment. "You will be careful around Fleur, won't you?"

"I'm not eighteen anymore, and if she taught me anything, it was to be wary of women like her." Drew stood and gave him a friendly swat on the shoulder. "Now, off to work before Denny sees you loitering and reports you to Mr. Padgett."

"Don't think he won't," Nick said, standing. "Guess I'd best get at it then."

"Unless . . ." Drew gave him the smallest hint of a grin. "Unless you'd care to pop up to Farlinford with me for a moment while Madeline's busy with her fitting."

"To do what?" Nick asked, eyes wary. "To *not* talk to Landis about the case?"

Drew nodded. "I suppose I would like to know what the police said to him. Maybe I could give him a few pointers on how to deal with old Birdsong. What do you think?"

"What about Madeline?"

"She doesn't have to know about it at all. It's not as if I'd actually be looking into the case, and I certainly wouldn't be seeing Fleur. Well, what do you say?"

Nick glanced furtively at the door, where his father had just been standing. "Better hurry, if we're going to go at all. Dad will no doubt see this as dereliction of duty and have me up on charges if he catches me at it."

"Right then." Drew motioned toward the open French doors overlooking the lawn. "This way, and don't dawdle."

Landis hurried out of his office, hand outstretched. "Good afternoon, Mr. Farthering. Mr. Dennison."

There were handshakes all around.

"Is there something I can do for you, Mr. Farthering?" Landis asked.

Drew smiled. "I hoped we might have a discussion about . . . recent events."

Landis's welcoming smile vanished. "Actually I wanted to speak to you on the matter myself. Would you like to come in?" He glanced at Nick. "Both of you."

Landis ushered them into his office and into the chairs facing his desk. "Mind if I smoke? I started off wrong this morning and can't seem to get turned the right way round. I hate getting into work behind my time." He lit a cigarette, then settled into his own chair. "I hope you'll forgive me for bothering you with this, Mr. Farthering, but I've heard about the murder investigations you've been involved with." He nodded at Nick. "Both of you. This is, well, something I'd rather not have to discuss with the boss, but I don't much know where else to turn."

Drew nodded. "About the Ravenswood murder."

"I'm afraid so."

"That's exactly what we came to talk to you about. First off, I would strongly advise that you find someone who's an expert at this sort of thing. Nick and I, as earnest as we are about delving into these kinds of cases, we're rank amateurs. You'd do far better to go to the police or a professional who knows what he's doing."

"Fleur told me you'd say that."

There was a touch of rue in the man's expression, and Drew couldn't help pitying him. "She told you she'd come to see me?"

"Yes." Landis shook his head. "I'm most terribly sorry she bothered you, Mr. Farthering. I didn't know about it until afterward. I told her she must never do such a thing again, but now . . . well, now things are different."

Drew narrowed his eyes. "Different? How?"

Landis exhaled sharply, sending smoke up toward the ceiling. "The police have been here to speak with me, and they've come to interview Fleur. Twice now. Just gathering information, they say, but it seems rather unlikely they'd waste their time if they didn't see her as a suspect."

"I suppose not," Drew said. "Do you know where she was at the time of the murder?"

"I do," Landis said. "She was at home all night. With me."

"Then there's nothing to worry about, right?"

Landis blew out his breath. "The police don't seem to be completely convinced."

"All the more reason for you to involve professionals in the matter."

"No!" Landis took two more puffs of his cigarette before he went on. "Forgive me, Mr. Farthering. As you might expect, what with one thing and another, I've been a bit on edge lately. But, really, as Fleur told you, we don't want this getting about. The scandal would ruin everything."

"You know it will get out if charges are pressed," Nick said quietly.

Landis nodded. "That's why we were hoping you two might look into this for us. On the hush-hush, as it were."

"Believe me," Drew told him with a touch of good humor, "I've had my share of notoriety these past few months. It doesn't generally last."

"It's not just the scandal." Landis tapped the ash off the end of his cigarette. "It's . . . a certain family situation."

Drew lifted one eyebrow, waiting for the man to go on.

"You may have heard of my uncle, Clive Vernet Brent. No? He made his fortune in the cotton mills up north some fifty years ago and has kept it through some fairly shrewd investments since then. He was eighty-eight last spring and, until a month or so ago, was as hale as I am. Now, though, his doctors tell me he won't likely see eighty-nine."

Nick frowned. "Surely he's not so fragile

that the mention of such a scandal would—"

"No, that's not it at all. But I am the only family he has left. He didn't want me to marry Fleur. In fact, he very nearly disinherited me over it. I calmed him down, convinced him that she was nothing like he thought and promised him she would never shame my name or his." The warmth came back into Landis's eyes. "When Peter was born, that scotched a lot of his objections, and he's seemed content since to know that when he's gone, his money will come to me and, in time, to Peter."

Drew picked up a photograph that stood there on the desk, and again that look of pride came into Landis's face. In the picture he was sitting in a large wicker peacock chair, with Fleur standing next to him. He had his hand at the small of her back, and she was looking straight ahead, smiling that dazzling smile and making the most of those eyes. Clearly the camera loved her as much as the footlights once had.

Their little boy, Peter, was beaming at his father, standing sturdy-legged in Landis's lap, both arms around his neck. Despite having his mother's pretty features, he clearly did not share her dark hair and eyes. Landis was dark too, though perhaps he'd been fair as a child.

"Yes," Landis said. "Uncle dotes on the boy. I'd hoped to take Peter to see him one last time, but it doesn't seem too likely now he's ill. Seems rather a shame."

"It does. But I can see why he'd be taken with the little fellow. How old did you say he was?"

"Four. And apart from wanting to climb everything in sight, the boy's good as gold."

Drew chuckled and put the picture back where he'd found it. "I suppose you don't want to risk the boy's inheritance by scandalizing your uncle, eh?"

"Precisely." Landis's expression turned sober. "He supports a school in Manchester for under-privileged boys. Of course, he'll leave them a nice legacy regardless, but he told me when I married Fleur that if ever she caused a scandal, every penny of his money would go to the school. I haven't money of my own to speak of, and I'd hate my boy to be left without anything."

"I understand," Drew said. "Still, I'm afraid I can't help you with this. Truly, you ought to have a professional, someone who can do you a proper job of it."

"Please," Landis said, "I've heard about the cases you were involved in—you two and your young lady, Miss Parker. You have a way of getting to the bottom of a thing."

Drew shook his head. "And I almost got myself killed last time."

"I doubt there's a lunatic involved here."

Drew studied him for a moment. "And why do you think Ravenswood was murdered, Mr. Landis?"

"Haven't the foggiest, I'm afraid. You know how theater people can be. Might be one of them wanted to take over as leading man at the Tivoli. Could be the wife had enough of his unofficial matinees with her understudy. Could be she'd just had enough of him in general."

"Have you ever met his wife?" Nick asked.

Landis chuckled. "Good heavens, no. I know nothing about her. I've seen her a couple of times on the stage, that's all. She may well be a saint. I was just throwing out a few possibilities. There's always the money angle. Find out where he got his and who'd benefit from his death, right? Even so, none of those reasons point to Fleur. That's all I'm saying."

"True." Drew studied Landis's eyes, his reactions. "Unless the two of them were still seeing each other."

Landis's face paled. "No. No, that was over years ago. Before Peter was born. I'm certain of it."

"Sorry. I had to ask."

"Yes, I know. And I know it's been years since you and she were friends, but I was hoping for her sake, well, that you three might consider looking into things. Peter and I, we just wouldn't know how to get on without Mummy."

Drew picked up the photograph again and focused on the little boy, who was looking with adoration at his father. Then with another glance at Landis, he set the picture down and nodded.

"I was a frightful climber at that age myself."

Landis looked puzzled for a moment, and then a smile touched his face. "You mean you will?"

Nick looked sidelong at Drew but said nothing.

"I can't make you any guarantees of course, Landis," Drew said, avoiding Nick's gaze, "but I can see what I can find out. On the hush-hush."

"Are you certain?" Landis looked pitifully relieved. "Truly?"

"You have my word on it," Drew said.

"We'd be very much grateful, Fleur and I, for anything you three could possibly—"

"Two at most, I'm afraid." Drew stood. "As you might well imagine, Miss Parker is quite involved in wedding plans these days."

"Oh, of course," Landis said, rising from his chair. "I wouldn't dream of asking her to interrupt what she's doing for this. But if the two of you could possibly . . ." He looked at them with hope in his eyes, and Drew nodded again.

"As I said, Mr. Landis, I can't give you any guarantees. But for the boy's sake, eh, Nick, old man?"

"I'm game if you are," Nick said as he got to his feet.

"It's very good of you, Mr. Farthering. Mr. Dennison." Landis offered his hand to each of them in turn. "I don't know how we could ever repay you."

Drew gave him a shrug. "Save that until you see whether or not we're of any help."

Drew drove for several minutes in silence, the Rolls humming along the road back to Farthering Place, and the sunlight glinting off the patchy snow.

Finally, Nick glanced over at him. "So much for only giving him a bit of advice."

Drew frowned. "Well, what could I have done?"

"You might have turned him down."

"I was going to. I was absolutely not going to have anything to do with this investigation. But then, well, when he said it was for the little boy's sake, what could I do? You, uh . . ." Drew kept his eyes on the road, forcing all emotion out of his voice. "You know how it's been since I found out about my mother. My real mother. It's perfectly maddening to know nothing about her, to be unable to find a trace of her still."

Nick nodded. "I'd've thought your solicitors would have something by now."

"Not a sausage," Drew replied flatly. "Anyway, little Peter is no doubt quite attached to his own mother, such as she is. And truly there is not that much to the case. Not that much to do with Fleur anyway. It's not as if I would be right at her side day in and day out."

"What's our Miss Parker going to think of this now?" Nick asked. "No doubt she's none too happy that Fleur has popped back into your life. I daresay she'd prefer you didn't pop back into hers."

Drew managed to keep the annoyance in his expression down to a mere hint. "There's been no popping on the part of either party. Neither of us is pleased to renew the acquaintance, and this investigation just makes it all the more awkward."

"But you're going to carry on anyway." Nick lifted one sandy eyebrow. "And Madeline is supposed to receive this news happily?"

"Not half," Drew muttered.

"What do you suppose she'll say?"

Drew kept his eyes on the road, not wanting to respond to Nick's question.

"She's not going to be pleased about this, you know," Nick said.

Drew sighed. "I know. I know. Perhaps if we had a bit more information, I can see if there's anything I can actually do. Like as not, there isn't and that will be that. No need to upset the bride-to-be, eh?"

"Tread carefully, my lad, or you're not likely to have a bride-to-be. Now just where are you hoping to obtain this additional information?"

"Well, what is one always advised to do if one is lost?"

Drew looked at Nick, and then they both spoke at once.

"Ask a policeman!"

— Four —

Madeline laid the catalogue on the bed. "I can't decide between the ivory with bluebirds and flowers and the cream with the pink rosebuds. What do you think?"

Aunt Ruth looked down her nose at the picture. "You're about to marry into a house with about forty different full sets of china. Why in the world would you want more?"

Madeline frowned. "I know. I thought I might want something that's just sweet and pretty. Something we might have used at home when I was growing up. Something we can use for midnight snacks and picnics on the lawn, but I don't know if I really want even that. I guess they expect it of me, though."

"Who's *they?*" Aunt Ruth's lips twitched into a smile. "It seems to me your young man likes you for your not being too concerned what *they* think or what *they* do."

"You're right." Madeline closed the catalogue. "But I do need to do some shopping."

"And what are you after today?"

"You know the tradition, Aunt Ruth. Something old, something new, something borrowed, something blue."

"I suppose we ought to get that straightened

out then. I always expected the something old—"

"Mother's veil. I've wanted to wear it for my wedding since I was a little girl."

Aunt Ruth nodded, her expression wistful. "She would like that, I know. It's a beautiful thing too—handmade Irish lace and seed pearls, down to your feet in front and six yards down the back. You'll be lovely in it. What about the new?"

"That's why I wanted to go shopping. Since Drew and Nick went to the office today, I thought it would be the perfect opportunity to find just the right thing."

"What are those two doing at the office? Not work, surely."

Madeline shrugged. "I don't know. They went to talk to Mr. Landis about something. I think Nick went only to get out from under Mr. Dennison's watchful eye."

"Not more of that detective nonsense, I hope."

"Not today, no. I think Drew's given that up. At least until after the wedding." Madeline shrugged. "More or less."

Aunt Ruth gave her a shrewd look. "In other words, he's not telling you what he's up to."

"It's not that. He told Mrs. Landis very plainly that he wouldn't be investigating that actor's murder. I think that's the end of it."

"You don't sound too sure." The older woman stood with her arms crossed. "And just why is that?"

Madeline sighed and sat down on the bed. "I know how much he likes solving these cases. He says, and I think he just might be right, that he feels it's something he's supposed to do."

"A rather odd sort of calling to have, isn't it?" Aunt Ruth smirked. "Detecting?"

Madeline laughed. "I suppose it is, put that way. But we're not all called to preach, are we? Besides, it's really only helping people who need it. Isn't that what we're all called to do?"

"True enough. But you say he's turned down this particular case, so why the worry?"

Madeline propped her chin on one hand. "I'm afraid it won't be the end of it. You saw him when Mr. Montford was murdered. He was going to stay out of that one too, but Mrs. Montford coaxed him into investigating anyway."

"Good thing she did too," Aunt Ruth said. "No telling how long it would have taken that Birdsong fellow to figure out what was going on. He nearly got your young man killed as it was."

"You can't blame that on the chief inspector. If Drew hadn't insisted on keeping his suspicions to himself, he wouldn't have gotten into trouble like that."

"Maybe so. Anyway, if he's promised you he'll stay out of this one, you shouldn't trouble yourself about it."

"Well, he didn't exactly promise," Madeline said. "He didn't even tell me he would stay out of it. He told Mrs. Landis he wasn't the right man for the job and that was all."

"So? I don't know what's wrong with that. What did you want him to do?"

Madeline squirmed under her aunt's stern gaze. "I don't know. I guess I just wanted him to tell her in no uncertain terms that he didn't ever want to see her again."

Aunt Ruth sat down on the bed next to her. "Their friendship was a little more than friendship, wasn't it?"

Madeline caught hold of her arm. "Don't tell him we talked about this. Please. It's not . . ."

Aunt Ruth patted her hand. "He'll never hear it from me. But it sounds as if he more or less did tell her he didn't want her to come back. So long as the past is firmly in the past, and he has made his peace with God over it, I don't know what more you can expect from him."

Madeline frowned. "Maybe I don't know what I expect, either. She's just . . . well, you saw Drew and Nick that night at dinner. Mr. Landis, too. Not that they all weren't perfectly polite, but you could see the effect she had on them. I don't expect there's much she wants that she doesn't get."

"Do you think he is still interested in her? In Mrs. Landis?"

Madeline shook her head. "I don't think that at all. I just don't like the idea of him still being in contact with her. Even if it's just in this investigation."

"For goodness' sake, Madeline, if you don't trust the man any more than that, you probably shouldn't be marrying him."

"It's not that I don't trust him." Madeline shook her head again, not knowing if she wanted to laugh or cry. "It's not that at all. I don't want her to be on his mind right now. We're about to get married. I want him to be thinking of the future, not of the past. He doesn't remember her fondly, and I don't want that tainting what ought to be a happy time for us both."

"No use borrowing trouble," Aunt Ruth said.

Madeline gave her a reluctant smile. "I suppose you're right. He's through with the whole matter. If Mrs. Landis didn't kill this Ravenswood person, then it's up to the police to figure out who did. Drew has more important things to do at the moment."

"Exactly." Aunt Ruth pulled her to her feet and thrust a handkerchief into her hand. "Now wash your face and put on a little powder and you'll be fresh as this morning's snow. We were talking about your 'something new,' weren't we?"

Madeline laughed, sniffled and blew her nose. Then she did as her aunt suggested and washed and powdered her face. She glanced in the mirror as she finished and patted her hair into place. It hadn't been a real cry, only just enough to add a touch of pink to her cheeks.

"Yes," she told Aunt Ruth when she came back into the bedroom. "We were talking about my something new. I thought it would be nice to have that be something I bought here. Sort of a symbol of my new life, a new start and all that. What do you think?"

"Yes, I suppose that would be very nice."

"Just one other thing . . ."

Aunt Ruth pursed her lips. "Yes?"

"Well, I thought . . ." Madeline took a deep breath. "I thought, since it is my wedding and such a joyous occasion, I thought maybe we could get you a dress in a happier color."

Aunt Ruth arched an eyebrow. "Are you saying what I would choose to wear isn't good enough for your shindig?"

"Oh, no, Aunt Ruth. Please don't be mad. It's just that, well, I thought just for once, you might not wear black."

Aunt Ruth tugged at the lapels of her black satin jacket, pulling it more snugly around her. "Black was evidently good enough for Queen Victoria, and I assume she attended a great many weddings in her time."

Madeline kissed her aunt's cheek. "You wear whatever you like, dear. I just thought that if you hadn't absolutely decided what you're going to wear, you might want to look around a little while we're out."

Aunt Ruth looked doubtful. "There isn't much

to choose from in the village, you know. What are you going to get? A string of those paste pearls they sell at the drugstore?"

Madeline giggled. "Of course not. But I thought we might go over to Mrs. Forest's shop and see what she has."

Aunt Ruth consulted the little watch brooch that was pinned to her blouse. "You'd better get a move on then, missy, or that fiancé of yours will be back, and you two and Mr. Dennison will end up dashing up to some village called Porridge-on-Toast, looking for a redheaded train conductor with a parrot and a wooden leg or some such nonsense."

"Don't be silly," Madeline said as she put on her coat. "Porridge-on-Toast is in Yorkshire, and we'd never get up there and back before tea-time."

It was a beautiful day, despite the snow, and Madeline was certain that if Drew were here, the two of them would have walked over to the village. But with her cane, Aunt Ruth wasn't used to going such distances on foot, so Madeline had Denton, the chauffeur, bring around the Bentley and drive them.

Forest's Ladies' Emporium was at the end of the High Street in Farthering St. John, just around the corner from the church. Like almost all the buildings in the village, it was a small, half-timbered structure at least three hundred years old. Mrs. Forest, a wizened little sparrow of a woman, came around from behind the counter to greet them.

"Good morning, ladies. How may I help?"

Though Madeline was already scanning the display cases, she looked up and smiled at the older woman. "I was looking for my 'something new' to wear when I marry Mr. Farthering."

"Ah, certainly," said Mrs. Forest. "Best wishes to you both. And do you have a sixpence for your shoe?"

"What's that?" Aunt Ruth asked, looking at her and then at Madeline. "A sixpence?"

"It's the tradition here," Madeline said, and Mrs. Forest nodded.

"Yes, indeed, ma'am. 'Something old, something new, something borrowed, something blue, and a sixpence in her shoe.' And if you don't have one already, you can go right over to the post office and change one of yours for a bright new one. Mr. Pringle keeps them specially. He's really quite a sentimental old dear, but don't tell him I said so."

Madeline chuckled. "Don't worry, I won't. But I'll certainly remember to go see him. I thought if I had a brand-new sixpence, I could keep it after the wedding. It would have our year on it and everything. Maybe I could have it put on Drew's watch chain for a remembrance."

"That would be lovely," Mrs. Forest agreed. "Now, about your something new . . ."

"Yes." Madeline eyed the display cases again. "Is there anything you would recommend?"

"We have some nice lace gloves."

"I'll be wearing my mother's gloves and veil. They're handmade Irish lace. I'd like to add something from Farthering St. John."

"Ah." Mrs. Forest led Madeline and Aunt Ruth over to a tall glass case in the corner of the shop. "Here is where I keep the jewelry. Of course, this isn't London. I don't have anything with large diamonds and the like. Just good pieces you could wear to a nice dinner and all. These are the newest."

She showed Madeline a tray of pretty rings and bracelets, nothing large or gaudy.

Madeline's breath caught in her throat. "Oooh, may I see that one?" she asked, pointing.

Mrs. Forest smiled. "You may, but it's not new. In fact, it's quite old."

She took out the piece, a tiny brooch of seed pearls around a delicate oval cameo of an angel. It wasn't even an inch long.

"That's so sweet." Madeline touched it with one finger and glanced up at her aunt. "I think it's just what I want."

Aunt Ruth snorted. "I thought you were after something new."

"Well, for me it's new. Besides, isn't that sort of

like my coming to England? While everything's very old here, it's all new to me."

Mrs. Forest brought out a piece of black velvet and laid it on the counter. Then she set the brooch on it.

"The lady who owned this, a Mrs. Featherstone, was also from America. She came here when she was just a girl, sent over by her parents due to the war between the North and the South. She met Mr. Featherstone and never went home again. They were married nearly seventy years and passed away about four years ago now. She went only a day after he did. I'm told he gave her this brooch on their wedding day."

"Isn't that a lovely story?" Madeline turned shining eyes to her aunt. "So romantic."

Aunt Ruth looked as if she didn't believe a word of it, but at least she was polite enough not to say so. "And how did you come by it, may I ask?"

"Once the old couple were gone, one of the man's distant relatives, a great-nephew or some such, sold off everything they had." There was a certain wistfulness in Mrs. Forest's rheumy eyes. "There were a few rather grand pieces of jewelry that were a bit much for my shop, but I did manage to get hold of some of the smaller ones. All of them sold now. All but this." She held up the brooch near Madeline's cheek. "You would look charming wearing it. It suits you."

Madeline beamed at her. "It's just what I

wanted, even if I didn't know it until just now. I'll take it."

"Hogwash," Aunt Ruth said the moment she and Madeline left the shop. "Utter and unadulterated hogwash."

Madeline giggled. "I don't care if it is. I like the brooch, and I want it for my wedding."

"Besides," Aunt Ruth said, "aren't those things, the something old and new and all the rest, aren't they supposed to be given to you? I didn't think you were supposed to buy them for yourself."

"What difference does it make? If you like, I'll give the brooch to you, and you can give it to me as a wedding present. How would that be?"

Madeline put the little box holding the brooch into her purse and snapped the clasp shut.

"Well, that Mrs. Forest can tell a tale," Aunt Ruth said, pulling her coat more snugly around her neck.

"I thought it was a very sweet story, and maybe it really is true." Madeline took her aunt's arm. "Come on. I want to go to the bookstore."

"Whatever for? You have stacks of books you haven't read yet, as well as a whole library at Farthering Place."

"I know." Madeline piloted her aunt across the slushy street and onto the sidewalk in front of the tea shop. "I just want to see how much it's changed since it was open last."

Aunt Ruth looked over at the bookstore and

frowned. "I'd think you would want to steer clear of it after what happened there."

"I can't go my whole life being afraid of the local bookstore. Besides, from what I hear, Mr. and Mrs. Ketterley are very nice."

"I'm certain you and your Englishman will be in and out of their shop more days than not. If you—" Aunt Ruth stopped short, her lips pursed. "I think we need to go back home instead, Madeline. I have something I need to see to."

For a moment, Madeline was puzzled. Then she saw the gleaming red bicycle leaning up against the side of the bookshop and suppressed a laugh. "Still avoiding him?"

Aunt Ruth shook her head. "Nothing of the sort. No man will ever influence where I choose to go or when I choose to go there. I just . . . feel like going home now."

"Yes, Aunt Ruth."

Madeline took her arm, still trying to hide her smile, and they hurried down the High Street. Just as they passed the bookshop, there was the jingle of a bell and the front door opened.

"Well, good morning, ladies." Mr. Llewellyn, owner of the bicycle, grinned and made a courtly bow. "What a delightful surprise to see you both."

"Good morning, Mr. Llewellyn," Madeline called as Aunt Ruth practically dragged her around the corner to where Denton was waiting with the Bentley.

"Aunt Ruth!" Madeline protested with a breathless laugh. "That really wasn't very polite."

"The old flatterer," Aunt Ruth muttered while scurrying into the backseat. "He must be seventy if he's a day!"

"That doesn't mean he doesn't know a fine woman when he sees one," Madeline said, getting in beside her. "And Drew was just saying we ought to fix you up with someone here."

"To get me out of the house, I suppose."

"Not at all, Aunt Ruth," Madeline said, squeezing her arm as Denton drove away. "To keep you here."

The color came up in her aunt's face, yet there was a touch of a pleased little smile on her lips. "I hardly think so."

"It's true. He's really quite fond of you. I think, not having much family of his own, he likes borrowing mine. He hasn't actually come out and said it, but I think he'll miss you when you have to go."

"Pish tosh," was all Aunt Ruth said, though she still looked rather pleased.

Drew peered around the half-open door and saw Chief Inspector Birdsong at his overburdened desk. His chin was propped up on his hand as he pored over a typewritten report, one from a rather formidable stack of the same.

With a glance at Nick, Drew tapped on the door. "Inspector?"

Birdsong looked up, heaved a martyr's sigh, then looked back at his report. "I thought you'd be here two or three hours ago."

"You did?"

Exchanging puzzled glances, Drew and Nick stepped into the room.

"And there's young Dennison of course," Birdsong added. "What? No Miss Parker?"

"No," Drew said. "She and her aunt are seeing to something for the wedding."

"That's still on, is it?" Still not looking up, Birdsong put the report back on the stack and took a file folder from his desk drawer instead.

"It is," Drew said cheerfully. "Why did you expect I would be here two or three hours ago?"

"That was when Mrs. Landis came to see you, wasn't it?"

"Yes . . . it was." Again Drew looked at Nick, who gave a shrug. "How did you know?"

"Her husband works for you. Seems rather obvious that she would come to you, what with you being the faddish choice these days for upper-crust crime solving. And there was the simple matter of my constable making enquiries of the cabbie who drove her to Farthering Place. Brilliant bit of police work, that."

Birdsong smirked at Drew and then opened the file and began shuffling through its contents.

"May as well sit down, the both of you," he added, pointing with the stub of a pencil at the pair of chairs in front of his desk. "Make it brief."

"I'll go straight to the point then." Drew sat down and pulled his chair just a bit closer to the desk. "Why haven't you arrested Mrs. Landis?"

Birdsong stopped messing with the papers and gave him a keen look. "Mrs. Landis is a person of interest in our investigation. We have not arrested her because we have not yet found enough evidence to do so."

Nick leaned on the back of the empty chair. "Not yet?"

"Not yet," Birdsong repeated. "Sit down."

With a chuckle, Nick complied. "But you have some concerns about her?"

"One of the witnesses claims to have seen her."

"Conor Benton." Drew nodded. "She told me about that, but she says he's doing it out of spite, that she was home all night."

"And that is why she is not currently in custody. Her husband corroborates her story."

"How certain did you say Benton was that he saw her and not someone else?"

"All right, he told me he didn't actually see her face," Birdsong admitted. "But he saw someone, a woman, he's certain, and he thinks it was Mrs. Landis. Rather, he insists it was Mrs. Landis. He says he knows by the way the woman moved that she was the one. And she was heard to make a threat against Ravenswood down the local pub the Monday before he was killed."

"What exactly did she say?"

Birdsong shuffled through his papers until he lighted on the one he wanted. " 'You don't want to do that, Johnnie, I swear you don't,' or very nearly that."

"That's not much of a threat. What does she say about it?"

The chief inspector shrugged. "Says they were discussing a new production and how Ravenswood's wife wants to do Shakespeare. Mrs. Landis claims it would be a flop if they did. I suppose it could have been that."

"Could be. It's not much to go on."

"Well, Benton's convinced at any rate. He recognized her cloak and just . . . how she was. He says in no uncertain terms that it was Mrs. Landis."

"Any other suspects?" Nick asked.

"Just the usual. Wife. Business manager. Other members of the troupe. Crime of passion like that? Anyone could have done it."

"Are you sure it wasn't premeditated?"

"Bash a fellow with a bottle that way?" Birdsong scoffed. "No fear."

Drew sighed. "I suppose you're right."

"Anyway, we're looking into all of them. Not enough evidence as yet to arrest anyone. Of course, we're doing our best to watch anyone we have reason to suspect."

Drew glanced at Nick and then gave the chief inspector a guileless smile. "And of course it's early days yet."

"It is, in fact, Mr. Farthering, thank you very much. So, did you come to let me know I would be receiving your *help* in this case?"

Drew grinned. "You appreciated my help the last time, Chief Inspector. Admit it."

"You did have an idea or two," the chief inspector allowed. "When you weren't putting yourself in danger of getting killed."

"He's certainly not going to do that again," Nick said sternly. "Not for a lark anyway."

"I've had that lecture from Madeline and from our dear chief inspector as well, Nick," Drew said. "No need to go over it all again."

Chief Inspector Birdsong narrowed his eyes at him. "Well, since you've been duly cautioned by all parties, I suppose there's little more to be said." He shook a thick index finger in Drew's face. "Do all the nosing about you please, but do not put yourself or anyone else in danger, and do keep us apprised of anything you happen to dig up, eh?"

"Certainly. But you needn't worry, Chief Inspector. I don't have much time for this sort of thing at the moment. I'm about to be a married man. My carefree days of bachelorhood are coming to an end, and I am not my own. Besides, if I get murdered now, Madeline will certainly kill me."

"And well she ought. Now go along, both of you. Stay out of the way of any officers doing their duty, do not trespass upon private property, and leave that pistol of your stepfather's locked up where it ought to be. Am I understood?"

"Will do, Chief Inspector." Drew stood. "Come on, Nick. We'd best get back to Farthering Place before we're caught being truant."

"You know, Detective Farthering," Birdsong drawled before they reached his office door, "I have been married a good many years myself. I haven't kept a happy wife by putting myself in harm's way unnecessarily."

"I will certainly bear that in mind, Chief Inspector."

"He's right, you know," Nick said once they turned on the road that led south back to Farthering Place. "Madeline might be all for the two of you investigating cases and helping the poor and innocent masses, but she's going to want you home nights and in reasonably good order."

"You don't think I want the same?"

"Oh, no doubt," Nick assured him. "But you don't always remind yourself of that when you're on the hunt."

"Well, I'm not really on the hunt this time, old man. I'll just see what I can see."

"I don't know how you'll have time with the

wedding coming up. You've got to see your tailor on Wednesday, and aren't you and Madeline supposed to motor up to Stratford tomorrow?"

"Yes. *Romeo and Juliet.* We've had the tickets for weeks now, and Madeline's wanted to see the town and all the attendant tourist attractions. And then, of course, the play, though she was disappointed to realize that the Globe Theater of Shakespeare's day was in London and not Stratford. Anyway, I'm not sure now if *Romeo and Juliet* was the best choice."

"What?" Nick said. "It's one of the most romantic plays ever written. What better for a bride- and groom-to-be?"

"I just wish there'd been a happier end to their story," Drew said. "I wouldn't want any of that tragedy to rub off, you know."

"Oh, no, no. I'm certain there won't be any of that." Nick grinned. "Provided you refrain from provoking the bride."

"Heaven forbid."

"Which brings us back to *The Mystery of the Actor and the Femme Fatale.*"

Drew shook his head. "No need to worry about that. I'll just poke about a bit, ask a few questions, and see if I can't clear Mrs. Landis. After that, I'll carry on preparing to marry the finest girl in the world. Madeline can hardly object to that, can she?"

Nick gave him only a shrug and another grin, neither of which was the least bit reassuring.

— *Five* —

Three days had passed since Monday, when Drew had promised to look into the Ravenswood case. He'd spent Tuesday in Stratford with Madeline, happy to see her happy, and glad to have nothing but her on his mind. Wednesday was the final fitting of his wedding attire: a black, gray, and white ascot tie, morning coat, pearl-gray waistcoat, slim-cut striped trousers, and handmade button boots.

"One cannot be too careful with the fitting of a body coat," Drew told Madeline as he escorted her downstairs to lunch. "And if I hadn't been aware of this before, I certainly am now."

She made an effort to look serious. "I imagine with Denny and Plumfield both accompanying you, you had to have appreciated the gravity of the situation."

"Well, Denny had to come to make certain his standards were upheld, and then of course Plumfield had to come along, as well. Everyone in Farthering St. John knows he's been looking after me the past little while. A misstep at so critical a juncture would ruin him for life."

Madeline took his arm. "You know, Drew, it's very good of you to take on Plumfield. Uncle

Mason would be pleased to know he is still here at Farthering Place."

"I wasn't sure I wanted a valet, you know. I think Denny is still a trifle offended to be replaced in that area, but that was never properly his job anyway. It's been a local scandal since I came back from Oxford that I haven't had a gentleman's gentleman."

"The lord of the manor must keep up appearances."

He wagged one finger at her. "You needn't be so amused, Miss Parker. When we're married, you simply must have a lady's maid or people will talk. Mrs. Farthering could never do without one."

"Yes, yes, I know. Beryl's already been helping me dress for when we have company. She's really very good with the hair, too. I suppose I'll keep her."

"My mother never had any complaints about her, which says quite a lot. And it's kind of you to keep her on. No need to send the poor thing looking for work when she's done so well here."

"I agree completely," she said.

He didn't say anything else for a few moments, until finally she narrowed her eyes at him. "What is it?"

"What is what, darling?"

"What's on your mind, and don't tell me nothing. I know that look."

"Already?" He sighed melodramatically. "How ever will I keep things from you when we've been twenty years married?"

"Drew . . ."

"It's just that I need to tell you something, and what with one thing or another, I haven't had the opportunity."

"I'm not going to like it, am I?"

They were at the top of the stairs now, where he leaned against the rail and drew her close to him. "No, I don't expect you will. But I hope it needn't be a great bother to you."

"What is it?"

He took a steadying breath and then gave her a bright smile. "I told Landis I'd look into the Ravenswood case for him."

"You mean for Fleur." There was a sudden tightness in her expression, a spark of anger in her eyes.

He squeezed her hand. "No, darling, for him. Mr. Landis. It's understandable, isn't it? A man wouldn't want his wife to be in a jam like this. Certainly he would do all he could to get her out of it." He stroked her cheek with the back of his fingers. "I know I would, if it were my wife under suspicion."

She seemed to soften a bit, but then her mouth tightened. "I thought you weren't going to have anything more to do with her."

"I'm not."

"Then why did you tell him you would try to clear her? Why did you even go talk to him about it?"

"Please try to understand, Madeline. I merely went to give him a little advice on how to deal with the chief inspector and to recommend our solicitor. I was going to turn him down if he asked me to help. I did turn him down, in point of fact. I told him exactly what I told her, that I couldn't help him. Then, well, he told me more about their little boy and how neither of them would much like it if she were taken away from them."

"What does that have to do with you?"

He was silent for a time, wondering how much to tell her.

"She asked me to forgive her," he said at last, "and I realized that, after all these years, I never had."

He looked into her eyes, pleading for her understanding, and after a taut moment, she sighed and pulled away from him.

"Okay, I agree. You ought to forgive her, but that doesn't mean you have to stay in touch with her."

"I'm not staying in touch. I'm simply looking into a case for her husband. For a good man who works for my company."

"Why?"

"We talked not too long ago about the possibility that investigating certain cases might be what I was meant to do with my life. To help people who needed it, people in a jam who didn't know where to turn for help." He took her hand in his. "I thought you agreed with me."

"I did. I do. It's just—"

"If she were a complete stranger, I would try to help her. If I've forgiven her, why shouldn't I help her now? I suppose . . ." He searched her face. "Part of it is this thing with my mother. It's been four months since I found out I'd been mistaken about Constance all my life, that someone else was my real mother. I thought it wouldn't matter really, but it does. I just . . . I don't want Landis's boy to wonder his whole life about his mother." He let out a slow breath. "You're angry with me, aren't you?"

She shook her head, not looking at him, but she tried to pull her hand away. He held it more tightly.

"Madeline."

"I . . . I don't know what to think. I want you to know about your mother, of course. If it's important to you. But I don't know why that means you have to help Fleur."

"Are you angry with me for agreeing to help her or because she exists at all?"

She looked at him, her forehead wrinkled. "I suppose I ought to forgive her, too." She laughed under her breath. "Until a few days ago I didn't even know she existed. And now, knowing how she treated you, knowing that she . . ." She broke off, refusing to say whatever else she was thinking.

"It was all a very long time ago, darling. Oughtn't we both to let it go?"

There was something distant and dark in her expression. "I can't stand even the thought of her."

"Poor darling." He kissed her temple. "If Landis weren't such a grand chap, I'm afraid I wouldn't have considered helping Mrs. Landis, either. What a pair of reprobates we are, eh?"

After a long pause, she said, "Maybe that's the point of this whole thing, Drew, helping anyone who needs us. Not just the ones we particularly like."

"Maybe." He smiled. "No, not maybe. I'm certain of it."

She nestled closer to him. "I'm sorry I was mad at you."

"I'm sorry you were too, darling. Sorry you have to deal with any of this just now actually. I expect all you want to do is enjoy being a bride and everything that comes with it."

They said nothing more until they were almost at the door to the dining room. He stopped her before they went in.

"You needn't be involved in this case at all if you'd rather not. I'm just going to see what I can find out. I expect Nick will lend a hand when he's not enmeshed in estate business or figuring out what to do about Barbie Chalfont. I'm certain, for the little bit I plan on doing, I won't really need him."

"Oh, no. You're not doing anything on this case without me. The more help you have, the quicker you'll be done with the whole thing."

He beamed at her. "Then you'll help me?"

"Of course I will," she said, but without even a hint of her usual cheekiness. "Try and stop me."

He brought her hand to his lips. "Wouldn't dream of it, darling. Wouldn't dream of it."

"So where do we start?"

He thought for a moment as he settled her in a chair. "I suppose the scene of the crime is the recommended place." He sat down beside her and put his napkin in his lap. "What did that article in the newspaper say? The Tivoli?"

"The Tivoli?" Nick said as he came into the room. "The Ravenswood murder, isn't it? Oh, I say, Drew, you are going to let me come along too, aren't you?"

Drew nodded. "Provided you can tear yourself away from estate business for the afternoon. We'd better get this all resolved before the other little maids from school arrive."

Madeline gave him a reluctant smile. "That's not for another two weeks."

"Plenty of time," Drew assured her. "If not, I would say bring Miss Holland along, but then I suppose Miss Brower would have to be asked too, and then we'd look rather like a touring party."

"I adore the girl, you know," Nick said, leaning against the doorframe, "but when it comes to fussing about with murder investigations, I'm sure Miss Holland would be most grateful to be spared. I know Barbie wouldn't hear of being part of so pedestrian a pastime."

"More than likely. Not every girl is as suited to sleuthing as mine. Have you and Barbie patched things up?"

"Ah." Nick winced just the slightest bit. "Not as such."

"Well, perhaps Miss Holland would be a better match anyway." Drew stood and tucked Madeline's arm into his. "What do you say, darling? Shall we see what secrets are hidden behind the stage curtain?"

The Tivoli was a rather small theater located on Jewry Street in Winchester. Bright posters advertised *The Mikado* by Gilbert and Sullivan, with *John Sullivan Ravenswood* written in bold letters at the top. But the word CLOSED had been pasted across each of the posters. The marquee was blank, and there was a handwritten sign in the ticket window:

Due to the recent tragedy, the Tivoli's presentation of *The Mikado* has been can- celed. Refunds for unused tickets will be given between the hours of two and four o'clock in the afternoon, Sundays and Mondays excepted.

The Management

"Not much of a place," Nick observed, looking up at the bland white-brick front. "Looks more like a hotel than a theater. Ever been inside?"

"A time or two." Drew shrugged. "I brought Daphne Pomphrey-Hughes here three or four years ago. She cried all through *The Pirates of Penzance*."

"Was the production that bad?" Madeline asked.

"Not at all," Drew said. "Quite good actually. She said she just felt very, very sorry for all those orphans."

"Orphans? The pirates? They ended up all right, didn't they?"

"True enough, but she was of the opinion that even if they were all noblemen who had gone wrong, returning to the House of Peers would not make up for the anguish caused by their parentless childhoods."

Madeline could only shake her head.

Drew laughed. "Dear Daphne is an earnest soul, yet the mysteries of comic opera are far above her head."

"In other words," Nick said, "she didn't get the joke."

Drew tried to open the front door and found it

locked, so they went round to the stage door. That too was locked, but then a spindly little man opened the door at Drew's third bout of knocking. He looked his three visitors up and down.

"Miss Cullimore," he said with a sniff, "don't give autographs exceptin' after performances. Good afternoon."

"Good afternoon," Drew said, tipping his hat and deliberately misunderstanding the pointed dismissal. "We didn't come for autographs."

The man looked at him with mild disgust. "She don't talk to nobody about Mr. Ravenswood neither 'less they're with the police. Are you with the police?"

"Not as such," Drew admitted. "However, I—"

"Thought not," the man said, grimly pleased. "Good afternoon."

Madeline gave him her prettiest smile. "I know it's your job to keep people from bothering the players, but we'd be awfully obliged to you if you'd let us have just the teensiest look around." Her smile turned conspiratorial. "You might not have noticed, but I'm from America. I'd just love to see the inside of this fine old theater. We don't have anything like it back in Chicago where I'm from. Have you ever been to Chicago?"

"No, miss," the man said. "Been to Finchley, but I don't reckon that's quite the same."

"Well, you must come sometime. You'd love it." She slipped her arm through his and walked into the theater beside him. "But tell me about this place. It looks more like a hotel than a theater."

"It was at one time, miss. Back sixty or seventy years ago. This lot have been putting on Gilbert and Sullivan here for five years now. In fact, it was their anniversary they was celebrating that night Mr. Ravenswood was killed."

Nick smirked at Drew as they followed Madeline inside.

"And before that it was variety," the man continued. "Mr. Memory, trained dogs, all that. Now, in my father's day, we had Miss Jenny Lind, we did. Saw her once myself, and bless me if she weren't a true nightingale. But that was some while ago."

"What about last week?" Drew said. "They were playing *The Mikado*, I believe."

"They were. And now Mr. Benton has got to take on all of Mr. Ravenswood's roles and train up Master Hazeldine for the juvenile leads."

"*Master* Hazeldine?" Nick raised one eyebrow. "Young, is he?"

Their guide made a noise somewhere between a laugh and a snort. "Says he's twenty-one. Don't know that he could be more than seventeen. Mightn't be that even, and likely a runaway. Still, he does fair enough, and I'm not saying he don't, even if he does come a bit flat on some of the higher notes. There's not so many as notices that, and the young ladies swoon over him already."

Drew tried to hide a grin. "And Benton?"

"Well, he can still play the young'uns, if you don't look too close."

"So he's doing all of Ravenswood's old roles now?" Nick asked. "Does he have that sort of voice?"

The man gave him a gap-toothed grin. "The orchestra's had to raise the key on some of the songs, but Mr. Benton's not half bad. Come along and hear for yourself."

Drew hurried after as the man led them presumably toward the stage. "Mr. . . . ?"

"Name's Grady."

"Very well, Mr. Grady, I would—"

"Not Mr. Grady. Grady Hibbert."

"I see. Mr. Hibbert then. I would—"

"Nope. Just Grady. My granddad was Mr. Hibbert. My dad was just Pop. He kept this stage in Queen Victoria's time, God bless her, and if he didn't need no surname, then I'll do without as well."

"Grady it is." Drew shook his hand to seal the bargain. "Now, I would very much like to find out about how the stage is set up and the arrangement of the dressing rooms and so forth. What would you say to letting me and my friends here have a look round inside? Scene of the crime and all that? We needn't stay long."

Grady scratched behind one ear. "I dunno. They're rehearsing. Going into *Penzance* and

Pinafore starting Saturday. Not that they don't know 'em already, but just polishing up, as it were."

"I see," Drew said. "Mind if we have a peep? We'll try to stay quiet at the back."

"They'll never know we're there," Madeline promised, bright-eyed.

"Well . . ."

Drew jingled the coins in his pocket, and Grady gave him that gap-toothed smile again.

"Well, if you put it that way, don't like to say no to a gentleman. Mind you, if you're seen you have to swear you snuck in on your own."

Drew slipped him a half a crown. "Your secret is safe with us. Come along, Madeline. Nick."

The four of them crept into a dim, narrow hallway. Grady tapped the side of his nose, warning them to silence, and led them around the side of the stage and down another longer hallway into the lobby.

"Quiet as mice now," he whispered.

He opened the door to the theater just enough for them to squeeze through. As stealthily as they could, Drew, Madeline, and Nick stole to the back row of seats and sank down. On the stage, swords crossed, stood two men. One was lithe and cat-like and looked to be thirty or so, handsome and well made. He had to be Conor Benton. Drew fought a smile. He did have a bit of a weak chin.

The other was not so graceful and looked quite

young, eighteen at most. There was still a bit of that awkwardness about him, though it would probably not have been so noticeable with anyone else onstage.

"No! No!" Benton said. "Don't clomp around as if you were mucking out a stable! A little grace, man! A touch of style, if you can manage it."

The young man jabbed his sword at the air next to Benton's head, and Benton turned it away with an easy flick of his wrist.

"Sorry," Hazeldine murmured, pushing his hair back from his damp forehead and taking a better grip on his blade. "Let me try again."

"All right." Benton crossed the stage and stood next to Hazeldine. "We'll do it together. The police say, 'So to Constabulary, pirates yield!' And then the girls have their line."

He looked at the rather bland young woman sitting at the corner of the stage, script in hand, her legs curled under her. She had her eyes fixed on him, and there was a certain wistfulness in her expression that Drew had seen before in stage-struck young ladies.

Benton raised his eyebrows. "The girls? Tess?"

"Oh, sorry, Conor. Sorry." She glanced at the script. " 'Oh, rapture!' "

He gave her an encouraging smile and then turned back to Hazeldine. "Right. Now, the minute the girls do their line, you lunge at Dave with your sword. Don't let it drag."

A sturdy-looking man with a handlebar mustache gave Hazeldine a nod.

"Now," Benton said. " 'So to Constabulary, pirates yield!' "

" 'Oh, rapture!' " the girl called Tess chimed in.

Benton and Hazeldine lunged in unison toward the man with the mustache. He gave a comic leap straight into the air and then parried both their swords with his truncheon.

"That's it," Benton said as he and Hazeldine continued the fight at a snail's pace, upstage and downstage. "Better, better. One, two, count in your head, five, six, seven, eight. Good."

Finally, Dave lay prostrate at Hazeldine's feet. The boy was looking at Benton again, waiting for Benton's assessment.

"Not so much like a cart horse that time," Benton said. "Now if our police sergeant would—"

Drew stepped forward. "I beg your pardon."

There was a sudden silence onstage, and then a lanky blonde stepped out from behind some scenery and shaded her eyes, squinting into the darkness of the house. "Who's there?"

Drew nudged Madeline, and she and Nick both stood.

"Miss Cullimore," Drew said. "Good afternoon. My name is Drew Farthering, and this is my fiancée, Madeline Parker, and my friend, Nick Dennison."

Benton narrowed his eyes. "This is a private rehearsal. How did you lot get in here?"

"How do you know my name?" the blond woman asked. "Are you with the police?"

"No," Drew said. "But we are looking into the death of your husband." Drew turned his hat in his hands. "I've seen you onstage before. Do accept my condolences."

"Farthering?" She looked him up and down. "Who sent you? You aren't newspapermen, are you?"

Nick chuckled, and she gave him a poisonous glare.

"No," Drew assured her. "We're making a private investigation, trying to make sure the guilty party is discovered as quickly as possible and that the innocent are let alone."

"Who are you working for?" Benton asked, arms crossed. "Whoever it is, we haven't time for your nonsense. We open day after tomorrow, and we'll hardly get everything done as it is. Now, if you'll let us carry on."

He looked pointedly toward the doors, but the blonde crossed over to him and put one hand on his arm. "Who did you say you were working for?" she asked Drew.

"I didn't, in point of fact, but it's a Mr. Landis. I doubt you've heard of him, but—"

The woman laughed. "The Landis who's married to Fleur Hargreaves? He sent you?" She nodded, eyes narrowed again. "I shouldn't wonder. He sent you to clear her?"

"That was rather his hope," Drew said. "I merely said I'd look into the thing. I couldn't possibly make him any guarantees."

"Farthering." She nodded several times. "I knew I'd heard that name before, and now I remember. You fancy yourselves detectives, don't you? You and your friend there? And that must be the American girl. Your fiancée, is she? Frightfully lucky girl."

"Come on, Simone," Benton said. "We don't have to—"

"No, let them stay."

She smirked at Drew, and Benton scowled in return.

"I've got better things to do just now than spend the afternoon talking to a bunch of toffs who fancy themselves Sherlock Holmes." He stalked down the center aisle and out the lobby door, calling back to them, "Don't think we're even near being ready to open on Saturday."

"Come along then," Miss Cullimore said, evidently amused by him. "Come up here, every-one, and we'll all have a nice chat." She motioned with both hands. "Gather round, children."

The players made a semicircle around her, and Drew realized there weren't all that many present. Benton, the Pirate King, had already taken himself off, but that left Hazeldine as Frederic, Dave as the First Policeman, the man they called Clive as the Sergeant. Drew assumed the rather rotund and red-faced older man was the Major General, and Miss Cullimore herself was playing the dewy-eyed Mabel. At least for rehearsal purposes, it seemed the script girl, Tess, was everyone else.

"Now," Simone said, "Mr. Farthering is going to ask us questions, and we're going to tell him everything we know. Won't that be fun?"

"Don't be ridiculous, Simone," said the older man. "You should let the police see to things about Johnnie's death."

"It's all right, Ronald. The police don't seem to be moving very quickly on this case. Perhaps Mr. Farthering and his friends can find some evidence they've overlooked."

Drew glanced at Nick. "And just who do you think is the guilty party?"

"Fleur," Simone said. "At least Conor says so."

Madeline glanced at Drew but kept silent.

"Do you believe him?" Nick asked.

"Why shouldn't I? I don't know who else would." Simone sat down on a plaster boulder. "She and my husband had been at odds for a while now. He didn't much care what she did, but she hated him with a true passion."

Drew looked up at her. "Because . . . ?"

"It was hardly a secret, you know. Not round here. He'd been seeing her off and on from the time they were in that company together in

Oxford—can't remember what it was called now—until about four or five years ago. Then she up and marries this Landis fellow. Only one explanation for that, if you ask me."

"Which is?"

She gave Drew a knowing look. "She was being an unbearable nuisance, making demands on him, insisting he leave me and marry her. I don't know why she'd think he'd do that. He didn't do that for any of the others. Why should he for her?"

"Then you knew about their . . . liaison at the time?"

"I always knew. He wasn't exactly very good at keeping secrets, and it's not as if he even tried to keep that sort of thing from me. He and I were over years ago. I think he married me only because I told him he couldn't have me any other way. And I meant it. But I shouldn't have expected to change him. I knew how he was. We weren't married long before he'd fairly much moved on to someone else. And someone else, and someone else." She glanced at the script girl. "Once he made one of his conquests, it didn't take long for him to start looking for the next challenge."

"Why didn't you divorce him?" Madeline asked.

"I should have." The actress managed a faint smile. "I really should have divorced him for it, but once I resigned myself to it all, somehow I didn't care. I was still rather fond of him, and I certainly didn't want to marry someone else. Not after seeing what marriage was like with him. I must give Fleur credit for keeping him amused longer than any of the others."

Tess kept her eyes on the script in her hands.

The leading lady's mouth turned up in a smirk. "He usually lost interest the minute they gave in to him. He was a charmer, I'll give him that. He could sweet-talk you into or out of anything. You saw him onstage in Oxford, didn't you?"

Drew nodded.

"Well, what you saw onstage was exactly how he was offstage," she said. "Bigger than life. Always a smile. Merrily doing as he ruddy well pleased."

Drew looked at her for a moment, trying to read her thoughts. Actors and actresses earned their bread pretending to be who they weren't.

"And that bothered Mrs. Landis—his doing as he pleased?"

Miss Cullimore nodded. "Or at least him not doing as *she* pleased. But really, I don't know any details. She has always bored me to tears, and I expect Johnnie felt the same way. Especially recently."

"Why recently?"

"She was rather annoying, to be frank. Dropping in at odd hours, insisting on talking to him. It's funny, because he was quite good-natured about it all, as if he were humoring her and still going to do just as he wanted."

"And what did she want him to do?" Madeline asked. "Or stop doing."

"Your guess is as good as mine," the actress said. "They were always squabbling, and I really didn't have the patience to listen to it. Nothing to do with me, at any rate."

"Then just who would know?" Drew asked pleasantly.

"You might talk to that newspaper reporter he was so thick with."

"Newspaper reporter?"

Miss Cullimore made a sour face. "Jo Tracy. Writes for the most awful scandal sheet I've ever read. Do you know it?"

"I have seen it a time or two," Drew admitted. "Not precisely *Times* quality, eh?"

"Not precisely. But she has quite a following."

"She?" Madeline said.

"Josephine, I believe, darling," said Drew. "One of those *très moderne* career women, it seems." He looked at the actress again. "She and your husband were friends?"

"Now," Miss Cullimore replied. "They were something more for a time, but I believe that fizzled out a couple of years ago. They were still quite chummy. She picked up a lot of material for her column just by listening to Johnnie ramble about our friends and acquaintances when he'd had too much to drink. I heard she wanted to be a novelist or something, and I suppose she observed a great deal about human nature, too. Actors *are* human, aren't they?"

"You tell me," Drew said.

She laughed. "I suppose the jury's out yet on that one. Anyway, she's the only one I can think of who might have any idea what Johnnie was up to. As I told the police, I went home after we had our little anniversary party with the cast."

"Five years at the Tivoli, was it?"

"That's right. Only Johnnie and I and Ronald, naturally, had been here the whole five years. Ronald, he does all the parts for gentlemen of a certain vintage, fathers, major generals and such. He's been at the Tivoli just ages. Poor chap."

"And no one saw anything out of the ordinary last night?" Drew asked, looking around the half circle of thespians. "What about the stagehands? Or those in the orchestra?"

Miss Cullimore shook her head. "They all clear out fairly quickly after a performance is over most nights. And Johnnie didn't invite any of them to our gathering that night, I know that much."

"All right," Drew said. "Mrs. Landis wasn't at the party, was she? Had anyone seen her at all earlier that night?"

"I hadn't." The leading lady looked at the others. "Anyone?"

The gathered players looked at one another, shaking their heads and murmuring in the negative.

"And yet you think she's the one who killed your husband?"

Miss Cullimore shrugged. "She was the only one he was at odds with as far as I can tell. And she could be awfully pushy when she wanted something."

Drew nodded. "But you don't know what it is she wanted."

"No. Sorry." The actress beamed at him. "Anything else you'd like to ask? While we're all here and feeling indulgent?"

"So none of you saw anything out of the ordinary that night?" Drew asked again.

Again the only response was in the negative.

"None of you remembers hearing anything telling between Mrs. Landis and Ravenswood in the recent past? Something that might not have seemed odd at the time, but might now in light of recent events? No?"

"Fleur always made a nuisance of herself about the place," the older man, the one called Ronald, said. "Nothing unusual about that."

Drew looked at young Hazeldine, suddenly reminded of Oxford and himself at that age. "Do you know Mrs. Landis?"

"Seen her about, but not much more than to speak to," the young man said. He blushed faintly. "She told me I ought to give up the stage and go back to the farm."

"Did you see her the night Ravenswood was

killed?" Drew persisted, but Hazeldine only shook his head.

"We've already told everything we know to the authorities," said Dave, the man playing the First Policeman. "There's really not all that much to say."

Drew handed out several of his cards. "Do let me know, any of you, if you happen to think of anything you neglected to mention. No matter how small."

"All right, kiddies," Miss Cullimore said. "We've lost our Pirate King, and I think we've made as much of a dog's dinner of *Penzance* as we can manage in an afternoon. Tomorrow, same time." She turned to the three visitors as the rest of the troupe hurried out, chattering on their way. "I don't know what else you can find out here, but I can show you Johnnie's dressing room if you like."

Drew glanced at Nick and Madeline, trying to keep his expression grave and not unbecomingly eager. "That would be most helpful, if it isn't too painful for you."

"It's been a shock," said Miss Cullimore, "and I have a feeling it will all sink in just when I'm not expecting it." There was a flicker of pain in her eyes, and then she flashed a tight smile. "For now, the show must go on. Come this way."

She led them across the stage and behind the curtain to the same hallway Grady had led them up earlier. Ravenswood's dressing room was done up as if it were his club. Besides the requisite makeup table and well-lit mirror, there was a wing-back chair in front of a cozy hearth and a well-used leather sofa along one wall. The walls themselves were covered with photographs, mostly of himself, from various productions.

"He spent most of his time in here," the actress said. She glanced at the sofa. "What with one thing or another."

Drew dropped to one knee beside a dark stain in the Persian carpet. "This is where they found him, I expect."

Miss Cullimore nodded, paling a bit. "I saw him before they came to take him away. He simply looked . . . asleep. He looked just as he had in dozens of roles, and for a moment I thought he would jump to his feet and laugh and tell me it was all a joke. But when I saw the back of his head . . ." She blinked hard and took a shuddering breath.

Madeline went to her, putting a comforting hand on her arm. "If you'd rather not talk about it right now, we'll certainly understand."

"She's right." Drew got to his feet, feeling an absolute cad for putting the woman through this. "We can have a look about on our own if you'd rather go. I give you my word we won't disturb anything."

Again she gave him that tight smile, and for

once she didn't look as if she were onstage. "It's all right. Really." She squared her shoulders and lifted her chin. "He was there, just as you said. Everything else was exactly as you see it now, except for the champagne bottle. The police took that away."

"It was found near the body, I suppose," Nick said, and the actress shook her head.

"In the dustbin. The neck of it was wiped clean, but there was blood enough on the rest of it, seeped into the label and everything. It was one of those large, heavy ones. The police said there wasn't even a crack in it."

"Where were you at the time of the murder, Miss Cullimore?" Drew asked, studying her face.

"I went home. It was Sunday night. We're always dark on Mondays, so I was planning a nice hot bath and then sleeping away a good portion of the next day. I got home and realized I'd left behind the book I was reading."

"What book was that?"

"It was Sayers. *Murder Must Advertise*. Have you read it?"

Drew nodded. "But she has a new one out now, doesn't she?"

"I think so. This one came out last year, but I'd only just gotten round to it, and I was keen to read more. Anyway, I called up to the theater and asked Grady if he would get it out of my dressing room and send it home with Johnnie."

"Mr. Ravenswood didn't usually accompany you home after performances?"

"He did at times, but usually not. If he didn't have some assignation planned, he often stayed late anyway, going over the performance that night, seeing if there were any notes he needed to give the cast, that sort of thing."

"You didn't think it odd for him to still be here that late?"

"Oh, no." Eyes wistful, she looked at one of the photographs. It was Ravenswood as a young Orlando. "Not at all."

"He was very handsome," Madeline said, studying the same picture.

"That was how he looked when I first met him, like a blond Errol Flynn. As fair as Apollo, and as fickle." The actress's smile turned rueful. "Whatever you do, Miss Parker, don't let yourself be taken in by a handsome face and a silver tongue."

Madeline glanced at Drew, a flicker of uncertainty in her eyes, and the leading lady's mouth turned up slightly.

"Present company excepted, of course."

Nobody said anything for a moment, and then Nick ran a hand over the splintered doorframe. "I understand they had to break down the door."

"To get in," Miss Cullimore said. "Yes. Grady has keys to every door in the building save this one. Johnnie was very particular about that. He didn't like anyone being able to come into his sanctuary without his permission. And now the key is missing."

"You didn't have a key?" Drew asked.

"No. Not even when we first came here. Not ever. He absolutely wouldn't have it."

Drew examined the label on the bottle of bay rum that sat on the dressing table. "And no one he may have had in here would have had a key? Not even Mrs. Landis?"

The blonde shook her head. "He wasn't like that with his lady friends. He didn't want them to feel at home here. This was his domain, and we weren't allowed to ever forget it."

"I suppose you've already been through all this with the police," Drew said. "Anything else you think important enough to mention?"

"Not that I can think of."

"I understand someone claims to have seen the killer. Do you know anything about that?"

"That would be Conor," the actress said, and she looked annoyed. "But you'll have to ask him about what he saw. It's possible that Fleur killed Johnnie, but I wouldn't have thought she'd be stupid enough to be seen doing it." She shook her head, her eyes shining now with tears. "Johnnie was really quite a monstrous cad, you know, but one couldn't help being charmed by him. At least for a while. I suppose now I will spend the rest of my life thinking more fondly of him than I did when he was alive."

— *Six* —

Miss Cullimore gave them permission to look about the theater on their own. Later, when Drew and Madeline and Nick returned to the stage, everyone was gone. Everyone but Tess, who was collecting the scripts left behind after the rehearsal and tidying up the place.

"Pardon me," Drew said, and she started.

"Oh. I'm sorry. I didn't realize you were still here. Is there something else you needed?"

"Are you terribly busy at the moment?" Drew asked.

"Not terribly, no." Her expression was wary. "May I help you?"

"You're the script girl, correct?"

She looked down at the stack of scripts in her arms. "Not officially. Millie eloped, and we haven't anyone to replace her yet. I'm actually wardrobe, but I help out wherever I can."

"I see. We were wondering if you could tell us about Mr. Ravenswood. You knew him fairly well, didn't you?"

She looked down, clutching the pages against her chest. "I've worked here for the past five months. I first met him when I started. I'd seen him onstage before that, of course, but never to speak to. So, no, I can't say I knew him well."

Nick glanced at Drew and then again at the girl. "Could you tell us your impression of him?"

Tess shrugged. "Like Miss Cullimore told you, he was very charming. Not that he ever meant a word he said, but he was very attractive saying it."

"Miss Cullimore seems to hold rather a low opinion of his moral convictions," Drew said, and the girl blushed.

"He was a man of the world, as they say, and he certainly had no end of admirers. But for all that, underneath I'd say he was a bit unfeeling. He was one to say the way he was going to have something be, and that was how it was. No good asking him to think about how someone else might see it. He wanted his own way and didn't much mind anything else."

"He directed the plays as well as acting in them?" Nick asked.

The girl nodded. "Sometimes he and Mr. Benton would quarrel over a bit of business or what have you. Nothing of any importance most times."

"What about Mr. Benton?" Drew asked, encouraging her with his eyes. "What's your impression of him?"

A faint color rose in the girl's cheeks. "Mr. Benton, he's . . . uh, I don't know him that well, though he's been very kind to me. I think he sings beautifully and he's quite a good actor."

Drew nodded. "These disagreements with Mr. Ravenswood, none of them was particularly serious, was it?"

The girl's smile was rather tentative. "Oh, no. It was just that Mr. Ravenswood had been doing everything the same way for so long now, and Mr. Benton, well, he wanted to change it up some. You know, make it a bit more up to date."

"And Mr. Ravenswood objected?"

"As I said, he was rather one to say how he wanted things and not expect anyone to say any different. I'm afraid I don't know what else to tell you."

"You will telephone me if you think of anything, won't you?" Drew asked. "You still have my card?"

"If I think of anything, I'll ring up."

"Tess, are you coming to my—?" Benton stopped, noticing Drew, Madeline, and Nick were still there near the stage. "I thought you three left an hour ago."

Tess looked up, and there was a touch of guilt in her expression. "I'm sorry, Conor. I'm just going now."

She hurried off the stage, still clutching the scripts, and Benton watched after her. Then he turned back to the three visitors and said, "Look, she's been through enough lately. No need for you lot to be badgering her, too."

"It was only a few questions," Drew said.

"We're just trying to find out what happened to Ravenswood."

"She's a frightfully decent girl, and she doesn't deserve all this."

"All this?" Drew asked. "All what? What is it she's been through lately?"

Nick slid onto the piano bench nearby and softly picked out a few notes, a line from one of the songs they'd been rehearsing.

> Pretty brook, thy dream is over,
> For thy love is but a rover . . .

Drew knew the words from the tune as almost anyone would. Being in the play, Benton clearly knew them better than most.

"It's none of your business," the actor snapped. "Nothing to do with the murder."

Still at the piano, Nick added more notes.

> Sad the lot of poplar trees,
> Courted by a fickle breeze!

Benton glared at him and then at Drew. "All right. You've figured it for yourselves anyway. Johnnie, as Simone already made plain, was an absolute swine when it came to women. Tess is a parson's daughter. She didn't stand a chance with a smooth talker like him."

"Threw her over right after, I expect," Drew said sympathetically.

"Didn't even have the kindness to speak to her about it. Just made sure she saw him with his next fling, one of the new girls from the chorus. Tess never said a hard word to him or about him as far as I know, but you could see the heartbreak in her eyes." Benton shook his head, his eyes full of pity and then a flash of anger. "I let him hear about it, though. I can tell you that straight out."

"And Ravenswood said . . . ?"

"Just shrugged and said she had to grow up sometime." Again Benton's eyes flashed. "As if that's what defines maturity. Is there anything more immature than selfishness? He didn't love her. He didn't care a thing for her."

Nick turned around on the piano bench, leaning back against the keys. "I wonder she's still around. I'd have thought a girl like that would bolt back home."

Benton sighed. "I told her she ought, but she was afraid what her father might think. I've never met him, but from what she says about him, he seems a good chap. Not the type to turn a girl out of the house and all, you know? But she says she's disappointed him and doesn't think she has any business being around him anymore."

"And here he's probably longing for her to come back," Drew said. "Does she have anyone here? Friends? Relations? Anyone?"

"Not a soul. She's friends with a couple of the girls in the cast, I believe, but most of them think she's hopelessly provincial, not *our* kind at all."

Drew and Madeline exchanged a glance.

"What do you think, Mr. Benton?" Madeline asked.

"She seems quite a nice girl, miss. Rotten how Ravenswood treated her. Someone like her shouldn't be in this business at all."

"So what happens now?" Drew asked. "Business-wise."

"We keep going, I expect." The actor's expression turned bright and brittle. "The show must go on, eh? I suppose Simone will inherit the old Tivoli. She's been wanting to make some changes as it is. I suppose we'll have them now."

"Changes?" Nick asked.

Benton evidently couldn't resist smirking. "Fancies herself Lady Macbeth. One thing Johnnie knew was his own limits. He played Gilbert and Sullivan well—better than anyone I've ever seen. Just the right touch of fun without being too broad about it. But he knew better than to try roles that didn't suit him. I saw him and Simone rehearsing a scene from *Hamlet* once. She kept scolding him for not being serious. Truth was, they were both no good, only he knew it and was having her on about it."

"Were they really that bad?" Nick asked.

Benton shrugged. "No, not really. Just not great. Very ordinary. Painfully ordinary. I expect, once she gets her feet under her managing things, we'll at least have a go at more serious stuff. Shakespeare, Ibsen, Chekhov, perhaps Shaw or O'Neill. Not exactly what the company is looking for."

"But Miss Cullimore is pleased, right?" Drew said. "Just how badly did she want to try something besides light opera?"

Benton looked puzzled for a moment and then barked out a humorless laugh. "Do you mean would she have killed him because of it? Don't be ridiculous. If she didn't kill him over all the women he had, I daresay she wouldn't over this. I don't know that she's particularly heartbroken over him, but I don't think she'd kill him."

"Do you have any theories about who did then?" Drew asked.

"Fleur Hargreaves, of course. Oh, pardon me." Benton made a low, mocking bow. "Mrs. Landis."

"How can you be so sure?"

Benton shrugged. "I saw her. I heard his dressing room door slam shut. It was loud enough to wake the dead, I tell you, though it didn't seem to help old Johnnie. Anyway, I looked into the corridor and saw her running out."

Drew gave him a piercing look. "You absolutely saw her, and there's no doubt in your mind."

"I didn't actually see her face, if that's what you're asking, but I saw her. She was wearing that black cloak she likes." Benton frowned. "The one with the hood. It was pulled up over her head, so I couldn't properly see her face, but I could tell. Who else would it be?"

"That's what we're trying to find out," Nick said. "Are you sure it couldn't have been someone pretending to be Mrs. Landis? I mean, if you didn't see her face and all?"

"I don't think so."

Madeline studied him for a moment. "You can't think of anyone else who might have wanted Mr. Ravenswood dead?"

"Johnnie was rather a rotter, but everyone more or less put up with him. I don't know who else would kill him other than Fleur. They were having an awful row on and off."

"But why?" Madeline pressed. "What would make her do such a thing?"

"Well, obviously, she didn't want him telling her husband about their affair."

"Are you saying they were still seeing each other?"

"Good heavens, no. That was over four or five years ago. Still, I'm certain Landis wouldn't like it if he knew. Perhaps Ravenswood threatened to tell him unless she paid him off."

Drew shook his head. "That would hardly be a threat. Landis has known about it for years. She confessed everything to him not long after their son was born. He forgave her, and she's been devoted since."

"Women like that, they never change. She may not have been seeing Ravenswood anymore, but she had someone else like as not."

Again Drew thought of his time at Oxford. "Young Hazeldine?"

Benton snorted. "Don't make me laugh. Little Billy? He fancies himself a Lothario. I expect, with the following he's got from the girls already, he will be one day. But he hasn't quite got the polish for it at this point. A bit too much of the country in him yet for our crowd."

"Then who is it, do you think, Mrs. Landis is seeing?"

"I haven't the foggiest," Benton said with a shrug. "All I know is a cheat is a cheat, once and always."

Drew looked at him coolly. "I suppose you speak from experience."

"I'm no saint," Benton said with a sneer. "I daresay I've made a false step or two, but I mean to give that over. It grows rather stale after a time." He glanced at the doorway Tess had just passed through. "I'd like to think there's something rather more meaningful to be had."

Nick gave them a sly look and turned again to the piano, picking out a few notes from a jauntier tune in the play.

He will be faithful to his sooth
Till we are wed, and even after.

Seeing Benton's sour look, Drew said, "Perhaps Mrs. Landis felt the same way. Landis seems the sort of fellow who might convince a woman to settle down. And there's the child, as well."

Benton crossed his arms over his chest. "That woman has no more mothering in her than I have."

"Just how well do you know Mrs. Landis?" Drew asked.

"Well enough. She's been flitting about with Ravenswood for the year and a half I've been with the troupe, telling him how to run the productions. Said she was onstage herself for some while. Seemed to think that gave her the right to order us all about."

"Ravenswood didn't object to that?"

"He'd only laugh and let her have her way. When it didn't interfere with his own way, of course. Simone was livid about it. Not that he was seeing Fleur, but that he was letting her as much as be the director, something he never let Simone do. No matter that Simone was his actual wife."

Nick leaned back against the piano again and crossed his legs. "But that wasn't recently?"

"No," Benton replied. "Only about three or four years ago, I'm given to understand. Maybe more. What I heard was that when Fleur was going to have her baby, when her figure started to change, he moved on to someone else, that lady reporter to be exact, and Fleur didn't come about anymore.

Not until a couple of years later. Evidently she missed the stage and her friends in the troupe and liked to help with the productions. That seemed to suit everyone until about a month ago."

"What happened a month ago?"

Benton frowned again. "I really don't know. I heard her in his dressing room a time or two, both of them talking low and . . . I don't know, *fierce* is the only word for it."

"They weren't seeing each other again?"

"No, I'm almost sure of it. There's a different feel to a lovers' quarrel. As an actor, it's my business to know this sort of thing. If I'm going to give a believable performance, there are certain undertones, gestures and looks that say more than the actual dialogue. I'd almost bet there was nothing between them in the least anymore. Not love anyway. But whatever she was after him to do, he only laughed it off. I hated that about him, you know. Everything was a joke."

"Jolly fellow," Nick said.

"And you don't know what she wanted him to do?" Drew asked.

"I have my suspicions," Benton said, "but no, I don't know for certain."

Drew lifted an eyebrow. "Suspicions?"

Benton laughed. "Did you ever see Ravenswood? Onstage?"

Nick shook his head.

"Yes, you did, old man," Drew corrected.

"Remember when you and I took a couple of girls round to see *Iolanthe*? Our first term at Oxford? Remember the Lord Chancellor?"

"No, not really."

"Of course you do. Tall, blond fellow. Got the most applause at the end. A girl rushed out of the audience and gave him roses."

Nick nodded. "Right. I remember now. He was all the ladies could talk about during the interval."

"That's the one."

"That was Ravenswood?"

"The same," Drew said.

"Exactly." Benton gave them a knowing look. "Blond. Blue-eyed. And Mrs. Landis's little boy?"

"Blond and blue-eyed," Drew said. "Still, that's not much proof of anything. I understand Mrs. Landis was blond as a child."

Benton shrugged. "Just a theory. But what happens to her happy marriage if Ravenswood decides to claim the boy as his own?"

Drew looked at Nick. It had been obvious from that night at dinner and afterward that Landis doted on the boy.

"Legally, the boy is Landis's," Drew said.

"Legally," Benton agreed. "That doesn't mean he wouldn't have tossed the child and his mother into the street if Ravenswood had made that claim and Landis believed it. It's been known to happen."

"Let's go back to the night of the murder," Drew suggested. "What do you remember?"

Benton knit his brows, thinking. "We did the show. Came off rather well that night, and we got an extra round of applause when Johnnie announced it was our fifth anniversary at the Tivoli."

"And after?" Madeline asked.

"We came back to his dressing room and had a bit of a party. Just the cast. The orchestra and the hands had gone. We had some remarkably fine champagne too, if you ask me. Even old Grady had a sip, and he's a temperance man," Benton said, smiling faintly. "Just a few drinks, a little reminiscing about when we each joined the company and who's not with us anymore. Didn't last long, as I remember. Everyone had fairly much cleared out by one."

"Why hadn't you gone yet?" Drew asked.

"I'd noticed there was something chewing at the wiring in my dressing room. A rat or something, I expect. I was talking to Grady about trapping it or poisoning it or whatever it is one does with the little beasts. Then I heard a noise and went to see what or who it was, and that was when I saw Fleur running down the corridor."

"Running where?" Drew asked.

"Out the door that goes into the alley. I don't know why it wasn't locked. It generally is. Anyway, she dashed out, and I didn't see her

125

after that. A few minutes later, Simone called to get Grady to give Johnnie a message. When we couldn't rouse him, Grady and I broke down the door. And, naturally, he was dead."

"How long after you saw Mrs. Landis did Miss Cullimore call?" Madeline asked.

"As I said, only a minute or two." Benton considered for a moment. "Couldn't have been more than five at the outside."

"And Grady saw this cloaked intruder?"

"No. He was behind me."

Nick grinned at the actor. "So how do we know you didn't set this all up yourself, and there was never anyone there but you? Did you kill Ravenswood?"

"I was with Grady the whole time. He had taken Johnnie his usual steamed towels, and I caught him as he was coming out. Johnnie was fine then. I saw him there on his sofa, smoking a cigarette. Grady and I were together the rest of the time, until we broke down the door and found the body."

"Steamed towels?" Madeline said.

"Oh, yes, Miss Parker. He was very particular about taking off his makeup every night. Didn't want to lose that youthful glow, you know. Had to have steamed towels and then cold cream. Afterward he would lie down for half an hour with a cold towel over his face. Never changed."

"So he was a man of regular habits, was he?" Drew asked, watching the actor's eyes.

"Ruddy machine, he was," Benton said, sneering again. "Once he set himself on something, there was no shifting him. Every prop, every bit of business, every line, every inflection in every word had to be the way he said and had to be the same night in and night out. The only thing he liked to change up regularly was his women."

Benton chuckled, and there was a touch of irritation in Madeline's eyes.

"What about the lady reporter?" Drew asked. "Josephine Tracy."

"What about her?"

"Was she at the party the night Ravenswood was killed?"

"Yes, I believe she was, come to mention it. She was talking to Johnnie and scribbling like a maniac in her notebook."

"Scribbling what?" Nick asked. "Do you know?"

Benton shook his head. "I assumed she was going to put something about the anniversary in her column and Johnnie was telling her what he wanted in the story. I'm surprised it wasn't in that rag the next day."

Drew frowned. "It wasn't?"

"No," said Benton, again shaking his head, this time directed at Drew. "Just the usual society rot. Same thing, different names, over and over again."

"You don't think this woman could have had anything to do with Ravenswood's death?"

"I shouldn't think so."

"Anyone else at this little bash you had after the show?" asked Nick. "I mean, it was the cast and the lady reporter and your stageman Grady. Who else?"

"Zurrie . . ." Benton thought for a moment and then nodded. "Yes, I'm certain he was there."

"Zurrie?" Drew said.

"Lew Zuraw. Manages the business side of things. Simone insisted Johnnie find someone to do it. He was frightful with figures and hadn't a clue whether we were making a profit or where that profit might have gone. The second time we had our lights cut off, she told him he had to engage a business manager. Simone's never liked the man, but he was better than leaving that sort of thing to Johnnie, so they kept him on."

"Why didn't she like him?" Madeline asked. "Didn't he do a good job?"

"I suppose so. We didn't have the lights cut off after that anyway. I don't know what it was exactly. Simone never cared for foreigners, I suppose. They just never quite hit it off. But as I said, he was better than Johnnie, so she didn't complain."

"Why didn't she just do the books herself?" Nick asked.

"Simone Cullimore? Keep books?" Benton snorted. "Miss Cullimore, in case you didn't know, is an actress. No, pardon me, she is an *artiste*. A leading lady. She has far better things to do with her time than tot up the receipts and pay bills."

Drew nodded. "How did this Mr. Zuraw get along with Ravenswood?"

"Well enough," Benton replied, looking a little disgusted. "Everyone did, you know."

"No quarrels between them?"

"Not that I ever heard. Zuraw was engaged here only four or five months ago. Quiet fellow. Thick mustache. Thick glasses. Thick middle. Polish, I believe. He has a bit of that accent, though I think he came here when he was young. Lived in Hounslow or something, British schools and all that."

"And where might we find him?" asked Drew.

"His office is down at the end of our storage rooms, but I don't believe he's in now. Ought to be tomorrow. He's rather a night owl and likes to keep the same hours we do. Made it nice for Simone and Johnnie, I suppose, to be able to pop in and check up on the receipts whenever they liked."

"I see. I'm a little unclear on this point. Did Ravenswood own the theater? The troupe?"

"He did," Benton said. "It wasn't much, but I fancy he would rather have run the whole thing at our little place here than work at someone else's posh theater in London. I suppose it's Simone's now, mortgaged as it is."

"Any idea how much of it was his free and clear?"

Benton shook his head. "Zurrie would know. He keeps to himself, though, so I don't know how much you'll be able to get out of him. Doesn't matter. If you're looking to find out who killed Johnnie, I've already told you it was Fleur. No matter that I couldn't see her face."

"She claims she was home," Drew said. "With her husband."

Benton laughed. "She claims."

"She says she turned down your advances, turned them down flat, and that's why you're claiming you saw her after the murder. For spite."

The actor snorted at the thought.

Madeline looked the man in the eye. "Is all this just to get back at her, Mr. Benton?"

He crossed his arms and was silent for a while. Finally, he said, "Very well, it's true. After a fashion. When I realized she and Johnnie weren't seeing each other, I thought perhaps she and I could have a bit of fun together. No strings, you know. But that was more than a year ago now."

"What did she say to you?" Drew asked.

"Just laughed and said she wasn't that desperate."

"Rather harsh, eh?"

Benton shrugged. "A bit of a slap, I'll grant you, and meant to be. It's not as if I were brokenhearted over her. I didn't fancy I loved her or any such nonsense. Didn't actually even like her, not even back then. But I figured there had to have been something about her that kept Johnnie coming back as long as he did. Looking as she does, I wanted to give it a go myself. That was all. I never really thought twice about it since."

"So you aren't just trying to get back at her by saying you saw her? Not at all?"

Benton's expression turned grim. "Not at all. I admit she wasn't very good for my ego, but I'd be rather a beast to try to get her hanged for it. This is murder we're talking about after all."

"True." Drew gave the actor his card. "If you think of anything else that might pertain to the case, do telephone."

"All right." Benton put the card in his waistcoat pocket. "But I already told you who did it. I don't know what else there is to say."

— Seven —

"He seems awfully certain," Drew said as they walked from the dim theater into the wan winter sunshine.

"But why would she have killed Ravenswood?" Nick asked. "It doesn't quite fit together."

"Benton said something about the little boy being blond like Ravenswood," Madeline said. "And they did break things off while she was expecting. You don't suppose Ravenswood was going to tell Mr. Landis that Peter is his child, do you?"

Drew opened the passenger side door and helped her in and then got behind the wheel. "I still don't know. If Mrs. Landis confessed her affair with Ravenswood after the boy was born, surely Landis had to admit the possibility that the child wasn't his. If he didn't send her off then, why should he now?"

Nick climbed into the backseat. "True enough. Unless she had convinced him the affair was over before the child was conceived."

Drew gave him a rueful smile. "Hardly a question a gentleman could ask a lady."

"Unless that gentleman happens to be with the police and specifically given the duty to ask, I suppose." Nick shook his head. "What a bit of work this Ravenswood must have been. That song in *Penzance* might have been written for him. 'Shocking tales the rogue could tell . . .' "

"Yes, well, evidently 'nobody can woo so well.' It's a wonder our Miss Cullimore stayed with him as long as she did."

"The theater," Madeline said in reply. "He gave her the starring roles, equal billing with him, as best I can tell, paid the bills and let her do fairly well as she pleased. Seems she found that enough reason not to leave him."

"As Tennyson said, 'The jingling of the guinea

helps the hurt that honor feels.' " Drew frowned, considering. "I wonder what this newspaper woman has to do with any of it. What do you say? Shall we go see if she's in?"

The offices of the *Winchester Tattletale* were on the fourth floor of a ramshackle building in the older part of Winchester's business section.

"They might at least have an elevator," Nick huffed as he reached the landing between the third and fourth floors. "I thought gossip columns and smut were all the rage. Oughtn't they be making money hand over fist?"

"Perhaps the owner merely keeps all the profits for himself," Drew said.

Madeline grinned at him. "Maybe the squalid setting keeps the writers in the right frame of mind. I mean, just look at the kinds of stories they specialize in."

She scampered up the last flight of stairs, with Nick and Drew right after her. They all stopped short before an open door with a glass insert. The lettering on the glass was backward from that side, yet Drew could still read *Winchester Tattletale* stenciled on it. Even if the lettering hadn't been there, he would have had no doubt that they were in the right place.

There was the clash of voices from a number of telephone conversations, half-shouted, rapid-fire questions, the scribble of blunt pencils on scratchpads, and the clattering away of several typewriters. Above that was the sound of arguing, the voices belonging to a large middle-aged man in a shiny suit and a short thirtyish woman with unnaturally red hair. Neither of them seemed the slightest bit concerned about the rather pungent vocabulary they were both using.

Drew knocked, quite politely, on the doorframe. "Pardon me."

Neither the man nor the woman noticed him, and the rest of the office roared on unabated.

Drew cleared his throat. "Pardon me, but I'm looking for Miss Tracy."

Again no one took notice, and finally Nick put two fingers into his mouth and gave a piercing whistle.

"Good afternoon," Drew said into the sudden silence, his voice pleasant. "May I presume you are Miss Tracy?"

"No," she said, penciled brows drawn tightly together. "I'm Audrey Sherman, her secretary. Who are you?"

Drew removed his hat. "I'm Drew Farthering. My friends and I would very much like to speak to Miss Tracy. Could you please direct us to where we might find her?"

The redhead placed her hands on her hips. "Well, I wish I knew. I've been trying to reach her all day. I suppose she's getting the story on Ravenswood, seeing they were such friends and all, but it's not like her to not at least call in. Not after three days."

"Oh, come along, Audrey," the man said, scowling at Drew. "I need you to type up my story for me. Won't take a minute. There's really nothing to it."

"If there's nothing to it, you type it. I've got to get Miss Tracy's column ready in case she doesn't get back in time again." She gave Drew an apologetic smile. "Sorry, but I really must get this seen to."

"Do you typically write her column for her?" Drew asked.

"Not write it, no, but I have been known to type up her notes now and again when she's out on a story. She was planning on a column about that duchess who's carrying on with her chauffeur behind her husband's back, you know the one, but I'm sure she dropped it when the Ravenswood news broke. Came in Monday morning at seven as always, read the front page, and was out like she was shot from a cannon."

"Did she say where she was going?" Madeline asked.

"Never said a word to me or anyone as far as I can tell," Audrey said. "Just grabbed up a stack of papers from her bottom drawer and dashed off. But she has a nose for a story, so I'm certain she's off about Ravenswood."

"Very well." Drew handed her one of his cards.

"I would be very much obliged if you would ask Miss Tracy to telephone me when she comes in. Tell her I won't keep her but a moment."

"All right." Audrey grabbed a paper clip from a nearby desk and clipped the card to her notepad. "Can't guarantee she'll call, but I'll tell her."

"She might like to know it's about the Ravenswood case," Drew added. "Unofficially, of course."

The man had said nothing all this while, but now he looked uneasy. "Are you with the police?"

"Just this morning, in point of fact," Drew said, ignoring Madeline's reproving look. "Do you know anything about the Ravenswood matter, Mr. . . . ?"

"Poste. Alvin Poste." The man looked a bit green. Drew nodded at Nick, who pulled out a small notebook and jotted down the name. "Look here, besides what's been in the paper, I don't know anything about Ravenswood."

"You work here at the *Winchester Tattletale*, do you, Mr. Poste?" Nick asked, his voice taking on an impersonal yet official tone as he scribbled away.

"I do." The man squirmed and fidgeted with his collar. "Notable deaths is my line."

Drew blinked. "And you aren't interested in the Ravenswood case? I should think, as local deaths go, his would be considered 'notable.' "

Poste shrugged. "I have what I need, and my

column on him was in yesterday's edition, thank you."

Audrey smirked. "He mostly takes what he reads in other papers, fancies it up a bit, and puts it in his column. Or were you planning to get additional information from Miss Tracy when she gets back in?"

Poste merely looked down his nose at her and then looked at Drew, eyes anxious. "See here, I don't want any trouble with the police."

Drew shook his head. "I can't promise you won't have, Mr. Poste, but you can rest easy about us. We are just making an unofficial inquiry. As a personal favor to someone and nothing to do with the police at all." He looked once again at the woman. "I hope to hear from Miss Tracy soon. It's quite important."

She tapped the card that was clipped to her notepad. "I won't forget."

— *Eight* —

"What do you think, darling?"

The workmen had finished the paint and wallpapering portion of the remodeling and gone to eat their midday meals. That gave Drew and Madeline some time to inspect the place alone.

"I think it's going to be lovely," she told him, "once the smell of paint and wallpaper paste and sawdust has gone away and all the furniture put back where it belongs."

He chuckled. "We have three weeks until the wedding. I'm certain it will smell of nothing but furniture polish and roses once we move in."

She wrapped her arms around him. "I think it's rather nice that neither of us have slept in here yet. It will make it all the more special when we do."

"Three weeks seems a very long time just now," he said with a sigh.

"I know." She kissed his cheek and then pulled away from him. "But it's not forever."

"Even if it seems so." He gave her a determined smile. "Very well, Mrs. Farthering-to-be, what if we turn our thoughts to matters we *can* do something about?"

She pursed her lips. "You mean the Ravenswood case."

"I do. Shall we go down to the library and see what we ought to do next?"

He took her arm and escorted her out of the room and down the hallway.

"I don't suppose you've heard from that lady reporter yet, have you?" she asked.

"Not yet, no. I'd like to solve this case and not have it to worry us anymore."

"So would I."

He was puzzled by the storminess in her expression, but then she smiled again.

"Where do we go next?"

He considered for a moment. "Well, as they say, we need to find out who would benefit from Ravenswood's death. Financially. What do you say, darling? Would you care to pop round to the Tivoli and talk to this business manager of his?"

"Well, all right. I just wish you weren't doing any investigating right now."

"But, darling, what about poor Landis? It wouldn't do him much good for us to look into the case any other time. And if his wife isn't guilty, it would be awfully sad for him to lose her, wouldn't it?"

She pouted. "Maybe he'd be better off without her."

"Darling! Whether or not I might agree with you, he loves her and very much wants her cleared of suspicion. We ought to at least want the truth to be known, eh?"

"Yes, I know. I know." Still she pouted. "I'd just feel better if she wasn't involved at all."

"Well, she won't be at the Tivoli, just a desperately dull bookkeeper who probably won't tell us much of anything useful. Now, would you or would you not like to come see him with me?"

Finally she smiled. "Who could resist such an invitation?"

Soon they were once again at the Tivoli's stage door. It took a few determined knocks, but eventually the door opened.

"Well, good afternoon, Mr. Farthering. Miss."

Grady beamed at them, leaning on the handle of his push broom. "Back again, are you? I'm afraid Miss Cullimore ain't in yet. Nor Mr. Benton, if that's who you come to see. Should be soon, but not yet."

"Actually," Drew said, "we were hoping to speak to Mr. Zuraw. Is he in?"

"Oh, him. Right." The stageman motioned them into the hallway and pointed. "Go round the corner there, to your right and all the way at the back. His office is the last on the right."

"Excellent."

Drew flipped half a crown into the air. Grady caught it neatly and tucked it into his waistcoat pocket. Whistling, he carried on with his sweeping.

Drew and Madeline followed his directions and soon found themselves at the end of a long, ill-lit corridor with doors at regular intervals along both sides.

"Storage rooms, it seems," Drew said, peeping into one and then continuing on down the hallway. "And the office of one Mr. Lew Zuraw."

He knocked on the last door on the right.

"Yes, yes," said a rather exasperated-sounding voice. "Come in. Come in."

Drew gave Madeline a wink. "Unless I am much mistaken, that is the accent of our slightly foreign Mr. Zuraw."

He opened the door, and he and Madeline stepped into a little hole of an office, remarkable for the amount of papers stacked on every available surface. Zuraw was just as Benton had described him: thick mustache, thick glasses, and thick middle. He squinted at them over the spectacles perched on his knobby nose.

"Did you want something?"

Drew removed his hat and gave the man his card. "My name is Drew Farthering, and this is Madeline Parker. We don't want to disturb your work, but we thought perhaps you could answer a few questions about Mr. Ravenswood's death."

"Ah, Miss Cullimore said you might wish to talk to me."

"I understand you were present at the little party after the last performance of *Mikado*," Drew said. "Is that correct?"

Zuraw nodded his balding head. "I've already told the police everything, but I suppose we must go through it all again." He jabbed a stub of a pencil toward a pair of well-worn chairs piled with papers. "Sit. Sit."

"Thank you, er . . ."

"Oh." Zuraw looked around as if noticing the mess for the first time. "Anywhere. Anywhere."

Drew stacked the papers on the already cluttered floor and then pulled the chairs closer to the desk.

"Could you tell us about that night?" he asked once he and Madeline were seated. "About the party."

Zuraw shrugged. "Nothing much to tell. After

the show, everyone gathered in Mr. Ravenswood's dressing room for champagne and congratulations. He made a speech, mostly telling us all what a fine fellow he was. There wasn't enough champagne but for everyone to have one drink, save himself, so it was rather a quiet affair and broke up early."

"Was Mr. Ravenswood intoxicated?" Madeline asked.

"Tipsy more like, I'd say." Zuraw pulled out a large handkerchief and polished his glasses. "I never saw Mr. Ravenswood actually drunk, though he certainly could put it away when he liked. The only way one could ever tell he'd really had too much was he got sullen. Not generally a sullen man as a rule. Not sober anyway."

"So he wasn't sullen that night?" Drew asked.

"Not at all. He seemed in a jolly humor. Thick as thieves with that reporter he's friends with, of course, but happy to talk to anyone." Zuraw grinned. "So long as it was about himself."

Drew nodded. "Besides the reporter, was there anyone else there who wasn't part of the company?"

"Not that I noticed. No. It wasn't much of a party at all."

Madeline looked at Drew, then smiled at Zuraw. "Do you know Fleur Landis?"

"I've met her. Well, Fleur Hargreaves they call her more often than not, but yes, I've met her. Mr.

Benton says she's the one who killed Mr. Ravenswood."

"And what do you think of that theory?"

"I can't really say, I'm afraid. I don't know her more than to say good day to, myself. They say she and Mr. Ravenswood were carrying on some years ago, but that was well before my time here."

"So she hasn't been around the theater lately?" Drew glanced at Madeline, but her expression didn't change. "I mean, you haven't seen her about during the rehearsals or anything?"

"No, no, I don't mean that at all. She's been about right enough." Zuraw nodded rapidly. "Always telling the actors what they ought to do and such. When I first saw her, I thought, with her looks and all, she must be an actress trying to get work. Just the past three or four weeks now, though, I didn't see her about much. I mean, I'm not really one to notice other people's business, so I'm not saying she wasn't here now and again, but I didn't see her about often."

"Right," Drew said. "Where did you see her when she was in?"

"About the theater, of course, usually during the afternoon. And I heard her and Mr. Ravenswood squabbling from time to time in his dressing room and sometimes in the hallway."

Madeline frowned. "Every afternoon?"

"No," Zuraw said. "Several afternoons, but not with any kind of regularity. Just now and again."

"What else was she doing besides squabbling?" Drew asked. "Just now and again."

"I saw her near Mr. Ravenswood's dressing room a couple of times while he was out. And when she was leaving the theater one time, I saw her then. Alone. Before that, I saw her talking to Miss Cullimore." Zuraw's forehead wrinkled. "That's all that comes to mind just now."

"Do you suppose she and Mr. Ravenswood were seeing each other again?" Madeline asked.

"Hard to say, miss, but I wouldn't have thought so. She seemed to be badgering him about something. Something she didn't want him to do."

Drew's eyes met Madeline's. That was more or less what Miss Cullimore had said. "Do you know what that was?"

Zuraw shook his head. "None of my business. Mr. Ravenswood paid me to see to the books, and that's what I did. So long as Miss Cullimore keeps me on, I'll carry on doing it. Anything else is between the parties in question and their own consciences."

"I see." Drew glanced at the stack of checks Zuraw was writing. "I see you're in charge of disbursements as well as simply keeping the books."

"That's right. I pay the bills, including the payroll. Manage the bank account. Everything to do with money, I see to."

"And you don't have trouble keeping everything

straight?" Drew gestured to the clutter. "In all this?"

Zuraw looked at him coldly. "I know where everything is, young man."

"Oh . . . certainly. So, how did you and Ravenswood get along?" Drew asked. "Any disagreements over how things ought to be managed?"

"Not at all. He didn't much care how everything was handled so long as it was handled. If the bills were paid and the troupe had their wages and he had enough left over to live as pleased him, he didn't much mind."

"And Miss Cullimore?" Madeline asked.

"She asked a question or two here and there, and I told her I was happy to show her the books. But she's an actress. She doesn't know a debit from a credit and doesn't care to be taught. I told her to have an audit if she liked, but she didn't seem to care for that idea, either. Mr. Ravenswood only laughed at her and said she shouldn't worry her pretty head over such things, that it was all seen to."

Drew looked again at the stack of checks on the man's desk. "I understand the theater was owned by Ravenswood."

"By him and the bank," Zuraw clarified. "Mostly the bank. You know how it is, Mr. Farthering, especially in the early years of a mortgage. Most of the payment goes for interest, and the principal stays almost the same. If you're asking if someone killed Mr. Ravenswood for his interest in the Tivoli, I'd say no. It would be precious little to commit a murder for."

"Do you have any idea why someone *would* have killed Ravenswood?"

"As I said, Mr. Farthering, I'm not much of one to get involved. I mind my business and do my job and leave them to theirs. Easier to stay out of trouble that way, that's been my experience. I'm sure you've heard it already, but Mr. Ravenswood was one for the ladies. It may be one of them didn't like being thrown over. It may be whatever that Fleur Hargreaves and he were arguing about. It may be one of the actors didn't like how the theater was run. Whatever it was, nobody told me about it, so I can't tell you. The last I saw Mr. Ravenswood, he was drinking champagne in his dressing room, surrounded by friends and loved ones. Beyond that, I can't say."

Drew stood and brought Madeline to her feet beside him. "You have my card. Mr. Zuraw, if you happen to think of anything else. Or, if you'd rather, telephone the police and let them know. Even the slightest bit of information may be the key to cracking the case."

He offered the man his hand. After wiping his own hand on his sleeve, Zuraw took it and gave it a rather tentative shake. Zuraw then nodded at Madeline. "Miss."

Drew escorted Madeline out of the office and back down the hallway to the stage door.

"Do you any good?" Grady asked, looking up from his dustpan.

"Not in any measurable amount, I'm afraid," Drew told him. "But thank you for letting us in."

"Ah, well, I might've saved you the trouble. Mr. Zuraw don't pay much attention to folk. He might be able to tell you how much money's in your pocket just from the jingle of the coins, but you could come in painted bright blue and never get anything out of him but a 'good morning.' "

Madeline gave him a warm smile. "Thank you all the same. We'll try not to bother you anymore."

He touched his forehead in respect. "No bother, miss, to be sure. Always happy to oblige. We'd all sleep a sight sounder if you and your gentleman figured out who'd done for Mr. Ravenswood."

"That's just what we mean to do," Drew assured him. "You keep your eyes open, you hear?"

"I'll be doing that, sir," Grady said, and then he opened the stage door to the street and made a bow to Madeline.

The next morning, Madeline kept Drew busy with planning their wedding.

"As long as, by the end of the thing, we are well and truly married, I don't mind what you do,

147

darling," he said as he escorted her to the table at midday. "Between you and Aunt Ruth, I am certain the affair will be stylish and tasteful and just opulent enough to be taken notice of without being a local scandal."

Madeline huffed. "Well, I thought you'd at least want to know about your own wedding. And I still don't have anyone to walk me down the aisle."

"We'll figure it out, love." He went over to the sideboard and started filling his plate with ham and game pie. "I know all I need to know, and that is that I will have the most glorious bride in the entire kingdom for my very own. What else matters?"

"I suppose you'd rather be looking into the Ravenswood murder," she said as she filled her plate.

"He's much better at that than figuring out seating arrangements and such," Nick observed, helping himself to the poached trout before he sat.

Madeline's expression softened. "Yes, I suppose he is. And this is what I get for agreeing to marry a mystery-reader-turned-amateur-sleuth."

Drew grinned at the twinkle in her eye. "You can't say you didn't know ahead of time, darling."

"You're just as bad, Madeline," her aunt added, joining them. "If it weren't for the wedding, the three of you would be sitting together, thick as thieves, plotting where to search next for clues."

Madeline laughed. "I suppose you're right, Aunt Ruth. And I don't suppose I will be able to get my groom to pay attention to our wedding plans until this case is over and done with. What do you boys think? After lunch, should we sit together, thick as thieves, and plot?"

Drew gave Aunt Ruth a grateful glance, and she nodded serenely in return. Then he nudged Nick with his elbow.

"What do you say, old man? Are you up to a bit of plotting? Or has old Padgett got you examining drains and checking fences for the day?"

"I think all is quiet on that front just now," Nick said. "When it comes time to collect rents, I cannot call my soul my own, but that day is not today."

"All right then." Drew took another helping of steamed carrots and then escorted Madeline to the table. "If we're to investigate further, where shall we start?"

"We ought to write down what we know," Madeline suggested as she settled into her chair, "and what we're wondering about."

Nick chuckled and recited, " 'I've got a little list—I've got a little list.' "

Madeline tried to look stern but failed. "Gilbert and Sullivan aside, we really should make one, unless you have a better idea."

"It's a capital idea, darling," Drew said. "And I know what I'd put on it first. I want to know what Ravenswood and this lady reporter were chatting about right before he was killed."

"I don't suppose she ever telephoned," Nick said, and Drew shook his head.

"I rang up the *Winchester Tattletale* yesterday, but she still wasn't in."

Nick dabbed his mouth with his napkin. "Do you suppose she's doing some sleuthing of her own?"

"It would make sense," Drew agreed. "She is a reporter after all, and Ravenswood was a particular friend of hers."

"She may not want to talk to you, you know," Madeline said.

Drew feigned horror and said, "That couldn't possibly be."

"No, really. As you say, she is a reporter. She might not want to tell you anything before she's had a chance to get the story into print herself. An exclusive, as they say."

"Maybe so," Drew said. "Well, I don't care about her deuced story. We'll keep it quiet, except for the police of course, whatever she might tell us. She may well be the key to this whole thing. I believe another visit to the *Winchester Tattletale* is in order. The elusive Miss Tracy has to be in sometime, and if she refuses to come to us, then we will go to her."

"Bustling as usual," Nick half shouted over the din of telephones and typewriters at the *Tattletale*. "Do you suppose she's in here somewhere?"

Drew shook his head. "Apart from you," he said to Madeline, "I don't see another female."

Audrey Sherman, the redhead they had spoken to before, looked up from the filing cabinet she was rummaging in. "Well, I like that!"

"Ah, Miss Sherman. Didn't see you there." Drew bowed slightly. "Good afternoon. You might remember us from the other day. Drew Farthering?"

"I remember," the woman said, glancing again at the open drawer. "I'm rather busy just now."

"We just wanted to speak to Miss Tracy if she's available," Madeline said. "Did you give her Mr. Farthering's card?"

The redhead slammed the drawer shut. "No, I didn't, because Miss Tracy hasn't been in since she left that morning after Ravenswood was killed."

Drew glanced at Nick. "Not at all?"

"Not at all."

"Is she out investigating a story?" Nick asked.

"Could be," Audrey said, "but she generally calls in if she's not coming to the office. I've never known her not to after this long, and I've worked for her for six years. Well, nearly six. I've had to write up her column for her for the past five days now. Good thing that duchess has been making a right fool of herself with her chauffeur. That will give us plenty to put in the paper until Miss Tracy comes back."

"Did you try her home?" Madeline asked.

"Did I try her home?" The other woman gave her a disgusted glance. "Of course I tried her home. Off and on all day yesterday and today. About every twenty minutes for the past three hours. I was looking just now to see if we had a number for her mother or someone like that. In case there's a problem."

Drew nodded. "And do you?"

"Nothing. Just her landlady. She says she hasn't seen Miss Tracy since Friday week, but she says she doesn't pay much mind to her comings and goings. Her rent's on time, and that's fairly much all she asks."

"Have you called the police?" Nick asked. "If she's missing, perhaps they ought to know."

"I did." Audrey sniffed. "They said they would send someone round to her flat to check into it, but they didn't sound any too keen, if you ask me."

Drew nodded slowly. "Who did you speak to? Was it the chief inspector?"

"No, just the constable at the desk. Might have been a sergeant, I don't know."

"Did you tell them it was connected to the Ravenswood murder?"

The woman's eyes went wide. "No. Should I have? You don't think Miss Tracy has something to do with that, do you?"

"Weren't she and Ravenswood friends?" Madeline asked.

"Yes," Audrey said, drawing the word out reluctantly. "They had been for years as best I ever heard."

"Had they quarreled?"

"Not that I knew of, and I think she would have told me. Not that they didn't squabble off and on most of the time, but from what she says, he didn't do much squabbling. Just said how he'd have things and then smiled and carried on doing everything his own way. That always irritated her, I'll admit. She's not shy about saying how she feels or who makes her mad."

Nick gave the redhead an arch look. "Has a temper, does she?"

Audrey lifted her chin. "No more or less than anyone else." She patted her too-brilliant hair. "Of course, we redheads are famous for our tempers, but not Miss Tracy. Not that she didn't speak her mind when provoked."

"First I heard of hair dye giving someone a temper," Madeline whispered to Drew.

He gave her a wink and then looked at Audrey. "Miss Tracy wasn't working on a story about him already, was she? I mean, before the murder?"

Audrey shook her head. "I'm almost certain she

wasn't. She'd done one in the summer, sort of a tell-all about his scandalous youth. It was one of her most popular pieces, I can tell you that. She got Mr. Beakins to give her a rise in her salary afterwards, too. She said she'd have it or go elsewhere with her work."

"Bit of a risk, that," Drew said. "Jobs being scarce and all."

"Well, she wasn't afraid. At least she wasn't going to tell him that. Besides, he does pretty good business off what she writes, and they both know it. People like a nice scandal, if it's not about themselves of course."

"No doubt," Drew said. "No doubt."

"I say, Audrey, have you seen today's *Times* anywhere?" Poste sauntered up to her, coffee cup in hand, and frowned when he noticed the trio of visitors. "Why are they here again? If you don't have enough to do, then come and type up my column."

"We're looking into the Ravenswood murder," Drew told him. "Do you have any idea where Miss Tracy might be right now?"

Poste's frown deepened. "Not the slightest. Out getting a story?"

"We're not exactly sure," Drew said. "And you didn't see her that morning before she left?"

"No."

The redhead smirked. "He's never in till ten most mornings."

Nick smiled at her, then asked, "Did anyone else see Miss Tracy that morning, Miss Sherman?"

Audrey shrugged. "Anyone on the floor, I suppose. It's bedlam round here most of the time. I can't say who might have actually noticed her, though."

"Did you see her speak to anyone else that morning?" Drew asked.

"No, but I asked if anyone had. Seems they were all busy with their own work. Nobody particularly remembers her coming in or leaving."

"All right. You still have my card, I believe."

The redhead nodded.

"Meanwhile, I'll see if I can't stir up a bit more interest in constabulary circles about her going missing."

"I thought you said you weren't with the police."

"True, but I do happen to know the chief inspector will be quite keen to find out if there's any connection between your Miss Tracy and the Ravenswood killing."

"Oh, I say." Poste looked awake for the first time Drew could remember. "You're not saying *she* might have done for the old boy, are you?"

Audrey elbowed him. "Of course not. Don't be daft, and don't talk about things you know nothing about." She looked at Nick. "If he minded that advice, we wouldn't likely hear a peep out of him for days on end."

Nick covered a laugh with a slight cough. "We'll see what else we can find out, but do have Miss Tracy ring up Farthering Place when she gets back. We'd be much obliged."

"*If* she gets back," Madeline said once they had gotten to the ground floor again. "If she had something to do with the murder, she might have taken herself off to the Argentine by now."

Drew nodded. It was entirely possible. "Come along. I think another visit with Chief Inspector Birdsong is in order."

— *Nine* —

"So this lady reporter's gone missing, has she?" Birdsong drew his heavy brows together and leaned forward on his desk. "And no one thought to notify the police?"

"Actually, her secretary, a Miss Sherman, phoned this morning. The desk sergeant said someone would look into it." Drew pulled up a chair for Madeline and, once she was seated, stood behind it. "I would have thought Miss Tracy would be on your list of people to speak to about Ravenswood. It seems they were great friends."

"She is on our list, Detective Farthering," the chief inspector assured him. "However, we do have more than one case to see to and not all the money in the world at our disposal." He sniffed. "Unlike some I know of."

"No one is laying blame," Drew said. "We just felt you ought to know Miss Tracy is not where she is generally expected to be and has not been since the morning Ravenswood was killed."

Nick pulled up a chair for himself. "It does seem a bit odd that she would pop off just after reading the headline about the murder. I mean, if she'd actually done the thing, she shouldn't have been surprised by the news, eh?"

"Maybe she was just surprised that the body had been found already," Madeline offered. "It was Sunday night, and the theater is dark on Mondays. Maybe she thought Ravenswood wouldn't be found until Tuesday afternoon at the earliest, when all the actors started coming in to get ready for the performance."

Birdsong narrowed his eyes. "You say she popped off just after she read the morning's headlines? How do you know?"

"Her secretary said so," Nick told him. "She said as soon as she saw the paper, Miss Tracy grabbed up some notes from one of the drawers in her desk and was off like a shot."

"And that was the last this secretary heard from her?" Birdsong chewed his lip, thinking. "Did you ask her what those papers were? The ones Miss Tracy had with her?"

"No," Drew admitted. "I hadn't actually thought

about them till just now. When the secretary mentioned them, no one realized yet that Miss Tracy had disappeared. We thought she was just out."

"Well then, there may be a need for my humble services after all," Birdsong said. "I'll send someone round to the *Winchester Tattletale* to speak to this secretary and see what she can tell us."

"You'll want to talk to Miss Tracy's landlady as well, I expect," Drew said. "Though the secretary says the woman doesn't notice much beyond whether or not the rent is paid on time."

"Not uncommon among those in her line." The chief inspector nodded. "We will make inquiries. Is there anything else you've uncovered that might help us in our investigation, Detective Farthering?"

Drew thought for a moment. "Did you know Tess Davidson is in love with Conor Benton?"

Birdsong pursed his lips. "She told you that, did she?"

"Not in so many words."

"You only have to look at her to see it," Nick put in. "The proverbial misty eyes and blushing cheeks."

"I see." Birdsong looked unimpressed. "What bearing does that have on the case?"

"Only in as much as Ravenswood played fast and loose with this Tess Davidson's heart quite recently," said Drew, "and Benton is rather protective of her."

"So he returns the sentiment, does he?"

"He hasn't actually said anything to her yet," Madeline told the chief inspector. "He told us he wanted to just be a friend to her until she had recovered from her involvement with Ravenswood."

Birdsong looked at Drew. "You're saying he killed Ravenswood for the sake of the girl's honor?"

"Might have done," Drew said, shrugging. "Just a theory."

"Any other theories?"

"I presume you know already that Ravenswood was a rake and didn't care who knew about it. His wife claims she didn't care, but that may or may not be the case."

"Right. We're looking into that. Anything else?"

Drew looked from Madeline to Nick and then back at the chief inspector. "Not in particular. But now you've got me wondering about those papers Miss Tracy took off with."

Birdsong nodded. "And so am I. I suppose all we can do is keep working at it."

"Precisely." Drew put on his hat, tipping it as he settled it on his head, and then he offered his hand to Madeline. "You know, these papers may be as simple a thing as her notes for her latest column or a book she's writing. Her secretary said she always wanted to write a book."

Birdsong stood as Madeline did. Then he looked

at Drew, his expression keen, something between warning and wariness. "Don't you go poking about on your own without keeping us informed. Am I understood?"

"Most certainly," Drew promised with a grin. "I'll be the very model of a modern sleuthing amateur."

Birdsong gave him a pained smile in return. "Go on, the three of you. And mind what I said, Detective Farthering."

Madeline giggled once they were safely out of the office. "Good thing he likes you, Drew, or you'd probably end up in one of his cells."

Drew laughed as Nick took them each by an arm and directed them toward the car. "Come along, you two. I forgot I'm meant to be accompanying Mr. Padgett and Dr. Wight on a check of the livestock."

"Oh, lucky you," Drew said.

"Dr. Wight?" Madeline asked.

"The local vet, darling. Good man. A bit strict, but kindly."

"Kindly, yes," Nick said, hurrying them along, "unless he's kept waiting."

They got back to Farthering Place with just enough time for Nick to make his appointment. Much later in the afternoon, Denny announced that Mr. Landis was on the telephone.

"Landis," Drew said when he picked up the phone in the study, "what can I do for you?"

"Pardon me for troubling you at home, Mr. Farthering." Landis's voice quavered. "It's, well . . ."

"Is it about Mrs. Landis?"

Landis drew an audible breath. "The police have taken her away."

"I'm sorry. Have you spoken with Clifton?"

"He's on his way here. To the police station."

Drew sat himself on the corner of the desk. "Tell me what I can do to help."

"I know you've dealt with Chief Inspector Birdsong in the past," Landis began. "Fleur couldn't possibly have killed anyone. I thought perhaps you could convince him to release her."

The chance of that happening was comically slight, but Drew kept any hint of amusement out of his voice. "I don't know if there is much I can do in that respect, I'm afraid. Our chief inspector does not arrest the guilty party on each and every occasion, but he does tend to have good reason for any arrests he does make."

Landis was silent for a long moment. "Very well. I am sorry to have troubled you with a personal matter."

"Now, don't misunderstand me, Landis. I'm not saying I won't try to help. Getting Mrs. Landis released is very likely beyond my powers, but that doesn't mean I can't try to find out what Birdsong has against her and do a bit more investigating on my own. Has he said why he decided to arrest her now? He wasn't prepared to before."

Again Landis was silent.

"Landis?"

"There's been another murder. Some girl at the theater. Script girl, wardrobe girl, I'm not certain which. Tess Davidson."

"Good heavens," Drew breathed. "When was this?"

"Last night sometime. Must have been after the performance when she was putting everything away."

"And Mrs. Landis doesn't have an alibi for last night?"

"She was at home."

"All night?"

"Yes, of course. And she would have no reason to kill this girl, would she?"

Drew cringed inwardly at the desperation in the man's voice. Would she? Drew didn't know, just as he didn't know what help he could be.

"No," Drew finally said. "No, of course not. And why are they just now making an arrest?"

"Evidently the girl was stuffed into a wardrobe or a closet of some kind. They didn't find her until late this morning."

"And then they came round and arrested Mrs. Landis."

"Yes. But I told them she couldn't have done it. I don't suppose you could make the chief inspector see reason."

"I would like to talk to him, in point of fact. I'll be right down, Landis. Stiff upper lip now."

Drew hung up the telephone and went back into the parlor. Madeline was reading the latest Albert Campion novel, and she smiled up at him.

"Anything important?"

"I'm afraid so, darling. There's been another murder."

Madeline's smile vanished. "Oh, no. Who is it?"

"Tess Davidson. From the theater. They've arrested Mrs. Landis for it."

Her expression grew cool. "And now you're supposed to go and get her released?"

"Landis would like me to speak to Birdsong."

She was still for a moment, and then she bit her lip. "I want to come."

"You don't have to. I realize you and she aren't exactly the best of friends."

"No, really, I want to go. I want this over and done with."

He pulled her to her feet. "Of course, darling. How could I ever manage without you?"

Her expression warmed. "Well, with Nick busy with the stock and everything, I think someone should come along and be Watson for you."

He tucked her arm into his. "You're much too pretty for Watson, you know. Tuppence, I think, better suits, though you're much too pretty for her as well, apart from sharing a determined chin." He tapped her chin and smiled. "Shall we be Tommy and Tuppence, then?"

"Fair enough," she said, "but you're rather too pretty for Tommy, too."

That startled a laugh out of him. "Pretty?"

She traced one finger down his nose to his lips. "Gorgeous."

"You're a shameless flatterer." He kissed her fingertip and hoped his face wasn't too frightfully flushed. "Be kind enough not to say that in front of my friends, eh? Bunny would get no end of amusement out of it and manage to bring it up at every awkward moment he was able. He might forget his own name from time to time, but things like that have a way of sticking with him."

Her eyes twinkled. "Oh, all right. I won't say it to anyone but you. But you're nothing like Tommy, as much as I enjoy reading about him. Red-haired and pleasantly ugly? No, that's not you in the least."

"And I am thankful for small favors. Now, we'd best get up to Winchester. Landis sounded as if he could use a friend at the moment, and no telling what our beloved chief inspector has up his battered sleeve."

They found Landis sitting on a bench just down the corridor from Birdsong's office, elbows propped on his knees and head in his hands. He leaped to his feet when he saw Drew and Madeline.

"Bless you both for coming," he said, reaching

out to shake Drew's hand and then turning to Madeline with an apologetic look. "I know you have your wedding to prepare for. This really is a terrible imposition."

"Not at all," Drew assured. He examined the man more closely. "Are you all right?"

Landis shrugged. "Been a bit sluggish all day. Slow start again this morning. I thought I might be coming down with something, but it doesn't really matter at the moment. I just need to see to Fleur."

"Has Mr. Clifton arrived yet?" Drew asked.

Landis nodded. "About fifteen minutes ago. He's in with Fleur right now."

"And the chief inspector?"

"I told him you would want to talk to him about the case."

"All right," Drew said. "I don't doubt they think this murder is tied to the first one. Ravenswood."

"I suppose." There was pleading in Landis's eyes. "But she couldn't have done the first murder, so why would she have done this one?"

"You're certain she was home all night when Ravenswood was killed."

The older man nodded.

"All night?" Drew pressed.

Again Landis nodded. "I was in bed next to her. She took her sleeping medicine and didn't move till morning."

"How about earlier that evening? Was everything amicable between the two of you?"

"Well, we, Fleur and I, had a bit of a row. Not much of anything, mind you."

Drew looked at Madeline again and then back at Landis. "I don't mean to pry into personal matters, but what did you quarrel about?"

Landis pushed his fingers through his hair. "It was nothing really. A misunderstanding more than anything."

"Did it have to do with Mr. Ravenswood?" Madeline asked.

"No. We didn't know about the murder at the time. Our quarrel was very silly. It was over Peter. Well, Winston, his nurse, to be absolutely precise."

"What?" Drew pressed.

"Oh, Fleur claimed she was spoiling the boy and letting him have his own way far too much. I told her I hadn't seen any sign of him being spoilt and that we couldn't possibly let her go. Peter's very attached to her, you know, and for all I've seen, she's quite good with him."

"And what time was this?"

"I'm not exactly sure," said Landis. "Eleven or later. She was already dressed for bed. I was about to change. I could tell she was unhappy about something. She's not much of one to hide it if things are not the way she wants them. I couldn't think of anything I might have done that would have provoked her, so I thought I'd come straight out and ask."

"That was all?" Drew asked.

"That was all."

"Had she and Miss Winston not been getting along?" Madeline asked.

Landis shrugged. "So far as I know, they have. It's not as though the two of them spend a great deal of time together. And, truly, Peter is a very well-mannered little boy. I don't say that just because he's mine, either. Whatever Winston is doing, she must be on the right track."

Drew nodded. "Is it possible that Mrs. Landis isn't pleased with her over something else and is just using the boy as an excuse?"

"I suppose it's possible, though I don't know what it could be. As I said, it's not as if the two of them spend much time together. What else could they quarrel over but the boy?"

"And that was all you and Mrs. Landis discussed?"

Landis looked down again, faint color coming into his face. "You know how it is, or I expect you will soon enough. We started with Winston spoiling Peter and quickly worked our way up the list to the point where she declared with some certainty that I had never really loved her and wished I had never married her."

Drew gave him a sympathetic smile. "That's rather a leap, isn't it? Over such a trivial matter?"

Landis looked sheepish. "That would be Fleur. One moment purring like a kitten, the next, claws out and yowling. One can never tell about the fair sex."

"Quite. So you didn't tell the police this when they originally questioned you?" Drew asked.

"I didn't think that it mattered. It had nothing to do with Ravenswood."

"What about last night, Mr. Landis?" Madeline asked. "Do you know where your wife was? Was she at home again?"

"Yes, of course she was."

"And you were with her?" Drew asked.

"She slept next to me all night."

"You'd have noticed if she got up, would you?"

"Oh, yes. I've always been a light sleeper. It doesn't take much to—"

Landis broke off when Birdsong emerged from his office giving instructions to a rather sturdy-looking constable. When the constable hurried off, Birdsong turned to Drew.

"There you are, Mr. Farthering." He shook Drew's hand and nodded to Madeline. "Miss Parker. Won't you both come into my office?"

Landis looked at him, a desperate hope in his eyes, and Birdsong's face was professionally sympathetic. "If you don't mind, Mr. Landis, would you wait out here? We'll be just a few minutes."

With a nod, Landis sank back down onto the bench as Drew and Madeline followed the chief inspector into his office.

— Ten —

Birdsong offered Drew and Madeline each a chair and then sat down at his desk. "I suppose Landis told you what's happened."

Drew nodded. "He said the wardrobe girl, Tess Davidson, was murdered last night."

"She was strangled with the cord from the iron, the one they use on the costumes."

Birdsong pushed a file folder across the desk. Drew opened it, looked inside, and swiftly closed it. "You may not want to see this, darling."

Madeline pressed her lips together. "Is it pictures of the body?"

Drew nodded.

"All right," she said. "I can take it."

He opened the folder again. The first photograph showed the girl huddled in the corner of what looked to be a closet in the wardrobe room at the theater. There were costumes hung on a rod along the back and a large box of military-looking hats in the corner. Judging from the cloth wadded in her hands, and the clothes hanger that had slid out onto the black-and-white linoleum floor, she must have pulled one of the pirate costumes down as she was being strangled. The cord from the iron was still around her neck.

"What happened to the iron itself?" Drew asked

as he thumbed through the other photographs, close-ups of the cord, the costume clutched in her stiff hands, her blanched, distorted face.

"The iron's still on the ironing board," Birdsong replied. "There in the wardrobe room. The killer evidently cut the cord off with the shears from the sewing kit they keep. I rather wondered why our murderer didn't bash the girl on the head with the iron, though. Just to make sure."

Drew studied one of the photographs again. She was just a wisp of a girl. It wouldn't take much for anyone, male or female, to make away with her. "Why do you think Mrs. Landis did it?" he asked.

Birdsong frowned. "She was a suspect in the Ravenswood murder. She was seen at the theater that night after the performance."

"Not really." Drew glanced at Madeline and then back at the chief inspector. "Even Benton doesn't claim he actually saw her face."

"Perhaps not," Birdsong said, "but it does make her a suspect in this case. Not likely to have two murders in the same little theater without them being connected, eh?"

"Landis tells me his wife was at home last night," Drew said. "Benton doesn't claim he saw her at the theater again, does he?"

"No."

"That's hardly enough to arrest someone on," Drew protested. "Why would Mrs. Landis want to have killed this girl anyway?"

Madeline narrowed her eyes at the chief inspector. "There's something else, isn't there? Something you haven't told us or you wouldn't have arrested her."

Birdsong nodded gravely. "It seems our killer left behind a tassel from her cloak. It's unquestionably Mrs. Landis's. Even her husband can't deny it or explain it away."

There was a knock, and then the door opened and a uniformed officer leaned in. "A Mr. Clifton to see you, sir, on the Landis case."

"Right," Birdsong said. "Send him in."

The officer stepped back, and a tall, somber-looking man came into the room and shut the door behind him. Drew and Birdsong both stood.

"Mr. Clifton," the chief inspector said, shaking the man's hand. "I believe you know Mr. Farthering here."

Clifton shook Drew's hand, too. "Indeed. Good afternoon, Mr. Farthering. Mr. Landis told me you were here."

"Good afternoon. Madeline, this is Mr. Clifton from our firm of solicitors. Mr. Clifton, may I present my fiancée, Miss Madeline Parker?"

"Miss Parker." Clifton nodded, then turned back to the chief inspector. "Mr. Landis says I'm to make Mr. Farthering and Miss Parker privy to anything we discuss. If that's all right with you, I have a few questions."

"Certainly," Birdsong said. "Won't you sit down?"

Clifton accepted the invitation. "Apart from the matter of the tassel, which could easily have been planted to incriminate my client, what else do you have against her, Chief Inspector?"

"Mrs. Landis was implicated in the Ravenswood killing. Now she is implicated in this one. It can hardly be a coincidence."

"And hardly proof positive, either," Clifton said. "Mr. and Mrs. Landis claim she was at home all evening."

The telephone on the desk rang, and after excusing himself, Birdsong answered it. His eyes grew shrewdly pleased at what he heard on the other end of the line.

"Perhaps we ought to have Mr. Landis in after all," he said once he had rung off. He quickly went to the door and opened it. "Mr. Landis, if you please."

Landis hurried in, and the chief inspector shut the door behind him. There were no more chairs, so Drew gave Landis his next to Clifton and moved to stand behind Madeline. Chief Inspector Birdsong sat behind his desk once more.

"Now, Mr. Landis, would you care to tell us where you and your wife were last night?"

"We were home." Landis glanced at Drew. "Asleep."

Birdsong nodded. "And tell us who is likely to have access to your car."

Landis looked puzzled. "My car? Our driver,

Phillips, of course. Me. Sometimes my wife."

"One of my men has been at your home, sir, questioning your staff. It seems your car was moved sometime in the night."

"Moved?"

"So your man says. He left a pan under it because he noticed an oil leak. This morning it wasn't in the same place."

"The pan?" Drew asked.

Birdsong shook his head. "The pan was where he put it, on top of a stain in the cement. But the car had been moved. Not much, but moved all the same. And not by him."

Landis opened his mouth to speak, but Clifton put a cautioning hand on his arm. Landis immediately shook him off.

"Excuse me, but I have nothing to hide. If that car was moved last night, it wasn't moved by me or my wife."

"So you absolutely vouch for your wife's whereabouts?"

"I do. She had taken a sleeping tablet and gone to bed. It was something she often takes, and she sleeps quite soundly afterward. She was still sleeping when I woke this morning. I tell you, it couldn't have been Fleur." Landis had both hands clenched into fists now, and his jaw was tight.

"And neither of you drove the car?" Clifton asked, his voice calm.

Landis shook his head. "No. She was asleep, I

tell you. She didn't even know when I got into bed with her."

Birdsong leaned forward. "Is there anything else you would like to add, Mr. Landis?"

Landis glanced at Drew and then shook his head again.

"Until I can speak to the judge about bail, I take it Mrs. Landis will remain in your custody, Chief Inspector," Clifton said.

"That's right." Birdsong stood. "Thank you for the information, Mr. Landis. We will be sure to keep you informed about the case."

"Very well then." Clifton stood, shook hands once more with Birdsong and with Drew and then bowed to Madeline. "Thank you all for your time. I think you'd be better off at home now, Mr. Landis." He took Landis by the arm and led him, unprotesting, out of the office.

"You've talked with all the staff at Landis's, have you?" Drew asked the chief inspector once they had gone.

"Yes."

"Did any of them see Mrs. Landis leave during the night?"

"No," Birdsong admitted. "That doesn't mean she didn't."

"Wouldn't this Phillips, the driver, have heard something if the car was moved in the night?"

Birdsong shook his head. "Sergeant Price says the man's rather hard of hearing."

"So he wouldn't have known if the car was moved the night Ravenswood was killed, either."

"Price did ask him that. And no, he wouldn't have. Anything else, Detective Farthering?"

"No." Drew and Madeline both stood. "Though I'm led to believe you have not yet given any reply to the wedding invitation you were sent. You aren't going to disappoint us, are you, Chief Inspector?"

"I, uh . . ." The chief inspector's thick mustache twitched, and there was an extra tinge of color in his face. "It is most kind of you both to invite my wife and me, but, well . . ."

"No need to make a fuss over it, Chief Inspector, neither you nor Mrs. Birdsong," Drew said. "We'd be delighted to have you come. Practically the whole village will be there at the church, and you needn't stay long."

"Well, of course, but—"

"You mustn't say no." Madeline took the chief inspector's arm, beaming at him. "You really mustn't. If it weren't for you, we would likely not be getting married at all."

"Me, miss?"

Drew fought a laugh, seeing the usually imperturbable chief inspector look even more flustered than before. "She's right, you know. That was a near thing, our last little adventure, and only then did my dear Madeline realize how desperately she loved me."

Madeline raised one eyebrow. "I was thinking more along the lines that you didn't actually die."

"Well, there is that," Drew said sunnily. "Come now, Chief Inspector, do say you'll come. We absolutely cannot get married without your august presence."

Birdsong gave them both a nod. "If you're certain, sir, miss, the wife and I would be most honored to accept."

"Excellent." Drew shook his hand. "Three o'clock on the tenth of next month, Holy Trinity in Farthering St. John."

He escorted Madeline out into the corridor, and Birdsong followed them to his doorway.

"Well, if it isn't the two of you together."

Drew turned and saw Conor Benton rise from the bench where he had obviously been waiting, the same bench where Landis had sat just minutes before.

"Mr. Benton," Drew said. "I didn't expect to see you here."

Benton stalked over to them, barely sparing Madeline a glance, glaring at the hand Drew offered. "Are you happy now? She's dead. She's dead because you wouldn't let them put that . . . that *woman* behind bars in the first place." His face went all red and patchy, and his lips trembled. "I told you, Inspector, and I even told Farthering here. Neither of you did the least bit of anything

176

about it, and now an innocent young girl lies dead."

"We are using every resource available to us in this investigation, Mr. Benton," Birdsong said, his voice calm and professional. "Your comments were duly noted when you made them. At that point in time, there was not enough evidence—"

"How about now?" Benton demanded. "Do you have enough evidence now? Tessie is lying on a slab in the morgue with only a sheet to cover her, strangled to death. Is that proof enough?"

"Come along now," Drew said, his voice gentle as he tried to take Benton's arm. "Sit down for a bit."

Benton shrugged him off with a gasping sob and then stood there shaking, fighting to compose himself.

"Mr. Benton," Birdsong said after a moment. "Do sit down. Please, sir."

Benton dropped back onto the bench and looked up at Birdsong. "She said she remembered hearing something Ravenswood said to Fleur before he was killed."

The chief inspector raised both eyebrows. "Miss Davidson did? What was it?"

"I . . . I don't know. She said it mightn't be anything, so she didn't like to say." Benton fidgeted, his fingers in a helpless knot. "But she must have known something . . . something that pointed to Fleur as Johnnie's killer."

Drew shook his head. "That's hardly proof, Benton. Why would she—?"

"Tess is dead! I told you, that's proof enough!" Tears spilled from Benton's red-rimmed eyes as he glared up at Drew. "I understand you're about to be married."

Drew nodded.

Benton jerked his chin at Madeline. "To her?"

Again Drew nodded, and he stepped a little to one side, putting himself between Benton and Madeline.

"Tell me, how would you like to be taken down to a cold, foul-smelling basement just to see her lying on a metal table with her face hardly recognizable?"

Madeline's eyes widened, and her hold on Drew's arm tightened. He pulled her closer. He hadn't seen the body in person, but in the photographs he had seen the girl huddled defenseless in the corner of the wardrobe room closet, her face distorted and full of blood. If that had been Madeline . . .

"You loved her, didn't you?" Drew said. "Did she know?"

"I hadn't . . ." Benton drew a painful, shuddering breath. "I hadn't come out and said it, if that's what you mean. I knew she was still hurting over Ravenswood, and I didn't want her to think I was the same. I . . . I tried to show her in little ways, you know? Only as a friend at first." He covered his eyes with one hand, and his shoulders shook. "She was just beginning to be happy again . . ."

"Why don't we discuss it further but in a more private setting?" Drew suggested, giving Benton his handkerchief. "Something more suitable than this hallway, eh?"

Benton nodded and stood, and the four of them went back into Birdsong's office. The actor took the seat the solicitor had been in, and the other three sat where they had before.

"Now," Drew said, "you told the chief inspector you are sure you saw Mrs. Landis hurrying out of the theater the night Ravenswood was killed. Are you still certain of that?"

"Yes. I'm certain it was Fleur. I recognized that cloak of hers with the tassels. She had the hood up and was nearly running, but it was Fleur all right. Even if I hadn't recognized the cloak, I could tell by the way she moved. I thought at the time it might have been Tess, but then I realized it wasn't. Tess was such a slip of a thing. Not so tall as Fleur and not so . . . well, not shaped the same way. I didn't know why Fleur would be there at all. She hadn't been at the performance or at the party. But, even running, she's always had a particular grace to her. I don't know what it is, almost hypnotizing in its perfection. It was like seeing one of Botticelli's angels step out of a painting and onto the pavement." He glanced at Drew. "You know what I mean?"

Drew nodded, avoiding Madeline's suddenly cool gaze. Fleur did have a way about her.

"And you saw no one else that night?"

Benton shook his head.

"All right," Drew said. "What about this morning? You didn't see anyone? Not Grady? None of the other actors?"

Benton pressed his lips tightly together and shook his head. "Nobody had come in yet. I was in my dressing room."

"So you came in earlier than usual?" Madeline asked. "Why?"

Benton looked at her, then at the chief inspector. No doubt Birdsong had asked all of these same questions at least once already, but he seemed content to hear Benton answer them again.

The actor blinked. "I was going over my lines."

"Why?" Drew asked. "You had to have done *The Pirates of Penzance* at least a hundred times before. More, I daresay. And you want us to believe you didn't know your lines?"

"I haven't ever played the Pirate King before." Benton shrugged. "Well, when I was at school I did once, but that was a long while back. At the Tivoli, Ravenswood was always the Pirate King. I was always Frederic. I did all the juvenile leads. Now we have Hazeldine taking on my parts and me taking on Ravenswood's. The lyrics aren't bad to remember; the music helps them stay in one's head. But the lines not so much. It's not that I

180

haven't heard them time and again, just that I only ever really paid attention to the bits that were cues for me. And I kept wanting to do Frederic rather than the Pirate King. I had a couple of near misses during the dress rehearsal last night, and I thought I had better run through the whole thing again on my own. Hazeldine was helping me."

"We've already questioned Mr. Hazeldine," Birdsong put in.

Drew nodded and turned again to Benton. "And did you go through everything?"

"No. We were only about a third of the way into it. Where the pirates first come across Mabel and her sisters."

"Why did you stop there?"

"I thought I heard someone in the corridor. The wardrobe room is down the hall from my dressing room. From all the dressing rooms. I thought perhaps Tess was coming in, so I opened my door to tell her good morning."

"That was when you saw—"

"I didn't see anything actually, so I went to the wardrobe room to see if she had already gone in, but I didn't see anyone in there."

"What made you open the closet?" Drew asked quietly.

"There was something caught in the door. I didn't know what it was, but I knew Tess wouldn't be happy about it. She was very careful of the costumes. So I opened the door and that's . . ."

Benton's face contorted again, and tears welled in his eyes. "I found her there at the bottom of the closet."

"You didn't see a sign of anyone else being there?" Madeline asked.

Benton shook his head.

"And was she still there when you left last night?" Drew glanced at the chief inspector. "Are you certain?"

"Yes, I told her good-night. She said she was going to be a bit longer. I don't know what she was working on exactly. Sometimes one of the costumes had to be mended, either from something that happened onstage or just from rough handling while being put on and taken off in a hurry. She generally tried to get it done and the wardrobe room tidied up before she'd leave for the night. I know because sometimes I would stay with her and talk until she was ready to go. That way I could make sure she got home all right. I didn't like to think of her on the street that late." He paused and wiped his eyes with the heels of his hands. "I didn't want anything to happen to her."

"But you didn't stay last night?" Madeline asked.

"No." He sniffled and caught a hard breath and then calmed somewhat. "No, I wanted to get to sleep since we were supposed to open today. Of all the nights to leave her there on her own . . ."

"Was anyone else there last night?" Drew asked. "After you left?"

Benton shrugged. "Just Alf. He would have been there."

"Alfred Penrose, the night watchman," Birdsong supplied. "We've spoken to him. He saw Mr. Benton leave. He was the last of the company to leave, excepting Miss Davidson of course. And Penrose spoke to her right after Benton left."

Drew nodded. "And he didn't see anyone come in?"

"No," Benton said. "Alf's been with the Tivoli a long time, same as Grady. He mostly finds himself a chair in a warm corner and sleeps. Everyone knew it." His expression turned bitter. "Even Fleur."

"Why do you think Mrs. Landis would want to kill Tess?" Drew said, watching his eyes.

"Because of Johnnie. Obviously."

Drew raised an eyebrow. "Obviously?"

"Tess must have seen Fleur when she killed him. That, or she had some evidence that would have proven Fleur killed him. Probably threatened to go to the police. Knowing little Tess, she'd have told Fleur to turn herself in and hope for mercy from the court. I expect Fleur found it more convenient just to kill her, too."

"And you know of no one else who might have had reason to?"

"No." Benton crossed his arms over his chest, looking as if he wanted to curl into himself. "Who would want to kill her except the person who killed Johnnie? Two murders here, one following after the other, and you expect me to believe they aren't tied together?"

Drew smiled just the slightest bit. "No, that would be quite a coincidence. Not at all likely. Still, are you certain? She didn't have someone she was seeing? Someone who might have been jealous?"

Benton shook his head slowly. "She wasn't the type. Mostly went straight home when she was done at the theater."

"Perhaps so," Drew mused. "But there was Ravenswood."

With a curse, Benton leaped to his feet and shoved Drew against the wall, chair and all, making a framed photograph hanging there go crashing to the floor.

"Here now!" Birdsong grabbed Benton's shoulder and pushed him back down.

Benton huddled in his seat, his head in his hands and his elbows on his knees. "He has no right to say those things about Tess. She was a good girl. So Ravenswood led her astray. She wasn't the first to fall for his charm, but you make it sound as though she would go with anyone. It's not right, I tell you, and I won't have it!"

"Yes, yes," Birdsong told him. "All right."

"I do beg your pardon, Benton." Drew bowed his head. "I meant nothing against Miss Davidson. Just trying to keep my facts straight."

"Mind you do then, that's all."

"Is there anything else you'd like to say about the case?" the chief inspector asked.

Benton drew a deep breath and then let it out, shoulders sagging. "I don't suppose there's any more to say. You have the killer locked up now, even if it is too late for poor Tess." His lips quivered, and tears again filled his eyes. "Poor Tess."

"Come along, Mr. Benton." Birdsong took him by the arm and helped him to his feet. "You go on home now, and someone will telephone you if there is anything else we need to know."

Benton dragged the back of his hand across his eyes and then under his nose. "You get it right this time, Inspector, do you understand? Fleur is behind this, I know she is, and I'll swear to it before the court, before God if you like."

"No doubt, no doubt." The chief inspector put his hand on the actor's shoulder. "We'll see to things from here."

"If you lot had seen to things, Tessie wouldn't be dead just now, would she?" Benton wrenched out of Birdsong's grasp and stormed out of the office.

"That went well," Drew said brightly.

Birdsong merely nodded, looking rather disgusted. "Well, he tells the story the same every time at any rate."

"The same words and all?" Drew asked. "As if he were speaking lines?"

"No, no. I can spot those a mile off. But he tells the details the same. Most of the time that means he saw what he says he saw."

"Then he saw Fleur," Madeline said. "Or thinks he did."

Drew took her hand and looked into the clear depths of her eyes. "You believe him?"

"I believe he's telling the truth," she said. "Whether or not he's mistaken, I don't know, but I don't think he's lying."

"I suppose the girl's family have been contacted by now, eh?" Drew asked. "I don't know who she had for family, except that her father was a parson of some kind."

"In Dover, according to our records," the chief inspector said. "We've sent someone to speak to him. Of course, he'll want to see to the arrangements."

Drew sighed. "Poor girl. Well, as the Mikado says, 'It's an unjust world, and virtue is triumphant only in theatrical performances.' "

He hadn't always agreed with the Mikado on this point, but as he and Madeline drove back to Farthering Place, he wondered if the Mikado hadn't been right all along.

Sunday was quiet, and Drew and Madeline stayed home except for the morning service at Holy Trinity. Funnily enough, the text had been that same one from Proverbs he and Nick had talked about just a few days before: "Can a man scoop fire into his lap without his clothes being burned?" Odd that old Bartlett would choose that verse just now. Drew had foolishly scooped fire into his lap when he met Fleur, but those embers had gone cold six years ago and the burnt clothes were thrown into the dustbin. He had the scars, of course, and even now it seemed there were consequences of his foolishness still to be borne. But he was thankful for the divine mercy that covered those scars and that foolishness and assured him he was forgiven. He wished he could be as sure of Madeline's forgiveness as he was of God's. There was something strained between them. There had been since Fleur had showed up.

The next day, while Madeline and Aunt Ruth were upstairs with the dressmaker, Drew made his way, as usual, from the back of the newspaper to the front. He couldn't help a sardonic grin when he saw that the Tivoli's production of *H.M.S. Pinafore* in repertory with *The Pirates of Penzance* was scheduled to open tomorrow. Apparently the show must indeed go on.

When he turned to the front page, he stopped short. *ARREST MADE IN RAVENSWOOD MURDER*, the headline blared. There was the usual photograph of Ravenswood, the one in profile from the marquee at the theater. There was also a photograph of Fleur. It must have been from her days onstage. She was younger then and looking fatally glamorous.

Drew glanced down the page and stopped at a third photograph, this one obviously more recent than the other two. It showed Brent Landis coming out of a church, a fair-haired little boy clutched in his arms, hiding his face against Landis's neck while a group of men with cameras and notepads surrounded them. Landis himself looked flustered and rather desperate to get away. Drew didn't blame him.

"This reporter finds it cause for concern that Mr. Landis, presumably with nothing to hide, declined to comment."

Jaw clenched, Drew tossed the paper onto the breakfast table. What absolute and utter swine reporters could be. He stopped to have a quick word with Denny and then went out to the Rolls. A few minutes later, he was at Farlinford Processing, being waved through by Landis's secretary, who was in the middle of a telephone conversation.

He knocked briskly on the frame of Landis's open office door. "Might I have a word?"

Landis was immediately on his feet. "Certainly, certainly. Come in, Mr. Farthering."

Drew shut the door behind him and sat in the chair Landis offered. "I understand you've had some unpleasantness with the press."

"I'm afraid so." Landis sank back down into

his own chair. "I suppose some of them must be decent enough chaps, but there were three or four yesterday afternoon who were rather unpleasant. I ask you, on a Sunday hardly outside the church?"

Drew frowned. Rather unpleasant indeed. "I'm sorry."

"And I had my boy with me. They scared him enough to make him cry, poor little fellow."

"Oh, I say, that *is* too bad. I, ah, I don't suppose you have someplace you and the boy could go? Just to keep out of the public eye, as it were. Until things have calmed a bit."

Landis shrugged. "Not really. I haven't any family even remotely close, save the uncle I told you about. Neither has my wife. But we'll do well enough. I have my work to do, of course, and I don't want to be too far from where they're keeping Fleur until all of this is put right."

"And Peter?"

"He's got his nurse to look after him. She's a good girl, devoted to him, you know."

"It would be a shame, though, to have the little fellow kept indoors all the time because of these reporters."

Drew had already thought this all out. Landis shouldn't have to go through this on top of what was happening with his wife. And there was the child to be thought of.

"You know, Landis, you and the boy might

come and stay with us at Farthering Place until all this is settled."

Landis blinked. "Oh, no, I couldn't possibly consider—"

"Why not?" Drew asked, a smile spreading across his face. "You'd still be close enough to the office and to Mrs. Landis. No one would bother you there. They needn't even know where you are."

"We'd be a terrible nuisance," Landis said, shaking his head. "It's grand of you to offer, I'm sure, but—"

"But what? We've just acres of spare rooms. Lots of places for the boy to play. Does he like animals?"

"Keen on them," Landis admitted. "But Fleur doesn't care to have them about the house."

"Well, we have dogs and horses and several cats. Sheep and cattle, as well. They could all do with some attention, I daresay."

"But we have no way of knowing how long it might be." Landis shook his head again. "Clifton says sometimes it takes weeks to sort these things out. Months even."

"All the more reason to come," Drew said. "At least for a while. In time, no doubt, there will be a shiny new intrigue for the press to chase after, and you and young Peter can go back home, none the worse for wear. What do you say?"

Landis studied him for a moment, no doubt

trying to gauge his sincerity. "Have you ever had a four-year-old living at Farthering Place?"

Drew chuckled. "Well, Nick and I, we were both four-year-olds there, at the same time too, and the old thing's still standing. I imagine Master Landis can't do the place much harm."

"I warn you, there's not much he won't try to climb. I've thought he might give me heart failure a time or two, and those are just the instances I've been told about. I daresay Miss Winston has spared me more than what she's told."

"Miss Winston, I take it, is his nursemaid?"

"Yes. Been with us four years now. She'd have to come with Peter, of course, if that suits. He'd hardly know what to do without her."

"Certainly," Drew said. "I suppose you'll have a valet to bring along, as well."

Landis laughed. "I'd hardly know what to do without *him*."

"It's a scandal, I know, but I've only recently taken on one myself," Drew admitted. "I'm afraid he's spoilt me already for seeing to things on my own."

"It happens," Landis said with a chuckle. "Harper has me hardly knowing where my socks are kept. But he's a good fellow. As conscientious as you could wish."

"Well, then ring him up. Tell him to pack what you'll need for at least a week or two, and the same for Master Landis and Miss Winston. Then have them pop round to Farthering Place. We'll be most pleased to have you all."

"It's awfully good of you. I can't thank you enough. But are you certain it will be all right? I know you and Miss Parker are planning your wedding. I shouldn't like to interfere or anything."

"No trouble at all. You know how brides are. They want the groom to be involved in every step of wedding planning, so long as he doesn't actually make any decisions."

"True enough," Landis said. "I'm thankful that Fleur wanted only a quiet affair at the registrar's office. I was never much one for a fuss."

"Ah, well, if the bride is pleased, the groom need worry about nothing else. Now, you will come stay at Farthering Place, won't you? At least for a time?"

"Provided that, the moment we become a nuisance, you promise to send us all packing," Landis insisted. "Are we agreed?"

"Done and done."

The two of them shook hands on the bargain.

— *Eleven* —

Landis and the others made their way to Farthering Place the next morning. Drew had spent most of the day with Nick and Mr. Padgett, seeing to some estate business, so he didn't see them arrive. And when he got back home late that afternoon, the only sign of their presence was the Landis Daimler parked in the drive.

Once he had ascertained that everyone was happily settled and that Madeline and Aunt Ruth had not yet returned from another of their shopping ventures, he settled on the parlor sofa with Madeline's copy of *Police at the Funeral*. He hadn't been overly impressed with the first Campion tale, but the sleuth had been just a minor character in that one. The next two books had been proper corkers, and this one was off to a whale of a start. If he could manage even half an hour's uninterrupted reading, he would count himself blessed.

He had gotten through only about three pages when he heard something that sounded suspiciously like unsuccessful tiptoeing. He peered around the edge of his book and into a pair of very blue eyes.

"Well, hello there."

The blue eyes blinked at him, and then the golden-haired little boy drew himself up very straight and put out his hand. "Good afternoon, sir. My name is Peter William Landis, and I am very pleased to meet you."

Holding back a chuckle at the piping small voice, Drew put his book aside and stood up to shake the boy's hand. "Master Landis, it is a pleasure to finally meet you. I am Ellison Andrew Farthering."

The boy blinked at him again, clearly unsure, now that he had done as he had been taught, what he should do next.

Drew gave him an encouraging smile. "Is there something I can do for you, Master Landis?"

Peter looked at him for a moment, and then with a careful glance toward the door he lowered his voice. "Did you know there's a kitty hiding in your house?"

Drew pretended to be shocked. "There is? Well, we'd better find it, hadn't we? What does it look like?"

"It's very little," Peter said, holding his hands about six inches apart. "It's white and has blue eyes just like me."

"Ah, that would be Mr. Chambers, I expect."

"Mr. Chambers?"

"Yes. He lives here, you know."

"In your house?"

"Yes."

The blue eyes got bigger. "Your mummy lets you keep him in your house?"

Drew gave him a slightly rueful smile and sat down again. "My mother isn't with any longer."

"Did she go to stay somewhere else?"

"In a manner of speaking."

"My mummy went on a trip, too." Peter crawled up onto the sofa and settled next to Drew. "But she will be back anytime now."

Drew gave the boy his most reassuring look. "That will be nice, won't it?"

Peter frowned a little, thinking. "When will your mummy come back?"

"Not ever, I'm afraid," Drew said gently.

"Did she . . . ?" Peter glanced back at the open door, and once again lowered his voice. "Did she get dead?"

Drew nodded.

"Did her boat sink in the ocean?"

"No." Drew put his hand on the boy's shoulder. "Do you know someone whose ship sank?"

"Colin used to have the garden next to ours. His mummy and daddy did. Then when they got dead, he had to live with his aunt 'Lizbeth, and now we can't play anymore."

"I'm sorry to hear that."

"He had a dog that lived in his house." Peter leaned against Drew's knee, blue eyes bright. "Will you play with me?"

"Won't someone be looking for you just about now?"

The boy's smile turned mischievous. "Nurse has her half day, and the other lady falled asleep."

"I see." Drew grinned back, standing once more. "Very well. Shall we see if Mr. Chambers would like to join us? Now, be very, very still and quiet for a moment. Can you do that?"

Peter nodded and, hands clasped together, stood stock-still. Drew reached into his pocket and jingled his keys. Almost at once the curtain rippled, and the tip of a tiny pink nose poked out from under it. Quick as he could, Drew stepped over to the door and pushed it closed. Now at least the little rogue couldn't lead them on a merry chase all over the house.

"Don't be difficult now," Drew said, moving closer to the curtain on silent feet. "Come along and play."

He was almost in reach now, and he held the keys out toward the kitten. Mesmerized, Chambers stretched out his neck so his nose was almost touching the glittery prize. Drew brought his free hand down, trapping him in the curtains. Peter squealed and bounced toward them, and Mr. Chambers hissed, digging his claws into Drew's arm.

Drew gritted his teeth as he untangled Mr. Chambers from the curtain and from his sleeve. Then he carried the squirming feline over to the sofa and sat down, holding him in his lap, making sure he wasn't in a position to scratch again. Peter came closer and put his face on the same level as the kitten's.

"My name is Peter William Landis, but I think you can call me Peter."

"On a first name basis already," Drew said. "How can that bode but well?"

"May I pet him?" Peter touched his hand to the back of Mr. Chambers's head, looking concerned.

"Don't be afraid, Mr. Chambers. I love you."

The kitten made a squeaking mew.

"What did he say?" Peter asked. "Do you know?"

"Well, I believe, if I've translated properly, he said you might pet him once more, very gently, and then we'd best let him go."

Peter touched one white ear, making it twitch. "Will he come back later? I won't hurt him."

Drew gave the little boy his keys. "You show him those, and he won't go too far. Just don't let him get too excited and scratch you."

The minute Drew released him, Mr. Chambers dove back into the curtains. With a giggle, Peter ran to him and dropped to his knees, jingling Drew's keys and then running them under the curtain again. Mr. Chambers popped out, ears forward and eyes round. Peter shrieked and dropped the keys, looking equally terrified and delighted. Then there was a knock at the parlor door, and the kitten darted back into his hiding place.

Drew stood up, pocketing his keys. "Come in."

The door opened, and Denny peered into the room. "I beg your pardon, sir, but Beryl . . . Ah. Master Landis. I will tell Beryl to dry her tears."

"Mr. Dennison," said an unfamiliar-but-worried voice from the hallway. "They told me Peter is missing."

"In here, miss."

Denny stepped back from the doorway, and a

young woman rushed in. Her brown eyes were flooded with relief when she saw Peter sitting on the floor. "There you are!"

"We were playing with the kitty," the boy piped.

The woman hurried over to take Peter's hand, smiling and apologetic. "You must be Mr. Farthering. I'm terribly sorry. We didn't mean to be a nuisance."

"Nonsense. The little chap and I were getting along famously." Drew held out his hand. "Miss Winston, is it?"

She dropped a brief curtsy and shook his hand. "Yes, sir. It's my half day. Your maid Beryl was supposed to be looking after the boy. I warned her that Peter's fond of exploring when left to his own devices."

Drew laughed softly. "Hunting this time, I believe. Big-game cats."

"He's all white and he lives in the house and his name is Mr. Chambers and I love him," Peter said, not stopping to take a breath.

"You mustn't bother Mr. Farthering again, Peter," the nursemaid told him, only a hint of scolding in her tone. "He's very busy."

"No, no," Drew assured her again, and she abruptly scooped the boy up into her arms.

"Peter, Peter." She kissed his golden hair and cuddled him close. "I was afraid something had happened to you. And then it would be all my fault because I left you."

He patted her face with one little hand. "I'm sorry I leaved the other lady. But she was 'sleep and so I couldn't tell her when I went to find the kitty."

"And what do you suppose your daddy would say if you went away from us? He would be very, very sad."

The boy bit his lower lip. "I don't want Daddy to be sad."

"Neither do I," she said, and then she smiled uncertainly at Drew. "The poor little mite. Mr. Landis dotes on him so."

"I saw that the first time we met," Drew said. "It's one of the things I liked best about him."

Miss Winston's expression was shy and earnest all at once. "I felt the same way when I first came to work for him and Mrs. Landis. So many men have no time for their children. Believe me, in my line of work, I know."

Drew studied her for a moment. She wasn't as young as he had first thought. A bit past thirty perhaps. Pleasant looking enough, but certainly no great beauty. Not like her mistress. But there was a gentle sweetness in her face that was very appealing, and Peter clearly adored her.

"How long have you been looking after our big-game hunter here?" Drew tapped Peter's nose, and the boy giggled, snuggling into the nursemaid's neck and then squirming to be put down.

"Nearly four years now," Miss Winston replied

as she set him back on his feet. "Stay right here. Do you understand, Peter?"

The boy nodded, eyes eager, and then started crawling down toward the bottom of the curtain, no doubt looking for the kitten again.

"He was such a little fellow when I first came to the Landises," the woman told Drew. "They were afraid for a time that he wouldn't make it past his first year. I had some nursing experience during the war. Of course, minding an infant isn't quite the same as patching up soldiers, but it still came in handy with the baby."

Drew could hardly imagine the meek woman in the bloody aftermath of battle. "You must have been quite young then," he observed, and a blush touched her cheeks.

"I told them I was eighteen when I wasn't even seventeen quite yet." She looked up at him, her brown eyes earnest. "But I did so want to help. All those men with no one to look after them after they had risked everything to keep us all safe. I had to help them."

"And your parents didn't mind?"

"Oh, I hadn't any. I was raised in an orphans' home. I couldn't wait to leave it."

He smiled a little. "Even without official permission?"

She shrugged, turning pinker. "They had plenty of children who actually needed to be looked after by then, and not that much space or resources. I really was grown up, you know. I had been taking care of the little ones at the home since I was ten or so. One thing I can thank them for is preparing me to make my own living."

"Always a good thing, I'd say. And how do you like working for the Landises?"

She gave Peter a fond glance as he lifted a corner of the heavy curtain and then tried unsuccessfully to push aside the lace sheers so he could look for Mr. Chambers.

"It's quite a good place actually. Peter's a darling. I can't imagine having a better child to look after. He tries so hard to please, though he does tend to climb things he ought not."

Drew chuckled. "So Mr. Landis told me. I suppose there are worse traits for a child to have."

Miss Winston nodded. "It only means being a bit more careful in watching him. I expect he'll grow out of it one day."

"Or become the first to reach the top of Mount Everest."

"There is that," she said, and her laugh was rich and sweet.

Peter looked up at her, smiling because she was happy, and Drew smiled, too. He was certainly an appealing child.

"He does favor his mother," Drew observed. "Apart from the blue eyes and fair hair. Though I understand she was blond as a child, as well."

"Did she tell you that?" The nursemaid laughed.

"Helen, that's her personal maid, she told me that Mrs. Landis's great-grandmother was a full-blooded Sikh brought back to London by one of Queen Victoria's soldiers sometime in the 1850s. That's where she gets those black eyes and black hair. She was never fair-haired, not even as a baby. I've seen photographs. And that name of hers. Fleur? She was born Florence Eugenia Frye. Florrie Frye? Can you imagine? No wonder she changed it."

She looked down when Peter flung himself against her skirts. "Can you find the kitty for me, Winnie? I think he's runned away."

Miss Winston gave him a severe look. "Now, Peter, what have I told you about interrupting when grown-ups are talking? Please ask Mr. Farthering to excuse you."

The boy bit his lip and looked down at the floor. Then he turned his big blue eyes up to Drew. "Please excuse me for interrupting, sir. It was quite rude of me."

Drew held back a smile at the carefully rehearsed speech and gave the child a nod. "Think nothing of it."

Peter threw his arms around Drew's legs, beaming at him. "Now can we find the kitty?"

"Peter!" Miss Winston gasped.

Drew had to turn his face away to keep from laughing outright. That would do nothing to help her efforts to teach the boy proper manners. Once he had assumed a suitably grave expression, he bent down to face the boy. "When Miss Winston and I have finished our conversation, Peter, we'll see if we can't get Mr. Chambers to come back and play, fair enough?"

Peter didn't seem at all certain about the fairness of this arrangement, but he nodded and made no protest when Miss Winston took his hand and had him stand next to her again.

"Perhaps I had better get him back to the nursery and ready for his supper," she said.

"Not quite yet, eh, Miss Winston?" came another voice.

"Daddy!"

Peter broke away from his nurse and ran to the parlor door.

Landis scooped up the boy, hugging him close and pressing a kiss to his fair hair. "And what is this, young man? I expected to find you in the nursery."

"I came to see Mr. Chambers. He's a white kitty and he lives in the house and I love him!"

Landis chuckled and carried the boy back into the parlor. "Good afternoon, Mr. Farthering. I trust we haven't upset things too much already."

"Not at all," Drew said. "Peter and Mr. Chambers and I are already fast friends."

"I'm sorry, Mr. Landis," Miss Winston said, a sudden tinge of fresh pink in her cheeks. "He got away from the girl who was looking after him while I was out." She gave Peter a look of gentle reproof. "While he was *supposed* to be napping."

Landis gave the boy a stern look and then turned to her, and her cheeks grew even pinker.

"I'm certain he won't do it again." Landis looked again at Peter. "He knows we must be on our best behavior while we are guests in Mr. Farthering's home, right?"

Peter nodded, biting his lip.

"All right then, there's my good boy." Landis kissed his hair again and then handed him to his nurse. "Now off you go. I have some things to see to."

"Will you come tell me good-night, Daddy?"

Miss Winston smiled hopefully. "It means a great deal. I mean, Peter always sleeps better after you've been by."

Landis winked at the boy. "You behave yourself and no more running off, and I'll come tuck you in later." He turned to Drew. "It's really very good of you to have us to stay while . . ." He glanced at Peter, who was watching him with bright eyes, taking in every word. "While there are difficulties."

"I take it there has been nothing new on the matter," Drew said.

"Nothing, no."

Miss Winston watched him with sympathetic eyes but didn't say anything.

Landis cleared his throat. "Well, I have a few

things to see to before I dress for dinner. Peter, you behave now."

The boy gave him a brilliant smile. "You betcha."

"All right," Landis said with a chuckle. "We were listening to an American program on the wireless a few weeks ago. It seems to have left an impression."

"And after I've tried so hard to teach him to speak properly," Miss Winston said. "Mr. Landis, you oughtn't to laugh. It only encourages him."

"Yes, I know, Miss Winston, I know."

He tried to look contrite and failed miserably, and the nursemaid finally shook her head. "You'd better go tend to your business, sir. It wouldn't do for you to be late to dinner your first night here."

"Very true. If you'll excuse me, Mr. Farthering."

"I suppose we ought to get back up to the nursery," Miss Winston said, once Landis had hurried off. "Tell Mr. Farthering thank you, Peter, for looking after you today."

"Thank you, sir," the boy said. "May I come play with you again?"

"Of course you may, Peter. Very soon."

"Will Mr. Chambers come, too?"

"We'll make certain of it. Now you have your supper and I will see you later." He made a bow. "We'd be very pleased to have you join us for dinner too, Miss Winston. One of the maids can sit with Peter, if you like. I'm certain there won't be another incident."

"If it's all right," she said, looking flustered. "If you're certain Mr. Landis—"

"He wouldn't mind, would he?"

"No, I don't mean that. Just, well . . ." A smile touched her lips. "I would be very pleased to come. Thank you again, Mr. Farthering." She shifted the boy against her hip, getting a better hold on him. "We'll try not to be such a nuisance in the future."

She turned, carrying her charge away, and he looked at Drew over her shoulder, blue eyes wide and uncertain. Obviously he had no wish to be a nuisance.

Drew tapped the side of his nose and said in a stage whisper, "Mum's the word, but I'll bring Mr. Chambers up to the nursery to play for a bit before you go to bed. How would that be?"

Peter giggled and put one finger to his lips. "Shh. Winnie will hear you."

She turned back to Drew, looking far more indulgent than stern. "If we eat all of our supper, including the vegetables, without a grumble, then we would very much enjoy another visit, Mr. Farthering."

Drew gave her a nod as she carried Peter into the hallway.

"*All* the vegetables, Winnie?" came the plaintive little voice, and Drew laughed.

— Twelve —

Before he went to dress for dinner, Drew decided to make good on his promise and take Mr. Chambers up to play with Peter for a short while. He hadn't been in the nursery for ages, but he felt a sudden fondness for the old place as he neared the door. He remembered it as bright and airy, full of cupboards and endless possibilities, and battered enough to be played in without too much scolding from the adults. It hadn't been redone since. Fleur may have been rather particular about Peter's playroom at home, but Drew wanted the boy to enjoy himself here at Farthering Place.

Drew paused as he reached the nursery door, holding Mr. Chambers against his shoulder. He heard Miss Winston's voice and then Landis's. After that, there was only a low laugh, hers, followed by the patter of little feet and Peter's piping voice.

"Daddy, may I play with this pony?"

"I don't know," Landis said. "Perhaps we'd best ask before—"

"Oh, not at all," Drew told them, stepping into the room. "You may play with any of the toys you find in the cupboards up here, Peter. You're very welcome."

"Mr. Drew!" The boy dropped Drew's fondly

remembered buckskin pony and ran to him. "You brought Mr. Chambers!"

"I most certainly did." Drew pushed the door shut behind him and set the kitten on the floor. "Now, Mr. Chambers, be a gentleman and show our guest around."

Mr. Chambers at once jumped up on the window seat, and Peter scrambled up after him, whispering to him until, purring, the kitten came to him and rubbed against his flannel nightshirt.

"Truly, Miss Winston," Drew said, watching them, "he is welcome to anything he finds up here. I don't believe it's been much changed since Nick and I played here as boys, and I seem to remember no end of fun and no end of toys."

"We brought a few of Peter's favorites from home of course," she said, "but little ones get bored very quickly. He'll love exploring, I'm sure. Thank you."

"Yes," said Landis. "You've made us all feel quite at home. I don't know how I shall ever repay you."

"You're all more than welcome," Drew assured him.

He and Landis discussed a few business matters while Peter and Mr. Chambers played, and then Drew gave Landis a nod.

"The bell for dinner is at seven." He picked up the kitten. "You do just as Miss Winston says, Peter, and get to bed when you're told, and Mr.

Chambers will come back and visit tomorrow. How is that?"

The boy smiled the dazzling smile he'd inherited from his mother. "I'll be good, Mr. Drew."

"Capital." Drew leaned down a bit so Peter could pet the kitten one last time, and then he opened the door to the hallway. "Good night for now. We'll see you again tomorrow."

"Oh, there you are." Nick leaned into the nursery. "I was just about to go dress. Your bride-to-be said that if I were to see you, I was to tell you not to be late and that you ought to invite Miss Winston to dinner if she would like."

Drew nodded. "I trust you will still be joining us, Miss Winston?"

She looked at Landis, her face coloring. "I . . . I ought to just have something up here in the nursery—"

"Nonsense," Drew said. "If you don't come, we shall be one lady short at the table. That just won't do."

"Do say you'll come, Miss Winston," Nick urged. "Otherwise I'll no doubt be sent off to the kitchen to beg for scraps."

She fought a smile. "They wouldn't do that."

"There's always a chance," Nick said, perfectly solemn. "I don't like to risk it."

She pursed her lips and looked toward Landis once more.

"What?" He looked up absently from where he

was chatting with his son. "Oh, certainly. You must come along, Miss Winston. Miss Parker and her aunt wouldn't want to have an odd number at the table."

"If you're certain no one will mind, Mr. Landis," the nursemaid said, and now there was a touch of pleasure in her eyes.

"Oh, no. You must come."

She turned to Drew. "Yes, thank you, Mr. Farthering."

"You'll hear the bell." Drew looked over at Landis. "Coming?"

"Of course. Good night, Peter. Say your prayers, and sweet dreams."

The boy hugged him around the neck. "Mr. Drew says he has horses, Daddy. Will you take me to see one tomorrow?"

"I must go to my office tomorrow, son. We may have to wait until Saturday."

"But maybe you can come home before it gets dark and we can go see the horses tomorrow?"

"Well, I . . ."

Drew chuckled at the eager expression on the boy's face. "I doubt there would be much harm in knocking off work an hour or so early, would there, Landis? Anything urgent going on at the office?"

"Not much, no. What do you say, Peter? Shall we visit all the animals tomorrow? I think there are sheep and some cows. And if I heard properly, someone has a dog. Now you get a good night's sleep or you will be too tired to go out tomorrow."

"Will Mummy come, too?"

"No, Peter, I'm afraid not. Most likely she won't have gotten back from her trip by tomorrow."

Peter's lower lip went out in a slight pout. "Doesn't Mummy want to come home?"

"Of course she does." Landis cuddled the boy closer. "More than anything."

Miss Winston's mouth tightened just a bit.

"When *will* she be home?" Peter asked. "Saturday?"

"Well, it might be Saturday," Landis told him, "but it might not." He kissed the top of his son's head. "Now, be a brave soldier, Peter, and tomorrow we'll go see the animals. How would that be?"

"Just you and me, Daddy?"

"That's right. Just you and me."

"Poor little thing," Madeline said when, as they were going down to dinner, Drew told her about Peter's questions about his mother. "Fleur doesn't seem to be much of a mother to him anyway. You wouldn't think he would miss her very much."

"I know how he feels," Drew said softly. "When I was a boy, I always wondered what was wrong with me and why my mother never seemed all that interested in me. Looking back, I guess she did rather a remarkable job of trying anyway. It doesn't appear as though Mrs. Landis is doing as much with her son, and he is without a doubt her own child."

She slipped her arm through his. "Have your lawyers still not found anything more about your mother, Drew?"

He shook his head. "Without even a name to go by, and after a quarter of a century, it seems rather unlikely we'll find anything helpful. It's unsettling, the not knowing, more than I thought it would be." He pulled her closer to his side. "Perhaps we'll look into it together sometime. Once we're married, I see no reason why we couldn't hop over to the Continent for a bit. You'd like Paris, I'm sure."

"I'm sure I would," she said, smiling, but then her smile faded. "What do you suppose you'll discover? If you find her, I mean."

He shrugged. "There's no telling. All I ever heard was that she was an ordinary shopgirl in a place that sold hats on the *Rue de la Paix*. It could be she owns the shop by now. Or perhaps she's married and has children, possibly grand-children, of her own."

"Could be."

"Perhaps she's passed on. She's likely not very old, surely not more than fifty. But we have no guarantees of reaching a certain age, have we?"

"Do you think you'd know her, Drew?" Madeline stopped in the foyer and tilted her head, studying his face. "Yes, she gave birth to you, but you never once saw her after that. I don't mean would you recognize her, but do you think there would be some kind of connection between you and your mother if you were to meet her? Do you think it matters after all this time?"

"I don't know."

He ran a hand through his hair. It was something he'd been wondering about ever since he learned that Constance Farthering Parker wasn't in fact his natural mother. Knowing that explained a lot, about her and about himself, but not enough. Yet finding this Frenchwoman wouldn't likely explain much more. The whole thing was maddening. He had to find out. He had to.

"I just don't know," he said again. "I hate to think of Peter going through the same thing one day concerning his own father."

Madeline put both arms around him. "Maybe Peter will never know anything besides that Mr. Landis *is* his father."

"Maybe," Drew said. "But Ravenswood was a public personage. It's almost bound to come out one day. And gossip can be so cruel, especially to the innocent."

She leaned up to kiss his cheek. "At least Peter can be certain the father he knows loves him. Mr. Landis makes no secret of that."

Drew smiled and started them walking again. "True enough, God bless him. And I hope you're right. All Peter needs to know is that Daddy loves him, and Ravenswood need never come into it at all."

Dinner that night, as well as the two nights after that, was quiet and pleasant. They didn't discuss the case or Fleur. Convivial small talk was the order of the day, and Miss Winston turned out to be quite an interesting companion. Her comments were mostly directed to Madeline and Aunt Ruth, and she was surprisingly well educated and knowledgeable about current affairs.

"I didn't expect that," Drew admitted once the meal was over on Thursday night, glad he and Madeline finally had a moment alone. "Miss Winston, I mean. I shouldn't have thought there'd be that much to her."

"I feel bad for her," Madeline said, her voice quiet.

"Why's that, darling?"

Drew escorted her onto the balcony that overlooked the meadow and Farthering St. John in the distance. It was a fine night, even though a tad cold, and she snuggled against his side.

"She doesn't have anyone in the world, and going on as she is, she isn't likely to."

"Oh, I don't know," Drew said, holding her closer when she shivered. "She's not entirely as she seems. Rather a wicked sense of humor for someone as naturally reserved as she appears to be. Not unkind but a bit pithier than I would have expected of her."

Madeline's mouth turned up on one side. "Better than being bitter, isn't it?"

"Bitter? Why should she be bitter?"

"Well, being an old maid and all . . ."

Drew laughed. "You act as if she's fifty rather than thirty. And even at fifty, who's to say when one might meet one's true love?"

"So you think even Aunt Ruth might find someone someday?"

"I do. He'd have to be a sharp fellow and always on his toes, but then again we wouldn't want her settling for anything less, eh? But perhaps she doesn't want anyone. She seems happy enough as she is. And better to be on one's own than tied to the wrong spouse, don't you think?"

"I suppose." Madeline looked up at him, biting her lower lip, eyes pensive. "Or to long for some-one else's."

"Yes," Drew said. "That's also rather tragic. Even if one remains nobly silent on the issue."

"Do you suppose he even knows?"

"Landis?" Drew shook his head. "As best I can tell, he's pleased with her work and appreciates her fondness for the boy, but that's all. He has seemed a bit surprised by her the past few days. I don't suppose she generally takes dinner with the family. But with Mrs. Landis in the picture, he's very unlikely to look at anyone else, eh?"

She shook her head slowly, her smile forced. "Men."

"Now, now, darling. Not all men are dazzled by a pretty face." He smirked. "Not forever."

"And if I had looked more like Miss Winston than I do, would you have bothered to even talk to me?"

He felt a touch of color rise into his face, and he laughed faintly. He had promised to be honest with her. "Well, I can't very well help it that you have the most glorious periwinkle eyes I've ever seen."

Her lashes fluttered to her cheeks. "Drew, I mean it."

He put one finger under her chin and turned her face up to him. "So do I. I won't deny that I thought you were perfectly lovely the first time I saw you and your friends jammed into that little roadster that pulled up to the house. It was enough to interest me, to be sure, but if I hadn't found you intelligent and kind and amusing and challenging and everything I hoped one day to find in a girl, none of the external things would have mattered. Mrs. Landis is quite possibly the most perfectly beautiful woman I've ever seen, but there is nothing about her that entices me anymore. Whether or not she's a murderess, there is simply nothing in her soul that connects with mine." He pulled her to him. "When I met you, it was truly as if I had found the other half of myself. I can't explain it any better, darling. I can't—"

"Pardon me, sir. There is a telephone call for you in the study."

Madeline pushed herself away from him and turned to lean against the balcony railing.

Drew cleared his throat. "Who is it?"

There was a definite aura of disdain on Dennison's normally impassive face. "The gentleman declined to say, sir. I told him that unless he was willing to identify himself, I would not be able to connect him. He claims you will want to speak to him regardless."

Drew glanced at Madeline, standing at the balcony railing, her arms around herself, looking fragile and uncertain. Before he could tell Denny he was otherwise occupied, she excused herself and hurried inside. Drew turned to the butler with an exasperated sigh.

"Shall I tell the caller you are not available to answer the telephone?" Dennison asked, perfectly composed.

"No, no, it's all right. I'll speak to him."

Drew went into the study and picked up the receiver.

"Is this Mr. Farthering?"

Drew didn't recognize the voice, but he couldn't help thinking he had heard it somewhere before. "Who's speaking, please?"

"This is Lew Zuraw from the Tivoli. You may

not remember me, but I manage things financially for Miss Cullimore."

"Oh, yes." Drew remembered the man's slight accent from their brief conversation. "Is there something I can do for you, Mr. Zuraw?"

There was a moment of silence on the other end of the line. "I was wondering if I could speak to you in person," the man said finally. "At my office in the theater. I've uncovered some evidence here that I think you will find . . . interesting."

"Very well." Drew checked his watch. "What time did you have in mind?"

"Now, if it isn't inconvenient. Go to the stage entrance and tell Grady to bring you round to my office. There's a performance going on, so I know nobody will bother us."

"I can be there in a few minutes. Mind if I bring along a friend or two?"

"That girl you had with you before?"

"Yes," Drew said. "And one more."

"All right. No harm in that. Just come quickly. While they're all busy with the show. I don't want . . . well, you've got to get here right away, that's all."

"Right. See you in a moment."

Drew hung up the phone and then hurried back into the parlor.

"I say, Nick, old man, care to take a little drive into Winchester?"

Nick's eyebrows went up. "If I didn't know

218

better, I'd mistake you for a man who's picked up a fresh scent."

Drew nodded, unable to keep the excitement out of his eyes. "Got it in one." He bowed formally in front of Madeline, who was sitting before the fire without her usual book. "How would you like to go to the theater, darling?"

She glanced at Nick and then stood. "Who was that on the telephone?"

"Mr. Zuraw, the business manager at the Tivoli. He says he's got something terribly important to tell us, and he wants us up there right away. Are you still in on the game?"

Again she looked to Nick, and her smile seemed suddenly more genuine. "The sooner we go, the sooner we'll have the case solved and be able to forget all about it."

They bundled into their wraps and were soon motoring up to Winchester. They made good time, and the Tivoli was blazing with lights when Drew pulled the Rolls up in front of the theater. Even from the street, the familiar music was discernible. *"Things are seldom what they seem . . ."*

"It's *Pinafore* tonight, I see."

They knocked at the stage door several times before Grady opened it.

"Oh, it's you." He scratched behind one ear and eyed both Madeline and Nick. "Brought everyone along this time, eh?"

"Good evening, Grady," Drew said. "We've come to see Mr. Zuraw."

Grady gawked at them for a moment longer and then shrugged. "Well, come in then, I suppose. Mr. Zuraw didn't say anything to me about visitors, but I'll take you round to his office if you like. Mind you keep the noise down while the show is on. Not such a problem when the music's going, but there are times when it's just dialogue, and then the audience can hear most anything that happens back here."

The music stopped just then, and they could hear the actors speaking their lines as well as the audience's laughter. One finger to his lips, Grady led the visitors down the dim corridor and stopped at the last door on the right.

"Mr. Zuraw?" He tapped softly when he got no answer. "Mr. Zuraw?"

"Zuraw?" Drew called a little more loudly, ignoring Grady's scowl. "Are you there?"

"Perhaps he's gone out," Madeline suggested, but Drew shook his head.

"He asked us to come. He wouldn't have left until after we talked." Drew tried the door, but it was firmly locked. "Do you have a key?"

Grady looked mildly offended to even be asked the question. "I have keys to all the locks in this building, save what was Mr. Ravenswood's dressing room."

He pulled a large ring from his pocket and

started sorting through the keys, finally separating a section of them from the rest.

"These here are for the storage rooms and offices. This door's number twelve." He selected a key and thrust it into the lock, but it wouldn't turn. "Hmmm."

He pulled the key out and squinted at it. He then counted from the key on the left until he got to twelve. He tried that key in the lock, the same one he'd tried before, Drew was certain, and still it would not turn.

"How many keys to that section?" Drew asked, making a swift count.

"Fifteen in this hallway," Grady replied. "Seven odds left, seven evens right, and number fifteen at the end. They're not marked that, but that's how I keep 'em straight."

"Only fourteen keys there now." Drew nodded toward the one in the lock. "May I?"

"Suit yourself," Grady grumbled.

Drew took the key from the lock and tried it in the last door on the left. It opened easily. "That's number thirteen, not twelve." He indicated the key next to it. "And I daresay this one is number eleven."

He tried that key in the door to the left of the one he'd just opened. It too swung open without protest.

"So someone took the key to Mr. Zuraw's office." Madeline tightened her hold on Drew's arm. "You don't suppose he's . . . in there, do you?"

"He'd just rung up to say he had some information on the case and now he's not answering the door?" There was a knowing glimmer in Nick's eyes. "I can tell you what would be in there if this were one of Mrs. Christie's stories."

Madeline pursed her lips. "Oh, Nick, stop."

"Does anyone besides Zuraw have a key?" Drew asked, knowing they were all thinking the same thing Nick was.

"The night watchman, Alf," Grady said. "But he won't be on duty until after midnight when I go off."

"Better break it down," Nick said, and Drew nodded.

"Here now!" Grady protested, but Nick was already throwing his shoulder against the door. In another moment, with a splintering crack, the door gave way.

The room was empty, silent but for the muted sound of Simone Cullimore singing. *"The hours creep on apace . . ."*

They made a quick check of the space under the desk and behind the curtain, but there were no bodies concealed anywhere. The only thing out of place was the green-shaded desk lamp. It was lying on its side and had no cord.

"No place else in here to hide anyone," Drew said, frowning at the lamp. "He seems to have tidied up a bit since we were here last. The desk at least."

Instead of the whirlwind of clutter, everything on the desk had been arranged into neat stacks now.

"He might have been embarrassed for us to have seen it that way," Madeline suggested.

Nick looked around the room again. "Perhaps he did just step out for a while. Terribly inconsiderate of him, if you ask me. So, do we wait until he comes back or—"

There was a clatter from somewhere outside the room.

"Drew!" Madeline gasped, and then there was the sound of a slamming door. "Down there. Hurry."

Drew sprinted down the corridor toward the door that led to the alley behind the theater. "Come on, Nick. Stay with Grady, darling."

"Oh, no, you don't," Madeline muttered.

With her right behind them, Drew and Nick burst through the door and then stopped short. The alley was empty and silent. A quick search told them there was no one lurking behind dustbins or in any of the locked doorways to either side of them or across the way. A second door from the alley to the theater was also locked.

Nick shook his head. "Gone. Whoever it was."

Drew turned back to Madeline and took her arm. "What exactly did you see, darling?"

"It was hardly anything." She shrugged. "I'm sure someone was there, but all I could see was a streak of black going down the hall and then turning to the door that leads out here."

"Black?"

"Yes, or at least very, very dark. And flowing. Like a cloak."

"Like Mrs. Landis's cloak?" Drew asked.

"I . . . I don't know. I didn't really see much."

He looked again up and down the alleyway, and then they all went back into the theater.

Grady was still standing in the doorway to Zuraw's office. "See anyone?"

Drew shook his head. "What are the rest of these rooms? Offices?"

"A couple of them. Most are storage rooms. If they're needed, though they usually aren't, they're sometimes dressing rooms for the chorus. They're a bit out of the way to be handy to the stage."

"I say, Drew?" Nick stood next to the first door on the left, number one. "This wasn't open before, was it?"

The door was open just a crack, and no light came from the room.

Drew glanced back at Grady. "A storage room, did you say? Is it usually kept locked?"

"Might be. Might not." The stageman shot out his lower lip and shook his head. "Depends on who's been in and out and if they do as they're supposed to and lock up behind themselves."

"I suppose that crash could have come from in here," Nick said. "Mind if we have a look?"

"I don't mind," Grady said, yet he looked as though he did.

With Drew and Madeline beside him, Nick pushed the door open with his foot and turned on the light. Sprawled in the middle of the floor was Lew Zuraw, his face black with blood, an electrical cord around his neck.

From the stage came the faint sound of a baritone singing. *"Kind Captain, I've important information. . . ."*

— *Thirteen* —

Grady peered into the room from the corridor, rheumy eyes wide. "Mr. Zuraw," he breathed. "Love a duck."

Drew looked at the two chairs that were overturned beside Zuraw, careful not to touch anything. "That's what must have made the clatter." He knelt beside the body and then looked over at Grady. "You might want to give the police a ring."

The stageman turned to go.

"I say, Grady," Drew added, "do they generally keep those in here?" He nodded at the low handcart in the corner of the room.

"Not usually," Grady said. "They're kept

backstage or in one of the main storerooms. Might be used anywhere in the theater, of course, but wouldn't be kept here. This is mostly costumes for the shows we don't have on at the moment. Everything from *Thespis* to *The Gondoliers*." He glanced at the body. "I'll have the police right out. I just hope they can keep the noise down until the show is over."

He hurried away, and Nick shook his head. "I should hate to see his reaction if the production had to be halted."

"Heaven forfend," Drew said. "Now, since we have a moment or two before the gendarmerie arrive, let's see what there is to see. What do we notice right away?"

"He's obviously been strangled," Nick said. "Nasty bit of work."

"Yes, but not here." Madeline stepped around the body, examining the crime scene from a different angle. "Everything here is too neat. I mean, boxes and racks and things look like they haven't been touched in a long time. Except for those chairs—and we heard them fall over before the killer ran out of the room—everything in here seems to be where it belongs. Mr. Zuraw had to have fought against whoever strangled him, even if he was taken by surprise."

Drew nodded. "Which explains why that cart is in here. The killer used it to move the body, but from where?"

"It wasn't his office. It was perfectly in order, except for the desk lamp and the cord missing from it," Nick said. "And there's little doubt what's become of that."

"I don't know." Drew knelt again beside the body. "Compared to when we saw it last, his office was too neat. Perhaps he was strangled there and brought here. But why? And by whom? It obviously wasn't Mrs. Landis."

"Someone who wanted us to think it was Fleur?" Nick mused.

"Yes, but why?" Drew's forehead wrinkled. "Locked up, Mrs. Landis has the only truly iron-clad alibi of the lot."

"But Drew," Madeline said, "I saw someone. I'm sure of it, and in a black cloak of some kind, like the one Fleur had."

"A black cloak that's locked up at the moment as well, I daresay." Drew leaned closer to the dead man, head tilted to one side.

"It's strange," Madeline said. "He didn't pay much attention to people at all, from what he said when we spoke to him earlier. I wonder what it was he wanted to tell us."

"Maybe it was something pretty obvious, if he noticed it," Nick offered. "That must be why he was killed."

"One would assume," Drew said.

"I see you've beaten me to it again."

Drew looked up to find Chief Inspector

Birdsong standing in the storage room doorway, arms crossed over his chest.

"Tell me, Mr. Farthering, do people ring you up to let you know they're about to be murdered, just so you can hurry over and find them afterwards?"

"I can see how it might look that way, Chief Inspector, but no. He did ring me up, but only to say he had some information I might want to hear."

"What did he say precisely?" Birdsong asked as one of his men began to photograph the body.

"He just said he wanted to talk to me while the performance was going on, and that it was important for us to get here right away. 'While they're all busy with the show.'"

Another song wafted in from the stage: *"Carefully on tiptoe stealing . . ."*

"What happened once you arrived?" Birdsong asked.

Drew motioned toward the stageman. "Grady here let us in, brought us back to Zuraw's office, but it was locked up tight. And someone had stolen the key off Grady's key ring."

Grady nodded, a look of disgust on his face. "Easy as you please, and no beggin' your pardon."

Birdsong took out his notebook and began writing. In the brief silence, the music from the stage grew in volume and became very clear.

"Goodness me," sang the chorus. *"Why, what was that?"*

A baritone voice answered, *"Silent be, it was the cat!"*

"Then what?" asked the chief inspector.

"We broke down the door to Zuraw's office and found the room empty. The cord was cut off the desk lamp." Drew glanced at the victim and then back up at Birdsong. "It's almost certainly this one."

"Right." The chief inspector jotted down something in his notebook. "And then?"

"We heard a clatter," Drew explained, "and Madeline caught a glimpse of someone running down the corridor to the alley door. We chased after, but there was no one there. We think whoever it was must have knocked over these chairs in getting away."

Nick gave him a grim smile. "It wasn't the cat, at any rate."

Madeline frowned at him and moved a little closer to the body. "Whoever I saw, Inspector, was wearing something dark and hooded, like a cloak."

Birdsong narrowed his eyes at her. "Could you tell anything about this person? Height? Weight? Male or female?"

"It was barely more than a glimpse, I'm afraid." She gave him an apologetic shrug. "He—or she—was around the corner and out the door in a flash."

"And out into the alleyway?" Birdsong asked.

Madeline nodded.

"You all searched out there, did you?"

"We did," Nick replied. "Locked doors all round and not a soul stirring."

Birdsong jerked his chin at the constable, who had accompanied him. "Take a torch and have a good look out there."

"Right, sir." The constable hurried away, almost running into the coroner as he came in.

"Well?" Birdsong asked after the man had made a brief examination.

"Strangulation," the coroner said matter-of-factly.

"Time of death?"

"I won't know for certain until I have him on the table, but I'd say between half an hour and two hours ago."

"I spoke to him on the telephone no more than an hour ago," Drew said.

"Very well," the coroner said. "Between a half hour and an hour ago. Once I've given the body a proper going-over, you'll have my report."

"Right." Birdsong made another note. "We're done with things here, I reckon." He signaled his men, who quickly moved into place and began lifting the body onto a stretcher.

"Wait!" said Drew. "What's that under him?"

"Don't touch it," Birdsong warned.

"Wouldn't dream of it," Drew assured him as he bent down to get a better look at the object, hands behind his back.

"What is it, old man?" Nick leaned over his shoulder, eyebrows drawn together.

"Another of those tassels like the one Tess Davidson had in her hand when she was strangled."

Madeline put one hand over her mouth.

"Tompkins," Birdsong called. "Get a picture here."

The photographer snapped two pictures, and afterward the chief inspector removed an envelope from one of his overcoat's pockets and carefully placed the tassel inside it.

"You know Mrs. Landis couldn't have done this one," Drew said. "Unless she's got a key to your jail."

"No." Birdsong's voice was grim. "She's there all right. Had a chat with her not three hours ago."

"May I ask what you spoke to her about?"

"I merely asked again who she thought might have a motive to kill Ravenswood and the Davidson girl if she hadn't done it. She said she didn't know, but she was wondering if someone wasn't trying to implicate her in both murders."

Drew nodded. "Could be."

"She couldn't possibly have killed Mr. Zuraw," Madeline said. "So why would someone kill him to frame her?"

"Perhaps this someone doesn't know Mrs. Landis has been arrested." Drew stood, looking around the room a final time. "I expect they'll have to release Mrs. Landis now."

"That doesn't mean she couldn't have done the first two murders, does it?" Madeline asked.

"True. But they don't actually have any hard evidence against her, just Benton's rather histrionic claim that he saw her. Best I can tell, he didn't actually see anything conclusive. I'm sure our Mr. Clifton will have his client out of custody before teatime tomorrow."

Chief Inspector Birdsong looked more than a bit put out when Drew appeared in his office two days later.

"Yes, Mr. Farthering, Mrs. Landis has been released. For the present. She was discharged yesterday afternoon. Do you have any suggestions regarding who might take her place as our chief suspect in these murders?"

"I'm afraid not, though I am doing my best to make sense of the deuced case. May I sit?"

Birdsong nodded toward the battered chair in front of his desk, and Drew made himself comfortable.

"I don't suppose you have any other information that might be of help?" Drew asked.

The chief inspector gave him a shrewd look and then tossed a manila folder onto the desk toward Drew. "According to the coroner, Zuraw was killed at approximately seven o'clock Thursday evening."

"That's not possible." Drew opened the file and

232

looked over the report. "I tell you I spoke to him at almost nine o'clock. Couldn't have been seven."

"And you couldn't have been mistaken about the time?"

"Not at all. I remember he was very specific about us being there right away, and I knew we were going to have to rush a bit to get there."

Birdsong knit his brows. "What was so important about the time? Did Zuraw say?"

"No." Drew chewed his lip, thinking. "Just that he wanted to talk to me before the performance was out."

"But that would have gone on till . . . when, ten o'clock? Half past?"

"More or less," Drew agreed. "Why did he want us there by then in particular? I'm guessing it was so no one in the production would know he was talking to us. Could the coroner be mistaken in this instance?"

"Possible," Birdsong said, "but highly unlikely. He's been at his job longer than I've been at mine, and he does it very well."

"I will add that to my list of things to think about. I've been considering the question of timing, however. Zuraw was insistent about our hurrying up there. I wondered too about what might have been happening onstage when he was killed and when our mysterious intruder was dashing out into the alleyway, so I took Madeline back to see *H.M.S. Pinafore* last night."

"It's a wonder you could get in," the chief inspector observed. "They've sold out every night since the murders started."

"Yes, well, I managed to convince a nice couple they would much rather have a healthy return on their investment in a pair of tickets than see a rather tired version of *Pinafore*." Drew grinned. "They eventually agreed."

"A golden key opens every lock, eh?" Birdsong gave him a sour look and then a reluctant smile. "I suppose you prove yourself valuable now and again, Detective Farthering. In your way and with certain methods we don't have at our disposal. And what did you discover?"

"Not a lot yet," Drew admitted. "I paid special attention to what was happening onstage at about the time we were there on Thursday night. Unfortunately, it was the entire cast singing 'He Is an Englishman,' which was no help at all. But then I recalled what I heard from the stage right when we heard the clatter in the storeroom. It was Miss Cullimore singing 'The Hours Creep on Apace.' "

"Which proves she could not have been your hooded phantom."

"Right. But it also proves that, as that is a solo piece, almost anyone else in the company could have been."

Birdsong pursed his lips, thinking. "It would take some rather good timing. And how would this person get back in time for his next cue?"

"I've wondered that myself," Drew said. "Turns out there's another door from the alley into the theater. It was locked when Nick and I checked, but that doesn't mean this particular person wasn't the one who locked it after himself, after he'd gone back inside. Mind you, that doesn't mean that actually was what happened, but it was at least possible. So Mrs. Landis and Miss Cullimore could not have murdered Zuraw." He paused for a moment. "No, that's not right. Mrs. Landis could not have done it. Miss Cullimore could have, though she could not have been our cloaked intruder."

"One other thing we know, seeing you've mentioned it, is that there's a second black cloak. The one belonging to Mrs. Landis is still locked up in our evidence room with the two tassels."

Drew nodded. "I thought as much. Might I see them? The tassels?"

"Why?"

"I would like to compare the two, of course." He gave the chief inspector his most charming smile. "If I might."

Birdsong gave him a stern look and then picked up the telephone. "Baker, bring me that cloak we have for the Landis case and those tassels. Yes, straightaway."

A few minutes later, a constable brought them the cloak and a small paper bag containing the tassels that had been found on the bodies.

Birdsong emptied them out onto the desk. "Now, let's give these a look."

The two tassels looked identical, except one was tagged DAVIDSON and the other ZURAW.

Drew frowned. "Notice anything odd about them?"

"Odd?"

Drew nodded. "Imagine you're in a death struggle with someone and you grab at that person's cloak and catch hold of a tassel. You wrench that tassel hard enough to pull it off. It's not going to have a neatly cut end, is it?"

"Shouldn't have, no."

"But look at that one. It looks as if cut with a scissors. As if it were put there to be found. You lot grabbed it up so fast I didn't have time to think about it much. But if you look at it again, you'll see what I mean."

Birdsong examined the one marked Davidson. "This one's clearly torn, but this one . . ." He touched the one marked Zuraw with the tip of his pencil. "This one was definitely cut. You have a keen eye, Detective Farthering."

"I shouldn't wonder, Chief Inspector, if the one on Zuraw wasn't planted there by someone. Now, what about the cloak itself?"

Birdsong spread it out on the desk, searching for the place where the tassel was missing.

"This is cut, too," he said once he'd found the place. "But it can't be the tassel we found at the

Zuraw scene. It's been locked up here." He looked over the rest of the cloak. "As best I can see, there aren't any others missing."

"Then there's definitely a duplicate cloak, just as we suspected. And some planning in advance. Do we know where this one came from? It doesn't much look like something Mrs. Landis would wear, if you ask me. Rather bourgeois, don't you think?"

"It came from Lewis's," Birdsong said. "They sell them by the dozen."

"Mrs. Landis shops at Lewis's?"

"It was a gift. Seems all right to me."

"A gift? From whom?"

"From her husband, or so she says. She claims she hated not to wear it, since it was from him and all."

Drew pressed his lips together. "Landis, eh?"

The chief inspector peered at him. "What are you thinking, Detective Farthering?"

"Nothing that makes me very happy, I'm afraid."

Birdsong's dark eyes narrowed. "You think Landis is up to something?"

"I don't see him as the type, no, but I can't help wondering all the same."

"Wondering if he's involved in all this?"

"Suppose someone is trying to incriminate Mrs. Landis," Drew said. "If there were to be duplicate cloaks, someone would have to make sure Mrs.

Landis had one and wore it often enough for the cloak to be identified with her, right? What better way to do that than to make a sentimental gift of it?"

"But why?" Birdsong asked. "What does it benefit Landis?"

"I haven't figured that out yet," Drew admitted. "From all I can tell, he's perfectly mad about his wife and would be devastated to lose her."

"It would seem so," Birdsong said, "but it has been my experience that there's many a murderer who can give a subtle performance that would put professional actors to shame."

When Drew returned to Farthering Place, he found the Landis car pulled up to the front door and their chauffeur loading several suitcases into the boot. Miss Winston and Peter were coming down the front steps.

"Miss Winston!" Drew called as he pulled the Rolls up behind the Daimler, and Peter ran up to him.

"Mr. Drew! Mr. Drew! Mummy's come back from her trip and we're going home!"

"So I've heard." Drew picked him up and then turned again to the nursemaid. "Leaving us already, Miss Winston?"

"Yes, I'm afraid so, Mr. Farthering. Now that Mrs. Landis is home, Mr. Landis feels we ought not impose upon you any longer."

"Nonsense. It's been no imposition in the least. Lovely to have all of you." Drew tapped the boy's turned-up nose. "Mr. Chambers hasn't had so fine a time in ages."

Peter looked toward the house. "He'll forget about me, won't he? He'll think I left him and didn't even tell him goodbye."

"No need to say goodbye, Peter," Drew said, "because you can come back to see Mr. Chambers again sometime."

The boy's expression brightened. "May I, please?"

"Just as often as you like."

"Can he come see me, too?"

"Well . . ."

"Now, Peter," Miss Winston broke in, "you know Mummy doesn't allow us to have animals in the house."

"But Mr. Chambers lives in Mr. Drew's house."

"That's Mr. Drew's house and not yours." Miss Winston reclaimed her charge. "Now tell Mr. Drew goodbye. Daddy and Mummy are waiting for us at home."

"We'll miss you, Peter," Drew said. "You come see us again, all right?"

Peter gave him a brilliant smile, a perfect copy of his mother's. "You betcha."

Miss Winston put him into the backseat, and he immediately stood up on it, leaning out the window. "Tell Mr. Chambers I love him and I won't forget him."

"Certainly," Drew told him. "Not to worry."

"Peter," Miss Winston scolded, "sit down at once! You know you're not to stand on the seats."

Crestfallen, Peter immediately sat.

"I'm certain he didn't mean any harm," Drew said out of his hearing.

"Oh, I know," Miss Winston said. "Poor little lamb, he's very attached to that cat already. He would so love to have a kitten or a puppy of his own to play with, but his mother won't allow it."

"What's his father say?"

That soft light came again into her eyes. "I think he would like to have a dog. He says he always had one before he married her, and he still speaks fondly of the last one he had. But she won't hear of him having another. She says she won't have pet hair on her furniture and clothes, especially on her black dresses."

"What's your opinion on the matter?" Drew asked.

"I was raised in an orphans' home, Mr. Farthering. None of us had pets. I always wished I had one." She laughed. "Or a dozen. But as you may well imagine, working in other people's homes, I can never have any of my own."

"You never know what the future holds," Drew said. "Perhaps one day you'll have a home and family and pets of your own."

"And if the sky falls, we shall all catch larks." She snorted softly and then hurried to the car. "We ought to be off now. Thank you again, Mr. Farthering."

She sat down beside Peter, and they both waved goodbye. Madeline came down the front steps just as they disappeared from sight.

"She's got it bad and how, as they say in the cinema." Drew shook his head. "Poor thing. How I would hate it if I knew you belonged to someone else."

"Do you suppose Mr. Landis is in the same boat?" Madeline asked, still watching the empty driveway.

"No, I'd hardly think so. It seems rather obvious to me."

There was a sudden wariness in her expression. "Because he's already got Fleur, is that what you mean?"

"Well, darling, there is quite a difference. Poor Miss Winston hardly stands a chance by comparison."

Her eyes flashed, and he knew he had chosen the wrong words.

"Not that looks are everything," Drew said, slipping his arm around her. "Of course they aren't. But he's married to Mrs. Landis. It wouldn't exactly be the decent thing to leave her for someone else, no matter how great her character and personality, eh?"

"No, I don't suppose it would," Madeline said. "No matter how much I dislike Fleur. We don't have to see her anymore, do we? I mean, she's out of jail and bound to be cleared before long. I don't know why you'd have to be involved in the case now."

"Well, it isn't actually solved yet, you know," he said. "I really ought to—"

"You really ought to concentrate on our wedding now, don't you think?" Her eyes flashed again, and then her expression softened and she put one hand up to his cheek. "Don't you think?"

He pulled her close and turned his head so his lips were touching her fingertips. "I do, darling." He kept his eyes fixed on hers. "As difficult as you make it for me to think at all."

"Drew," she breathed, before melting into his arms, her face hidden against his neck. "Are you sure? Are you very, very sure?"

With a soft laugh he kissed her hair. "Sure of what, darling? Sure that I adore you? Sure that I want to marry you and spend the rest of my life learning everything there is to know about you? Sure there's no one else in the world so perfectly suited to be mistress of Farthering Place? Yes, I'm very, very sure. I've no doubt whatsoever."

She giggled and looked up at him through a glimmer of tears. "Muriel was right about you from the start, you know. You're definitely a smooth talker, and I'd better keep my eyes open."

"Good idea, darling. Then you can't help seeing how much I love you."

For a fleeting moment she searched his eyes. "I'm glad you don't have to be involved in this case anymore, Drew."

"Not with Mrs. Landis's bit of it, at any rate." He tapped her pouting lips. "Come along now, love. I'm certain Mrs. Devon must be waiting tea for us."

— *Fourteen* —

The following Monday, Drew slipped away from Farthering Place and dropped in at Brent Landis's office.

"I have a question for you, Landis." Drew's voice was light and pleasant as he made himself comfortable in the chair facing Landis's desk. "That cloak of your wife's, where did it come from?"

Landis looked rather embarrassed. "From Lewis's. I bought it for Fleur."

"I see. Was it for a particular occasion? A birthday or an anniversary?"

"No. I thought it would be nice to give her something for no particular reason." His face reddened. "Just because I love her. Surely with Miss Parker and all, you understand."

"Oh, yes, of course. But why that? Did she typically shop at Lewis's?"

"No, not at all. I was surprised, actually, because she has always been rather particular about where she shops. But I was given to understand that she wanted that cloak especially, so that's what I got for her. Good heavens, I never expected it would be part of this whole awful affair."

"Did Mrs. Landis tell you that was the cloak she wanted?"

"No, in fact. It was just a gift. Fleur had been a bit down around that time, and I wanted to do something to cheer her up. But I couldn't think of anything she'd mentioned she wanted. The cloak seemed to please her very much, more than I thought it would."

Drew nodded. "You said you were 'given to understand' that she wanted that one. Who gave you that understanding?"

"Miss Winston, actually. We were talking about how difficult it can be at times to choose just the right gift. She said Fleur had had her eye on that particular cloak. I'm not certain why. But if it pleased her, I thought it would be just the thing."

Drew considered for a moment. "Have you told the police all this?"

"Oh, certainly," Landis said. "It was one of the first things they asked about before Fleur was released—where I bought the cloak, how long ago and all that."

"Yes, but did you tell them about your little talk with Miss Winston?"

Landis shook his head. "I suppose it never occurred to me to mention it. I mean, they know Fleur was, well, out of play when that business manager was killed. All they have to do is figure out who bought another cloak like that one. Well, someone involved in the case, rather. I'm certain there are many of the same sort of cloak about."

"You're probably right," Drew said. "Tell me, did Miss Winston and Mrs. Landis discuss fashion as a rule?"

"Not that I ever heard, no. To be frank, I'm not sure Fleur very much likes Miss Winston. I suppose they're just too different, the two of them, to get along. Fleur is, well, you've seen her, stylish and dramatic and"—his expression turned wistful—"all woman."

Drew lifted one eyebrow. "And Miss Winston?"

Landis chuckled. "Miss Winston's a good girl, practical and dependable. She would have made someone a fine wife. Good mother to his children and all that."

"Would have?"

"Not to say she wouldn't still, of course," Landis corrected at once. "Perhaps a nice man who's lost his wife and who has small children who need looking after. Miss Winston would be just the one for the place, eh? But she doesn't seem much interested in finding anyone at this point. All work and no play, you know?"

"Why do you suppose that is?"

"Happy just as she is, I guess. Perhaps she's given up trying to find anyone. Either way, I'm glad to have her with us. She's a wonder with the boy, and that's all that matters to me. There aren't many others I'd trust him to."

"And he's definitely quite fond of her, as well," Drew said. "She must have been a real find."

"She was, especially with her nursing background. There's rarely anything we need the doctor for with her around. You know, I sometimes wonder if Fleur isn't a bit jealous of her. About Peter, I mean. Of course, as much as she loves our boy, Fleur's never been one to be tied down to home and hearth. She's always been a social butterfly, and I would certainly never try to confine her."

"Couldn't be done," Drew said as he got to his feet.

Landis stood, too. "Isn't there anything else you wanted, Mr. Farthering?"

Drew shook his head. "Just a word. Everything settled at home? Now that you're all together again?"

"Fairly well back to normal, thank you. This has all been a bit distressing, as you may well imagine."

"No doubt."

Landis exhaled and gave Drew an unsteady smile. "Just having Fleur back was a great relief. It's a bit frightening to be at the mercy of the law."

"True enough." Drew put on his hat. "But these things are sorted out in time. If not, there is the great Judge who always sees the truth and without any obscurity."

"I suppose none of this comes as any surprise to Him, eh?"

"Not at all." Drew gave him a nod. "Well, I'd best let you get back to work. You'll want to finish up and get home to Mrs. Landis as quickly as possible."

Landis escorted Drew to the door. "Thank you, I do."

With a farewell to Miss Stokes, Drew hurried out of the office and down to the Rolls.

"They'll be back before long, old man," Drew said a day later. "We really ought to get this all sorted before then."

Mr. Chambers merely yawned, his spine making a nearly perfect crescent-moon shape as he stretched himself on the lush parlor carpet.

Drew scowled and got down on his hands and knees next to him. "Have you been at all paying attention to what I've been saying? How are we possibly going to solve this case if you don't pay attention to all the clues?"

The kitten blinked unrepentantly and reached

over to play with Drew's silver cuff link. With a chuckle, Drew stretched out on the floor beside him, tickling the tip of his tail to make him turn over.

"Now pay attention, and we'll start at the beginning once more. When Ravenswood was killed—"

Denny cleared his throat, and Drew looked up, a guilty warmth seeping into his face.

"Are you at home to Mrs. Landis, sir?" the butler asked, his disapproval faint but unmistakable.

Drew shook his head, frowning, but she was already in the room, pushing past Denny.

"Drew, please."

He scrambled to his feet, the heat in his face intensifying. "Really, Mrs. Landis, I would rather not—"

"Drew." She held up her hands, pleading. "Just a moment. Just give me a moment. It's desperately important." Tears stood in her impossibly black eyes.

Drew looked at Denny. "We haven't heard from that, uh, party we're expecting, have we?" The last thing he needed was for Madeline and Aunt Ruth to come home to find him alone with Fleur Hargreaves.

Denny's expression remained suitably grave. "No, sir, though it should not be long before they arrive."

"All right, Denny. That will be all."

"Shall I have tea served, sir?"

Drew glanced at Fleur as she stood there trembling and then back at Denny. "No. We'll be only a moment, I'm certain."

"Very good, sir." With a bow, Denny disappeared.

Fleur moved closer to Drew, taking his sleeve in both hands. "Thank God. Please, Drew. Hear me out."

"I thought we had an agreement," he said, his voice cold. "Anything you need me to know, you can ask your husband to tell me."

"Not this, Drew. I need your help. Someone is trying to kill me, and poor little Peter . . ." She caught a hard, choking breath and collapsed against him.

"What about Peter?" He took hold of her arms. "Fleur, what about Peter?"

She froze, eyes wide, and he released her. She managed a ghost of a smile. "Brent sent me chocolates—he does spoil me so—and I didn't think anything of it. Why should I? I was just so happy to be out of that horrid prison, I thought everything was all back to normal and this was over. Anyway, I've been trying to reduce a bit, so I didn't eat any of them right away. I just left them in the little sitting room I use to write my letters and such. Peter knows he's not to go into that room. I've told him at least a hundred times, but he went in anyway. He went straight to that candy and ate some of it. And then . . . Oh, Drew."

She clung to him, weeping openly now, and a sickening fear twisted into him. He shook her harder than he meant to, forcing her to look up at him.

"What happened to Peter?"

"It was so horrible. He couldn't breathe and he turned so frightfully pink. Nurse snatched him up at once, thank God, along with the chocolates, and made Brent drive them to Dr. Klarner's."

"Is he all right? What happened?"

"Drew, it was cyanide! The candy was full of it."

"Peter—"

"He's going to be all right," she quickly added. "If Nurse hadn't caught him eating the piece he had, and if she hadn't been there to recognize the symptoms, I don't know what would have happened. But, Drew, how would she know . . . and so certainly? I mean, who thinks of cyanide poisoning right off? And if she hadn't known at once, Peter would have died."

"Have you told the police this?"

She put one trembling hand over her mouth. "Yes, I spoke with them, but I couldn't tell them everything. I couldn't tell them . . ." She shrank against him again. "Oh, I don't even want to say it, it's so horrible."

"Say what?"

"That . . . that it was Brent who sent me those

chocolates. He always does, you know, and he admits he sent them this time. You don't think he could have possibly . . . ?" She hid her face against Drew's shoulder. "No, no, no . . ."

"He could have what?" Drew asked, prying her away from him. "What are you saying?"

She looked up at him, trembling and fragile in his hands, and he felt all sorts of a cad for wanting to shake her again.

"What are you saying?" he demanded. "You don't think your husband poisoned those chocolates, do you?"

"No, he couldn't have. He wouldn't have! Why would he do such a thing?"

"You tell me," Drew said warily.

"There is no reason," she said, her red lips quivering. "No reason. I'm just . . . my nerves are on edge, that's all. Yes, that's all."

"Well, *someone* poisoned those chocolates," Drew said. "If it wasn't your husband, who was it? Who do you think would want to kill you?"

"Oh, I don't know. No one now."

"Now?"

"Well, you know Johnnie's wife would have. I mean, if she had ever taken the time to plan it out."

Drew studied her face. "Would she? Why?"

She shrugged. "Well, Johnnie and I, obviously."

"I thought you said that was over years ago."

"It was. I swear it was, but she was always

suspicious even if she does go on about not caring what he did. And she didn't much like me still being around the theater. Helping with the production and all. I still can't help wondering if she wasn't the one who killed him after all, and she just needed someone to blame."

Drew shook his head. "She was already at home. She phoned the theater right before the body was found."

"She could have made that call from anywhere." Fleur pouted. "All right, fine. Maybe she isn't the one. Or maybe she had someone else kill her husband for her. That Conor Benton would be just the type."

"It couldn't have been Benton, either. You know that."

"If he thinks I killed Tess, he might want to kill me, no matter who might have killed Johnnie."

"I suppose so. Doesn't seem the way he'd go about it, though. How would he know about the chocolates if your husband had them sent directly from the shop? He hasn't been anywhere near your home, has he?"

"Not that I know of." Fleur pouted again. "Well then, I don't know. But someone is trying to kill me. Now that Johnnie is gone, I don't know who it would be or why. Maybe it's someone the police haven't even considered. But, please, Drew, you have to find out. You have to stop whoever it is."

"All right," he said, leading her toward the door.

"I'm doing my best as it is." He stopped at the threshold, his face as stern as he could make it. "For your husband's sake and the boy's, do you understand?"

She nodded, a touch of hurt in her eyes, and she let him escort her out to her car.

"I do appreciate it, Drew. Truly." She gave him a winsome smile as she got behind the wheel. "I know you're not exactly fond of me anymore, so it means a great deal to me that you would still be willing to help."

He shrugged, once more feeling rather a cad. "If you're innocent, Mrs. Landis, then it is only right that we should find out who is behind all this. I know your husband and your son would hate to be without you."

She reached out of the car window to clutch his hand, but he moved away.

"Please believe me, Drew. I am not the girl who treated you so abominably six years ago. I wish there was something I could do to make amends."

"All that is over. I want nothing more than to never think of it again."

She had the grace to look embarrassed. "I'm sorry. Of course you wouldn't want to go over all that anymore. But I *am* grateful to you."

"Fair enough. Now, please, you ought to go. If there's anything else you think I need to know, please be kind enough to send the message through your husband."

"All right. I was just so scared by this thing with the chocolates."

She gave him another pleading look, and Drew couldn't help wondering, on the off chance that Landis was behind this, if he was wise to trust the man to give him whatever messages Fleur might have.

"On second thought," he said, "perhaps from now on, you should just ring me up direct if you have something you need to tell me."

"All right." She started the car and put it into gear. "Please, find out who's behind all of this, Drew. Please."

"I'll do my best. Now you'd best go along home and look after Peter."

"I have an appointment I must get to, tea with some old friends, but I'll go straight home after that."

"Mind you do, then."

She drove away, still with that troubled wrinkle in her forehead. Before he could do more than walk back up the front steps, he saw the Bentley coming up the drive, Madeline and Aunt Ruth returning from wherever they had been. They would have to come home just in time to see Fleur leaving. Smashing. Perfectly jolly.

He smoothed his hair and straightened his tie and then went back down the steps in time for Denton to stop the car with Madeline's door just in reach. He opened it and handed her out.

"Hello, darling. Have you and Auntie had a busy day?"

"Lovely," she said, but she seemed a bit distracted. "Denton, could you please see the packages are sent up to our room?"

Denton touched his cap. "Right away, miss."

He helped Aunt Ruth out of the other side of the car and then drove off.

Drew escorted both ladies into the house. "I trust there is something left in the shops still."

The older woman tried to hide her smile. "We may have missed one or two things, young man, but you cannot expect to host the wedding of the year without a considerable amount of foofaraw and fluff."

"Wedding of the year?" he said, putting his arm around Madeline. "Did you hear that, darling? We've been downgraded to wedding of the year." Madeline looked more distracted than amused. "Wedding of the century, don't you think, Aunt Ruth?"

Aunt Ruth only huffed. "I'll let you two sort that out. My feet hurt."

She clumped up the steps with her cane, leaving Drew and Madeline alone. Madeline didn't say anything for a minute, and then she gave Drew a very bright smile. "Who was that? In that car that was driving away when we got home?"

"You'll be quite surprised to know that was Landis's wife. I know I was."

Her smile tightened. "I thought you weren't going to see her, even about the case."

"I know, darling, and that's what I meant to do. I didn't know she was coming. And when Denny asked if I was home to her, I tried to tell him no. But she pushed her way in before he could even get my answer."

"And what did she want this time?"

He hesitated. "Why don't we go into the library for a bit?"

"What?" she asked, pulling back from him. "What's happened?"

"She was very upset, naturally. Someone had poisoned the chocolates Landis sent her, and Peter got into them."

"Peter! Oh, Drew, is he all right?"

"Evidently they got him to the doctor in time. He ought to recover quite nicely."

"Thank God." She closed her eyes for a moment. "Who could have done such a thing?"

"It's unlikely the poison was meant for him. The chocolates were sent to Mrs. Landis, after all. Would you like to come with me to examine the scene of the crime?"

"Do you suppose they'll let us see Peter?"

"We can certainly ask." He kissed her cheek. "Wait here and I'll bring the Rolls around."

Soon they were pulling up in front of the Landises' Georgian town house in a comfortable if not ostentatious neighborhood in Winchester. A red-eyed little housemaid answered the front door.

"Good afternoon, sir."

Drew removed his hat. "Good afternoon. Drew Farthering and Madeline Parker to see Miss Winston, if we may."

"Oh, I dunno, sir." The girl glanced up the curving staircase. "She's up with the boy just now, and I'm certain she don't want to leave him."

Madeline's hold on his arm tightened. "He hasn't . . ." She looked up at him with worried eyes and then turned back to the maid. "He hasn't taken a turn for the worse, has he?"

"No, miss." The maid gave her chapped nose a dab with a wadded-up handkerchief. "You mustn't mind me, miss. It's the dusting. Makes me sneeze something awful."

Madeline exhaled. "I'm sorry to hear that."

"Not your fault, miss, and thank you all the same."

Drew took a card from his pocket. "If you would be so kind, would you take that up to Miss Winston and ask her if we may come up and see Master Landis for just a moment?"

"I can't make you no guarantees, sir. Nurse hasn't much let anyone near him but the doctor and Mr. Landis himself."

"Not Mrs. Landis?"

"Oh, yes, of course, sir. Of course Mrs. Landis, but she hasn't been in much. Says she can't bear to see him so very ill."

Drew glanced at Madeline. "I think Miss Winston will see me," he said to the girl.

"Just as you say, sir. If you'll give me your things, miss, you'll want to wait in the parlor until I've asked if you can come up."

Drew smiled at the girl. "May we have a look at the room where Peter found the chocolates? Mrs. Landis's sitting room, I believe."

The girl looked puzzled. "If you like, sir. I suppose it would be all right."

Madeline shrugged out of her coat, as did Drew. He fished a paper-wrapped parcel out of one pocket, and then they both gave their coats and hats to the girl and followed her into a room as stylishly decorated as the foyer and what they could see of the rest of the house but decidedly more feminine.

"Do you know where Mrs. Landis had the box with the chocolates in it?" Drew asked.

"Here, sir." The maid indicated a wide book-shelf at Drew's eye level. "If you'll both wait, please, I'll go see Nurse."

"The boy must be a climber indeed," he said when the girl was gone. "How do you suppose he managed it?"

Madeline looked around. "Maybe a chair to get up onto the desk and then he reached the shelves from there?"

"I suppose so. Mrs. Landis seemed awfully determined to keep those sweets to herself."

"Doesn't surprise me."

Drew was startled by the coldness in her tone. "What do you mean?"

Madeline only shrugged. "Women like her. Selfish things, all of them."

Before he could reply, the girl came back into the room and bobbed a curtsy. "Nurse says you're both to come up at once."

— *Fifteen* —

Drew and Madeline followed the maid up the stairs and to the end of a long hallway. They waited as she tapped on the door and then opened it.

"Mr. Farthering and Miss Parker."

The room was large and airy, papered in a pale blue and cream stripe with a border of marching ducklings, every fifth or sixth one wearing a newspaper hat. Peter lay on the bed, sound asleep, purple smudges under his eyes, his dark-gold lashes resting on his pale cheeks, and a stuffed rabbit under the covers and grappled to his chest. Miss Winston was sitting in a chair beside him, a discarded book in her lap and, like the maid, a handkerchief crushed in her hand.

"Good afternoon." Drew kept his voice low. "How is the little fellow?"

She started to stand, but he shook his head.

"No need to get up. You look rather all in."

"I'm all right," she said with a teary smile. "I'm just glad he's still here for me to look after."

"He's not still in danger, is he?" Madeline asked, and Miss Winston shook her head.

"Only recovering now, thank God. Since we knew what it was, the doctor knew exactly what to do. Good thing he lives just round the corner." She shuddered. "Cyanide of all things, and it acts so quickly."

"I suppose in your nursing work you've seen a cyanide poisoning case like this," Drew said, watching her expression.

"I never saw anyone affected by cyanide before, but we were taught about it when I was in training during the war. There was some use of it as a weapon, but it was evidently not very effective. I never heard of any casualties from it, at any rate. But I did remember what I was told about it, the symptoms and all, and that faint almondy smell." Tears came into her eyes, and she stroked the boy's fair hair. "And him suddenly turning red, poor angel, and gasping for breath and all the rest of the horrible symptoms. Thank God what I knew about cyanide came back to me just then. He wouldn't have lasted much longer if he hadn't had treatment right away."

"How did he get into the chocolates?" Drew asked.

"It's all my fault." The nurse's face contorted as

she struggled to compose herself. "They were up on a shelf in Mrs. Landis's sitting room downstairs. Peter knows he's not allowed in there, and he knows he's not to take his mother's candy without permission. She didn't like him to have it at all, in fact, which is why she put it up." She turned up her nose. "She never much let anyone have any, even though Mr. Landis might snatch a piece or two when she's not by. You wouldn't think it to look at her, but she's a perfect fiend for the stuff, and he often has her some sent out."

"How often?" Madeline asked.

Miss Winston shrugged. "Every five or six weeks, I suppose. Sometimes not that often. They were never large boxes, just enough to make her happy. Anyway, I was taking Peter out to play in the garden, and I realized I had forgotten his hat and gloves. So I told him to stay right where he was, that was in the downstairs hallway, and I hurried up to get his things and came right back down. I couldn't have been gone but a few minutes. But the door to the sitting room was open, and Peter knows what comes in those little white boxes." Tears sprang to her eyes again. "He's always been a terrible climber. Since he could barely toddle, he climbed everything he could. I got back to the sitting room and found him halfway up the shelf, with the candy box open and two pieces in his mouth." She squeezed her eyes shut and pressed the handkerchief against them.

"Mrs. Landis says someone is trying to kill her," Drew said after a moment, his voice soft. "And one is forced to come to that conclusion, given the circumstances. Do you know who might wish to do that?"

Miss Winston gave a startled laugh. "Shall I write you out a list?"

Drew glanced at Madeline, then turned again to the nurse. "And who would you put on that list?"

Miss Winston gaped at him, and her face went red. "I didn't mean a literal list."

"But if you were to make one out?" Drew pressed.

"Well, I'm not sure. I suppose the wife of that actor, that Simone Cullimore. Or that Mr. Benton. Hasn't he insisted all along that Fleur was guilty? That's what the newspaper says. I don't know who would want to kill her. I just know that she's a wretched excuse for a wife and mother. I . . ." She stopped herself, pressing her lips into a tight line. "I don't know who I would put on that list."

"Yourself?"

Her eyes flashed, and then to his surprise, she nodded. "All right, since we're talking about wishes, I can't say the idea never crossed my mind. Well, not killing her, actually, but wishing I knew how to make her just go away." She looked at the still-sleeping child, the defiance in her features softening into fondness. "He's such a dear boy. He ought to have a proper mother."

"Yes," Madeline agreed. "He should."

Drew considered both women. Madeline was sleek-limbed and stylish, pert and pretty and whip smart. Adele Winston, on the other hand, was hardly beautiful. She was pleasant enough, to be sure. Tidy and fit and quite intelligent, she was what he would call a sturdy woman. Unflappable in a crisis, immovable once she had decided upon a course of action, absolutely loyal. Both of them had steel underneath the softness. And what else?

"In what ways is Mrs. Landis not a proper mother?" he asked.

"That may have been a bit harsh on my part." The nurse looked down at the floor. "She's hardly any different from most women in society, I suppose. So many of them are too busy to be the mothers their little ones need. I've never thought it right."

"I daresay that's true."

Miss Winston laughed half under her breath. "But then I suppose if every woman mothered her own children, I would be rather out of a job."

Drew smiled just the slightest bit. "And Peter? What does he think of his mother?"

"I think he's a bit afraid of her."

Drew narrowed his eyes. "She isn't rough with the boy, is she?"

"Good heavens, no. I never meant to imply anything of the sort. It's just that she hardly spends any time with him, and when she does, she seems rather put out the whole while. I shouldn't have said Peter is afraid of her. *Awed* may be a better word to describe it, as if some rare bird of paradise landed on the breakfast table. Mr. Landis, now, will take him for his walks or play with him before his bedtime, and he takes him to church now and again." Miss Winston's fond smile returned then. "It makes Peter feel awfully grown up, you know, to go out with Daddy alone."

"Was Mrs. Landis there when Peter ate the candy?"

Miss Winston turned pale. "She came into the room right after I did. I thought she was going to have a screaming fit when she saw Peter had gotten into the candy. Well, she did a bit, in fact. She was shrieking at me to do something when I was doing everything I could already. I thought she'd pull the bell wire right down before Sullivan could get in there. Sullivan's the parlormaid. She's the one who called the doctor to let him know we were coming and what was wrong with Peter."

"The girl who let us in?" Madeline asked.

"Yes, that's right. I was rather proud of her, in fact. Mrs. Landis was screeching at her, and Sullivan told her, as polite and respectful as you please, to sit down and shut up."

"So Mrs. Landis didn't see Peter when he was climbing up to get the candy?" Drew asked.

"No. She had gone up to her bedroom to get her

address book. She came back in just as I was taking the candy away from Peter."

"She didn't actually see him eat it, then."

"No," Miss Winston replied. "She came in just after, and right away started screaming. I had just realized something was wrong. There was that smell, you know. And then the poor lamb couldn't breathe." She swallowed painfully. "But, thank God, it all came right in the end."

Drew nodded. "Yes, thank God. And where was Mr. Landis? Was he out?"

"No, he had just come in and gone up to change for dinner. I'm sure he heard all the commotion and came down to see what it was."

Drew glanced at Madeline. "That loud, was it?"

The nurse snorted. "You know Mrs. Landis was in the theater not so long ago. Her voice certainly carries to the back of the audience when she wants it to."

"What was Mr. Landis's reaction when he saw what was happening?" Madeline asked.

"White as a ghost, poor man," Miss Winston said. "Little Peter is his moon and stars, you know. He stood there watching me trying to get Peter breathing again, and Mrs. Landis was hanging on him, wailing and telling him to do something. He tried to soothe her, tried to be strong in front of her, but I think he was rather relieved when I told him we'd have to get the boy over to the doctor's right away and Mrs. Landis said she couldn't bear to come. She was that upset, and she made Sullivan bring her the nerve medicine her doctor gives her. Pure alcohol, if you ask me, but there's something else in it too, I suppose, because she goes right to sleep when she takes it. Anyway, Mr. Landis and I took Peter to the doctor. It was a near thing, but Peter hadn't done much more than pop the candy into his mouth when I caught him at it. Good thing too. The police said . . ." Seeing the boy stir, she abruptly put her finger to her lips and shushed them.

"Winnie?"

She placed her hand on his forehead. "How are you feeling, Peter, dear?"

"Can I get up now? It's light outside."

She smiled at him. "Not quite yet, love. But you can *sit* up. You have some visitors. Isn't that nice?"

He blinked, noticing Drew and Madeline for the first time. "Mr. Drew. Miss Madeline."

He sat up, and Drew put a hand on his shoulder to keep him in bed. "Steady on, old man. You know the chain of command on this ship. Barring the captain and his lady, First Officer Winston is in charge. And if she says you're to stay in bed, then you'll stay in bed. Right?"

Peter giggled. "You betcha."

Drew sat on the bed next to him. "Now, Midshipman Landis, tell us. Is everything ship-shape and Bristol fashion?"

The boy wrinkled his forehead. "Huh?"

"He means," Madeline said, "are you feeling better?"

"I feel better." Peter frowned. "I don't think I want any more of that candy."

Miss Winston crossed her arms over her chest. "Maybe you'll remember that the next time you want to take something you've been forbidden."

"I'm sure he won't ever do it again," Madeline said, caressing the boy's pale face.

"I don't think I like candy anymore," Peter said.

Drew gave him a wink. "I have a feeling that won't last long. But I am nevertheless happy to report that this package does not contain candy of any variety." He let a smile crinkle the corners of his eyes as he laid the package on the bed next to the boy. "Mr. Chambers couldn't come along with us to see you, so he sent us out to get you that instead."

Peter looked at his nurse, and she nodded her approval. In an instant he had the paper off and was beaming at a little stuffed cat made of white muslin.

"It looks like him," he crowed, poking one finger into the cat's embroidered blue eye. "Is he mine, Mr. Drew? Can I keep him?"

Drew nodded. "He'd be most awfully unhappy if you didn't. Mr. Chambers told us to give him very strict instructions to look after you and Miss Winston, too."

Peter snatched up the cat and hugged it close, his rabbit temporarily forgotten. "What's his name? Are he and Mr. Chambers friends?"

"Oh, certainly. But you'll have to ask him what his name is. He wouldn't tell me. He said you were to be his little boy from now on, and the matter of names was between the two of you."

Peter nodded, his face solemn.

"And you'll let me know when you find out, will you?"

Again the boy nodded.

Drew gave him a warm smile and got him to lie back again. "Now, you get well, and we'll have you out to see Mr. Chambers again. How would that be?"

"I'd like that, Mr. Drew."

"Good man. See you soon," Drew said.

Madeline leaned down to kiss the boy's forehead. "Goodbye, darling. You will come see us again, won't you?"

Peter nodded. "Can I come see you even after you and Mr. Drew get married?"

"Of course you can. We'd be very happy to have you."

"Even if you have your own little boy?"

Drew smiled at her, though she managed to keep a straight face. "Well, that wouldn't be for quite a while yet, but yes, anytime. Now you and your new kitty go back to sleep, and make sure he doesn't wake up your rabbit."

Peter's drooping eyes popped open again. "Do you think he might?"

"Nonsense," Drew told him. "They'll be the greatest of friends by teatime. Now, best have your rest."

The boy yawned and nestled down in his pillows, and Drew and Madeline hurried to the bedroom door.

"Thank you for coming to see him," Miss Winston whispered, going with them. "I know it made him very happy." She looked back at the bed. "Look, he's already asleep again. I'll walk you down to the front door."

She led them down the stairs. "I do hope Peter wasn't too impertinent asking you about children and all, Miss Parker."

Madeline laughed softly. "Oh, no. That's always the next question, isn't it? First it's when are you going steady? Then when will you get engaged? When will the wedding be? And you've no sooner said 'I do' than they want to know the names of your first five children."

Miss Winston nodded. "That is the way, isn't it?"

"What about you?" Drew asked. "You seem rather a wonder with the little chap, and one might think you'd want children of your own."

She stopped on the stairway, and there was a touch of rue in her smile. "I'm thirty-two, Mr. Farthering. I'm afraid my chances of marriage and children grow dimmer by the day."

"Oh, but surely a woman like you must have prospects."

"I could have settled." She shrugged. "But, no. No husband is better than the wrong one. And it seems all the men worth anything have already been snapped up." There was a sudden defiance in her eyes. "And I have Peter to look after. At least until he's old enough to be sent to school. I couldn't wish for a better child, my own or not. Besides, now that Mr. Landis has come into his money, I'm certain Mrs. Landis will be more popular than ever with the *haut monde*, and she doesn't have time for the boy as it is."

"Come into his money?" Madeline asked.

"I take it Landis's uncle has passed on, then?" Drew glanced at Madeline. "You remember, darling. The uncle who was adamant about not having a scandal touch the family. I suppose the news of Mrs. Landis's . . . difficulties with the police never reached his ears."

"I believe he was very ill in his last days," Miss Winston said. "I doubt his doctors would have allowed such news to upset him at that point. Even if he had been told, I think it most unlikely that he would have been able to hear or understand the words. At any rate, I believe Mr. Landis's solicitor has assured him that the will names him as his uncle's chief heir apart from a few bequests."

"I see," Drew said. "How does Mr. Landis feel about that?"

"I wouldn't know," she admitted. "I don't think, with everything else that's been going on, he's had much chance to think about it. I have a feeling he wants to put most of the money away for Peter. For his education and all, you know."

"And how does *Mrs.* Landis feel about it?" Madeline asked.

The nursemaid scoffed. "I'm afraid I wouldn't know about that, either. But I don't expect she's pleased about it."

Madeline looked down into the foyer with its marble floor and thick Persian rug. "She seems rather well cared for as it is."

"I couldn't say," Miss Winston said, starting to walk again. "There are some who would throw aside what others would find most satisfactory."

The parlormaid Sullivan was waiting at the door with their things.

"Thank you for letting us come up," Drew told Miss Winston as he helped Madeline into her coat. "We wanted to make sure the little fellow was safe and on the mend."

The nurse shook her head. "I'll never forgive myself for taking my eyes off him. It won't happen again, I can promise you that. I won't let it."

"I'm sure you won't."

She took hold of Drew's arm, earnestness in her eyes. "Mr. Farthering, you must find out what is going on. I can't bear the thought of something like this happening again. We might not have so happy an outcome."

"I will. I promise." Drew patted her hand and put on his own coat and then his hat. "Thanks again. Do bring the boy to visit us once he's fully recovered."

"We'd love to see him," Madeline added.

Drew tipped his hat and then stopped. "Oh, I was just wondering, Miss Winston, do you know where Mr. Landis happened to get the idea that his wife would like that particular cloak? The one with the tassels."

The nursemaid blinked. "Well, uh, yes, actually it was from me. But only because he asked me what I thought she might like, and she had mentioned wanting that particular one. She mentioned it two or three times, now I come to think of it. I . . . I didn't think anything of it."

"No, of course not. Thank you very much."

With another tip of his hat, Drew escorted Madeline out the front door and back to the car.

"So, what did you think?" Drew asked after they had driven for a few minutes in silence, heading south toward Farthering Place. "Decidedly an accident."

Madeline raised both eyebrows at him. "Chocolates laced with cyanide? Hardly an accident. And it wasn't meant as a practical joke, that's for certain."

"An accident that the boy got into them, I

think," Drew amended. "I don't believe whoever poisoned the chocolates meant them for Peter, but do you think they were meant for Mrs. Landis?"

"They were sent to her," Madeline said. "I don't know who else they would have been meant for."

"But she said she was trying to reduce. Perhaps someone knew that and meant them for someone else."

"But not for Peter . . ." Madeline put both hands to her mouth. "It couldn't have been."

"No, no, darling. I do think that was just an accident. The candies were put up on a shelf he shouldn't have been able to reach, in a room he was never supposed to enter. And it was well known that Mrs. Landis didn't like to share with him."

"Or anyone else," Madeline added.

"So very like her." Drew's expression grew grim. "Thank God Miss Winston recognized the symptoms of cyanide poisoning right away."

"That was awfully quick thinking on her part," Madeline said. "Not normally the first thing you think when you see a little boy gasping for breath."

"No," Drew said. "I don't suppose it is. But she was trained to recognize the stuff, and there is that smell."

Madeline smiled slightly. "Yes, that famous almond smell. It's supposed to be very faint, though."

"So I hear. You know, there's always a whiff of it in the murder mysteries. Perhaps our Miss Winston is a reader."

Madeline took his arm. "Drew, you don't think she could be trying to kill Fleur, do you?"

"It's possible. I can't be the only one who's noticed how she is about Landis. Much as she tries to hide it."

"No." Madeline sighed. "I feel rather sorry for her about that. I'd think she was a sight better for him and for Peter than Fleur."

"Not if she's a murderess."

Madeline wrinkled her nose at him. "No, not if she's a murderess. And, all right, let's suppose she is. It would be easy enough, with her nursing knowledge, and especially what she has freely admitted she knows about cyanide, for her to poison those chocolates. I would think she'd know how to use a syringe to inject them, too. Maybe she wants to be the next Mrs. Landis."

"Women have killed for less."

"Definitely. But that wouldn't explain why she would kill Ravenswood or Tess Davidson or Zuraw."

"Hmmm." Drew thought for a moment. "Someone was apparently trying to implicate Mrs. Landis in those murders. Maybe our Miss Winston figured that having Mrs. Landis tried, if not hanged, for murder would be enough to end her marriage to Landis."

He slowed the car to a stop along the side of the road.

"What are you doing?" Madeline asked. "There's not something wrong with the car, is there?"

"The Rolls?" he said, feigning outrage. "Don't be daft. I merely thought, unless you have some pressing engagement, that we might make a brief detour to the chief inspector's office."

"What for this time?"

"I'd like to ask him what he's found out about those chocolates and if he knows where the poison may have come from. What do you say?"

"I say that, if you mean to go to the chief inspector's office, you're headed the wrong way."

"Perceptive as always, darling."

— *Sixteen* —

Drew put the car back into gear and turned the Rolls northward once again. He and Madeline had gotten only as far as asking the desk sergeant if Chief Inspector Birdsong was in when the man himself appeared.

"Ah, Detective Farthering. Just the man I was hoping to see."

Drew beamed at him. "Really?"

"No, but come in anyway." Birdsong nodded at Madeline and then escorted her and Drew into his office, where they sat in the chairs he offered. "How can I help the two of you?"

"We've just been to see Peter Landis."

The chief inspector's expression hardened. "Nasty business, that. A sure miracle the boy's still with us."

"True," Drew said. "Cyanide is nothing to play with. Any idea where it came from?"

Birdsong opened up a file folder and shuffled through its contents. "We checked out all the chemists within twenty miles of the Landis residence. According to the poison books, four of them sold cyanide in the past two weeks. One of the buyers was a jeweler and one was a photographer, both of them regular customers using the cyanide for their work. The other two wanted the cyanide for pesticide, ants in one case and wasps in the other."

"And your men checked all of them out?"

"The jeweler and the photographer, yes. As I said, they were regular customers where they bought the stuff, and neither of them has any connection to the Landises or to the theater."

Drew nodded. "And the others?"

"The man who bought the cyanide for ants was also well known at the chemist's. He has no connection, either to the Landises or to the Tivoli, and does have a rather impressive anthill in his back garden."

"That leaves the one with the wasps."

"Ah. That one is our puzzler. The shop itself is not very close to the Landis home, though it's still in Winchester. One of the less fashionable quarters of the city, in fact. Of course, one would be mad to waltz into the local chemist's and buy something as deadly as cyanide and not expect to be remembered."

"Did the chemist remember?" Drew asked.

"Not all that much, I'm afraid," Birdsong said. "He said the lady wasn't in the shop very long at all."

"Lady?" Madeline glanced at Drew. "Did he get a name?"

"Oh, yes, miss." Birdsong set aside one of the imposing stacks of documents piled on his desk and took out a worn-looking ledger book, red and gray. "Anyone purchasing this sort of thing must sign the poison book." He flipped a few pages and then turned the book around for them to see. "Last entry there."

Drew squinted at the spidery writing. "On the seventeenth. Thursday. Do we know what time?"

Birdsong glanced at his report. "Midafternoon was all the chemist remembered. He put it between three and four when pressed, but he couldn't be sure."

"Anne Winchester," Drew said, scanning the register again. "Not all that original. And this address?"

The chief inspector pursed his lips. "A rooming

house near the train station. The proprietress there says she never had an Anne Winchester to stay. Not recently. Not ever. She checked her records to be certain."

"I don't suppose the chemist had a description of this Anne Winchester, did he?"

Birdsong shrugged. "Woman, of course. Wearing a coat and hat. Very ordinary, he says. Brownish hair. A bit dowdy. Glasses. Not a lot to go on."

"That could fit just about anyone. Did he say if the woman was young? Old? Heavyset? Thin?"

"Average, to hear him tell it," the chief inspector replied, looking as if he had the beginnings of a headache. "Not fat. Not thin. Not at all old. Perhaps thirtyish. Hard to say. He said it was a busy afternoon."

"Thirtyish?" Drew looked at Madeline. "Sound like anyone we know?"

"Miss Winston," Madeline said, eyes wide.

Drew nodded. "And what's her first name? Adele? Adele Winston. Anne Winchester." He gave her a grim smile. "Of Winchester. It's not all that original."

"Clever, the two of you," Birdsong said. "But we're rather ahead of you on that one, I'm afraid. She was practically in hysterics when she told us about the boy nearly dying and that. Oh, we think, it's obvious—she tried to poison Mrs. Landis and almost killed the child in the process. It's plain she's fond of him, as if he were her own, so naturally she'd be terrified at the idea of accidentally killing him."

"I did wonder about that when we talked to her," Drew said.

"But . . . ?" Madeline narrowed her eyes at the chief inspector. "You've clearly changed your mind about that theory."

"We showed Miss Winston's photograph to the chemist, along with a few others of women approximately her age and description. He couldn't pick her out. So we brought her down to the police station and lined her up with four others, again roughly her age and description. The chemist said he couldn't say for sure that any of the women was the one he saw, though he did pick out one he thought was the most likely."

"Miss Winston?" Drew ventured.

The chief inspector snorted. "Kitty Blakeley from our typing pool. He said he picked her because she was the tallest of the lot."

Drew frowned, thinking. "So the woman who bought the cyanide was tall?"

"Evidently. Not extremely tall, mind you, the chemist said. But taller, he thinks, than our Miss Winston."

"Could she have been wearing heels that day?" Madeline asked. "Many women do, you know."

The chief inspector nodded. "Possibly. She doesn't have much of an alibi for that afternoon. It was her half day off, and she went to do errands."

Drew lifted one eyebrow. "That's rather unhelpful, isn't it?"

"Rather," Birdsong agreed. "She had been in the places she mentioned. Mostly where she's a regular customer."

"Seems all right, for now," Drew said. "Suppose we leave off considering Miss Winston just for the moment. Who else might have bought the poison?"

"Mr. Landis sent her the chocolates, didn't he?" Madeline began.

"Yes, but they came straight from the shop, and he wasn't home from the time they were delivered until just before Peter ate some," Drew said. "Besides, I don't think, even with glasses, Mr. Landis could convince anyone he was a woman."

"Don't be silly," Madeline said. "Still, wouldn't he be the obvious suspect in this instance?"

"A bit too obvious, if you ask me. He'd have to know he would be the first one the police would suspect."

"So, he makes it so obvious that no one even considers it." Madeline looked at him, both eyebrows raised. "Why not?"

"All right, but why?" Drew countered. "He poisons the candy to kill his wife. Why would he want to kill his wife? He loves her. He's mad about her, it seems to me. Why would he kill her?"

"Perhaps he's tired of her. You said it yourself—

it's impossible to get close to her. Perhaps Mr. Landis found someone he could really love, and he and this woman decided to get rid of Fleur so they could get married."

"Divorce might be a bit less complicated," Drew observed.

Birdsong looked at Madeline. "And you think this would be the woman who bought the cyanide?"

"It could be," Madeline said. "Why not?"

Drew didn't say anything for a moment. *Landis? Sweet heavens, not Landis . . .*

"So this mystery woman," he said at last, "she might have been the one Benton saw after Ravenswood was killed."

"And the one I saw after Zuraw was murdered," Madeline said. "It makes perfect sense."

Drew shook his head. "No. I don't believe it of him. I've never heard a whiff of rumor about him. These things usually get out, don't they? If there were such a woman, who would she be? I mean, Landis doesn't do much of anything. He works and then goes home to his family. If Miss Winston *were* the mystery woman, then it would fall together rather nicely. Someone in house, as it were. But if she's not the one—"

"So then it's one of the others."

Drew chuckled. "No doubt there's a cook and a scullery girl, maybe one or two more. Who's your money on?"

"That parlormaid who took our things and went to find out if we could go up to see Peter? Sullivan, wasn't it?"

Drew shook his head. "I would never have thought that one in particular. Not any of them really. Not every household features a torrid affair between the master and one of the staff, darling."

Her mouth turned down. "I realize that. I just don't know who it could be. Have your men been watching him, Chief Inspector?"

"They have, miss," Birdsong said. "He does just as Mr. Farthering here says. He goes to his office, works, and then comes home to his family. Regular as clockwork."

"All right," Drew said, "let's put him aside for the moment, too. What other questions do we have unanswered? Who do we yet have unaccounted?"

Madeline leaned forward in her chair. "Did you ever find out what happened to that lady reporter, Chief Inspector? Jo Tracy? Or what those papers were?"

Birdsong scowled. "I'm afraid not. We have bulletins out to police stations all over the country, but they haven't turned up anything as yet. We've spoken to her landlady and to her secretary twice, but neither of them could tell us anything. It may have nothing to do with the case at all, but it would be very strange if she just happened to disappear after finding out about Ravenswood."

"You don't suppose the killer has gotten to her too, do you?"

"It's possible she's still alive, miss. Somewhere."

The chief inspector didn't look hopeful. Perhaps, Drew thought, they were looking at this Tracy woman the wrong way round.

"Did she have any reason to put Ravenswood out of the way, Chief Inspector? Perhaps something to do with these papers of hers? Something he wouldn't let her print?"

Birdsong considered that. "I would certainly like to know where she's been all this time and what those papers were. Ravenswood did seem more the type to enjoy shocking the public with his exploits rather than trying to hush them up."

"And you say Miss Tracy has no family?"

"None to speak of," said Birdsong. "Some cousins in York. A great-aunt in Newcastle. They've all been checked out."

"Friends?" Drew asked.

"Several, but none of them has seen her, either. Women matching her description have been spotted everywhere from Land's End to Inverness, but none of those has come to anything."

"Any more clues about what those papers might have been, Chief Inspector?"

Birdsong let out a sigh. "None at all. The Sherman girl, her secretary, says she believes they were notes for a novel or some such she was writing. All very hush-hush. This Jo Tracy would never tell her what the book was about."

"I feel rather sorry for our chief inspector," Drew mentioned once he and Madeline were back at Farthering Place.

She gave him an odd look. "You do?"

"We have only one thorny puzzle to solve. He has to look into all of them." Drew sighed. "A policeman's lot, as they say, is not a happy one."

She smiled, but the smile was faint and distracted. "Drew?"

He sat on the parlor sofa, pulling her down beside him, and kissed her cheek. "What is it, darling?"

She lowered her eyes for a moment, then looked up at him. "I want you to let the police solve this case."

He wrinkled his forehead. "Why?"

"We're about to get married, Drew. I want you to help me plan everything. I want you to be thinking about us and not about . . . about anything else."

"But, darling," he said with a laugh, "you and Aunt Ruth have had everything planned for weeks now. What you have already decided will be glorious. And I *am* thinking about us. I think about us all the time, about how I don't deserve to be as deliriously happy as I am."

"Please, just this once. For me. Don't have anything more to do with this case."

"What's wrong? I thought we were going to make a career of solving cases together. Are you tired of it already?"

"No." She shook her head. "No, I do think this is something we can do for people who need our help. But not this time, Drew, please."

"Why, love?"

"I'm afraid something's going to happen. Something awful." She looked away. "I'm afraid I'm going to lose you."

He held her close. "You don't have to worry about this being like the last time. Whoever our killer is, he's not after me."

Again she shook her head, but she didn't say anything. He merely held her there, but soon she sat up and moved away from him.

"Do you really have to keep on with this investigation, Drew?"

"I did promise Landis and Miss Winston. You wouldn't want me to break my word to them, would you?"

"No," she said, standing.

"Madeline?"

She blinked hard, and her eyes were bright with tears. "I'm not saying you're in love with Mrs. Landis. I'm just saying . . . oh, I don't know what I'm saying. I just don't want you to be around her or her family."

"I thought you liked Landis. Surely you can't dislike Peter."

"No, of course not. He's a precious little boy. I've enjoyed having him here. And I do like Mr. Landis. But Fleur . . ." She exhaled, looking frustrated with Drew and with herself. "Fleur will use you until there's nothing else she wants from you, and then she'll kick you aside."

He could only shrug. "I've known more admirable women. That doesn't mean she's a murderess."

"I suppose not." She gave him a wounded look. "Couldn't you just drop the thing, just because I'm asking you to? Isn't that enough?"

He let his expression soften. "I suppose I could ask to be let off, if it means that much to you. But I don't know if I much care for going back on my word."

"It wouldn't be going back on your word if they agree to release you. Please, Drew. For me."

"All right then. For you, sweet."

"Promise?"

"I promise. I'll speak to Landis and Miss Winston tomorrow." He rose to stand next to her and kissed her cheek again. "Now come along. It's about time we dressed for dinner."

The next morning, Drew had an early breakfast before Madeline and her aunt came downstairs. Afterward he climbed into the Rolls and headed

up to Winchester. He'd just as well get this over
and done, starting with Landis. He didn't like
begging off, but this case really wasn't his problem to solve. He regretted Landis and especially
Peter having to go through such a difficult time. It
couldn't be easy for the boy, not with a mother
like Fleur, but Drew couldn't exactly help that.

Had his own mother been like Fleur? Surely
not. Then again, he had fallen for Fleur himself.
Why shouldn't his father have been equally
susceptible to someone like her? He slapped one
hand against the steering wheel. It was utterly
maddening not knowing who he was. What he was.

A French shopgirl was the sum total of his
knowledge about his natural mother. Was she a
schemer like Fleur? An innocent led astray? Or
had she done the leading?

Whoever and whatever she was, once this mess
with Fleur was over and Landis had the company
well in hand, Drew would have to find out
something about her himself. He didn't know
what it would be or even where he'd start. His
solicitors had been making inquiries for months
now, and they had turned up nothing. *A French
shopgirl.* How many must there be? How many
had there been twenty-five years ago?

"Please, God," he pleaded over the rumble of
the car's engine, "just a clue, a hint. Something.
Anything."

No beacon of light shone down upon him. He

heard no audible voice, not even a whisper. Well, God had many ways of speaking to His people. Drew would just have to remain patient until an answer came.

Before long, he was walking up the stairs toward Landis's office. One of the secretaries intercepted him.

"Pardon me, Mr. Farthering, but there's a lady waiting to see you. She wouldn't give a name, said you'd want to talk to her. I told her you didn't normally come to the office, but that you were to see Mr. Landis this morning. I suppose I shouldn't have said as much, but she was quite insistent."

Drew frowned. Fleur wouldn't just pop up to the office like this without telling her husband, would she? Surely she wouldn't be in disguise again. Well, however she came, that was all right. He needed to tell her he wouldn't be doing any more investigating on the case anyway.

"And where is she?"

The girl looked as if she feared she would be scolded. "She wouldn't wait in the lounge, sir. I'm sorry. She's in your office."

"My—"

Oh, yes. He still thought of it as his stepfather's office. But Drew was the sole director of the company now. The office was rightly his own, even if he had hardly been in it since Mason's death this past summer.

"My office. Yes. Right. Well, not to worry. I'll see to her."

With blushing thanks and another apology, the girl hurried off, and Drew went up to his office. He padded up to the closed door and eased it silently open. The woman sitting in the Morris chair near the window was . . .

Drew blinked. "Miss Cullimore. You're . . . well, I never expected to see you here."

The leading lady's secretive smile would have put the Mona Lisa to shame. "I don't suppose you would. I wasn't sure you'd come if I just rang you up and asked to meet with you."

"I'm already neck-deep in hot water with my young lady at the moment, mostly due to my being summoned to clandestine meetings by beautiful women, and I promised her I'd put an immediate stop to the practice." He made a bow in her direction. "So if you'll excuse me—"

"Won't you even hear me out?"

He tipped his hat. "I'd rather continue looking forward to a happy honeymoon."

"I thought you wanted to help people." Her eyes were wide and blue and guileless. "I'm being treated monstrously by the authorities and by the insurance company."

"Won't they pay on your policy?"

She frowned. "Not until I'm absolutely cleared. And the police aren't prepared to rule me out until they can positively rule someone else in."

"And you want me to find out who that is."

"Please, Mr. Farthering. My husband is dead, and I have no one to speak on my behalf. Surely you would not abandon a poor widow who merely wishes to see justice done."

"I fancy you'd like to see that insurance money, as well." He shrugged. "Well, it's a pretty speech, Miss Cullimore, but I am simply not the man for the job. Good afternoon." He turned to go.

"Mr. Farthering?"

He stopped, not turning back.

"Farthering," she repeated. "You know, it's not a very common name, Farthering. When I was a girl just starting out in the chorus, I had a friend who knew a man called Farthering. It was in Paris."

Drew turned to her, eyes narrowed. His father had met his mother in Paris. After so long without a lead, was it possible Simone Cullimore could tell Drew something about her at last? Was this his answer? He said nothing, waiting for her to go on.

"Of course I'd heard about your little sleuthing adventures this summer," she said. "It always bothered me, trying to remember where I'd heard the name before, and then I remembered my friend. I was just a girl, not yet sixteen, but I knew what was what even then. She was seeing this Farthering fellow. Andrew Farthering." She looked him up and down, a decided smugness in her expression. "I checked. Andrew was your father's name, wasn't it?"

Drew kept his expression blank. "It was."

"It would be a shame, wouldn't it, if it came out that he had been seeing someone on the side? Even after all these years, him being dead and all. Now, I can promise no one will ever hear a word of it, if you'll agree to stay on the case."

Drew only looked at her.

"I've been thinking back," she said. "My friend, her name was Marie, she was rather smitten with this man. Foolish really. He swept her off her feet and then abandoned her when she was in trouble."

Drew forced himself to stay calm. "Did he?"

"It wouldn't do your family or your business any good to have that bruited about, now, would it?"

"And who was she, this Marie? How do I know you're not making this all up?"

"Oh, it's true enough."

"I'd like her full name," Drew said, "and the shop where she worked. Anything to find—"

"The shop where she worked? I never said she worked in a shop. I said only that I knew her when I was starting out in chorus. Why would you assume she was working in a shop?" The actress gave him a faint smirk. "You already know about her, don't you?"

"Know *of* her. I'd like to know her name. The name of the shop too, where she lived, anything."

She studied him for a moment, brows drawn together. "How old are you, Mr. Farthering? The papers say twenty-four. My friend was in trouble back in 1907. I remember because I was about to turn sixteen. You were born when, 1908?" She laughed. "Oh, it's too priceless. *You're* the child. Your father must have handled it rather cleverly, passing you off as his wife's. Well done, I must say. I suppose he paid my friend well enough to keep her quiet."

"I'd . . ." He liked to congratulate himself on keeping cool in moments of crisis, but before this woman's absolute poise, he felt helplessly young and exposed. "I'd like to know as much about her as I can. I haven't a clue besides she worked in a Paris shop. Hats or something. This is the first time I've even heard her Christian name. I can make it worth your while."

"Money?" Again she laughed. "I think maybe a little trade might be better, hmmm?"

"Trade?"

"I need your help, obviously. The police will take forever to sort this all out, and the stupid insurance people will take forever after that. I have a theater to see to now, a lot of changes to be made, and that takes money."

"I'm willing to pay—"

"Not enough, love. Not what my insurance is worth, not to mention my good name and the reputation of the Tivoli. And I really wouldn't ask it of you. I'm not in it for the money. Not yours anyway. All I want is a little help. Solve this, and

I'll tell you what you want to know. That's fair enough, isn't it? For something that has been eating at you all this while?"

"Miss Cullimore . . ."

Her face hardened. "Those are my terms."

"I promised my fiancée—"

"Ah, yes, the girl. She doesn't like you to be around Fleur, is that it? Poor thing, but I can't help it. If you want to know about your mother, as well as keeping all this about your father quiet, then solve the case, Mr. Farthering."

He sighed. "All right, if you're serious, perhaps you'd like to tell me where you were on the afternoon of the seventeenth."

"The seventeenth?"

"Last Thursday but one."

She shrugged. "Getting ready for a performance, I expect. That or at home. How early in the afternoon?"

"Three or four o'clock."

"I don't know. I don't remember in particular. I . . ." Her sudden smile wasn't all that convincing. "Oh, that must have been the day I went up to London to shop. I bet . . ." She rummaged in her purse and then brought out a ticket stub. "Yes, that was the day. I wasn't sure I still had it, but there." She put the stub in his hand; it was punched and dated the seventeenth of November. "I don't know how I could have forgotten."

He inspected the ticket stub for a moment and

then looked at her. What was he to do now? She knew. She knew what he needed to know. But he had promised Madeline . . .

"You don't understand. I know practically nothing about my own mother. I don't even know the color of her eyes. I don't—"

"Find out who murdered my husband, at least prove it wasn't me, and I'll tell you all about Marie." That Mona Lisa smile was again on the leading lady's face. "There are a lot of shops in Paris, and a lot of Maries."

He tightened his grip on the brim of his hat. He *had* to know. Everything he'd believed about his father, about his mother, about himself had all been smashed to bits this past summer when he found out about this French girl his father had been seeing. Only a week, Drew had been told, but time enough to father a child.

He had to know. Who was his natural mother? Was she still alive? Did she have her own family now? Had she loved his father? Did she ever wonder about the boy she had given up? *Please, God, I have to know.*

He looked at the actress again. Surely Madeline would understand.

"I'll do what I can," he said.

Drew didn't go to talk to Landis or Miss Winston. There was no need now. He didn't have to ask to be released from his promises to them. He just had to explain to Madeline why he would be continuing to look into the case. But she would understand. Madeline loved him, and she knew how much he wanted to know about his mother. His real mother.

He found her in the kitchen of all places, smeared with some sort of dough and pink-cheeked with laughter.

"Oh, Drew." She hurried over to give him a floury kiss. "I'm going to make you the most wretched wife ever. Mrs. Devon has been trying to teach me to cook some good English dishes, and I'm afraid the only thing I've managed to make is a mess."

"Now, it's not so bad as that, Miss Madeline," Mrs. Devon said, "but perhaps you've had enough for one day. We'll try again another time, eh? I really ought to be getting lunch ready."

"She's quite right, darling." Drew took Madeline's arm and led her over to the sink to scrub up. "Besides, I have a bit of news for you."

"Did you go into the office?" she asked as she washed her hands and face. "What did Mr. Landis say?"

"I, uh . . ." Drew glanced over at Mrs. Devon, who at once busied herself with the vegetables. "I didn't exactly get a chance to talk to him. I ran into a little snag on that front."

She shut off the water, silent as she dried her hands. "What happened?"

"It's actually something rather wonderful, darling." Again he glanced at Mrs. Devon. "Why don't we go into the library so I can tell you all about it?"

Madeline looked wary when, once she was seated before the library fire, he made sure to shut the door.

"I'm not going to like this, am I, Drew?"

"I hope you will, darling." He sat beside her, forcing himself to look more confident than he felt. "I can't help but think it was an answer to prayer."

She pursed her lips. "Prayer?"

He took her hand. "I went to the office to tell Landis I wouldn't be involved in the case anymore. But before I got to him, I was stopped by Miss Leigh. Have you met her? She's one of the secretaries. She told me there was someone in my office waiting to speak to me."

Madeline's mouth tightened. "Fleur."

"I thought so, too," he said, not letting her pull her hand away. "But it was Simone Cullimore."

"Simone Cullimore? And she was the answer to your prayer?"

"Only in a roundabout way. Darling, you'll hardly believe the wonderful news. She knew my mother, my natural mother, in Paris. Before I was born."

Madeline's eyes lit up. "Really? Oh, Drew, that *is* wonderful news. Definitely an answer to our prayers. What did she tell you? Do they still keep in touch?" Now she was squeezing his hand. "What did she tell you?"

"Her name is Marie. That's all."

The sparkle in Madeline's expression faded to puzzlement. "That's it? Just Marie? She can't remember her last name or where she lives or anything else?"

"Oh, she remembers all right. I'm certain she does. She's just not saying."

"But why?" Madeline pressed her lips together. "I see. She wants something from you in exchange. She wants you to find out who killed her husband."

"Got it in one," he admitted. "I don't want to let you down, darling, but you know how this not knowing has bothered me. And there's just been nothing at all, not all this while, not until today. I could hardly—"

"You could hardly keep your word to me and just let the thing go."

He drew a steadying breath. "I was rather hoping you'd let me out of that promise. You will, won't you?"

She only sat there, her mouth in a tight line, and he looked at her in disbelief.

"Madeline, you don't . . . you don't expect me to turn her down now, do you?"

"You promised me."

"But surely you understand what this means to me."

She pulled away from him and got to her feet. "I do, but really, Drew, all that's in the past. What difference does it make? I'm more concerned about our future than your past. You're still yourself, no matter who your mother was."

"I thought you'd understand," he said, forcing his voice to stay low and calm, "but I see you don't." He managed a faint smile. "How could you really? You know who your parents were. You know who you are. For my mother, all I have is a Christian name and a description, *French shopgirl*. Not much, is it?"

He didn't get the understanding sympathy he was expecting. There was only a mix of hurt and anger in her expression.

"I thought we had an agreement, Drew. You promised." Tears filled her eyes. "You promised."

"I know. I'm sorry. I wouldn't hurt you for the world, but—"

"But you're going to anyway."

"Madeline—" He broke off when the telephone rang. "Excuse me." He picked up the receiver. "Hello?"

"Drew, I've just found something you ought to know about."

No, no, no. Not Fleur. Not now . . .

"I thought we agreed—"

"Wait. Please." Fleur's voice was little more than a hurried whisper. "I don't want anyone to hear me. Just in case, I mean."

He looked at Madeline, who was watching him with narrowed eyes.

"All right," he said into the telephone after a moment. "What is it?"

"I found a syringe," Fleur told him. "Stuffed into one of the drawers in my sitting room. I don't know how the police could have missed it. Drew, someone right here in the house had to have poisoned those chocolates. I wasn't sure before."

"How do you know there's poison in it?"

Madeline's eyes widened when he said it, and she moved closer to the phone.

"The smell. That awful almondy smell I remember from when Peter . . ." Fleur's voice broke. "Please, I'm so afraid. You have to do something."

"I'll telephone Chief Inspector Birdsong. He'll send someone over there at once. Is Peter all right?"

There was a flash of anger in Madeline's eyes. She had to know now that he was speaking to Fleur. Fabulous.

"I'm sure he is," Fleur said.

"Very well. Hold tight and don't touch anything. I'll ring up the chief inspector right away." He replaced the receiver and turned to Madeline. "That was—"

"I know who that was. And now I suppose you'll have to rush to her side."

"And if I did?" he asked, a little more brusquely

than was warranted. "Look here, Madeline, I've told you as clearly as I am able that I'm not in love with Mrs. Landis. I'll tell you again now. I'll have my solicitor send it to you in a letter if you like, witnessed and notarized. I am not in love with Mrs. Landis. I am not infatuated with her. I am not the slightest bit interested in her. I would like nothing more than to never see her or hear about her ever again."

"And yet you still jump every time she snaps her fingers."

There was a heightened color in Madeline's face, tears in her eyes, and a tremor in her voice. He pressed his lips together. Why couldn't she understand?

"Madeline," he said when he felt certain he could make a civil reply, "I need to call Chief Inspector Birdsong and tell him what Mrs. Landis just told me. He's got to get someone out there to the Landis place right away."

"You're going to let someone else hold Fleur's hand this time?"

"I am just going to let him know what she told me," Drew said evenly. "She found a syringe. Most likely the one used to poison the chocolates. That makes it clear that someone in the house had to have used it. Someone who might well not be through killing."

Her lips trembled, but then she nodded. "I'm sorry. Of course you need to see to this."

"Darling . . . ?"

"Go ahead and make your call. I'm just going to take a little walk in the garden."

He watched after her as she hurried off. It wasn't like her to be jealous. It wasn't like her to be demanding and suspicious and . . . oh, he didn't know what else. It wasn't Madeline.

He rang up the chief inspector and told him what Mrs. Landis had said.

"A syringe in her sitting room, by George. And my men missed it?" Birdsong grumbled under his breath. "I suppose I'd better go round there and see what's what. You coming?"

"Not this time, I'm afraid. I have a little mystery here that needs solving. But I would like to know what you find out, if you'd ring me back when you have a moment."

"I certainly will. Um . . . everything all right there, Mr. Farthering?"

Drew couldn't help smiling at the poorly disguised concern in the gruff voice. "I hope so, Chief Inspector. I truly do."

He hung up and went to find Madeline. He found her at the back of the garden, a thin cardigan wrapped around her, her shoulders hunched against the cold as she stared at one of the rosebushes.

"It was so lovely this summer," she said, not looking at him. "Now it's bare and dead."

"Not dead." He moved closer to her. "Just bare

at the moment. You'll see. Come spring it will be bursting with blooms again."

"Not if it's dead."

"Madeline—"

"Things die, Drew." She gave him a sorrowful look. "Even the beautiful things."

"Madeline—"

Her sorrow changed then to a determined cheerfulness. "Did you talk to the chief inspector?"

"Yes. He's going out to see Mrs. Landis."

"I suppose you'll want to join him."

"He's a qualified police inspector. I expect he can handle this sort of inquiry. I've something else I must look into." He took both of her hands in his. "I want to know what's really upsetting you. It has to be more than Mrs. Landis."

"I don't want you to be around Fleur. Is that so hard to understand?"

"What do you think I'm going to do, Madeline? Run off to the Argentine with her? Why don't you believe me when I say I'm not the slightest bit interested in her?"

"I believed you when you promised you wouldn't pursue the case, and I was wrong, wasn't I?"

He bit back a sharp retort. They never quarreled. Not really. Surely he could get her to understand. Surely she wasn't serious about making him drop the case. Not when he was so close to getting some real information about his mother.

There had to be something else on her mind.

"You've been unhappy," he said, studying her face. "For the past couple of weeks now. What is it?"

She shook her head, not speaking.

"What are you afraid of, Madeline?"

Something flickered in her eyes, and then she looked away again. He merely stood there, listening to her breathing, the breaths coming more quickly than usual. Finally she spoke.

"I haven't been honest with you, Drew."

She looked at him with that directness he admired but with none of her usual playfulness mixed into it, just pain and remorse all at once.

"Go on."

"I told you some time ago that I don't have anyone waiting for me back in America. That's true. I don't. But I did once."

"That's hardly surprising," he said, trying to keep his tone light. "Girls like you don't come along every day."

A touch of color came into her cheeks, and she huddled deeper into her cardigan. "His name was Jimmy Adams. We'd known each other for ages, and everyone just assumed we'd eventually marry. I thought so, too. He had started giving me hints that he wanted to ask me, and I was all ready to say yes. We were such great friends and got along so well, it seemed the right thing to do."

"Obviously something happened."

She nodded. "Her name was Diane, but they called her Dinah. Short for dynamite. She was too. There was always a commotion wherever she was, and the boys were wild for her."

"And I suppose your sweetheart fell for her. I'm so sorry, darling."

"It's a pretty common story, isn't it? He told me for weeks that he didn't care anything about her, that she was worse than a flirt and he would never want his name linked with hers."

Drew squeezed her hands, trying to rub some warmth into them. "I suppose you broke with him when you found out he was seeing her."

Madeline shook her head. "I didn't know about it until they were in a car smash. She was behind the wheel. They'd been to one of the roadhouses out on the highway, someplace none of our friends ever went, and both of them had too much to drink. She hit a tree, and he was thrown out. He died two days later."

"And the girl?"

Madeline's eyes flashed. "She was only bruised. I don't know what happened to her after that. Moved on to someone else, I suppose. I hadn't really thought about her for a long time. Not until—"

"Not until Fleur." He brought her hands to his lips. "No wonder this has been difficult for you. But, truly, love, believe me—"

"I do! Drew, I do believe you. That's what makes

this so awful. I don't think you're interested in Fleur. I don't think you'd betray me. I just . . ." Her breath hitched. "I don't think I can marry you."

"Please, darling, don't say that." He squeezed her hands more tightly, fighting the dread that swept over him. "You can't mean it."

"I'm sorry."

"You still love him," Drew said, forcing the emotion from his voice. "Is that it?"

"No." Her eyes brimmed over with tears once more. "I never loved him." She laughed softly, shaking her head. "I mean, yes, I loved him. I truly did, but I wasn't *in love* with him. Not the way a wife should love her husband." Again she looked away. "Not the way I love you."

"Then why . . . ?"

"I knew him for most of my life, Drew. And I still didn't really know him. If I hadn't seen him dead there in the hospital, if I hadn't read the police report about the accident for myself, I would never have believed it. I would have sworn it was all a mistake, that it was someone else. You and I . . ." She reached up to touch his cheek. "We haven't even known each other six months."

"So what are you saying?" he asked. "That you want to put things off a while until you're sure? Or that you want to end things entirely?"

She lowered her eyes. "It doesn't matter how much I love you. I just can't marry you. I'm sorry.

I shouldn't have been so hasty about saying I would, but I can't. I know that now."

"I thought we were past this. I thought—"

"I wouldn't have said yes if I hadn't meant it. Then Fleur showed up and made me realize I just . . . I can't go through with something like I did with Jimmy. Not again. Not when I love you so much more."

"Madeline—"

"We've had fun together, Drew, these past few months. Why can't we just go on the way we have been?"

"Fun?" He squeezed his eyes shut and pressed his clenched fist to his forehead, gritting his teeth until the surge of pain had passed. "Is that all it's been? Is that all you want?"

She looked at him again, and there was hurt in her eyes. Then that look was gone, replaced by cool resolve. She gave him a tight smile.

"It's been exciting and even rather frightening at times, but I guess I got too caught up in all the excitement to be practical." She shook her head, catching an unsteady breath and then smiling again. "It doesn't matter. I love you, Drew, I really do, but I'm not going to marry you."

She slipped the diamond off her finger and, leaning over to kiss his cheek, pressed it into his hand. He seized the opportunity to pull her into his arms, holding her as close as he could.

"Please, darling, don't do this. Don't go. You're

not yourself right now. You're . . . I don't know, but whatever it is, it's not you. Please, before you do anything rash, just stop and think. I love you. I want you." He pressed his face against the curve of her neck. "I need you. Madeline, don't do this. Please."

Her arms went around him, and she laid her cheek against his.

"Drew . . ." she whispered.

Her fingers felt light on his skin, tender and loving, and he was almost sure she was going to tell him she had changed her mind, that everything she'd just said was only the result of nuptial nerves. But then she abruptly pulled away and took several steps back, increasing the distance between them.

"I'll make sure everything is canceled," she said. "Aunt Ruth and I made all the arrangements. We'll make sure they're all unmade as quickly as possible. You don't have to do anything. I hope . . ." Tears glistened in her eyes, but she blinked them away, her face a mask of serene resignation. "I hope you'll see, and very soon, that this is best for the both of us. Friends still?"

He stared at her outstretched hand, the entire world suddenly turning bleak. "Madeline, please . . ."

"I'm not going to quarrel with you over this. It is the way it is. If you don't want to be my friend anymore, I can understand that. Just tell me."

He took her hand and pressed his lips to it. "I love you, darling. I would never try to force you to do anything you don't want to do." *Madeline, don't go. Please don't.* He clutched her hand more tightly. "Are you sure this is what you want? I mean, truly sure?"

She shook her head, lips quivering, and then took her hand from his. "But it's what's best."

Drew nodded slowly. "All right, darling, if you're sure you don't want to think things over. I suppose I don't have much choice, do I?"

She reached toward him and then clasped her hands together in front of herself. "You know I wouldn't do anything to hurt you, Drew. Not if I could help it."

"I'm certain you wouldn't mean to, but you have. You are." He studied her for a moment. "Would it make a difference if I agreed to drop the case? If we totally forgot about Fleur?"

"No. You should go on with the case. Miss Cullimore won't tell you anything about your mother if you don't."

"But you're right. Our future is more important than anything in the past, yours or mine. If I don't find out about my mother, then I don't. We can still—"

"Finish the case. Then find out about your mother. I'll still help you, if you like." She bit her lip and offered her hand once again. "So, friends then?"

"Of course." He shook her hand. "Friends."

"And I am right, and you are right, and all is right as right can be!" The words from that infernal *Mikado* wouldn't leave his head.

She stood there for a moment, clearly unsure of what to do next. Then she gave him a little nod. "I had better go see to some things now. I suppose I'll see you at dinner?"

He made a slight bow, one he would have used in the most formal of occasions. "Of course."

Without another word she strode back into the house. He followed her inside and sank down onto the library sofa. Numb. That was all. Even before the blazing hearth fire, he felt numb. The real pain would come in time. Right now he was too stunned to think. *Thank you, Fleur.*

"Well, it's all over."

He looked up to see Nick standing in the doorway.

"What?" Drew blinked. "Come in, old man. What is it?"

"Between Barbie and me. The whole thing's come a cropper. Not that I wasn't expecting it, not that I mightn't even think it's for the best, but—"

"Same with me and Madeline."

Nick's mouth fell open. "What?"

"I don't know how to make it any clearer. As of this moment, everything is off. Madeline has decided she was a bit too hasty in accepting my proposal and would rather we remain merely friends."

"I can hardly believe it. I thought she was utterly mad about you."

"As did I. She claims she is still, but she won't marry me."

He realized he was still holding the engagement ring, holding it so tightly that it was digging into his hand. He slipped it into his coat pocket.

Nick shook his head. "Bad luck, old man. I'm sorry. Still, I've been given to understand that it would hardly be a really serious engagement if it hasn't been broken off at least once. Perhaps she's been reading too much Oscar Wilde. Do you think she absolutely means it?"

"She says she does." Drew blew all the breath from his lungs. "I don't quite know what to make of it myself."

"What exactly did she say?"

"She wanted me to abandon the Ravenswood case."

Nick winced. "I was wondering when it would be too much for her."

"Having Fleur about? Yes, I was hoping it wouldn't come to that, but it has. Fleur gives me another firm kick to the jaw." Drew shook his head. "No, that's not fair. I can't blame Fleur for this. Not really. Yes, she has treated a number of men most abominably, myself included. She's still spoilt and brazen in many ways, but that doesn't mean she hasn't changed. Or at least that she doesn't want to be better than she has been. She claims she does. I mean, don't we all?"

Drew braced one elbow on his knee and leaned his chin in his hand. After all, was not his whole faith founded on the idea that no matter how steeped in sin, willing hearts could be made clean and new? He had found it so himself, and he could not rightly deny her the same grace. No, he couldn't blame this quarrel with Madeline on Fleur.

"So why don't you?" Nick asked.

Drew straightened, looking up at his friend. "Why don't I what?"

"Why don't you drop the case? Surely Madeline is more important to you than this murder investigation."

"Of course she is. Actually I was on my way to tell Landis I was done with it when I got a visit from Miss Cullimore." Drew paused. "Nick, she knew my mother. My real mother. Before I was born."

Nick grinned. "A break at last. Splendid."

"Yes and no. Miss Cullimore won't tell me anything unless I solve this case, or at least prove positively that she's not mixed up in it."

"So you can't drop the case, after all."

"I offered to, if that would patch things up between me and Madeline, but it didn't seem to help."

"Madeline's that angry over it?"

"Not angry," Drew said. "Scared, I think. A while ago, someone rather like Fleur came between her and the man she expected to marry, and then it all ended by cracking him up in a car. Being around Fleur brought it all back to her."

Nick frowned. "I'm not sure I see the connection."

"I'm not entirely sure I do, either," Drew admitted. "I think she's afraid that if she was wrong about someone she'd known all her life, she shouldn't be making commitments to someone she hasn't known half a year yet. But what can I do? I can't make her marry me if she doesn't want to."

Nick shook his head. "It's just not right, Drew. You're perfect for each other. Besides, I don't know of another girl I could stand having about the place all the time. Well, Carrie, I think, but she would be for me and not for you."

Drew gave him a rueful grin. "Certainly. Well, try convincing Madeline of that."

"That doesn't seem too likely." Nick's forehead wrinkled. "Well, is there anything I *can* do to help?"

"Thanks awfully, old man, but I don't expect there is. You might send up a prayer or two before you turn in tonight."

"And what if the answer is no?"

After a long moment, Drew gave him a thin

312

smile. "I don't much like to think of that."

"It could be, you know,"

"Yes, I know. I know it very well."

They were both silent for a while, and then Nick turned to leave. "I'll let you alone now, eh?"

Drew nodded, and an instant later he heard the soft click of the library door shutting. He was alone.

Alone.

His eyes stung, but he blinked them hard, clenching his jaw until he feared the bones would crack.

Madeline was going. She would stop all the wedding plans, send out cancellation notices to the guests, and soon after, go back to America. Might as well be China or the South Pole.

"Oh, God," he breathed, "show me what to do."

Though it was a meager prayer, it was the only one Drew could manage.

— *Seventeen* —

Madeline hurried up the stairs to her bedroom. She had to get inside while she could still hold back the tears. Drew. How could she leave him now? But she couldn't marry him. Not if she wasn't absolutely sure. She had been sure. At least until that Fleur Landis came around, knocking out every bit of self-confidence and certainty she had.

"There you are." Aunt Ruth approached her outside their bedroom door, fashion magazine in hand. "If I *were* to wear something special to your wedding, what do you think of . . . ? Whatever's wrong, child?"

Madeline shook her head, not trusting her voice enough to speak. Instead she bustled her aunt into the bedroom and shut the door behind them.

"Well?" the older woman asked.

Madeline plopped herself onto the bed and wiped her nose with her pocket handkerchief. "Nothing."

Aunt Ruth narrowed her eyes. "I know you better than to believe that, Madeline. Now, what is it?"

Madeline forced a tight smile. "Drew and I have decided we won't be getting married after all."

Aunt Ruth's eyes widened. "What? What happened?"

"It doesn't matter. I just want to cancel everything. Do you have a list of everyone we invited? I'll have to let each of them know it's off. I suppose I should have some sort of card printed up and mailed out. How do they handle these things?"

"Just a simple announcement that the wedding will not be taking place." Aunt Ruth sat down beside her. "Are you sure it's as bad as all that? I thought you loved him?"

Tears sprang into Madeline's eyes. "I do. I just

don't think . . . I shouldn't have said I would marry him. I'm not ready."

Aunt Ruth pursed her lips. "Well, you could have fooled me all this time. And just what makes you sure you aren't ready?"

"It's . . . it's Fleur. I'm afraid . . ." Her throat tightened. "I'm afraid."

"You don't think he's still interested in her, do you? Mrs. Landis? Poppycock. Why would you even consider such a thing?"

"No. It's not that. Not exactly."

"Then what?"

"Oh, I don't know." Madeline drew her knees to her chest and hunched her shoulders over them. "She just reminds me of that girl Dinah. The one Jimmy . . ."

Aunt Ruth nodded. "I've been wondering if you saw the resemblance. Not physical, of course, but the two of them were certainly stamped from the same mold. Well, if that was enough to shake you up, maybe you ought to slow things down after all."

"Exactly. When Drew and I first met, he was interested in me. All right, I was interested in him too, but I told you before that I was trying to make sure of him. Of us. And I thought I had. But what if I'm wrong again, like I was with Jimmy?"

For a long moment, Aunt Ruth only looked at her, her mouth in a grim line. This past summer she had arrived at Farthering Place unannounced and determined to extinguish any spark of love between Madeline and her spoiled foreigner. Now she looked as if she were offended the young man she'd warned Madeline against was now being refused by her.

"Have you discussed this with Drew? Whatever you decide, you owe him at least that much."

Madeline nodded, feeling half ashamed. "He says he doesn't want me to marry him if I'm not sure. I just . . . well, how well do we really know each other?"

Aunt Ruth chuckled. "Just how many murders do you have to solve together before you really know a man?"

"It's not funny." Madeline sniffled and dabbed her eyes with her handkerchief. "How do you know?"

Aunt Ruth put an arm around her. "You don't know, honey. I told you about Bert, the man I was supposed to marry, oh, a million years ago. When I found out there was going to be a scandal about his father's bank, I broke our engagement. What if I couldn't handle people talking about him? About us? What if he ended up being dishonest, just like his father? What if everything he ever told me was a lie? I broke it off because I was scared. And then, before I could sort out all my emotions about it, he died. He died, and I didn't have the luxury of changing my mind again."

"Would you have?" Madeline asked, her voice

thick. "Would you have married him after all?"

"I would have." There was a wistful look in the older woman's eyes. "I never found anyone I felt the same way about. Not in all the years since then. Or maybe I just remember him as a little more perfect than he really was or ever could have been."

Madeline studied her face, recalling pictures she had seen from twenty or thirty years ago. Ruth Jansen had been a beauty in her day. Now she was old, and those days would never return. Madeline didn't want to end up like her, with nothing but what might have been to look back on.

"Have you prayed about all this?" Aunt Ruth asked.

Madeline exhaled heavily. "Over and over. Until Fleur showed up, I felt sure Drew and I were meant to be together. Now . . . I don't know anymore. I feel like everything's wrong."

"You aren't expecting any money-back guarantees, are you?"

"No, but—"

"You can't know, honey. You can only believe and go forward and trust God one day at a time."

Until everything falls apart. Madeline felt that same pounding dread that had flooded over her when they told her about Jimmy when she was eighteen. She felt that same uncertainty, that same insecurity, that same sense of not being good enough. *Oh, what do I do now?*

"What do you think of Drew?"

Aunt Ruth chuckled again. "Oh, no. I'm not making this decision for you. You have to make it on your own, and then you have to live with it."

"All right. I guess the wisest thing to do is to break things off now," Madeline said, her eyes on the floor, "before we both make a terrible mistake. Anyway, I just need to know if you have the list of people we sent invitations to. I must let them know as soon as possible that they need to cancel their plans."

"You don't think you ought to think about this a while longer before you make a final decision?"

Madeline swallowed hard and blinked back tears. "I've been thinking about it since all this happened with Fleur. I just can't be sure I'm not making a mistake."

Aunt Ruth put one finger under Madeline's chin and tilted up her face. "You're certain this is what you want to do? And you absolutely will not marry this man you've been mooning over for the past six months?"

Tears welled in her eyes again, but there was no going back now. It was over. She nodded her head, unable to say anything more.

"Well then." Her aunt's voice became gentle and sympathetic as she pulled Madeline into a hug. "I don't want you to worry about any of it, all right? I'll see that everything's taken care of."

Madeline clung to her aunt, shaken with grief.

She loved Drew. More than she could have thought possible, she loved him. She wanted him. But she couldn't marry him and then find out it was all a huge mistake. It was best if she stopped wanting him.

She sat up, blew her nose, and straightened her shoulders. Best to decide such things now before it was too late.

"Thank you, Aunt Ruth. We should start thinking about going back home now." She sniffled and made herself smile. "I suppose Denny or Nick would make the reservations for us."

"Don't you worry about that either, Madeline. I don't want to be in such a hurry that we end up on the first tramp steamer going west. When I go home, I intend it to be on a respectable ocean liner, so we might not be leaving right away. That'll be all right, won't it? Or should we go stay at the inn until I can get all the arrangements made?"

Madeline shook her head, feeling rather foolish. "No, it's not as bad as that. Just a little awkward maybe. With Drew and with everyone else in the house. You know how the servants talk."

"Pshaw, let them talk if they like. If you don't mind being around the young man for a few days more, then we'll stay here. One thing's for sure, he'll be polite about everything. Whatever else you might say about him, you can't fault his manners."

Tears spilled over onto Madeline's cheeks. She couldn't fault his manners or much else about him. But if in a month or a year or two it all fell apart . . .

Making soothing clucking noises, Aunt Ruth put her arm around Madeline's shoulders again. "You go ahead and cry, honey. You've had a lot on your mind lately. There's nothing like a good cry to make you see things a little more clearly."

The next day, after Madeline disappeared into her bedroom following an uncomfortably quiet lunch, Dennison informed Drew that he had a telephone call. A few minutes later, Drew hunted up Nick, who was going over the estate accounts in Mr. Padgett's office at the back of the house.

"Can that wait a bit, old man?"

Nick looked up. "Just trying to figure out whether or not the farrier got paid properly, but it's not urgent. What are you on to?"

"I received a call from Grady over at the Tivoli. He claims he's found something we ought to take a look at."

"You know it was Grady for certain, do you?" Nick went to get their hats and coats. "You don't think he'll be dead by the time we get there, do you?"

Drew laughed grimly as they headed out to the Rolls.

Grady was waiting for them when they arrived

at the theater and escorted them to the wardrobe room at once.

"I was cleaning out this room, now that the police have done with it and all," he said, "and I came across this." He handed Drew a piece of paper, folded into thirds. It was a letter.

Drew opened it, scanning the cramped, angular writing.

Darling,
    Thursday. At the same little inn we stayed at during Ascot.
    Mad about you, my flower.

                    Your wanton wolf,
                    C

Drew passed the letter to Nick and then turned to Grady. "Where exactly did you find this note? I would have thought the police would give this room a thorough going-over."

"I expect they did," Grady said with a thoughtful scratch of one ear. "But it was stuck behind a drawer in the sewing table. I opened it to put away some pins and a thimble I found on the floor, and I couldn't get it to shut properly. So I took the drawer out, and there was the letter. Neat as you please."

"So Benton's involvement with Tess was not quite as advertised," Nick observed, handing the letter back to Drew.

"I don't know." Drew looked the letter over again. "I say, Grady, how long had Miss Davidson been working here at the Tivoli?"

"Since the first of August, I believe. I remember feeling a bit sorry, because she said it was her birthday and she didn't have anyone to celebrate it with."

"She didn't know anyone in the troupe?" Drew asked.

"Not that I knew of," Grady replied. "She'd been in Dover before then. Born and raised there, I understand."

"And she didn't know Mr. Benton before she came here?"

"Not in the least." Grady shook his head. "Far as I could tell, he had hardly a word with her until a week or two ago. He never was much for speaking to anyone beneath him, our Mr. Benton. Like he was doing a bloke a favor if he so much as said good morning to him. Not like Mr. Ravenswood. Mr. Ravenswood knew, of course, that he was fairly better than anyone, save the Archbishop of Canterbury, but at least he'd stand you to a drink and tell you so."

"But not Benton?"

"Oh, no, sir, though I would say he got a bit chummy this last two or three weeks. Perhaps he'd seen the error of his ways or some such."

"Hmmm." Drew glanced at Nick and then turned again to the stageman. "Tell me, was Mr.

Benton seeing anyone in particular before Ravenswood was killed? Anyone at all?"

"Particular? Not that I knew of. I mean, he and Mr. Ravenswood always had their pick of the girls. In the troupe. In the audience. Didn't much matter to them. Sometimes the same ones." Grady gave a disdainful sniff. "But I don't know as either of them was steady with just one. To be fair, I'd have to say I didn't notice it much with Mr. Benton lately."

"Since Miss Davidson signed on?"

"Well before then. Nearly a year now." Grady chuckled. "I thought maybe he'd got religion or something."

Drew tapped the letter thoughtfully, not responding to Nick's inquiring glance. "Right. Or something . . ."

The stageman seemed rather disappointed. "I thought maybe I'd found something grand there, Mr. Farthering, sir, but I guess it didn't end up being much after all."

"It's hard to say at this point," Drew told him, "but I'm certainly glad you found it. Now, what have the police said about it?"

"Oh." Grady looked sheepish. "I suppose I ought to have rung them up first, eh? That chief inspector isn't going to be too pleased, is he?"

Nick shook his head. "Knowing him, he may have you brought up on charges. Interfering with a police investigation?"

"You don't think he would, do you?" the stageman asked. "I would have told him. I just didn't think."

"Don't you worry now," Drew soothed. "Chief Inspector Birdsong is a reasonable man. Go ahead and ring him up and tell him what you've found here. No need to tell him we saw it first."

Grady nodded. "No, not at all. Not at all. Thank you, sir."

"Before we go, you wouldn't mind if we copied out what's in the note, would you? Just so we can study it more later?"

"No, sir," Grady said.

"Excellent." Drew handed the note back to Nick. "You have your notebook, don't you, old man? Mind seeing to that?"

"Not at all." Nick settled himself at the corner of the table and started writing.

"You didn't happen on anything else, did you, Grady? Sworn confessions or anything? Photographic evidence?"

"No. Just the thimble and the pins. Miss Tess, she was kind enough to let me call her that, she kept this wardrobe room neat as you please. But there's always something goes astray here and there, especially, you know, after . . ."

Drew gave him a grave nod. "Why do you suppose the police didn't find it? They searched the room, you said?"

"They did, sir."

"Might I have a quick look about the room?"

"If you like." The stageman opened the bottom drawer in a well-used sewing table in the corner. "It was this one."

Drew examined the drawer. The table itself wasn't very well made. The drawers were no more than wooden boxes that fit into cubbyholes. There was still a bit of adhesive tape stuck to the back of the one he was looking at.

"I suppose they missed it," Grady said. "It wasn't much of anything, mind you. After I swept up those things and was putting them away, I felt a little bit of a scrape or something when I tried to close the drawer. Didn't feel anything out of place in the drawer itself, so I figured it must have been behind it or under it. And there it was. I could see how it might be missed by a constable in a hurry, especially as the . . . uh, means of death was readily seen."

Drew nodded, then turned to Nick. "Got it all down, old man?"

"Just done." Nick handed the note back to the stageman. "There you are."

"Remember, no need to mention our little visit when you ring the police," Drew said. "Not if it doesn't come naturally into the conversation."

Grady winked. "Right you are, sir."

Drew paused. "One last thing, Grady."

"Yes, sir?"

"What sort of actor is Mr. Benton? I mean, what's he especially good at?"

Grady frowned a bit. "I dunno, sir. He's a fine singer. Far as I've heard, he always knows his lines and his cues and the bits of business he's got."

"Did you ever see him do any character roles? You know, silly walks, funny voices, impersonations?"

"No, sir. Mostly juvenile lead roles, though now he's taken on Mr. Ravenswood's parts of course. He does like to devil Miss Cullimore with imitating her when they argue. It would make Mr. Ravenswood laugh till he cried, and I wasn't sure if it was due to the imitation or just because it riled her so."

"Did her well, did he?"

"Oh, spot on, sir. Tone of voice, walk, everything. I think that's mostly what riled her."

Drew chuckled. "Very likely so. Well, thanks awfully for all the help."

"Sorry it didn't amount to much, sir, but if there's anything else I come across, I'll make sure you hear about it straight off."

"We'll be much obliged."

Drew tossed the man a half crown, and then he and Nick went on their way.

Madeline stood staring into the wardrobe in the room she and her aunt had been sharing. Drew's mother's old room, stylish and expensive and still very much belonging to Constance Farthering, despite its living occupants.

It was odd, since Madeline had come here planning to spend only a few days, how her things managed to end up everywhere. Of course, since her stay had stretched longer and longer, she had bought several outfits, not to mention shoes and hats and underthings and all the rest. And she did tend to amass books. Even with the large library downstairs and the smaller one on this floor and even the rather substantial one in Drew's study, she had managed to collect quite a few books of her own.

She sighed. Perhaps she should leave them here. Or perhaps she could hand them out in the village. Surely some of Drew's neighbors who couldn't afford much in the way of reading material would enjoy them. Perhaps the church could take them and use them to raise money in their next rummage sale. No, what did they call it? A jumble sale. Yes, that might be best.

She began ferreting out the books she had stashed all over the room. The ones on lace making, she would keep. There were only two or three of those, and they would fit easily in her luggage. The others, mostly mysteries, she would leave behind. She felt a familiar tightness in her throat as she gathered them up. Agatha Christie's *Peril at End House*. Maybe she'd hold on to that one. A memento. She remembered vexing Drew by snatching that one out of his mail and reading it before he had a chance to. But he'd really been very sweet about it and let her keep it.

She put a few more books into the pile she planned on leaving behind, and then she found another one that made her pause. *Have His Carcase* by Dorothy L. Sayers. Drew had brought her that one the day Aunt Ruth had come to stay. He had told her later that he meant to keep that one to himself and not even let her have a peep at it until he had read it through. But, seeing how miserable she was with Aunt Ruth so insistent she return to Chicago right away and accusing Drew of all kinds of misconduct, he had given her the book then and there. She wasn't sure if he'd ever gotten a chance to read it.

Perhaps she ought to give it to him now. No, he could get another copy. Perhaps she'd even buy one and send it to him or give it to him before she left. But this one was special. She didn't want to leave it behind.

The telephone rang downstairs, and she couldn't help wondering if it was Fleur again. With a little hissing breath, she put the Sayers book with the Christie one into the pile with the rest. She wouldn't keep them. Best to leave everything behind. He was very sweet and so much fun to be with, but that was precious little on which to build a marriage. She was twenty-two. Still a child, if her aunt was to be believed. What business did she have making so serious a decision as marriage when anything could happen?

Drew was twenty-four, only two years older than she. Certainly he hadn't been as sheltered from the world as she had, but did he truly know what he wanted? What he wanted for all the rest of his life? What if one day he changed his mind? What if one day he ran into another Fleur? What if? What if? What if?

She'd ask Anna to find a box for the books and then send them all to the church. At least there would be some good come of them. These old churches always seemed to need something done to them to keep them from falling over. Little wonder they were forever having these jumble sales. Well, this would help and be no loss to her.

She touched her fingers to the paper cover of the Sayers book, thinking back. Remembering the bookstore in the village where he had bought it, remembering things that had happened afterward. *"I'd marry you right here, this minute and in my bathrobe if I had to,"* she'd told him then when, by God's mercy, he had come back to her after she thought him dead. She remembered him then, warm and alive in her arms when she had feared he would never be again, and she'd promised to marry him. Silly, emotional, childish thing to do —to promise to marry a man just because he wasn't dead.

Still, people failed. They left. They died. How could she promise tomorrow when nothing was certain?

She tossed the book on the stack with the others and turned her back on it. It was done. It was all done.

She turned back to the wardrobe, staring at it for a long moment before, with equal parts care and reluctance, pulling out the long white box that was on the top shelf. She laid it on the bed and in a swift motion removed the lid. It was her mother's wedding veil. It was to have been her own.

She stroked the frothy bundle. It was nearly eight yards of handmade Irish lace, delicate and airy, carefully put away for her all these years, waiting for her own special day. It would just have to wait longer.

Tears welled in her eyes at the thought. How much longer? She had never met anyone like Drew. There *was* no one like him. Not for her. Would she end up just like Miss Winston? Like Aunt Ruth?

A tear slipped down her cheek and fell onto the veil. She gathered the lace into her arms, holding it against her, cradling it as if it were her groom, her lover, her—

She spun around at the knock on the half-open door.

"Drew . . ."

— *Eighteen* —

Drew gave Madeline the tiniest hint of a smile. "Hello. Are you terribly busy just now?"

She stuffed the veil into the box, not wanting him to see it. *No, I suppose that doesn't matter now. There is no tradition about the ex-groom seeing his ex-bride's wedding finery.* Still, she put the lid on the box and swiftly wiped her eyes before she turned to him again.

"No, not busy." She managed a faint smile, too. "Just packing up a few things. Did you want something?"

"No. Uh, yes, in point of fact." His expression turned apologetic. "With . . . well, with everything that's happened between us, I'm having a deuced time thinking straight. I thought perhaps you might help me go over the case once more, just to see if there's anything I've missed. I'd say you're a sight more clearheaded than I am just now."

"I am?" Her laugh was miserably thin. "I'm not exactly ready to swear to that in court."

"I, for one, have been *quite* ready to swear," he said, and there was a glimmer of humor in his expression. "But I try to suppress it. Wouldn't be at all gentlemanly, now, would it?"

"No, it wouldn't. And it wouldn't be like you at all."

"But then again, as you say, perhaps we don't know each other as well as we think."

She looked down. "No, I'm sure of that much. I think Fleur was right. Death before dishonor, utterly devoted, isn't that what she said?" She looked up at him again. "Quietly and deeply passionate."

There was more than a touch of rue in his soft laugh. "Perhaps she should have added 'practical enough to know when his attentions are no longer welcome.'"

Tears stung behind her eyes, but she refused to let them out. She smiled instead. "Yes, we ought to be practical now. Just because we aren't getting married, that doesn't mean we can't be friends."

"Quite right. And infinitely practical. That's why I thought you wouldn't mind helping me with the case. If you'd still like to."

"I told you I would." Still she forced that smile. "Now, what did you want to discuss?"

"The chief inspector just rang up. He wanted me to know what he found out about that syringe in Mrs. Landis's sitting room."

"Yes?"

"I'm afraid it was one of Miss Winston's."

Madeline felt faintly ill. "Oh, Drew, no. I didn't want it to be her. I really didn't."

"I know. I rather like her myself and can't imagine she could be behind any of this, but we have to remember that just because it was hers, that doesn't mean someone in the house couldn't have taken it from the medical kit she keeps." He was silent for a moment. "I'm wondering if maybe we aren't looking at this all the wrong way round."

"What do you mean?"

He glanced around the room. "Perhaps it would be best if we adjourned to more neutral ground. The library? I still like to consider myself a gentleman, and this is a lady's boudoir after all."

She took the arm he offered, and in another moment they were settled on the sofa before the library fire. It was a lovely room, filled with books and things of grace and beauty. She loved this room. She loved this house. She loved—

"Now," Drew said, "back to what I was saying. What if we have been looking at this the wrong way round? Suppose the problem isn't that Landis didn't notice Mrs. Landis going out the nights Ravenswood and Tess were murdered."

Madeline nodded rapidly. "Yes, I've had a nagging thought about that. Suppose it was her being too drugged to notice *him* going out that's the problem."

Drew took a deep breath. "I haven't wanted to think it of him. I haven't at all, but suppose that it's true. If she was asleep, if she was drugged, she'd never know whether or not he was there."

"But whoever it was Mr. Benton saw running away the night Mr. Ravenswood was killed, he

333

said it couldn't have been a man. Mr. Landis is definitely not slight enough to be mistaken for Fleur or any other woman. And he wasn't home when those chocolates were delivered, so even if he took the syringe, he couldn't have put the poison in them."

"Right," Drew said. "But, again, maybe we're thinking of things the wrong way round. Suppose it's not a man *or* a woman."

Madeline wrinkled her forehead.

"No," Drew said. "Suppose it's a man *and* a woman."

Her eyes were wary. "All right."

"Now tell me again, Madeline. When we were all in Zuraw's office and you heard that clatter in the storeroom, what exactly did you see?"

"Not much at all, as I told you. Really just someone in a black cloak running across the hall to the alley exit."

"Right. And you're absolutely certain you couldn't say if it was a man or a woman."

"That's right."

Drew frowned, thinking. "And Benton claims he saw Mrs. Landis, or at least someone in her cloak, running away after the Ravenswood murder, but nobody else saw anything."

"You don't suppose he killed Ravenswood, after all?"

"No, he was with Grady from the time they both left Ravenswood alive in his dressing room until they broke down the door and found him dead. But suppose he's so adamant about it being Mrs. Landis because he wants to deflect suspicion from the real killer."

"That's certainly possible."

"Here's the other thing. The chief inspector told me the coroner believes Zuraw was dead by at least seven the day he was killed. I got that phone call about nine. You remember Grady, right?"

She nodded.

"He told me Benton has been known to imitate Simone and that he does it quite well. What if she weren't the only one?"

"Oh, Drew, you don't think—"

"We spoke to Zuraw only that once and only for a few minutes. An older man with a faint accent? I never thought it might not be him, but I can't swear now that it was. Benton's an actor. He played the part of the bereaved lover well enough. Why couldn't he play the part of Lew Zuraw, as well?"

"But who would he have been diverting suspicion from?" Madeline asked. "If he didn't kill Ravenswood . . ."

"His lover."

Madeline raised her eyebrows. "Do you think Tess killed Ravenswood?"

"No, not Tess." He fished in his pocket and brought out the copy of the note Grady had found. "Tess had the original of this hidden behind

335

one of the drawers in her sewing table. I think she knew something was up. Read it."

Madeline took the note and looked it over. "This isn't to Tess?"

"Couldn't be. She had never been to Winchester until August of this year. Benton hardly spoke to her until a week or two ago. Why would he lie? Why would he say he was desperately in love with her unless he was protecting the woman he wrote that note to? The woman who murdered Ravenswood."

"But Tess . . ." Madeline tightened her hold on the paper. "She was in love with Benton. Or thought she was. If she found this note, this note to his lover who was not herself, she must have meant to tell someone. Us or the police or I don't know who."

Drew nodded. "After her rough go with Ravenswood, I would think she'd be especially sensitive about being deceived. A woman scorned, as they say."

"Oh, Drew, it must have been why she was killed."

"It seems very likely. Very likely indeed. Now, who is this mystery lover of Benton's? Ravenswood's murder did him no appreciable good. He had to have thought he would benefit by helping his sweetheart somehow."

"You don't think it might have been Simone after all, do you? Ravenswood was a pretty terrible husband to her. Maybe the theater wasn't what she was after as much as repaying him for years of infidelity."

"And Benton, desperately in love with her, would do anything to keep her from hanging."

"But, no, she couldn't have killed Ravenswood. She was home. She called from there."

Drew frowned. "Might have. Might not. She says she was at home, but she might have just as easily called from a nearby phone box, claiming to be at home. Rather convenient she rang up just in time to give herself an alibi, eh? But let's look at it the other way round. Benton might have been willing to kill Mrs. Landis. They disliked each other enough, but who might have helped him do it?"

"We're back to the candy again," Madeline said. "If Mr. Landis had it sent straight to their house, I don't know how Mr. Benton could have gotten to it to tamper with it."

"Right. That leaves only his partner in crime. The only one at the house who would have knowledge of cyanide and know how to inject it into those chocolates."

Madeline shook her head. "No. Not Miss Winston. She loves Mr. Landis, I'm certain of it. And she loves Peter. She couldn't have—"

"Couldn't she? If she and Benton both wanted Mrs. Landis to hang?"

"Even if they each wanted Fleur out of the

way for their own separate reasons, that doesn't explain why either of them would kill Ravenswood. Just to frame Fleur? That seems a little extreme."

Drew sighed. "It does, doesn't it? And if the connection between Benton and this mystery woman isn't a romantic one, then this letter doesn't make sense. And Tess keeping it doesn't make sense, either. Oh, I wish I'd never gotten involved in the whole stupid mess."

Madeline gave him a small smile. "I do too."

He felt a breath of hope at the soft regret on her face. Was she reconsidering?

That hope died when her expression again took on the cheerful determination to which he had grown far too accustomed.

"But, no, not really. If it helped us see things clearly and kept us from making a mistake, I suppose it was a good thing after all."

He moved closer to her, hesitated, and then took her hand. "Are you certain *this* isn't the mistake?"

Though tears filled her eyes, she still forced herself to look cheerful. "You make it awfully hard to be mad at you, Drew. You really do."

"Mad at me? Here now, why should you be mad at me? Even if you won't marry me, I thought we were still to be friends."

She shrugged, looking down, but she didn't take her hand away. "I'm mad at you for making it so hard to be mad at you."

He couldn't help a bitter laugh from escaping. "I don't even know how to reply to that particular revelation."

"Maybe you'd just better not try," she said, taking her hand away at last. "I think I'd better go. I can't have you thinking I'm more flighty and indecisive than you do already."

He forced a smile. "Just as you say." *Darling,* he wanted to add, but he didn't. She didn't particularly want to be his darling just now. "But don't go. Please."

"What else?"

"I don't know. There has to be something. Think back again to what you saw the night Zuraw was murdered."

She sighed and sat down again. "I've told you before, I didn't really see anything. Just a glimpse of someone in a black cloak running across the hallway and toward the exit."

"Right. Right. But think really hard. Close your eyes and imagine."

Madeline complied.

"Now," Drew said, "think about height. Tall or short?"

"Mmmm, I don't know. Kind of medium, I think, but it's hard to tell with someone hunched over like that."

"Hunched over? You didn't mention that before."

Her eyes popped open. "Well, I didn't think of it

before. And I don't know if *hunched* is quite the right word. You know how it is if someone is hurrying and he leans forward."

"Yes, exactly. All right, eyes closed again. Now what about girth? Heavy? Thin?"

She squeezed her eyes tight. "I just don't know. It was so fast. Definitely not heavy. Not at all. Lithe, I'd say, rather than thin. And fast."

"Good," Drew said. "No, don't open your eyes. Now, you couldn't see a face at all, yes?"

"That's right. Whoever it was had a hood on."

"And the cloak, as well?"

"Yes."

"How far down did the cloak come?"

Madeline considered, still with her eyes closed. "Almost to the floor, I think."

"Almost to the floor. So you couldn't see the legs?"

"Not really. Not that I remember."

"Shoes?"

"I do remember seeing the feet move under the cloak. They were black. Or at least very dark."

"So dark shoes likely," Drew said.

Madeline nodded. "Probably."

"Ladies' shoes?"

She opened her eyes with an exasperated huff. "You act like I had all day to stand there and take notes."

He held up one hand. "My error. Forgive me."

Her expression softened. "I just didn't see very much. I'm sorry."

He sat thinking for a moment and then gave her a hopeful smile. "Care to engage in a bit of an experiment with me?"

"What do you have in mind?"

He stood and offered her his hand. "I thought perhaps you and I and Nick could pop round to the Tivoli and test out some of our theories."

She narrowed her eyes. "What do you mean?"

"I thought we could gather up all of our candidates for the mystery woman and have them, one by one, dash across the hall wearing Mrs. Landis's cloak. Perhaps that would stir something in your memory."

"But we know Fleur couldn't have been there."

"Yes, but we'll have each of them run across without you knowing which is which. That way, if you happen to think Mrs. Landis looks to be the most likely, we'll know it's all a bust and have a good laugh at my expense, eh?"

"And if it's not any of them? If it's someone we haven't even considered yet?"

He looked into her eyes. "Had you rather not come? After all, you're the only one besides Benton who claims to have seen anything at all." He searched her face for the slightest bit of yielding. "It might be the difference between catching the killers and letting them off scot-free."

She exhaled. "All right, I'll go. You make whatever arrangements you have to make, and I'll go with you. I suppose Chief Inspector Birdsong would want to be present."

"I imagine he will," Drew said. "It's fairly likely he'll have to be the one to summon all the guests to our little party. They may not be willing to come at my humble invitation."

— *Nineteen* —

"Have you a better idea?" Drew asked, trying his best not to sound cheeky.

Chief Inspector Birdsong glanced around the dimly lit back hall at the Tivoli. "I'm not entirely sure this is the best use of police resources."

"And what would you suggest?"

"Apart from jailing the whole lot and calling it good? Nothing comes to mind, so I suppose we'd better try your way for now. We won't be inconveniencing you, will we, Hibbert?"

Grady looked rather dubious about that, but he merely shrugged. "Not as anyone would notice, Chief Inspector. Anything to help."

Birdsong nodded at Madeline. "If you would, miss, stand there at Mr. Zuraw's office door as you were the night he was killed. You were not in the hallway?"

"No." Madeline went into the office but leaned

out where they could still see her. "I was standing inside the doorway. I didn't look out until I heard the crash."

"Fine. If you would, stand just as you were, and please don't look out until you're asked."

"All right."

Madeline disappeared into the room. Birdsong turned to the three women lined up against the corridor wall: Adele Winston, Simone Cullimore, and Fleur Landis.

"Right. Now, ladies, if you please, step into the storeroom." He nodded at Nick. "Go with them, young Dennison, and have one of them put on the cloak. Don't tell us which. When I give the signal, have her run across here to the exit."

"This way, ladies," Nick said, motioning toward the storeroom.

Fleur pouted and pushed herself away from the wall she was leaning on. "I don't know why I have to do this. It couldn't have been me, Chief Inspector. I was in your nasty jail at the time."

"And I was in the middle of a performance." Miss Cullimore crossed her arms over her chest. "This is ridiculous."

"It's not so much to ask," Miss Winston said, herding them forward. "If it helps somehow, why not?"

Landis took his wife's arm. "She's right, darling. If it helps, and since we know it couldn't have been you, why not humor the chief inspector?

343

We want to find out what's going on, don't we? I mean, after what happened to Peter?"

Fleur's sulky expression vanished. "Yes. All right."

"There's a girl." Landis urged her toward the storeroom. "Now go on and do as they ask, so we can get this all sorted quickly."

"That would be good," Miss Winston said. "I'd like to get back to Peter as soon as possible. Sullivan always lets him go out without his gloves."

"What's going on here?"

"Ah, Mr. Benton," the chief inspector drawled as the actor was escorted in, "so glad you could join us."

"You didn't give me much choice in the matter, did you, sending your press gang round to fetch me?" He shook free of the policeman, who still had him by the arm, and then glared at Fleur. "What's she doing here? You told me she couldn't have had anything to do with the murders."

"Just a bit of an experiment," Birdsong explained, "if you'll be kind enough to bear with us."

Madeline came back into the corridor. "Mr. Benton. I didn't know you would be here."

Benton sneered at her and at Nick and Drew and then at the chief inspector. "Letting amateurs do your job again, Inspector?"

"Never you mind that, Mr. Benton. Just your cheerful cooperation, if you please."

"Fine." Benton plastered on a smile. "What is it you want me to do?"

"You claim you saw someone running away from Mr. Ravenswood's dressing room the night he was killed," Drew began, and Benton's sneer returned.

"I don't *claim* to have seen her. I *did* see her."

"You said you were certain it was Mrs. Landis. Do you still think that?"

Benton glared at Fleur and then huffed. "No, I don't suppose I'm certain now. She couldn't have done for Mr. Zuraw, that's plain."

"Good of you," Fleur said, lips tightly pursed.

"And I don't know why someone else would have killed him if she had killed Ravenswood and . . ." Benton pressed his quivering lips together, stilling them. "And Tess."

Drew looked at him coolly. "Were you in love with Miss Davidson?"

Benton's eyes filled with both fury and tears. "You know I was! I told you already."

"When did you and Miss Davidson meet?" Drew asked. "I don't believe you ever said."

Benton blinked hard and took a deep breath. "When she came here in August. When she started work."

"You never saw her before that?"

"No. Not to my knowledge."

Birdsong narrowed his eyes. "Tell me, Mr. Benton, is this your handwriting?" He showed

Benton the paper Grady had found stuffed behind the drawer in the wardrobe room.

The actor shrugged. "Suppose it is. What's that matter?"

"Do you recall writing this note, sir?"

Benton nodded.

"And when was that?"

"I don't know." Benton looked at the note more closely. "Maybe two weeks ago? Three? I really can't remember."

"Do you remember who it was to?" Drew asked, watching his eyes.

Benton's lip curled. "I should say. I addressed it to 'my darling.' "

"Just who did you mean by that, sir?" Birdsong asked.

"I told you already." Benton spoke very slowly and clearly. "I was in love with Tess Davidson. Who else would it be?"

"You pretended to be in love with her." Drew took a step closer to him. "So you could cover up the affair you were really having."

Benton glanced toward the three women still standing near the corridor wall. "You're insane."

" 'At the same little inn we stayed at during Ascot,' " Drew read from the letter. "You said you hadn't even declared yourself to Miss Davidson before she died."

"All right." Benton's face reddened. "Maybe our involvement was a little more than innocent. Is that a crime? I didn't want to sully her reputation. She is dead after all. Isn't that enough?"

Drew shook his head. "That would be terribly noble of you, I can appreciate that, except it's simply not the truth, is it? You didn't meet her until August. How could you have gone with her to Ascot in June?"

"Who said it was June?" Benton snapped. "The town's there even when there isn't a race."

"But you wrote *during* Ascot, not *in* Ascot. What could that mean except you had been there for the races during Ascot week in June? Who are you really in love with? And why did you help her kill all those people?"

Benton's eyes widened. "I don't know what you mean. Surely you can't think that I had anything to do with all of this. I tell you, Tess and I—"

"She found out about you and this other woman. That's why she hid this note, and that's why you killed her."

"That's an outrageous lie! I absolutely did not kill Tess Davidson!"

"After Ravenswood used her and threw her over, she didn't much like finding out she'd been used again, did she?" Drew said, his voice taut. "Did you kill her because she threatened to go to the police?"

Madeline's eyes were hard. "She was in love with you. Did you have to kill her?"

"And Zuraw," Drew added.

"Look here," Benton huffed. "I was in the middle of a performance. How was I to kill Zuraw and then be back onstage in time for my cue? The police don't even think he was killed where he was found. I would have had to move the body, as well. All during Simone's solo? It would be impossible."

"But he was killed before then," Nick said affably. "Well before you telephoned us to come up to the theater. To be your alibi, I believe."

Drew nodded. "All you need to have done during the show was make a little racket in the storeroom, where you had stashed the body, and then nip across the hallway into the alley and back into the theater in time for your next cue."

Benton stared at him, wide-eyed. Then he shoved aside the police constable who stood at his elbow and bolted down the corridor that led to the stage.

"My men have surrounded the theater, Mr. Benton," the chief inspector called, his voice wearily patient as the constable dashed after the actor. "You can't get away now." He sighed and glanced back at Drew. "Might as well come on then. All of you."

They all scurried onto the stage. It had been cleared in preparation for changing between productions. The curtain was up and so were the backdrops, exposing the backstage and all its mysteries.

The fugitive skidded to a stop, looking right and left and seeing several of Birdsong's men whichever way he looked.

"Come along now, sir," the chief inspector said, still patient and unhurried. "It's all over."

Benton shook his head, backing toward the center of the rear wall, policemen closing in on him from both sides and from the aisles of the house.

Drew and Madeline and Nick were right behind the chief inspector, with Landis and the three ladies on their heels. Fleur clung to Landis's arm, while Grady stood watching at the back.

Miss Cullimore looked from them to Birdsong to Drew and then to Benton. "What have you done, Conor? What in the world have you done?"

He only shook his head.

Birdsong moved to stand in front of him and put his hand on the actor's shoulder. "Edgar Benton Crowley, I arrest you for the murders of Henry Percival Sutherland, Theresa Rachel Davidson, Herschel Lew Zuraw, and the attempted murder of Peter William Landis."

"No!" Benton cried, backing away from him. "No . . ."

Birdsong nodded at the two constables, who stepped closer to their prisoner until he was forced against the back wall, in between the props and ropes, against the pinrail that held the tackle and pulleys.

"Come now, Mr. Benton," Grady coaxed. "This won't do you no good."

"There's no way out there," Birdsong said calmly. "Don't give us any trouble, and we won't have to give you any, eh?"

Drew stared at Benton as the man shrank against the bricks. He was a good actor, there was no denying it, but there was fear and rage now in his dark eyes, deep and true and real.

"Stay here, darling," Landis told Fleur, and he moved to where Benton cowered, looking ready to stand between him and the door should the need arise. "Best go quietly, Benton. You can't get away."

"You *are* a fool, aren't you, Landis?" Benton sneered, though his lips trembled. "I never killed those people!"

"No use lying," Drew said. "There's no way all this was done by one person. You and your lady friend have been switching back and forth, alibiing each other. It wasn't Miss Winston. She loves . . ." He glanced at the blushing nursemaid and shook his head. "There's no romantic connection between the two of you. After living with Ravenswood's endless peccadilloes, I daresay Miss Cullimore is more interested in the theater than any intrigues of her own. And then there is our elusive Miss Tracy. Everyone thinks she's one of the victims here, killed for what she knew, for what was in those papers she took away with her.

But suppose she has merely been in hiding all this time, helping you commit murder, free to come and go as she pleases and never looked for. I suppose now that you've been found out, she'll leave you to take all the blame. Your lover would never do that to you, would she, Benton? Leave you to hang for murders you didn't do?"

Benton stood there, gnawing his lip, and then he shook his head. "I tell you I never killed those people." He looked coolly at Fleur. "*We* did. Together."

They all turned to where Fleur stood toward the back of the stage, her graceful white-gloved hands clasped in front of her open mouth.

"I . . ." She gaped at her husband and then at the chief inspector. "I knew he hated me, but I didn't think even he would stoop to this. Trying to ruin me for spite?"

"Don't lie, Fleur!" The color came up into Benton's face. "For once in your miserable life, don't lie."

"Your legal name is Edgar Benton Crowley," Drew said when no one else spoke. "I see where you get the Benton portion of your stage name. Why did you choose Conor?"

Benton looked at him as if he'd lost his mind. "It's an old Irish name. Means *wolf*. Why in the world does that matter?"

Drew smiled. "So that's why you signed your note 'your wanton wolf,' is it?"

"So? What's that got to do with anything?"

"The note said 'my flower.' Florence. Fleur." Drew turned to Fleur. "It has to be you, Mrs. Landis."

She shook her head slowly, dark eyes wide and bewildered. "I think you're absolutely mad."

"No," Drew said. "It's the only way it makes sense. I've been thinking, ever since Peter was poisoned . . . Miss Winston, please tell us again about when Peter got into that candy."

The nursemaid looked rather flustered. "Well, as I said, I came into the room and found Peter popping a bit of it into his mouth. I scolded him for it and told him to give it to me at once."

"And when did Mrs. Landis come in?"

"Practically at the same time," Miss Winston replied. "She started screaming as soon as she saw what he had."

Drew nodded. "Precisely. Mrs. Landis went into hysterics the minute she saw he had gotten into the candy. She wasn't angry; she was panicked. Why would she be so upset before Peter had a chance to show any sign of distress? The only explanation is that she knew the candy was poisoned. Because she had put the poison in it herself. I'm terribly sorry, Landis. I didn't want it to be this way, but there it is."

Landis was ash pale and looked as if he had somehow sunken into himself. "Fleur?"

She looked at him as if struggling to speak.

352

Finally she blinked and said, "It's not like they make it sound, Brent. Really, it isn't. They both hate me because I wouldn't have them. Now they're trying to spoil things between you and me."

"You didn't actually kill anyone, did you, Fleur? Not . . . Merciful God, you couldn't have wanted to kill Peter. He's no more than a baby. Your own child!"

Tears filled her eyes. "That was an accident! He wasn't meant to get into those chocolates. I put them up on the shelf so no one would get into them."

"You poisoned the candy for what reason, Mrs. Landis?"

The chief inspector's voice was devoid of emotion, and when Fleur turned her pleading eyes on him, his expression didn't change.

She looked away. "Well, I had to make it look as if someone were trying to kill *me,* didn't I? I mean, if someone were trying to kill me, then it wouldn't be likely that I was the killer, wouldn't you think?"

Birdsong gave her a nod. "Perhaps you had better start at the beginning, Mrs. Landis. With the first murder. Ravenswood."

She shrugged, looking petulant now. "Johnnie was being terribly difficult. I just wanted him to be reasonable, but he wouldn't listen to me. He only laughed and said the truth must be told. I didn't know why it should be, and I told him so. But he still laughed. I couldn't bear it any longer."

"So you saw that champagne bottle there by his mirror and . . ." Landis glanced hopefully at the chief inspector. "It's not as if you meant to, is it, Fleur? Of course you didn't go there meaning to do anything like that."

Fleur shook her head. "It just . . . happened, and then, well, you know the rest. I just didn't know how to get out of the mess I'd made."

"That's not the truth, Mrs. Landis," Drew said. "It wasn't a crime of passion, a spur-of-the-moment thing. You planned this out. You and Benton. How else could he have been there when Ravenswood was murdered, with Grady specifically to alibi him? And why would you have so neatly slipped your sleeping draught into your husband's drink so you could leave the house without his knowing? You knew what a light sleeper he is."

"That's why I couldn't wake up properly the morning after he was murdered. And the morning after the girl was, as well." Landis closed his eyes. "I was so certain Fleur hadn't stirred all night."

"Too bad you hadn't noticed the pan under the car that second night, Mrs. Landis," Nick put in. "You counted on your driver being hard of hearing but not on his noticing an oil leak."

Fleur scowled at him but said nothing.

"And why Miss Davidson?" Birdsong asked.

Fleur huffed. "She knew about Conor, you see. She found that note and realized I had been seeing him. Poor little mouse. In her place I'd have scratched my eyes out." She smirked. "Of course I'm not likely to ever find myself thrown over as she was. Especially not for someone like her. She was angry enough, I suppose, but all she did was cry and tell me I ought to turn myself in or she would have to speak to the police about it. Well, I couldn't have that, could I?"

"You didn't realize she had pulled that tassel off your cloak, did you?" Drew asked. "But planting one on Zuraw when you couldn't possibly be the one who killed him would definitely make it seem someone else had done the other murders, too. The torn end of that tassel was cut off before you were arrested. Did you notice it on your way home?"

Benton glared at her when she made no answer. "That's exactly what she did. And I cut one off the second cloak and left it under Zuraw, so it would look as if someone were trying to frame her."

Birdsong's expression was coolly professional. "What about Zuraw? He told Mr. Farthering he had information to give."

"Only he didn't." Drew shook his head. "Because when I got that telephone call, he was already dead."

"We had to have some way of proving I couldn't

have killed those people," Fleur said, as if nothing else could be more obvious. "With that accent Mr. Zuraw had, dear Conor didn't have to be much of an actor to imitate him."

"And the chocolates," Birdsong said. "You say you poisoned those to make it look as if someone were trying to kill you?"

"That's not the only reason," Benton said with a glance at Fleur. "Tell them."

Fleur shrugged. "I don't know what you mean."

"Tell them!"

"I think I know," Drew said, turning back to Fleur. "Once Uncle's inheritance was safely deposited, if someone sent you poisoned chocolates and your husband just happened to eat them, that would solve two problems at once, eh?"

Landis stared dumbly at his wife, his face a picture of shock and disbelief.

"And if Miss Winston and her syringe were to be blamed for it," Drew added, "well, that would just be the whipped cream on the trifle."

Fleur looked Miss Winston up and down, painted lips curled. "As if she could possibly imagine any man of mine being interested in her. After being married to me? She would bore him to distraction."

The nursemaid only watched in stunned silence.

"Fleur . . ." Landis said, his voice half choked. "You couldn't have intended to—"

"You won't desert me now, will you, Brent?"

Drew couldn't help remembering a line from *The Mikado*, spoken by the vain, self-seeking Katisha. *"And you won't hate me because I'm just a little teeny weeny wee bit bloodthirsty, will you?"*

Landis shook his head. "Oh, Fleur."

"No one is going to take the blame for you now, Fleur," Benton said, his words venomous. "You've got no one left who'll cover for you. You'll have to face the music this time, and it's not a snappy little rumba they're playing."

"Say what you like, Conor. You know how juries are. And judges. Men, mostly. I may spend a year or two behind bars, but I won't hang." She patted her sleek black hair. "I won't hang."

Birdsong looked faintly disgusted and started toward her. "Florence Hargreaves Landis, I arrest you for the murders of—"

He broke off as Benton yanked one of the belaying pins out of its slot in the pinrail behind him. The rope whirred in the pulley and whipped up across the fly loft as the sandbag hurtled toward the stage.

"Fleur!"

Landis's cry split the air as he lunged toward his wife, as Drew and Birdsong lunged toward them both. They got there only in time to save Landis. It was too late, too horribly late, for Fleur.

"Don't look," Drew urged, pulling Landis back.

Landis fought to go to her, but Birdsong turned him away from the grim sight, propelling him toward Drew. "See to him."

"Fleur?" Landis stopped struggling, and he looked at Drew, eyes pleading. "No. She isn't . . . she can't be . . ."

Drew glanced over at Birdsong, who was kneeling down with his fingers pressed to Fleur's limp wrist. The chief inspector shook his head.

"Come now," Drew urged Landis. "There's nothing more to be done for her."

Landis squeezed his eyes shut, his breath coming now in sobbing gasps. "Fleur. My beautiful Fleur . . ."

He pushed himself away from Drew, catching hold of a ship's wheel that was part of the set decoration, clinging to it as he tried to regain control of himself.

Drew still held on to his arm, wishing there were something more he could do. Madeline and Miss Cullimore and Miss Winston merely stood there, for the moment paralyzed. Then Miss Winston hurried to Landis's side. She draped his arm across her shoulders and helped him to a metal folding chair near the back wall.

Drew glanced up and saw Benton watching them, as if he were the audience to their little drama. The two constables had him by the arms with his wrists handcuffed behind him. He gave Drew a pleased sneer.

"He ought to thank me, you know," Benton spat. "Landis ought. She'd have gotten rid of him next. Since he's already come into that money."

Drew turned to the other side of the stage. Birdsong still stood near Fleur's body, but he had laid a cloth of some sort over her head and shoulders. It made him a bit queasy to see it was the pirate flag from *Penzance*, the skull and crossbones.

Landis was looking that way too, one fist pressed to his mouth. He moved toward Benton. "You'll hang. Whatever else they can or can't prove, you can't get away from this one. Not in front of all these witnesses."

Again Benton smirked. "I might have hanged with her, but blast me if I was going to hang *for* her. And she was right. With her looks, they'd never have hanged her. Not in a million years."

"Get him out of here," Birdsong ordered, and his men escorted Benton down the center aisle and through the lobby doors.

Landis watched until the doors swung closed behind the prisoner. Then with a wrenching sob he pulled away from Miss Winston, stumbled to where Fleur lay, and sank to his knees. He didn't say anything. Instead he held Fleur's hand in its white lace glove, clutching it in his own two hands as tears coursed down his cheeks. Miss Winston stood behind him, steadying hands on his shoulders.

"Best let me have her seen to now, sir," Birdsong said, taking a step nearer. "Be grateful she couldn't have felt a thing."

"I loved her, you know," Landis said. "I mean, I wanted to love her. She would never quite let me close to her. I thought . . . I thought if I loved her enough, she would be content, she would change. I knew what she was, but I thought she wanted to be different. She told me she wanted to be. For Peter. For me . . ."

He looked down at the hand he still held, soft and slim and perfect, and pressed a kiss to the palm.

"I was a fool. A blind fool." His laugh was almost soundless. "No, I was worse than blind. I chose not to see. I so much wanted her to be what I needed her to be, I couldn't see what she was. But I loved her." With one more kiss he laid her hand gracefully over her heart.

Drew helped Landis to his feet while nodding at the chief inspector.

"Take him home," Birdsong told Miss Winston. "Take care of him. We'll see to everything here."

Miss Winston took Landis's arm.

"Drive them, will you, Nick?" Drew said.

"Right."

Nick led Miss Winston and Landis down the aisle and out of the theater.

Drew looked at the form lying on the stage, at the skull on the flag draped over Fleur's no-longer-beautiful face. The skull seemed to be grinning at him in triumph, and once again the words of *The Mikado* came to mind. *"And let the punishment fit the crime, the punishment fit the crime."*

He was suddenly aware of Madeline pressed against his side, her eyes also fixed on the tragic figure there before the footlights. He had to get her out of here. They both had to get out.

"Madeline . . ." He shook his head, feeling helpless and weary, and she put her arm through his, saying nothing. "I would never have wished this on her, no matter what she's done."

"No," Madeline whispered. "No, of course not." After a pause, she added, "I'm so sorry—sorry for him and for her, for all of them."

"Mr. Farthering?"

Drew took a quick breath, steadying himself before he turned. It was Miss Cullimore. She surprised him by taking his hand in hers.

"Her name was Marie Fabron. She worked at a milliner's off the *Rue de la Paix*. But after so long, I can't remember if the owner was Madame Thibault or Tolbert or Travere. Something like that. It was next to a jeweler's. Marie rarely spoke of her family, but she said they were from Grenoble. She had a younger brother in Marseilles. She was so pretty, and I recall she was very kind, too. I can't remember anything other than that."

He stood silent for a long moment, taking it all in, and then he opened his mouth.

"That's all I know," she said before he could ask, regret plain on her face. "You've kept your part of the bargain. Thank you. I wish I could tell you more." She squeezed his hand. "She had blue eyes."

"I'm sorry, Drew," Madeline said when Miss Cullimore was gone. "I too wish she could have told you more."

"So do I," he said, "but at least it's something to go on. A place to start."

She sighed. "I suppose that's all there is to it, then. The case, I mean. It's all over."

"No. It's not all over. There's still Benton to be seen to, and exactly why Fleur wanted to kill Ravenswood in the first place, and whatever happened to that lady reporter. And I—"

"We'll see to all that in time," Birdsong interrupted. "After we've looked after things here. Mr. Hibbert, once the coroner has seen to the body . . . ?"

"Right you are, Chief Inspector," said Grady, touching his forehead. "I'll see to things here. Like I always have."

"Right." Birdsong turned again to Drew. "You ought to take the young lady home now. The rest will wait."

Drew didn't argue with him. He gave the chief inspector a grateful nod and escorted Madeline out to the Rolls, and together they headed back to Farthering Place.

● ● ●

Dinner that evening was quiet and rather melancholy, and afterward everyone went early to bed. It wasn't long after breakfast the next day that the chief inspector rang up and asked Drew and Madeline to come to his office to discuss the remainder of the Landis case.

"Benton's confessed his part in it all," Birdsong told them. "As you suspected, Mrs. Landis killed Ravenswood and Tess Davidson. He killed Zuraw to alibi Mrs. Landis."

"Zuraw didn't actually know anything about anything, did he?" Drew said.

"No. He was merely convenient."

Madeline glanced at Drew, her expression troubled. "But why did she kill Ravenswood in the first place? Nobody knew about her and Benton, did they?"

"Not as far as Benton knows," Birdsong said. "Miss Cullimore claims it wasn't common knowledge around the Tivoli. Evidently . . ." The telephone on his desk rang. Excusing himself, he picked up the receiver. "Birdsong here." He paused, and then the annoyance in his expression turned into incredulity. "Oh, she is, is she? Well, certainly. Send her in." He hung up, looking smug.

"Good news, I see," Drew observed.

There was a knock at the door, and Birdsong hurried to open it, admitting a constable and a petite blonde wearing tweeds and carrying a leather satchel. The chief inspector dismissed the officer and invited the woman in, shutting the door behind her.

Drew immediately got to his feet, and Birdsong made the introduction.

"This is Miss Madeline Parker and Mr. Drew Farthering. They've been looking into the Ravenswood case with us."

The woman nodded as Birdsong's smile grew even more smug. "Mr. Farthering, Miss Parker, I'd like to introduce you to Miss Josephine Tracy, journalist."

Drew glanced at Madeline, one eyebrow lifted, and then he made a slight bow. "Miss Tracy, we're *very* pleased to meet you."

Birdsong offered Miss Tracy a chair, and they all took their seats, with the chief inspector once more ensconcing himself behind his desk.

"Now, Miss Tracy," said Birdsong, "if you would, perhaps you could tell us where you've been for the past seventeen days."

"Aberystwyth," she said with a smile.

Madeline gave Drew a blank look. "Aber *what?*"

"Aberystwyth is in Wales," Birdsong replied.

The journalist nodded. "When I heard Johnnie Ravenswood was murdered, I knew I had to make myself scarce. I knew he was going to stir up trouble, but I didn't think it would get him killed."

"What do you mean, 'stir up trouble'? How?" Drew asked.

She slapped the satchel onto Birdsong's desk and opened it. "This."

She pulled out a sheaf of unbound typewritten pages. Written on the first page were the words *John Sullivan Ravenswood, A Life, by John Sullivan Ravenswood with Josephine Tracy.*

"A tell-all?" Madeline said.

Miss Tracy chuckled. "And we certainly told *all.*"

"Including your own escapades?" Drew asked.

The journalist shrugged. "He and I didn't last long as an item. I knew we wouldn't. He never stayed interested in anyone very long. It wasn't his way." Her mouth turned up at one side. "At least not after he'd had his way. But that didn't keep us from collaborating on the book. You know what my column is like. People eat it up, and the more lurid the better."

"But Fleur . . ."

"Well, apparently, at least for a while, Fleur Hargreaves was an exception. *The* exception, if you exclude his actual wife. She and Johnnie couldn't get enough of each other, even when there were others off and on. Even when they fought. They were no good together, of course. And when he threw her over—once she started to lose her figure when her baby was coming—everything she felt for him turned to hate. It was worse when he wouldn't hate her in return. He only laughed her off, no matter what she did, but she finally hit him where it hurt."

"By marrying Mr. Landis?" Madeline asked, and Drew nodded.

"He couldn't imagine her claiming to be in love with anyone but himself, and that's why he decided to pay her out with this book."

"Benton claims she killed him for daring to send her off," Birdsong said.

"That may be what she told him, but it was more than that." Miss Tracy gave him a knowing glance. "Johnnie knew about that uncle of her husband's and knew how much Fleur was counting on ending up with his money. The book would certainly have spoilt that for her. Obviously she didn't want that, and when I heard Johnnie was dead, I didn't want to be next on her list."

"This is what she threatened Ravenswood about in the pub a week before he was murdered," Drew said.

The reporter nodded.

"Why didn't you report this to the police, miss?" Birdsong asked.

The reporter shook her head. "You wouldn't have believed me. You didn't believe Benton when he told you straight out that it was Fleur. That's what they were counting on, I suppose. I didn't dare come back until I read this morning's paper and saw that she was dead."

Drew studied her for a moment. "Is there anything in your book about the child?"

"Well, of course there is. It's one of the juiciest bits."

"Did Ravenswood claim paternity? In the book, I mean."

"Oh, yes, and he was fairly certain of it," Miss Tracy said. "I never saw Peter, of course. I don't know if Johnnie ever did, either. But he knew Landis's rich uncle wouldn't have given them a penny once Johnnie staked his claim on the boy."

Drew glanced at Madeline and saw a touch of worry in her eyes. "I suppose you're still set on publishing this book," he said to the reporter.

"I've spent five months on it," Miss Tracy said. "And now that Johnnie's dead, the book will sell ten times better than it ever would have before. Especially once I add the part about Fleur and Benton and the murders."

"And Peter?" Drew asked.

"Oh, he'll definitely be in it."

"Drew," Madeline murmured, her eyes pleading.

Drew gave her a nod and turned again to the reporter. "Could you perhaps leave that bit out? As a personal favor to all of us."

"About the boy being Johnnie's? Why ever should I?"

"Is it really necessary to burden the little chap

with that his whole life? I'd think the story is lurid enough as it is."

Miss Tracy frowned. "It will no doubt come out whether or not I say anything."

"But that may not be for some time yet. Poor Landis has lost enough just now, don't you think? Perhaps we can leave him just this little bit of consolation?"

"Absolutely not," Miss Tracy said.

"But suppose," Drew said, "we come to some agreement where you promise to leave any mention of Brent Landis and Peter Landis out of all your future publications, and I promise to make it worth your while."

Miss Tracy folded her hands in front of herself. "I'm listening."

"You're very sweet," Madeline said when they were more than halfway home.

He glanced over at her and dredged up a smile. "Am I?"

"You are. Taking care of Peter like that. And Mr. Landis."

"Well, it was small enough payment to spare them both."

"It might still come out one day, you know," she said. "People do talk, and they do make assumptions."

"Yes, I suppose they do." His smile was warmer now, and she realized how much she had missed it. "But that's a worry for another time. I've heard that today's evils are enough for today. Don't you agree?"

"Yes." She sat huddled on her side of the front seat, feeling more awkward beside him than she ever had. Finally she shook her head. "And I'm sorry I've hurt you. I think maybe I understand a bit more than I did before. About her. About how you were taken in by her."

"How can I explain it?" he said. "You make my blood race just by coming into the room, and yet I'm never so comfortable as when I'm with you. It was never that way with Fleur. Yes, she fascinated me. Certainly I was infatuated with her. But I could never relax around her. I could never just be myself and know that would be good enough for her. I dared be nothing less than sparkling and witty every moment I was in her presence. And you remember how she was that night at dinner. She was always like that. Always onstage, always in character. Who was she really? I don't know. I don't expect many people do. Poor Landis certainly never seemed to."

She sighed a little. "It's all kind of sad, isn't it, Drew? He always seemed as if he was trying desperately to love her enough to fill that space between them."

"And that's exactly what I felt when I thought I loved her, that if I tried hard enough, if I was stylish and witty and clever enough, if I could devote myself to her enough and be everything she wanted, that glorious, exotic creature would love me in return. Ah, well, one is eighteen only once, thank the Lord."

He gave her a rueful smile, and she quickly looked away. Eighteen. She had been eighteen when Jimmy had deceived her and when dazzling Dinah had taken him away forever. But she had recovered. She'd learned to be strong and confident and practical, to value her own intrinsic worth apart from what anyone else said or did. At least she had until . . .

"I guess I'm not as secure as I thought I was," she said.

"What's that?"

She turned back to him, gaze steady, chin lifted. "I was pretty sure of myself until Fleur showed up."

"Madeline, I don't—"

"You still don't understand. I don't know if I did till now. It wasn't how you felt about her that bothered me. It was how I felt. She made me feel dull and plain and stupid and totally unworthy of being loved." She blinked hard, trying not to cry. "Just like that woman who took Jimmy away from me."

"I never thought you were any of those things," he said softly. "Seeing you next to Fleur only showed me how right you were for me and how very, very wrong she had been."

"It's more than that." She fished a handkerchief out of her skirt pocket. "You once asked my forgiveness for not being the paragon I was looking for. Well, what if I'm not what you think I am? What would you have done when you found out I'm petty and willful and jealous and everything else? I knew I was most of that already, but I didn't think I would be jealous. I can't stand jealous women. And I never really felt jealous about any of the girls who flirted with you. No one but Fleur. Oh, Drew, I hated her for hurting you the way she did, and because . . ." Her gaze faltered, and she looked down again. "Because you were hers first."

"Madeline," he breathed.

Her eyes stung with tears. "Pretty, huh? The charming Miss Parker in all her glory."

She didn't really start to cry until he pulled the car over and took her into his arms, whispering her name, kissing her hair.

"Madeline, darling, I'm so sorry. I'm sorry I've made you feel that I expect you to be perfect. Heaven knows, you've put up with me, even with all my faults and foolishness. How could I do any less?"

"But you don't know . . ."

He held her away from him, making his face comically fierce. "You haven't swindled money from widows and orphans, have you?"

She laughed and then sniffed. "No."

"No radical political views I ought to know about?"

She shook her head. "Nothing like that. Just ordinary, everyday pride and lust and envy and anger and greed and laziness."

He grinned just the slightest bit. "Thank heavens you're not a glutton."

"Well, I do like chocolate much more than I should."

She sniffled again, smiling weakly. His expression grew stern, yet there was a barely discernible glint of humor in his eyes.

"So, what you mean to tell me, Miss Parker, is that you won't marry me because I might eventually find out you're human?"

She blinked hard, fighting tears once more. "I don't think you know what you're getting into."

He pulled her close again. "And I would be quite unhappy if I never had the opportunity to find out."

His voice was low and caressing. His eyes were tender, vulnerable, honest.

Honest.

"You can't know. You can only believe and go forward and trust God one day at a time." Aunt Ruth's words came back to her.

Madeline took a little hiccupping breath. *Oh, God, show me what to do.*

"Drew, are you sure? Are you really and truly sure?"

"Darling, the longer I know you, the more certain I am that we were meant for each other. I will wait for you if you like. If you insist, I will let you go. But I will always love you. No one I have ever met has charmed me and challenged me, soothed me and nettled me, or fit so perfectly into my heart and life as you. If you leave me, I will not die." He swallowed hard. "But I don't think I will ever be quite whole again." He nuzzled her ear. "Please, Madeline darling, marry me. Unless truly you don't love me, marry me."

"Oh, Drew." She pressed her face into the curve of his neck, wetting it with her tears. "I've always loved you. I just don't want you to be sorry."

"I could never be sorry about that, darling. Please say yes."

She nodded against him, and then she felt the low rumble of his laugh.

"With everything canceled, we may have to get married at the registrar's office. Would you mind terribly?"

She looked up at him. "See? No telling how many times I will put you through something like this once we're married."

"But will you love me?"

Again there was that sweet tenderness in his eyes, that searching vulnerability. She put her hand to his cheek. Life was fleeting and unsure, how well she knew that just now, but she couldn't be afraid to live it. She couldn't be afraid to take those blessings God had sent her.

"Always, Drew. Always."

She couldn't seal the pledge any better than with a kiss. Then Drew pulled back onto the road and drove them home to Farthering Place.

— *Twenty* —

The moment they arrived at Farthering Place, Madeline gave Drew another kiss and then scurried up the stairs and tapped on her aunt's door, knowing her face was flushed with happiness. If Aunt Ruth wanted to berate her for being fickle and foolish, well, that would be all right. She *was* fickle and she *was* foolish, but she was loved, so none of the rest mattered.

"All right. All right. Give a body a moment to get decent."

Aunt Ruth opened the door, wearing her bathrobe and slippers, her silvery hair damp and hanging nearly to her waist.

"What's the matter?" Aunt Ruth hurried Madeline over to the bed and sat down beside her. "Good thing you're going home and not staying here to always be rubbing elbows with killers and lunatics."

Madeline felt the tears well up again in her eyes, but she somehow managed to laugh, too.

"What's ailing you?" Aunt Ruth demanded.

"Well, Drew and I were talking. I think we worked things out and, well . . ." Madeline gave her aunt an apologetic look and showed her the ring was again on her finger.

Aunt Ruth pursed her lips. "I suppose you want the whole thing on again, eh?"

Madeline bit her lip and nodded, feeling like a mischievous child but far too happy to care. "Do you think it's too late to make all the arrangements and invite everyone again?"

Aunt Ruth frowned. "And I suppose I'm the one who's supposed to run around like I haven't got sense and try to put everything back together for you. Well, I won't do it. I won't do it, and you won't, either. Do you think you can just snap your fingers and it's all done?"

"Fine. Drew and I will go to the registrar's office and be married there. Not a church wedding, of course, but we'll be married all the same. He says he doesn't mind what we do."

Aunt Ruth gaped at her. "The registrar's? In that cathedral-length veil? No, ma'am. You just put that idea right out of your mind."

"Don't you want us to get married at all?"

"I do want you to be married. I want you properly married under the roof of a church, and I want you to get married there on the tenth of December just as you planned."

"But the guests, the caterers, the flowers—"

"They're all arranged. Have been for weeks now."

Madeline narrowed her eyes, and then a slow smile tugged at the corners of her mouth. "You never canceled anything, did you?"

"I did not." Aunt Ruth's expression was both serene and smug. "Don't you think I've seen the pair of you all this time? I knew the wedding would be on again before long."

"And what if it hadn't been? What were you going to do?"

Aunt Ruth shrugged. "I'd have seen to it, if need be. But I wasn't worried. I've seen wedding jitters before." She put her hands on either side of Madeline's face, smiling into her eyes. "Whatever else I may have said, and no matter how he seems to attract trouble, I can't imagine anyone so perfect for you as this Englishman of yours."

Madeline beamed at her, feeling a blush touch her cheeks.

"No one else has ever put that look on your face. Jimmy Adams certainly never did, poor boy." Aunt Ruth stroked back Madeline's hair and kissed her forehead. "Now I want you to stop worrying about wedding plans and relax. It's all taken care of."

Madeline nodded, still smiling.

"Now go on and find your detective and let me get into something warm before I catch my death.

No doubt he's owed a bit of pampering after what you've put him through."

Madeline threw her arms around her aunt. "Thank you for not canceling everything when I told you to."

There was a twinkle in Aunt Ruth's eyes. "That's what sensible maiden aunts are for."

With a giggle and a wave, Madeline went to look for Drew.

Drew and Madeline were lingering over their after-lunch coffee when Dennison came into the dining room and announced Mr. Landis.

"I'll come straight to the point, Mr. Farthering, if you'll both excuse me," Landis said. "I don't suppose you'll want me at the office any longer, what with the scandal and all." There was a deep weariness in his pale face. "I'm terribly sorry."

"Nonsense." Drew gestured to the chair next to his. "Do sit down. Coffee?"

Landis sat. "Just some tea, if you don't mind."

Madeline poured his tea, and then she cut a slice of cake and set it on a plate in front of him.

"Now," Drew said, "I don't want you to think for a moment that you can wriggle out of your contract with Farlinford. Our solicitors are quite good, and they saw to it that you'd be with us for some while to come."

Landis held his teacup in both hands, not

drinking. "That's just it. I don't . . . I don't think I can go back to the office quite yet."

"Naturally, and we can survive a while without you," said Drew, and he took a bite of cake himself. "Come back when you're ready."

A relieved touch of color came into Landis's face. "That's very kind of you, sir. I . . . I just need to get away from everything for a while."

"And the boy? I suppose Miss Winston can look after him while you're gone. They could stay here. I know Peter likes it at the old place, and we're quite pleased to have him."

"Oh, no, sir." Landis waved his hand in protest, and on his face was the first genuine smile Drew had seen from him since that day at the Tivoli. "I couldn't do without him. At the moment I'm finding it rather difficult to believe there are many things right with the world, but I know he's one of them. No, I couldn't possibly do without him."

"Are you certain?" Drew asked, watching the man's eyes.

Landis looked rather determined. "You mean do I realize he's not actually mine?"

Drew couldn't help feeling bad for him. "Well, there's been talk. I wasn't certain whether you would want to—"

"Peter is my son. In every way that matters, he is. Legally as well. He was born during my marriage to Fleur, so he is absolutely mine. And I thank God for him."

"Where will you go?" Madeline asked, pushing the platter containing macaroons within his reach.

With a nod, Landis took one. "I've decided on Venice. There's a cousin on my father's side who lives there with his Italian wife and their seven children. They haven't got two beans, but they're happy as larks and always asking me to come and stay for a bit. Peter will have a lovely time meeting them all, I'm sure."

"Sounds a fine idea," Drew said. "Take as long as you like. Your position will be waiting for you at Farlinford when you're ready."

"I think a fortnight, perhaps three weeks, should make all the difference," Landis said, taking a tentative bite of the macaroon and then, almost as if his enjoyment of it surprised him, two more. "I've made plans to leave this afternoon, if you don't object."

"We'll be sorry to see you go."

Madeline nodded. "I'm sorry we won't get to say goodbye to Peter."

"You may, if you'd like," Landis said. "He's out in the car with Miss Winston. We're headed down to Southampton straightaway."

Madeline grabbed Drew's hand and practically pulled him outside and down the front steps. At the sight of them, Peter bounced up and down in the Daimler's backseat, until Miss Winston opened the door and let him out. Then he hugged them both around the legs.

"We're going to Italy!" the boy announced. "How many 'talian cousins do we have, Daddy?"

Landis chuckled. "Lots and lots. Now tell Mr. Drew and Miss Madeline thank you."

Peter hugged his arms around Madeline's skirt once more. "Can't you and Mr. Drew come to Italy, too?"

She patted his cheek. "I'm afraid not, Peter. We have to have our wedding."

"Then can you come to Italy?"

She hugged him and handed him to Drew.

"Now what is Mr. Chambers going to do without you?" Drew asked the boy.

"Can *he* come to Italy with us?"

Drew laughed. "I'm afraid not, but I'm certain he will miss you."

Peter looked at him, forehead puckered. "Will you miss me, Mr. Drew?"

"Very much," Drew admitted. "But you'll have a fine time with your cousins, and before you know it, you'll be right back in England and back in your own house with Miss Winston and your father. How will you like that?"

"But not Mummy. Mummy isn't coming back."

Drew hugged him close. "No, I'm afraid she isn't."

Landis cleared his throat. "Peter . . ."

"Come along now, Peter," Miss Winston said, her voice cheerful, and she took the boy from Drew. "Tell Mr. Drew goodbye."

"Let me have him," Landis said, perfectly composed. "We Landises have to stick together, don't we, son?"

Peter beamed at him. "You betcha."

Landis gave Drew a grateful nod and carried the boy back to the car.

Miss Winston paused at the car. "Goodbye, miss. Sir."

"Goodbye," Madeline said. "Do take good care of him."

The nursemaid smiled. "I will. Don't you worry."

Her face reddened just the slightest bit when Landis took her hand to help her inside next to Peter. With Peter waving out the back window, the Daimler roared away and was soon out of sight.

Drew stood for a moment, looking down the drive toward the now-empty road. He smiled when he felt Madeline slip her arm through his and twine their fingers together.

"Do you suppose she meant Peter or Mr. Landis?"

He raised an eyebrow. "What?"

"When she said she would take good care of him. Miss Winston, I mean."

Drew pulled her a little closer to his side. "Both, I hope. Perhaps he'll be able to appreciate her before long. In a year or two, maybe even love her."

She looked out at the road. "She does love him, doesn't she?"

"I think so. And terribly. In a 'for better or for worse' sort of way."

A wistful sort of sadness came into Madeline's eyes. "I don't suppose he would have ever gotten that kind of love from Fleur."

"I don't think Fleur had it in her." Drew squeezed her hand. "He'll get along just fine, though. He's loved."

"You are too."

He looked down into her beautiful, earnest eyes and saw a glimmer of tears. "Bless you, darling."

"I'm sorry, Drew . . . for being so jealous. I do know I can trust you."

He kissed her forehead. "That's all behind us now." A moment later he shook his head. "But poor Landis. He's a good chap, and I can't say he deserved all that Fleur put him through."

Madeline nestled closer to him. "Maybe it wasn't really about him. Maybe it was for the sake of someone else."

"Someone . . ." Drew nodded. "The little fellow is in good hands after all, isn't he?"

"The very best," Madeline said, looking again toward the road. "The very best."

"There she is!"

Madeline rushed over to the edge of the dock,

waving her white handkerchief and smiling, even though the cold wind off the sea stung her eyes. There on the upper deck of the ship, leaning over the rail, was a petite strawberry blonde searching the crowd onshore.

"Madeline!" she called, waving back.

Nick gave Drew a nudge as he moved closer to the ship, his eyes on the diminutive girl. Her eyes met his and somehow managed to grow even brighter. Before long she was working her way through the crowd coming down the gangplank.

Madeline ran to her and embraced her tightly. "I didn't think you'd ever get here." She pulled Drew up next to them. "Drew, you remember Carrie."

Drew removed his hat. "Indeed I do. Welcome back. And of course you remember Nick Dennison."

Madeline gave Nick a little push toward Carrie, and he gave her an unsteady smile, belatedly remembering to remove his own hat.

Madeline frowned, still searching the crowd. "Where's Muriel?"

"Oh." Carrie put one white-gloved hand over her mouth and giggled. "Well, it was like this—"

"Carrie? You're going to lose me in this crowd if you're not careful."

Madeline blinked at the rather stout older man who approached them just then, a valise and a suitcase in his hands. "Mr. Holland, how nice to see you!" She hugged him, then looked at Carrie. "I thought . . ."

Again Carrie giggled. "So did I. Daddy, this is Drew Farthering, Madeline's fiancé, and his friend Nick Dennison. Boys, this is my daddy."

"Pleased to meet you, sir," Drew said at once, shaking his hand.

Nick swallowed hard and followed suit. "Yes. Pleased to meet you, sir."

"It's so nice to have you," Madeline said. "Almost like having my own father here. But where in the world is Muriel?"

"Muriel decided to elope with a drummer she met at the hotel we were staying at in New York," explained Carrie. "Daddy absolutely wouldn't let me come alone, so I told him he'd better come with me, and well, he did!"

"You didn't meet any drummers, did you, Miss Holland?" Nick asked, looking as if his future life and happiness depended on her answer.

Drew suppressed a smile. Perhaps Madeline was right, and Nick had been pining. He was glad it was for Carrie and not for Barbie Chalfont, after all.

"I leave all that to Muriel," Carrie said with a laugh.

Nick grinned, obviously relieved. "Shall I go and collect your luggage?"

Carrie glanced at Madeline and then looked up

at Nick. "Thank you. Maybe I'd better go with you—I mean, to make sure you get everything."

Madeline looked at Drew as they walked away, and he could see the I-told-you-so in her eyes, though she didn't say anything. Instead she took Mr. Holland's arm.

"What a surprise to see you," she said. "But a wonderful one."

He nodded while still trying to keep his eye on his daughter.

"You don't have to worry," Madeline assured him. "Nick's a perfect gentleman. And while they're seeing to the luggage, I have a favor to ask you."

The tenth day of December came in crisply cold yet blue as May. Drew peered out from a dining room window, across the snowy meadow toward Farthering St. John, toward the Church of the Holy Trinity and All Angels. It was perfection, and a grand day for a wedding.

He couldn't believe that he and Madeline had met only six months ago, six months almost to the day. It had been a scandalously short engagement according to conventional wisdom, but when he considered all they had been through together in such a short time, he couldn't imagine waiting would make him any more certain of her than he was already. He could imagine no one else at his side, no matter what the future held.

"There is a telephone call for you, sir."

Drew sighed and set his teacup back on its saucer with a rattle. "What is it now, Denny? Of all the days that I should be let alone, surely this one is paramount."

"I'm very sorry, sir. But I believe it is most urgent."

Drew glanced at Nick, who was smirking at him over his lunch, and tossed his napkin onto the table and stood. "Very well. Who is it?"

Denny's usual grave expression didn't change. "The young lady declined to say, sir."

Drew scowled. "I promise you, if it's Daphne Pomphrey-Hughes ringing up again to find out where the wedding will be, I will carry Madeline bodily from her room and take her to a registrar in London. The rest of you can have the grand supper and that cake which looks more like Everest than a dessert."

Nick laughed. "Go on and take your call. But if it's another mystery that wants solving, you'd best tell the woman she has the wrong number."

Drew's eyes widened. "There will be absolutely no cases whatsoever until Madeline and I are well and truly married."

He hurried into the study and picked up the telephone. "Hello?"

"Hello, darling."

He sank into the chair behind the desk with a relieved sigh. "Madeline. I'm so glad it's you.

I . . . no, wait a minute. Are we supposed to speak to each other before the wedding?"

"It's all right. I just wanted to thank you, Drew. The pearls are gorgeous. And I have a feeling they come with a history."

"Indeed they do. My father's grandmother was given them for her wedding sometime in the middle of the last century. Since then, all the Farthering brides have worn them. None, I daresay, as fetchingly as you." He leaned back in his chair. "And how is my bride on this her wedding day?"

"Deliriously happy. Terrified. Eager. A little nauseous. I think that mostly covers it."

He laughed softly at her cheerful confession. "My poor darling. And still with three hours to go."

"What about you?" she asked. "Have you changed your mind yet?"

"Oh, no. Definitely not."

"Not the slightest doubt?" she asked.

There was just the hint of a quaver in her voice, and he wished he could rush upstairs and take her into his arms, tradition be hanged.

"Do you want to wait, sweetheart?" He didn't really want to ask the question, but he thought it would be better asked now than later. Postponing the wedding at this point, awkward as that would be, was far better than having the bride not turn up at the altar. Or, heaven help them, having her flee from it. If she wasn't certain still, he didn't want her to feel pressured into anything.

"Darling?" he asked when she didn't reply. "Are you crying?"

"No," she said with a sniffle. "No, I'm just . . ." *She is crying.*

"Madeline? I don't want you to do this if you aren't ready."

"I *am* ready, Drew." She giggled. "Really. The only thing that scares me is how happy I am. I think it can't be true, and I'm afraid you'll decide you'd rather not marry me, after all. Especially since I can't decide whether to laugh or cry."

He let out a breath. "Just jitters, darling. I suppose all brides have them."

"You're not nervous, Drew? Not at all?"

"No. I've been sure of you since I first met you. It's as if I've been trying to solve a puzzle for ever so long, and with you all the pieces just seemed to have fallen into place." He chuckled. "But you did devil me terribly when you were deciding if you felt the same way."

"I wasn't deciding. I just wanted to make sure you were serious and that I wasn't just infatuated."

"Your aunt wouldn't have allowed such nonsense for long, I don't think," Drew said. "And you'd likely still be wondering about me if she hadn't insisted I was a cad and up to no good."

"Well, she was right."

"Steady on there."

She giggled. "I mean she was right that if I wasn't sure enough about you to defend you to her, I had no business marrying you. And I do want to marry you. I'm just a little giddy, that's all. I can't quite believe it's happening at last."

"It very definitely is happening. Now go do whatever it is you brides do before you appear in all your radiant glory, and I'll just sit here counting the minutes until the time arrives."

"I love you, Drew," she said, "and I will see you at three."

She made a little smack of a kiss into the telephone and then rang off, and he had to smile. Three o'clock could not arrive soon enough.

The low winter sun shone bright through the windows, staining the stone floor of the church, adding touches of color to the white of the candles, the great bouquets of roses, and the organza that had been draped from pew to pew. Between the invited guests and the parishioners who had also come, there wasn't a spare seat in the place, and most everyone else from the village were lined up on either side of the path that led from the road to the church door. They huddled together with coats and wraps over their Sunday best, smiling and chattering away as they waited for the much-anticipated arrival of the bride.

How long had Drew been standing here? Only a

few minutes, no doubt, although it seemed much longer than that. He scanned the pews for the hundredth time.

"Where's Bunny?"

"Late as always," Nick said. "Or he forgot the date. Or where the church was located. Or he noticed someone's new motor car outside the post office or something."

"Or something," Drew grumbled.

Aunt Ruth was there in the front pew, looking lovely in rose-colored silk, so Madeline must be dressed and ready. He ran one finger inside his suddenly tight collar.

Nick grinned at him. "Not at all nervous, eh?"

Drew narrowed his eyes, not wanting anyone in the congregation to see him scowling just now. "It's deuced hot, that's all."

"It's cold as stone in here and you know it." Nick chuckled. "She'll be here. Don't worry."

Drew looked up at the window above the altar, at the lovely old stained glass that colored the sunshine. Christ in His glory, beckoning all who would come to Him, His expression gentle, merciful, loving.

Drew closed his eyes. How could he possibly thank Him for Madeline? He thought of Landis and the torment Fleur had put him through, a torment that, despite his stumbling, Drew had been spared. He thought of Simone Cullimore, who had lived for years with her husband's unfaithfulness. He thought of Tess Davidson, who hadn't been loved at all.

And then there was Madeline.

He swallowed down the tightness in his throat. There was Madeline. *Help me, dear God, to love her as you love her, to give myself for her as you did, and to thank you daily for the gift you've given me in her.*

As Mrs. Bartlett began playing the wedding march, Nick gave him a subtle elbow to the ribs. Drew opened his eyes, suddenly aware of nothing but the slender, graceful vision in lace and white slipper satin walking arm in arm beside Carrie's father, her veil falling almost to her feet in front and stretched for yards behind her, and a little cameo of an angel over her heart. His bride at last. *Oh, sweet Madeline.*

He stood there frozen, until Nick nudged him again and gave him a little push toward where she was standing. Evidently, Mr. Holland was giving this woman to be married here today, and Drew was certainly not going to miss out on the offer.

He moved to Madeline's side and took her hand. It was trembling slightly in his, and somehow that steadied him as he said his vows. By some miracle they came out clear, composed and coherent, and before he knew it, he was sliding a smooth band of gold onto Madeline's finger. Then he swiftly brought the back of her hand to his lips, pressing it with a fervent kiss. It wasn't really part of the ceremony, but he didn't care.

She touched her free hand to his cheek and then, when he was standing straight again, she took up his ring, her hand warm and soft as she put the gleaming gold on his finger. He drew a hard breath at her touch, blinking to clear his blurred sight, and afterward they both lifted their eyes to Mr. Bartlett.

"Insomuch as Ellison Andrew and Madeline Felicity have consented to live forever together in wedlock, I pronounce that they are husband and wife." He nodded serenely to the bride and groom. "You may now seal the promises you have made to each other with a kiss."

Drew gathered up her veil, lifted the frothy white lace over her head, and let it fall back with the part that trailed behind her. Her eyes sought his, bluer and more lovely than ever for the tears that stood in them. Her mouth was turned up, poised for his kiss. He took both of her hands in his and leaned down, touching her lips with a reverent and holy kiss. Then, because one was not nearly enough, he grinned slyly and kissed her again. She caught her breath and threw her arms around him, laughing for pure joy.

There was a murmur of surprise and a ripple of laughter through the congregation. From the front pew, Aunt Ruth gave Drew a look of stern reproof, yet there was a twinkle in her eyes, too.

Drew and Madeline quickly signed the register, and then together they began walking down the center aisle again. Madeline stopped to give her aunt a kiss and a hug. Drew took the older woman's hand and bent to kiss it, but she pulled him into a hug, as well.

"You be good to my girl," she said, her voice soft.

He gave her a wink and a kiss on the cheek, then took Madeline's hand again. With the congregation pouring out behind them and the merry church bells ringing, they stepped into the December sunshine. Waiting for them there in the middle of more well-wishers stood a chimney sweep, brushes, soot and all.

Madeline's brow wrinkled. "Drew?"

Drew laughed as he reached to shake the young man's hand. "Well, well, if it isn't Geordie Jenkins." He turned to Madeline. "Darling, this is Geordie Jenkins, and he is about to kiss you."

Madeline smiled, but he could see the wariness in her eyes.

"It has long been thought to be very good luck," he explained, "for a bride to see a chimney sweep on her wedding day. Even better if the groom gets a handshake and the bride a kiss."

The chimney sweep touched his cap, his teeth showing white in his blackened face. "If you please, missus. I'll mind not to get soot on your lovely dress."

"Go on, missus," someone from the crowd called, and others began to urge her on.

With a giggle she offered the sweep her cheek. Just as he touched his lips to it, there was the flash of a camera. After a few more pictures and many more farewells, Drew spotted someone trying to sneak away at the back of the crowd.

"Oh, no, you don't!"

But Chief Inspector Birdsong only gave him an approving nod and a tip of his best hat before hurrying off, his placid-looking wife in tow.

Madeline grinned at Drew as Carrie went to hug her.

"You two be happy, you hear me?" Carrie said.

"We will," Madeline promised, and Drew kissed Carrie's cheek.

"Here now," Nick protested, "you've already got a girl."

Madeline leaned over and kissed Nick's cheek before he realized what she was doing. "There," she said. "We're all even now."

Nick gave Drew a smug look, and Drew shoved his shoulder.

"Those are all legally mine at this point," Drew said, "and I'm keeping detailed records from here on out."

"Fair enough," said Nick, throwing an arm around his friend's shoulders. "All the best, old man. You've done well for yourself, and don't you forget it."

"Believe me, Nick, I know. I know."

With a laugh, Drew pulled Madeline into his arms and kissed her once more. Then, under a shower of rice and cheers and laughter, they ran hand in hand down the path to the road.

— *Acknowledgments* —

To my very dear agent and friend, Wendy Lawton, for her much-needed wisdom.

To all my writer friends, near and far, for being a wonderful source of information and encouragement.

And, always, to my dad, my number-one fan.

I thank God for you all.

— *About the Author* —

Julianna Deering, author of *Rules of Murder* and *Death by the Book*, is the pen name of the multi-published novelist DeAnna Julie Dodson. DeAnna has always been an avid reader and a lover of storytelling, whether on the page, the screen, or the stage. This, together with her keen interest in history and her Christian faith, shows in her tales of love, forgiveness, and triumph over adversity. A fifth-generation Texan, she makes her home north of Dallas, along with three spoiled cats. When not writing, DeAnna spends her free time quilting, cross-stitching, and watching NHL hockey. Learn more at JuliannaDeering.com.

Center Point Large Print
600 Brooks Road / PO Box 1
Thorndike ME 04986-0001 USA

(207) 568-3717

US & Canada:
1 800 929-9108
www.centerpointlargeprint.com